EX·LIBRIS

Lori Amsbary

559-355-2738

OTHER BOOKS BY BEN BEHUNIN

Remembering Isaac

Discovering Isaac

Becoming Isaac

Forget-Me-Notes

Borrowing Fire

Put A Cherry On Top

The Lost Art of Wooing Rabbits and Other Wild Hares

The Disciple of the Wind

How to Seduce a Sasquatch

Ben's books are available from his website,
www.potterboy.com, www.amazon.com and
wherever above average books are sold.

AUTHENTICALLY RUBY

The Illustrious Matchmaker of Niederbipp

by Ben Behunin

Authentically Ruby
The Illustrious Matchmaker of Niederbipp

First printing, December 2018

Published by
Abendmahl Press
P.O. Box 581083
Salt Lake City, Utah 84158-1083

ISBN 978-0-9998516-0-9

Photography by Harry von Lederhösen
Designed by Ben Behunin and Bert Compton
Layout by Bert Compton

To Nettie,
and our children,
Isaac and Eve.

TABLE OF CONTENTS

PRELUDE

It's hard to believe that it's been more than twenty-one years since the good people of Niederbipp began having tea parties in my head, begging for their stories to be told. It was difficult in the beginning to find the time to do them the justice they deserved. And it's unlikely I ever would have gotten around to it at all if life had gone the way I'd planned. But I've learned, as I suppose we all do in the end, that life very rarely goes as we plan.

I decided years ago, however, that life is generally good. Sure, there are always challenges and disappointments, but it seems to me that our attitudes significantly determine our outcomes, whether it be in our relationships, our work, or our general happiness. And those attitudes, I've discovered, are very often influenced by the books we read and the media we consume. And so when I began hearing voices encouraging me to write more than twenty-one years ago, I was glad that the voices were positive, full of hope and grace and passion.

With the 2009 release of *Remembering Isaac: The Wise and Joyful Potter of Niederbipp*, the world was first introduced to the utopia called Niederbipp. This new series is independent of the Niederbipp Trilogy, meaning you don't have to know the first books to enjoy this second series. But because they both take place in the village of Niederbipp, and because it's a small town filled with quirky individuals who like to stick their noses into other people's business, there are plenty of ties to the Niederbipp Trilogy for those who are looking to reconnect with old friends.

In the decade that has passed since my first book was published, tens of thousands of people have spent time in Niederbipp. Some have passed through quickly on their way to somewhere else. Others have become regular visitors, making annual pilgrimages to this upbeat utopia. And many, many others have set up a summer residence in the tiny hamlet and told all their friends about it, spreading the joys of Niederbipp far and wide. To those of you who have put Niederbipp on the map, I thank you. I could not have given voice to the Niederbippians without your encouragement.

I began working on this book at least eight years ago. Ruby and Lorenzo told me they wanted their story told too. But despite their regular visits to my pottery studio and many other places where I seek stillness, six other books somehow butted in front of them. I've enjoyed writing each of those other books, but coming back to this one—coming home to Niederbipp—has been a real treat. At the time of publishing this first book, I'm still uncertain how many books will be in this series— two at least, maybe three, maybe more. I've learned it's often pointless to make plans because they usually all take off on strange, surprising tangents anyway. And so we'll see. But the characters in this book are loud and competitive, and I doubt I'll be able to sleep much until their stories have been told.

I never dreamed I would write a book. And I certainly had no idea what I was getting myself into when all of this started. But with the release of this tenth book in just under ten years, I'm realizing that maybe I'm a writer after all. Thank you for reading. Thank you for sharing my books with your friends and family. Thank you for believing the world can be big and bright and beautiful and for doing your part to make it so. I hope my books will help spread some sunshine along your way.

Viva Niederbipp!
Ben 2018

CHAPTER 1

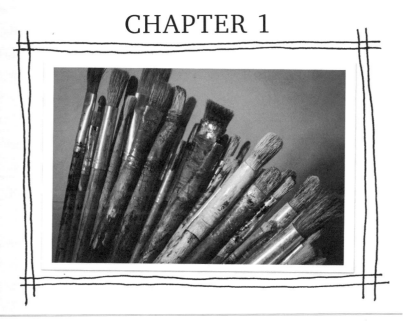

Genevieve

I learned long ago, never to wrestle with a pig.
You get dirty, and besides, the pig likes it.
– George Bernard Shaw –

Hello, Pottery Niederbipp."

"Uh, yeah, hi. I was hoping to reach Amy Eckstein."

"That's me," Amy replied, quickly realizing that no one had used her maiden name in several years.

"Oh, thank gawwwd, finally!" the woman on the other end said with a sigh. "I don't know if you remember me, but you and I were roommates freshman year at Endicott College."

"Julie?" Amy said, her voice rising with excitement.

"Uh, no, your other roommate."

"Kristen!"

"Umm, no. This is Genevieve Patterson."

"Oh...wow! It's...been a long time. Didn't you transfer to Northwestern after freshman year?" Amy asked, straining her mind to remember the last time she had seen Genevieve, or even what she looked like.

"Impressive memory! I considered Northwestern, but Syracuse was a much better fit for me, especially because of their rankings, you know. It's taken me a couple of days to track you down. Gosh, how are you?"

"I'm good, thanks. How are you?"

"Fabulous. Just livin' the dream here in Manhattan. I'm a writer now for an international women's magazine."

"Oh, that's great. That's what you wanted, right? I remember all those fashion magazines you used to have around the apartment. That's great that you've followed your dreams."

"Yeah, it's amazing, right? I couldn't be happier. I can't imagine a more perfect life for me. The money's great; I live in a beautiful loft in SoHo; I get to travel the world doing what I love to do, interviewing some of most fascinating people ever. It's really quite extraordinary. I honestly can't believe how ridiculously wonderful my life is. Thanks for asking."

"Uhh, yeah, that's great," Amy responded, suddenly remembering all the reasons she'd found it easy to dislike Genevieve. "So, what's going on?" Amy asked, setting down her paintbrush.

"You mean you haven't gotten my messages?"

"Uh, no," Amy said, glancing at the dusty answering machine, its message indicator light blinking more times than she could count at a glance. "We've been out for the weekend," she offered. "And we're closed Mondays."

"Oh, that's so cute. I guess you can do stuff like that in a small town," Genevieve responded patronizingly. "I spoke to your mother on Saturday. She said you're a painter. Are you painting houses or pictures? Ha ha ha."

"Uh, pictures," Amy said, her hackles rising. "You know, like I did back at Endicott?"

"Oh, that's right! It's just been so long. I looked on your Facebook and LinkedIn pages, but it didn't look like you're updated. I tried messaging you last week on Facebook, but I guess you didn't get it."

"No, I didn't. I haven't done much with Facebook since college. What's going on?" Amy asked, growing impatient.

"Well, I've received an assignment that should bring me close to you. I…I sent out a query last week to all of my many friends and contacts to see if anyone had heard of Neiderbopp."

"You mean Niederbipp?" Amy asked.

"Whatever. I've heard it both ways," Genevieve continued. "Anyway, Chandra Reynolds—she messaged back that you were living there. Is that right?"

"Yes. I've been here for just over eight years."

"And your mom told me that you're married! That's so cute."

Amy didn't answer, shaking her head as she remembered Genevieve's constantly condescending nature. "Yeah, it'll be eight years in July," she managed.

"Wow, impressive. I've never met a man I could possibly put up with for eight years. However have you done it?"

Amy bit her tongue.

"Who is it?" Jake asked, looking up from the potter's wheel, his hands covered in clay.

"It's my old roommate," Amy said, covering the receiver with her hand.

"Amy, are you there?" Genevieve asked.

"Yeah, I'm here; just distracted by my super cute husband," Amy said, winking at Jake. "Are you planning a trip to Niederbipp?"

"As a matter of fact, I am. I've tried to do some research before I head out, but there's not much on the website beyond some cheesy tourist information."

"Thanks, our best friend is the webmaster for the town site," Amy said, quickly approaching her boiling point. "I'll let him know that you don't like it."

"Oh no, it's not so much that I don't like it," Genevieve said, backpedaling. "It's just that I was looking for more information about the town and the people who live there. What is it you call yourselves—Neiderboops or something?"

"Niederbippians," Amy responded. "What would you like to know?"

"Well for starters, I've been looking for adequate lodging, and there doesn't seem to be anything but two-and three-star accommodations. Perhaps you could give me some suggestions for something a little more...classy, if you know what I mean?"

Amy smiled. "I don't know. I've never stayed anywhere in town besides our apartment and my aunt's place, but the bed-and-breakfasts are quite nice. The best one would probably be The Parkin House, but then they only cater to married couples."

"Oh, I'm sure they wouldn't consider discriminating against single people. Could you give me their number?"

Amy took a deep breath, trying to keep from screaming. She did not want the Parkins to associate her with Genevieve, but she didn't know how to get out of the situation. She opened the small phonebook and flipped through the pages until she came to the ad for The Parkin House. She read off the number, tempted to switch a digit or two, but she refrained, worried that it might only backfire.

"So, are you writing a travel story?" Amy asked, trying to imagine what a writer for a women's magazine would want to write about Niederbipp.

Genevieve laughed. "No, I've been asked to write an article about the Matchmaker of Neiderbopp, Ruby Swarovski. Do you know her?"

"Of course. Niederbipp is a small enough town that we all kind of know each other. She and her husband, Lorenzo, live just outside of town, up on Harmony Hill. What kind of article are you writing?"

"That has yet to be determined," she said curtly, suddenly sounding all business. "My editors have simply assigned me to do an interview and determine if she's a fraud or if she has any legitimate matchmaking skills. You might imagine that in today's world, with marriage on the decline and online dating services popping up everywhere, there's a steady interest from our readers in anything related to the field of matrimony."

"The field of matrimony, huh?" Amy responded, distracted as she imagined what a painting of such a field might look like.

"Yes, well, I don't need to tell you how rare it is among us millennials to even consider marriage anymore. I can't say I blame anyone; I mean the commitment alone is so burdensome, and then all the details: money, kids, jobs. Is it any wonder why no one really wants to be bothered by it anymore?"

Amy didn't answer. She had nothing to say. The nearly eight years since she and Jake had been married were undoubtedly the happiest years of her life, but she could tell that Genevieve had already made up her mind about marriage. And Amy had learned many years before that arguing with Genevieve Patterson was a complete waste of time and energy.

"Well, good luck to you then," Amy said, anxious to get off the phone and back to her painting.

"I'll be in town this weekend," Genevieve reported. "I'd like to get together for drinks and catch up if we could."

"Uh, sure," Amy said, not wanting to go into all the reasons why that would be quite impossible.

"Brilliant. It will be fun to see you. Thanks for your help. I'll see you on Friday. Toodles."

"Goodbye," Amy said, shaking her head as she hung up the phone.

"What was that all about?" Jake asked, smiling at Amy, who looked like she was quite ready to boil over.

She shook her head, trying to smile back. "Worlds are colliding," she answered, walking closer to Jake and wrapping her arms around him the best she could with her growing belly between them.

He hugged her back, careful to keep his clay-covered hands away from her hair. "What's this all about?" he asked again.

"Did I ever tell you about Genevieve, my roommate at Endicott?"

"Are you talking about the one who ruined your iron making grilled cheese sandwiches?"

Amy laughed. "No, that was Mindy."

"Is Genevieve the one who used to steal your laundry money?"

Amy shook her head, laughing again. "Maybe. She was high on my suspicion list. Genevieve was the one who always left dirty dishes in the sink but hired a maid to make her bed and do her laundry."

"Was she the one who crashed her BMW into the dean's car and made her dad buy her a new one the next day?"

Amy nodded. "That's the one—Genevieve Patterson. Undoubtedly the most difficult, condescending person I've ever met."

"And she's coming here?" Jake asked.

"Yeah. It sounds like she's bent on making a mockery of Ruby."

"Swarovski?"

"Yeah."

Jake laughed.

"What's so funny?"

"She has her work cut out for her if she thinks she can mess with Ruby."

"You don't know Genevieve."

Jake nodded. "Maybe not, but you know Ruby. She may look like a mild little granny, but she has more spunk than any ten women half her age combined. I'm guessing she's dealt with plenty of girls like Genevieve before."

She laughed, shaking her head again. "You don't know Genevieve Patterson."

"Do you think we should warn Ruby?"

"Absolutely," Amy responded. "She needs to know what kind of hurricane is coming to Niederbipp. I'd feel awful if we didn't warn her."

Jake nodded thoughtfully. "Well, unless things have changed, their closest phone is in that phone booth on the road above their home. It's fine for outgoing calls, but it'd be pointless to try to reach them by calling it. Are you up for a ride on the scooter, or should we borrow Kai's van?"

"Let's take the scooter," Amy said, squeezing Jake's ribs. "I don't know how much longer we'll be able to fit."

CHAPTER 2

The Warning

The aim of life is to live, and to live means to be aware,
joyously, drunkenly, serenely, divinely aware.
- Henry Miller -

Jake smiled to himself as he looked in the scooter's rearview mirrors and saw Amy's hair dancing about like a hundred wispy, red serpents. He had always loved these rides and the physical closeness he felt toward her when her arms were wrapped around his chest. For the past eight years, this scooter had been their only motorized transportation, and it pained him to recognize that these evening joyrides would soon be ending.

As they approached the turnoff for the farm after their belabored ascent up Harmony Hill, Amy tapped Jake on the shoulder and pointed to the valley below. They pulled up next to the phone booth and parked the scooter. From here, they could see the entire Niederbipp Valley; up and down the Allegheny; and over the forested eastern hills that continued to roll on as far as the eye could see, changing from green to blue to purple with each progressive layer. The sun hung low over the western horizon, bathing the landscape in amber light and making the river look like a meandering ribbon of gold.

"Let's walk from here," she said after a long silence, undoing the helmet's strap under her chin.

Jake nodded. They had been here several times over the years and had grown to appreciate the quiet of the farm, interrupted only by the sounds of its resident animals. The farmstead offered a unique sense of calm, and Jake and Amy had usually walked the last quarter mile down the rutted-out drive. It was a rough passage on the best days, and Jake knew Amy's suggestion to walk was a good one for many reasons.

After stowing their helmets, they headed down the colorful lane, hand in hand. What the long driveway lacked in maintenance was more than made up for by the whimsy and charm that greeted them. The fence posts were wrapped in bright, colorful wool socks and crowned with either obsolete farm implements or old glass telephone insulators in a wide range of colors. Jake and Amy each had their favorite fence posts, but they always discovered what seemed like new ones with each visit. Amy had once come here with her easel and paints to capture the colorful lane with oil on canvas but was frustrated when the painting couldn't capture the creative spirit of this magical place.

The bark of a dog drew their attention away from the fence, turning them to the large, white farmhouse at the end of the dusty lane. Jake raised his hand and waved to the two figures sitting on the porch. They waved back as the Border collie raced out to meet them.

"Get back here, Rex," Ruby shouted from the porch, and the obedient dog reluctantly turned and sauntered home.

"Who goes there?" Lorenzo asked, brandishing the broken shotgun he used to greet all his visitors.

"It's just us, Lorenzo. Jake and Amy."

"Who?"

"Jake and Amy Kimball from Niederbipp. You know, the artists," Jake shouted.

"Well, why didn't you say so? Come on up. The lemonade's almost gone, but there's enough here for the two of you to share a glass."

They walked across the freshly shorn front lawn and climbed the sandstone steps to the big covered porch.

"Welcome," Ruby said, putting down her knitting, offering a warm smile. "What brings you kids to Harmony Hill tonight?"

Amy glanced at Jake before turning back to Ruby. "I'm afraid we might have some bad news. We thought we better come and warn you about it before it hits."

"Sounds serious. Is there a fire raging in Niederbipp?"

Amy smiled. "No, but it may be worse. An old...acquaintance... called this afternoon to tell me she's coming here to do an interview for her magazine."

"That's nice. Who's she going to interview?"

"She told me she was coming from New York to interview you."

Ruby glanced sideways at her husband then quickly turned back to their visitors. "I haven't given an interview in at least...twenty-five years."

"Well, you might want to stick with that record. Genevieve Patterson is not a nice person. She usually gets what she wants by either force or manipulation. I felt like I needed warn you. She's supposed to be coming into town this Friday."

"Friday? Didn't we tell them Wednesday?"

"I'm sure we did," Lorenzo confirmed. "The new recruits will be arriving on Saturday. Friday won't work at all."

"So you know they're coming, then?" Jake asked, looking confused.

"Oh, they've been wanting to come since the last time Rubes gave an interview," Lorenzo replied. "It's hard to keep it all straight, but Friday definitely won't work. Why don't you let your friend know?"

"Uh, I don't know how to get in touch with her. And just to set the record straight, we're definitely not friends. That's why we came," Amy responded. "She's really terrible, and she said something about trying to figure out if you're a...well, she said she wonders if you're a..."

"Spit it out, child. If I'm a what?"

Amy looked stressed. "If you're a legitimate matchmaker...or a fraud."

"Ha ha ha!" she cackled. "I thought you were going to say a witch."

"You would've been spot on," Lorenzo said, laughing himself into a coughing fit.

"Are you finished?" Ruby asked, obviously not amused.

"Relax. I was only teasin', Mom. Of course she's a matchmaker. But you don't get to be a successful matchmaker without a little magic. And you've got to have more of that magic than the average matchmaker to have 532 successful marriages to show for a lifetime of doing this kind of work."

"That's pretty impressive," Jake said. "Five hundred and thirty-two marriages? How did you manage that?"

"Ahh, therein lies the magic." Lorenzo said, lifting his finger to his nose.

"It's really not much different than matching socks," Ruby answered.

Jake laughed, a little confused. "I've never seen a pair of your socks that matches."

"Mine do," Lorenzo said, kicking his feet up and lifting the hem of his overalls to show off his colorful socks. His right ankle was covered with horizontal stripes in six or seven different colors, and his left ankle was navy blue with yellow stars."

"Don't get me wrong," Jake said, unable to keep from smiling, "we love your socks. As you know, Amy and I both have several pair, but they're pretty unique."

"I should hope so. In all my years of knitting hosiery, I've never made two socks alike, at least not on purpose," Ruby quipped.

"The same way the good Lord never made two people exactly alike," Lorenzo added, his finger raised as he shared his bold observation. "He never even made two feet alike—thank goodness. I've probably checked a thousand times just to be sure I don't have two left feet, but every time I look inside those crazy, old socks, I discover I've got two very different feet that have kept me going for almost eighty-five years."

Amy smiled at Lorenzo and Ruby. "Jake and I have a lot of respect for both of you. We wouldn't have come tonight if I wasn't worried about Genevieve. She can be a real beast. If you don't want to give her an interview, make sure you're firm about it."

"Honey, I'm not worried. In my ninety-four years, I've had to deal with more than my share of cheeky monkeys. Lorenzo's probably the biggest one of all."

Lorenzo only smiled at this, making a face that looked remarkably like a chimpanzee.

"Pour yourself some lemonade, and let's enjoy the evening while our old bones aren't aching too bad. Everything changes next week."

"So you filled up the bunks again?" Jake asked.

"Of course we did," Lorenzo responded. "There's no way to keep the farm going without the help. Fortunately, we normally have a waiting list of folks chompin' at the bit to spend the summer with us. One of the fellas coming this year has applied for the past three summers."

"That's gotta feel good to be so popular," Jake replied.

"Yep, after more than three hundred years, the secrets of this farm are still drawing folks in. We were warned years ago that the internet was going to put a quick end to Ruby's matchmaking, but this year we had a record number apply—more than 860."

"Seriously?" Amy asked.

Ruby nodded.

"How do you decide which ones to take?"

"That's all Ruby's department," Lorenzo reported. "It's part of the magic. A matchmaker can't do anything without people being ready."

"But how do you know if they are?" asked Jake.

"You gotta feel it," Ruby answered. "We've just been going over the kids who are coming this year," she said, pointing to a stack of oversized index cards lying on the white wicker table.

Jake looked at the two stacks, divided by genders. "Does it look like a good group?"

"Oh, fairly average, I'd say," Ruby answered. "A bunch of lonely souls in search of a soul mate." She nodded, pointing to the stacks of cards. "Six of each."

"Do you mind if I look?" Amy asked.

"Help yourself."

She leaned forward and picked up the women's stack. A photograph was stapled to the top left-hand corner of each of the cards, and she shuffled though them quickly, looking for any commonalities. Outside of them all being fairly attractive, she couldn't see any similarities among the women, their ages ranging from twenty-somethings to thirty-somethings.

Jake looked over her shoulder, and she handed him the cards before reaching for the men's stack. These had pictures of equally attractive men in a similar age range, one perhaps looking a little older.

"We've seen your...*kids* around town every summer, and I guess I've always wondered what is it you look for?" Amy asked.

"I first look for a smile," Ruby replied.

"Really?" Jake asked sounding surprised. "You don't look for education or work experience...or income?"

"Oh, that all factors into my final decision, but if a person hasn't learned to smile in his first twenty-five years, there's hardly a ding-dang thing I can do to help 'em. I suppose part of that's probably selfish on our part, but it's a whole lot easier workin' with happy folks."

"Have you ever misjudged a person by their picture?" Jake asked, looking at the photos of the women, all of whom had pleasant smiles.

"Oh, sure. Some folks are pretty good fakers. I can usually screen 'em out by the rest of their application, but every once in a while, one gets past me and we have to spend the summer workin' with a grump—at least until we can get them to turn around. Some never do, of course, but I've found if we can start with good eggs in the beginning, we usually end up with an eligible group of folks who are ready to get married."

Amy looked up from the stack of cards, obviously confused. "Aren't these people eligible already?"

"If they believed they were, they wouldn't be seeking my help."

"So…what exactly is it that you do?" Amy asked.

"We give them a place where they can work on themselves, and we give them the right tools to help them on their way. Most of these kids just need a little more confidence."

"Some need a little less," Lorenzo interjected.

Ruby nodded. "But most of these kids just need to stand in front of an honest mirror for a few months. Most of 'em just need a tweak here or a little polishing there. That comes naturally if the conditions are right."

"She has 532 happy marriages to show it works," Lorenzo added. "And if you count the second- and third-generation marriages, well…"

"Wait. Second- and third-generation marriages?" Jake asked.

"Sure, the kids and grandkids that grow up with parents in a happy marriage and go on to create one of their own. We gave up trying to keep track of those a long time ago. It's a beautiful thing to work with an individual who goes on to create their own happy marriage, but the reward is even grander when you see those kids taking the stuff Ruby teaches 'em and living in such a way that the next generation can also benefit from it. It's rewarding to be able to help one generation, but it's even better to know that folks we've never even met are livin' better lives 'cause of the secrets we taught their parents and grandparents."

"But do people from these two groups ever get together?" Amy asked, holding the two sets of cards.

"Naturally," Ruby replied. "That's why we only have 532 marriages so far. It would have been close to two hundred more if they'd all married spouses from outside."

"I assume that number would also have been higher if you didn't have a few divorces in there too?" Jake suggested.

"Indeed. That's always a disappointment. To our knowledge, we've already had six divorces," Ruby lamented.

"Only six? Jake responded, quickly doing the math in his head. "That's barely one percent! That's amazing! I thought there were more people getting divorced these days than there are getting married."

"It's a tragedy of epic proportions, isn't it?" Ruby responded. "We've felt bad enough about our six kids that have gotten divorced that we've invited all of them to come back during the off-season so we could help them remember what we taught 'em. Four of them have come, and those four have found love again. We've also had close to fifty kids who have lost their spouses to death. Most of them have remarried too. It's a beautiful thing to find love once, but to find it twice…it's nothing short of a miracle."

"Do you call them all your kids?" Amy asked, charmed by the idea of it.

"Most of them," Ruby said, smiling. "When you work that closely with someone for nearly five months, you learn to love 'em. We invest a lot in them, and it's easy to think of them as our own kids by the end of the summer—most of them anyway. Some of them are tough to love, but those are the exceptions, to be sure."

"I just realized I've never asked if you have any children of your own— biologically, I mean," Amy said.

"Nope. It wasn't in the cards for us. I was almost forty when we finally got married."

"But we still had some fun tryin'," Lorenzo responded with a smile. "We learned a long time ago that life doesn't always work out the way you think it will when you're young. And maybe that's okay, because despite the disappointments, most times it works out even better than you think it will."

"There's lotsa ways to find happiness if you're sincerely looking for it," Ruby added. "We were just saying before you two arrived how nice it is to have each other, to have spent so much time here on the farm helping other people to find their happily ever after. Nope, life ain't hardly ever the way you plan it, but I never could have imagined that my life here on the farm would be so rewarding. I don't think I could have written a happier ending to this love story if I'd tried." She smiled, turning to Lorenzo and patting his hand as they sat next to each other in the old wicker chairs. "This couldn't have worked out any other way. Timing, location, mindset—it all had to be right for any of this to work out."

Jake looked at Amy and nodded knowingly. "So, how did the two of you meet?"

"We met right here on the farm, fifty-six years ago," Lorenzo replied.

Ruby nodded. "Fifty-seven actually. We've been married fifty-six years. I'd given up on the idea of marriage—decided I'd probably die a spinster. It was my sister who talked me into coming to the farm for the summer."

"Wait, I thought this farm had been in your family for several generations," Jake said, looking confused.

"It has, just not in the typical way of understanding family and ownership. We're simply stewards—caretakers, really—in a long, successive line of caretakers."

Jake glanced at Amy and found she was just as confused as he was.

"The farm's only ours until we pass it on," Lorenzo explained. "The same as it was for the Smurthwaites before us. When they retired, we moved into the big house and took over their duties. And someday we'll pass the farm on to another couple who'll keep the tradition going. It's been that way for almost three hundred years, ever since Mary and Johann Zwahlen homesteaded here back when Niederbipp was barely an outpost on the edge of the frontier. 'Course it was only eighty acres back then. But when the Zwahlens' only daughter married the only son of Siegfried and Maria Klunker—their only neighbors up here on Harmony Hill—the farms were combined somewhere in the middle of the eighteenth century, and they picked up the north forty some sixty years later. Since Rubes and I've been stewards over the farm, we've known the time would come when we'd have to pick our replacements and prepare to lie down next to our predecessors in the orchard."

Jake nodded slowly. "It's been the same way with the Pottery since the beginning."

"It's the same way with everything," responded Ruby. "No one gets to take anything with them except for the love and the memories. That's the way it is for everyone who lives and loves. Most folks don't think about it much when they're young and life is fresh, but by the time you get to be older than dirt, you can't help but think about how soon you'll be pushing up daisies."

"Yep, but I think we did it right," Lorenzo said, patting Ruby's hand. "We timed it so we might be pushing up daisies together."

Ruby smiled. "There are plenty of perks to marrying a younger man. The good book says that if you train up a child in the way he should go, when he's old and chubby, he won't wander far from it."

Jake smiled, wondering which good book she was talking about.

"I think most people get it backwards," Ruby continued. "Young brides marrying older men—it doesn't make much sense. Most of those boys die years before their brides, leaving them alone for too many years. The way I figure it, the nine years I have on Lorenzo probably means we'll kick the bucket about the same time. We've done almost everything together for the last five and a half decades. It'd be a shame for either of us to have to fly solo for any longer than necessary. A difference of nine years might not work for everyone, but it's worked for us."

"I've never considered it until now, but your marriage is kind of like your socks, isn't it?" Amy mused.

"That's right. A perfect match," Ruby replied. "Too many folks get caught up in finding a sock that's the same color, shape and size. In reality, there is no identical match, and we should all be grateful there isn't. I'm a pretty sweet old gal, but I'd go mad if I had to be married to myself."

"Now you know how I feel," Lorenzo whispered to Jake and Amy, smiling jovially.

"We all need to find the yin for our yang," Ruby continued, obviously ignoring her husband. "Sometimes it comes in a familiar-looking package, but more often than not, we have to open our eyes a little wider before we can see what's right in front of us. If I have any magic, I learned it from Millie Smurthwaite, who learned it from Margaret Keller, and on down the line all the way back to Mary Zwahlen, the very first matchmaker of Niederbipp. The simple truth is that a man can never be complete without a complementary woman at his side, and neither is a woman complete without a complementary man. The magic comes when we can open our hearts and eyes and can see that life can be better if we let love in. And we can only do that if we first make room for it by giving love away."

Jake looked at Amy and nodded, remembering their short but magical courtship. "Isn't that basic common sense?"

"You might think so, but in a selfish world, common sense isn't nearly as common as you'd like it to be," Ruby responded. "If it were, we wouldn't be gettin' eight hundred applications a year to spend almost five months working on a farm in exchange for a little help in figurin' these things out. We've never advertised, but people continue to hear about us. Our biggest regret is that we can't help more of 'em—only twelve lucky souls a summer."

"Have you ever considered expanding it?" Amy asked.

"Oh, plenty of times. We tried sixteen one year. It didn't work too well. In fact, two of those divorces came from that summer. The work is part of the magic and the medicine, and we're opposed to making up busy work that doesn't mean anything. No, it takes fourteen people to keep this farm in shipshape. Any more and we trip over each other. Any less and we have to fight the daylight to get it all done before the sun goes down."

"Plus we only have room in the bunkhouses for six of each," Lorenzo added.

Ruby nodded. "As it turns out, running a farm with twelve sets of volunteer hands is an odd hybrid of backyard rocket science and herding chickens, but we like to think that the orchestra we throw together each summer plays beautiful tunes."

"I can't imagine any reporter being able to argue with the results you've had" Jake responded.

"No, I don't suspect they could. It's nice of you kids to come all the way up here to warn us, but between Lorenzo's shotgun and my trusty sling shot, I think we're pretty well protected," Ruby replied, cracking a smile. "Now sit back, drink that lemonade, and tell us about how you're feeling about becoming parents."

Jake smiled at Amy, pouring a glass of lemonade and handing it to her. She took a long drink before sitting back in the wicker chair. She looked out at the tranquil farm, trying hard to relax but finding it difficult, knowing that Genevieve Patterson would be there in less than four days.

CHAPTER 3

Improper Introductions

There are always flowers for those who
want to see them.
— Henri Matisse —

"**W**ill you please stop?!" Jake said, as he watched Amy nervously rearranging the items on the front counter for the third time that day. "What's gotten into you? The Pottery has never been cleaner, and you haven't painted since Tuesday. I've heard of nesting, but this is a little over the top, don't you think?"

Amy forced a smile and leaned against the counter, feeling tired. "She could be here any minute, you know?"

"Amy, the last I heard, you can't even stand this girl. Why are you letting her mess with your head like this?"

She let out a long, exasperated sigh, shaking her head. "I don't know, Jake. I guess it's because I always felt judged by her."

"Babe, it's been more than ten years since you last saw each other. I'm sure you've both grown up."

Amy shook her head and sat down on the barstool she had been using for the past several months to give her a legs a break while she painted. "I feel like a water buffalo. Why couldn't she have come last summer when I skinny?" She looked like she was on the verge of tears.

Jake rinsed his hands off in the sink and removed his apron before walking back to the front counter to comfort his wife. He came behind her and put his arms around her middle, resting his chin on her shoulder. "You're more beautiful now than you've ever been," he whispered. "Don't let her get to you."

"I know! I'm just so hormonal right now. I wish I could crawl into a hole and hide for a while."

Jake smiled. "Should we invite her to dinner? I could make pancakes, and we could show her how real Niederbippians live."

Amy laughed. "I was hoping I wouldn't have to see her at all."

"Oh, really? Is that why you've been cleaning nonstop since Wednesday morning?"

She grimaced. "I'll be a lot happier when she's gone and I can get back to living without worrying what she's thinking about me."

"You talk like you're afraid she's going to think we're all a bunch of hayseeds. I could go put on an old pair of overalls and a straw hat if you think it would help."

"No," she said, shaking her head as she cleaned out the dirt from under her fingernails. "You're right. I'm sure I'm just overreacting."

"Let's not wait around for her. If she was going to visit, she should have had the courtesy to let us know when she'd be stopping by. Why don't we close up early and go for a walk down by the river? It would give you a chance to think about other things."

"Only if you promise to push me on the swing."

"You don't even need to ask. Do you want to take a picnic and your easel? It looks like it could be a nice sunset."

"That sounds nice, but what are you going to do?"

"I'm going to sit and watch you work. Kai told me the other day that it's a good idea to make memories before the kids come and change the dynamics of everything."

Amy nodded thoughtfully. "Are you ready for this?"

"Absolutely!"

"Seriously?"

He shook his head, smiling. "I'm actually scared out of my mind. Kai told me the other day that if people knew how much their life would change after they had kids, they'd probably plan a little differently. Ready or not, here it comes, right? I've got two months to grow up."

"You're going to be a great dad," Amy said, squeezing his arm.

The bells on the front door jangled, and Jake and Amy both looked up to see a woman talking loudly on a cell phone and holding the door slightly ajar with her free hand. She didn't come in, releasing the door instead as she began to pace back and forth on the cobblestones. Her words were muffled, but her hand gestures and the volume of her voice made it clear she was not in a good mood.

Amy turned away after a moment of observation. "Oh no."

"What's wrong?"

"That's Genevieve Patterson. Quick, turn off the lights. Maybe she'll go away."

"Amy!" Jake responded, smiling, and they watched her, wondering what she was doing.

"When did Niederbipp get cell service?" Amy asked after another thirty seconds.

"I was just wondering why that looked so strange," Jake responded. "Who do you think she's talking to? She looks really mad." They watched as she continued to holler into her phone, her free hand gesticulating. It was funny from this perspective, almost like watching a silent movie, but the few muffled words that got through the glass made it clear she was not happy about her rental car.

"Wow, I'd hate to be on the other end of that," Jake said as the tantrum rolled into another minute.

"I tried to warn you."

"She was like this when you were roommates?"

Amy folded her arms across her chest and shrugged. "It seems like she's become a little more animated since I saw her last."

"I really thought you were just exaggerating. I'm glad we warned Ruby and Lorenzo that she was coming."

"Me too."

"Imbeciles!" Genevieve muttered loudly as she threw open the door.

Jake and Amy walked around the counter to greet her.

"Genevieve Patterson," Amy said, forcing a smile.

"Amy Eckstein! I can't believe it. How the hell are you?"

"Sounds like I'm better than you. Is everything all right?" she asked, pointing to her cell phone.

Genevieve shook her head. "I just filled up the gas tank of my rental car, and the idiots in Pittsburgh didn't tell me it was a diesel. I mean, is there really that much of a difference?"

Amy looked at Jake.

"Uh well, yes, as a matter of fact there is. How far did you drive it?"

"From Pittsburgh," she said, looking confused.

"Really? You made it that far? Usually the car would stop working after about three blocks."

"Oh, you mean since I put the gas in? Yeah, I only made it about a half mile. I thought I must have run over a raccoon or possum or some other monster you people have out here in the uncivilized hinterlands. The car was gyrating all over the road before it stopped. I had to walk, and these stupid cobblestone streets are murder in high heels. They're going to pay for these too." She pointed to the skinny heels of her shoes where the leather had been ripped way, exposing thin metal posts.

"What are you going to do?" Amy asked.

"I'm going to find myself a cozy bar and a tall drink and charge it to those fools too. I really should sue them. I could have died. It'll be an hour and a half before they get here with a new car. Where can I get a drink while I wait?"

Jake looked at Amy this time, trying not to smile.

"Uh, Niederbipp is a dry town?" Amy replied.

"What does that mean?"

"It means the closest bar is probably in Tionesta, about twenty miles north of here."

"You're kidding me, right?" she asked, looking down at her phone. "Where the hell am I?"

"Welcome to Niederbipp," Jake said, walking forward to shake her hand. "I'm Jake Kimball."

She glanced up from her phone, obviously distracted and preoccupied. "Nice to meet you, Jack," she muttered.

He thought about correcting her but decided it probably wouldn't make any difference.

"I didn't think cell phones worked here," Amy said.

"Yeah, can you believe that? I didn't know there were still places in America where you can't get a cell signal. I insisted that the magazine rent me a satellite phone for this assignment. I feel like I'm on a campout in the backwoods," she said, her attention glued to the phone. "Wow, this is great!"

"What's up?" asked Amy.

"It's the email I've been hoping for. My editor finally made the arrangements for me to meet with Ruby Swarovski. It looks like all the stars are finally aligning."

Jake looked nervously at Amy, who forced another smile.

"So, I'm suddenly in a much better mood," Genevieve reported, finally looking up with a saccharine smile. "If you don't drink around here, what do you do to celebrate?"

Amy looked to Jake for the answer.

"Sometimes, when we're really feeling good about life, we go out to the bridge and jump into the river," he said with a hillbilly twang.

Amy laughed out loud before stopping herself, deciding to play along. "Well, gee whiz, it's still a little early in the season to float the river, ain't it? And b'sides, our guest inner tube's got a slow leak."

Jake winked at Amy. "That makes for a soggy bottom, don't it? And this time o' year, when the water's so cold, a big-city girl could catch pneumonia through her backside. We best just stick around town and eat some flapjacks."

Jake's accent was too much for Amy, and she busted up.

Genevieve looked like she didn't know how to respond, which was somewhat comforting to Amy.

"Where are you staying?" Jake asked, trying to make conversation.

"At The Parkin House. Thanks for the recommendation."

"I didn't know they rented rooms to single…"

"They don't. I'm registered as Mr. and Mrs. Patterson this weekend. I'm hoping to find something a little less rustic. The air seems like it would be a little thin out there, and they don't have any rooms with king-size beds. Do you have any other recommendations?"

"Umm, there's a Holiday Inn in Warren, but that's at least a half hour away. What is it you're looking for?" Amy asked.

"A Marriot—if not a Hilton. Certainly not a Holiday Inn, not that I've ever stayed in one. I was hoping for something with both room service and a spa."

"Yeah, you'll probably have to go back to Pittsburgh or maybe Erie for stuff like that. Either way, you're looking at about an hour and a half, if traffic's good."

Genevieve pinched the bridge of her nose and closed her eyes. "I've landed on the dark side of the moon."

"Oh, it's really not that bad," Jake responded. "Tourists come from all over the world to visit Niederbipp. It's a pretty great place if you give it a chance."

"On my way into town, I saw a billboard advertising a farm for neglected snails. Please tell me that's some sort of disgusting joke."

"Well, it's not entirely a joke, but they went out of business before either of us got here," Amy said.

"Are there any restaurants in town?

"Yeah. There's a newish pizza parlor just north of town, and Robintino's, a great little Italian place down the street from here. And then there's kabobs and ice cream," Amy reported.

"Does this Italian place serve wine?" Genevieve asked hopefully.

Amy shook her head. "But the food's really good."

"I've never heard of an Italian restaurant that didn't serve wine."

"Neither had the owners before they bought it, but they get all sorts of awards for their food. On the weekends, there's often an hour wait to be seated."

Genevieve shook her head and laughed. "I have a $200 per diem for food, and I have one decent restaurant and no alcohol for miles. I can already tell how much fun this is going to be. Where do single folks make connections around here?"

"Well, let's see," Jake said, turning to Amy. "There's that bowling alley in Warren, or hmm…yeah, what is it you're looking for exactly?"

"Forget it. Can I take you two to dinner? There's no sense in wasting my per diem on bowling."

"Uh, sure," Jake responded, turning to find Amy looking quite unhappy.

Genevieve's phone rang loudly, and she answered it, turning her back toward them.

"I don't know if I can do an evening with her." Amy whispered.

Jake shrugged. "Then you can tell her that you're tired and need to put your feet up. She just invited us to dinner, though. It would be rude to tell her to go away, wouldn't it?"

Amy grimaced, nodding. "I'd rather go out than be stuck with her in our apartment."

"Hey, look on the bright side. At least we don't have to cook."

Amy nodded thoughtlessly, obviously distracted by Genevieve's conversation. They listened to her pour on the sweetness, so unlike the conversation they had previously watched. It was clear that she was talking to someone who held some authority over her, and they smiled at each other as she went on about her safe arrival, conveniently skipping over how she had already ruined a car and wouldn't be able to find a drink. By the time she hung up, it was very clear to both of them that the woman who stood before them was capable of wearing multiple faces—an actress of the most dangerous sort.

"So, how about dinner?" Genevieve asked, turning back to them. "My treat."

"Sure," Amy said, forcing a smile as she took off her apron, laying it on the counter.

"Oh my gosh, you're...pregnant."

Amy nodded. "It's hard to miss any more, I guess."

"Wow, that's really...cute."

Amy flinched at her tone and word choice. "Jake and I need to change out of our work clothes. Why don't we just meet you down at Robintino's in fifteen minutes and give you a chance to get a feel for the town."

"Sure. I'll let the rental agency know where they can find me," she said, lifting her satellite phone. "Perhaps I should also put our names on the wait-list at the restaurant."

"That would be great," Jake responded, walking Genevieve to the door. He locked the door behind her and waved to her through the glass before turning back to Amy.

"You know that I'd rather have a root canal than eat dinner with her, right?" Amy said.

Jake laughed, taking her hand. "Come on, it'll be fun."

"Yeah, to have it over with. I wonder how long she's staying."

"I don't know, but I hope it's not long. I don't like seeing this mean streak in you."

Amy closed her eyes. "Let's just pretend this is all a bad dream."

Jake leaned forward and kissed her nose, causing a smile to form on her stressed-out face. "Come on. Let's go change and get this party started."

CHAPTER 4

Karma

An optimist may see a light where there is none, but why must the pessimist always run to blow it out?
- Rene Descartes -

They found Genevieve sitting on the stone bench connected to the fountain just across from the restaurant. Her head was down, her thumbs busily typing on her phone, all but present on one of the first warm evenings of spring. At least a dozen people milled about as they waited to be seated, but Genevieve seemed to be oblivious to all of them, sitting in the middle of the bench, her handbag on one side and her impractical, spoiled shoes on the other, leaving no room to share the space. Jake and Amy watched her silently for a long moment and were just about to approach her when the hostess at the restaurant called out her name from the door.

She didn't look up, obviously lost in a parallel world until Jake touched her shoulder.

"I think they're calling your name," he said, raising his hand to notify the hostess. Genevieve gathered up her things slowly, not noticing the two couples who were waiting to take her place on the bench. She slipped on her shoes and teetered obnoxiously over the cobblestones, grabbing Jake's elbow twice to keep from falling over.

They were quickly seated at a table near the back in a dimly lit corner. Jake pulled the chair out for Genevieve, but she didn't notice, her eyes still pinned to her phone as she slid instead onto the soft bench on the opposite side of the table. Amy smiled weakly, and sat down on the chair Jake had pulled out. They looked at each other, waiting for Genevieve to acknowledge them.

"So, tell us about your interview," Jake said after feeling ignored for nearly a minute.

She responded by raising her index finger quickly before returning to her phone, where she used what looked like all ten fingers in a blur of motion. "Do you have any idea how difficult it is to communicate solely on a five-inch screen?" she finally asked, looking up.

Jake looked at Amy, then back at Genevieve. "Uh, no, I guess I don't."

"Yeah, this is ridiculous. My laptop is useless here. There's absolutely no Wi-Fi to speak of. I feel like I just stepped back into the Dark Ages. How do you people live here?"

"Well, *we people* seem to do okay by talking to our neighbors and trying to pay attention to the folks that are right in front of us," Jake responded with a weak smile. "It's hard sometimes, and it kinda feels old-fashioned. But it can be quite rewarding. You should try it sometime."

Genevieve offered her trademark saccharine grin in reply. "No, I'm serious. How could two college-educated—I assume you're both college educated—how could any normal person live in a town like this?"

Amy squeezed Jake's hand hard as if she were indicating the level of pressure she was applying to her own tongue in an effort to tame it.

"Sometimes it takes a little getting used to, but believe it or not, people come from all over the world to unplug here," Jake responded.

"You're serious?" she said, one sculpted eyebrow raised impossibly high on her forehead.

"I'm sorry for the wait," the waitress said, interrupting the tepid conversation. She unloaded from her tray three tall glasses filled with water and then handed out menus. After reading off the daily specials from a notebook she pulled from her long apron, she said she would return in a moment to take their order.

"So, this is as good as it gets around here, huh?" Genevieve said, looking at the walls around them. "At least the art's decent. That one almost looks like an original," she said, pointing to a gold-framed painting hanging on the wall above Jake's head. Amy didn't need to turn to know it was one of her own paintings: an early landscape from her first summer in Niederbipp. "This restaurant wouldn't last ten minutes in Manhattan."

Jake squeezed Amy's hand hard.

"You weren't kidding that they don't serve wine here?" she asked, looking down at the water glasses.

He shook his head.

"Yeah, then I'll take back my generous prediction— they wouldn't last five minutes." She laughed out loud, a haughty, proud laugh, as she opened the menu. "Is there anything here you'd recommend?"

"What do you like to eat in Manhattan? They've got an awesome venison ravioli."

"Is that vegetarian?"

"Uh, no," Jake responded, trying not to laugh. "It has venison in it. Venison is…meat. Are you a vegetarian?"

She nodded, but didn't look up. "Kind of. I only eat free-range chicken, wild fish, and organic veal."

He smiled, wondering what brand of vegetarianism that might be considered.

The waitress returned a few minutes later with a basket of warm garlic bread and took their order, or at least attempted to. Genevieve was last to place her order, and after sending the waitress back to the kitchen three times to check on the fat content and countries of origin of the cheeses used in the lasagna, she decided on the spinach fettuccini with sun-dried tomatoes, on the condition that either Italian or domestic capers would be substituted for the Greek ones since she had once dated a personal trainer who happened to be Greek and didn't want to be reminded of him now. The garlic bread was long cold by the time they got to it, which Genevieve was quick to point out to the flustered waitress when she returned with their salads.

"You must be new at this," Genevieve muttered in a condescending voice as the waitress twisted the top of a giant pepper mill, dusting their salads with fresh-ground pepper.

"Uh, almost three months, I guess," the poor girl responded nervously.

"I can tell. You probably didn't notice, but my water has been more than half empty for nearly five minutes."

"I'm sorry," she responded, looking even more flustered. She hurried away, returning with a silver pitcher wrapped with a white linen napkin. She was visibly shaken, which did nothing to help steady her hand as she did her best to fill the cups, leaving several drips across the tablecloth.

"This is ridiculous," Genevieve said before the waitress had even left the table. "It's got to be hard to find good help around here."

Amy shook her head, embarrassed to be seated at the same table as this woman.

"So, tell us about your interview," Jake said, hoping a change of subject might temper his desire to accidentally kick Genevieve in the shins under the table. "When do you get to interview Ruby?"

"Tomorrow. My boss said she agreed to spend the whole day with me. She said it might run over into Sunday too."

"Really?" Jake looked surprised. "I thought she and Lorenzo had orientation tomorrow. How...?"

"Yeah, well, the email I got earlier said that the old lady had decided it was finally time to share with the media some of her traditional matchmaking secrets that have been passed down for who knows how long."

"Really?" Jake asked again. "That surprises me."

"We just saw her on Tuesday. They didn't say anything about that," Amy reported.

"Yeah, well, I have no idea who this lady is," Genevieve responded through a mouthful of salad, "but apparently she's turned down interview requests from every major newspaper and magazine in the country for the past twenty-five years. My boss had to pull some major strings to make this happen. I feel like this might be the interview that could finally give me the international acclaim I deserve."

"So, is this interview about Ruby...or about you?" Jake asked, perturbed.

"Well, her, of course. But can't it be both?"

"I don't know. I guess I've never been in your position, but it seems like..."

"Well, it's no picnic, I'll tell you that. I've had to travel extensively over the last couple of years: Paris, Milan, London. It's been absolutely exhausting—champagne parties till dawn, night after night. If I weren't in such great shape, I'm sure I'd have had a coronary by now with all the stress. Yeah, I've been to some pretty crazy places, but this place takes the cake."

"In what way?" Amy asked, bracing herself for the answer.

"Well, it's like I said. I had no idea that places like this still existed in the world, especially not in the United States—so technologically backward and so old-fashioned in nearly every other sense. It's so cute that you two chose to live here. I imagine it's got to be a lot like living on the set of a Shakespearean play, right? I mean, honestly, I thought pottery was like a totally dead art form. It's like, oh my freakin' gosh, I'm in some kind of living museum. However did you find such a silly place?"

Amy looked at Jake then back to Genevieve, not sure what to say but certain that the sincere feelings she had about Niederbipp would be lost on Genevieve. She turned again to Jake, who had taken an unusual interest in his salad and was stuffing his mouth so full of the greens that she wondered how he was breathing.

Before Amy could find a suitable answer, Genevieve's purse began ringing. She grabbed the designer handbag and slid across the vinyl-covered bench without a word, obviously distracted, and disappeared around the corner.

"I've never experienced this level of snobbery," Jake managed through a mouthful of lettuce. "If she says "cute" one more time, I think I'm gonna snap."

"Try living with her," Amy responded. "I remembered it being bad, but I think she's only gotten worse."

"How do you think Ruby's gonna handle her?"

"I'm pretty sure the only way to handle her is the same way you'd handle a hot potato."

"You mean like a radioactive hot potato—drop her and run as far away as you can get?"

Amy smiled. "Exactly. What are we going to do?"

"We're gonna eat as fast as we can, wish her a happy weekend, and hope we never have to see her again."

"But what about Ruby and Lorenzo?"

Jake shook his head. "I don't know. We tried to warn them. They've lived this long; I'm sure they can endure anything for a weekend, right?"

The waitress returned with their entrees, and Jake and Amy took the opportunity to apologize for Genevieve, which seemed to only slightly dull the poor girl's flustrations. When Genevieve didn't return right away, they wondered if they should go ahead and eat without her, but they decided one rudeness did not deserve another. Instead they waited, trying to imagine how this weekend would play out for their elderly friends. Five minutes passed, then ten, their meals getting colder with each passing moment. Finally, after nearly twenty minutes, Genevieve returned to the table, obviously ruffled.

"Is everything okay?" Amy asked.

"Fine. Everything's just fine." She dropped into her seat, grabbed her fork without looking up, and began twisting the green fettuccini into a glob the size of a tennis ball. They watched as she opened her mouth and somehow fit the whole thing in. Diverting their eyes to keep themselves from both laughing and choking, they dove into their own meals, enjoying them much less than they might have twenty minutes earlier when they were hot. Jake found himself wondering how someone like Genevieve, who had something negative to say about nearly everything, could stomach cold fettuccini without a complaint, but the quiet was so refreshing, he decided not to ask.

She was just finishing her last strands of noodles when her phone chimed again, and she immediately turned her attention back to it, her manicured fingernails gliding quickly over the keys in response. It had been a long time since Jake or Amy had seen anyone using a cell phone, and neither of them could remember ever interacting with anyone quite so rude.

"So, how long will you be staying in Niederbipp?" Jake asked, breaking the long silence.

Genevieve shook her head, but didn't look up from her phone. "I'm a little confused about that. I've got to be back in New York on Tuesday so I can pack for Brussels Fashion Show on Wednesday."

"Oh, that's great! You'll be out of here soon then, huh?" Amy asked, not trying to mask her excitement.

"Yeah, but I just got a schedule from the photographer who normally accompanies me. Apparently he's planning on making four trips to Neiderbopp over the next five months."

"Uh, it's actually pronounced Need-er-bipp," Jake corrected her.

"I've heard it both ways."

The phone chimed again, and they all looked at the screen this time to see what it said: "Check your email immediately!"

Genevieve tapped a couple of the keys and lifted the phone closer to her face to read from the small screen. As she read, the color faded from her face, and a look of panic replaced it."

"Is everything okay?" Amy asked.

"No, everything is not okay! Apparently the old lady has decided that she'll only agree to an interview if I agree to spend the summer working for her on her stupid farm."

Jake and Amy glanced at each other out of the corner of their eyes, trying hard not to laugh.

"So…?" Amy asked.

Genevieve shook her head, her eyes focused on the small screen. "I can't believe this!"

"What's wrong?"

"My boss already committed me to do it."

"But what about Brussels?" Amy asked, anxiously.

"She's reassigned it to another writer. I can't believe this. There's no way in hell!"

"What are you going to do?" Jake asked.

She shook her head, her bright fingernails tapping out an angry, ferocious dance on the keys. The response came quickly, too quickly, almost as if her dispute had been anticipated. She set the phone down on the table and sat back on the bench, looking pale and lifeless. Jake and Amy both looked down at the screen.

I have gone to extreme lengths to make this possible. Your job, as well as all future assignments, will be determined by your performance on this project. Do not disappoint me!

They turned and looked at each other for a quick moment before the phone chimed again and a new message appeared. Genevieve leaned forward, and they all read the message together.

Stay where you are. We've tracked your location. Mr. and Mrs. Swarovski will be arriving soon to pick you up.

"She can't do this!" Genevieve muttered.

"What are you going to do?" Amy asked.

"I'm going to forward this to my attorney," she responded, reaching for the phone. But before her angry fingers could even begin, the phone rattled again and another message appeared.

If you're thinking of involving your attorneys, let me save you the trouble and remind you of the contract you signed when you were hired. Page 4, paragraph 2: "I agree to accept any assignment at any time and do hereby commit myself to giving my best work under all circumstances. Failure to do so will likely result in immediate termination, forfeiture of living accommodations, and a forced reversal of remittance of any and all travel expenditures associated with current assignment." :)

"What the...?" But before she could continue, the phone buzzed again, and another message appeared.

We are saving room in the November issue for this assignment. Ten thousand words plus photos. This is the opportunity you have been waiting for. Do not disappoint me!

"Wow, can she do that?" Amy asked.

"Apparently she can if it's in her contract," Jake responded.

"This is nothing short of blackmail," Genevieve seethed. She shook her head, fuming. "It's been done before. The girl I replaced refused to do an article on the first female termite charmer in the Serengeti."

"And they fired her?" Jake asked

"She was homeless before she even made it back to the States," said Genevieve

"Seriously?" Jake asked.

Genevieve nodded, looking down at her phone. "I'm living in her apartment."

"So what are you going to do?" Amy asked.

"I don't really have a choice, do I?" Genevieve responded.

"Of course you do. I'm sure you've made contacts in other places. You could…" Amy trailed off, feeling anxious to be rid of her.

"Ahh, there you are," a kind voice said from behind them. Jake and Amy turned to see the familiar faces of Lorenzo and Ruby Swarovski, dressed in their farm duds and looking very out of place in the fanciest restaurant in Niederbipp.

CHAPTER 5

The Turning of the Tides

we are all cells in the body of humanity—all of us, all over
the world. Each one has a contribution to make, and will
know from within what this contribution is.
- Peace Pilgrim -

Lorenzo patted Jake on the shoulder as he and Ruby moved along the side of the table to the bench where Genevieve was sitting. "I'm Ruby Swarovski." Ruby extended her hand to Genevieve. "And this is my husband, Lorenzo. Mrs. Galiveto informed us that you had arrived early and are in need of a ride."

"You spoke to Julia?" Genevieve asked, looking surprised.

"Of course. Lovely woman, isn't she?" Ruby responded. "May we join you?" She didn't wait for a response, taking a seat next to Genevieve and scooting her down the bench to make room for Lorenzo. "It's such a pleasure to meet you. As I'm sure you know, it's very rare for me to accept an invitation to do an interview. I'm glad you came in early so we could get to know each other before the others arrive."

"This way you get used to the thin air, too," Lorenzo added. "Hey look, Mom, it doesn't look like the kids have had dessert yet. The tiramisu is to die for." He winked at Jake, who smiled back, grateful to have another couple of voices to dilute Genevieve's acidity.

Dessert was ordered and delivered before introductions were even finished, and by the time they dug in, it was clear to everyone present that Genevieve was not only way out of her element but was also scared to the edge of mortality. Jake and Amy were surprised to observe how the negativity and rudeness they had witnessed in Genevieve earlier were all but extinguished by the arrival of the Swarovskis. But in all fairness, she really didn't speak much after that—mostly just sat like a trapped animal between the corner of the bench and the woman with whom she would be spending most of the next five months. Looking both dazed and confused, she barely touched her tiramisu, which Lorenzo was quick to notice and even quicker to polish off.

The phone rang only once more that evening, and since Genevieve was trapped in the corner, she answered it at the table. It was the rental car agency telling her they had arrived to trade out her vehicle. Jake winced as he listened to her awkwardly tell the man who had gone to so much trouble that she would not be needing either of the cars. She suggested that if he could wait for her to get her things out, they could take both of the cars back to Pittsburgh.

"Well, I hate to keep the folks from the big city waiting," Ruby said as soon as Genevieve hung up. "I suppose we best be on our way and gather up your things. There's still loads of work that needs doin' before the kids arrive in the morning. It'll be nice to have an extra set of hands."

Genevieve frowned and closed her eyes as if she were already dead. Jake was quick to thank her for dinner, which she barely acknowledged. He escorted Amy quickly out of the restaurant after bidding everyone farewell, anxious to be done with one of the most obnoxious people he had ever had the misfortune of meeting.

"Do you think she'll be okay?" Amy asked as they turned the corner.

Jake laughed. "I'm gonna worry about her every day for the next five months."

"You are?"

"Aren't you?"

"Wait, are you talking about Genevieve or Ruby?" Amy asked, looking a little confused.

"Ruby, of course. You thought I was concerned about that monster?"

Amy laughed. "She really is terrible. Do you think we've seen the last of her?"

"One can only hope?" Jake said, wrapping his arm around Amy's shoulder. "One can only hope."

CHAPTER 6

The Farm

we have forgotten the gracious hand which has preserved
us in peace and multiplied and enriched and strengthened
us, and have vainly imagined in the deceitfulness of our
hearts that all these blessings were produced by some
superior wisdom and virtue of our own. Intoxicated with
unbroken success, we have become too self-sufficient to
feel the necessity of redeeming and preserving Grace,
too proud to pray to the God that made us.
- Abraham Lincoln -

The crow of the rooster was Genevieve's first clue that she wasn't in Manhattan anymore. She closed her eyes tightly as if by doing so she could make it all go away. She tried to imagine an alternative reality but simply couldn't, the sharpness of her actual reality overwhelming all imagination. The rooster's second crow shattered her hopes that this was all just a bad dream: Niederbipp—that black hole of a town; bouncing around on the busted-out bench seat of an old pickup truck, sandwiched between two of the oldest geezers she had ever met; and the longest night on the hardest, skinniest mattress on which she had ever attempted to sleep.

She listened with her eyes closed tight as the third soul-piercing crow came, followed by what sounded like laughter. She listened closer. The rooster was laughing! And it wasn't just generic laughter—he was laughing at her. Somewhere close, up above her head, a rooster was laughing at her!

Angry, she forced open her eyelids to find it was still quite dark; only pale light tumbled in through the three windows and overhead skylights. She sat up, straightening her pajamas, which were twisted and knotted around her legs and abdomen from the long night's wrestling match. The rooster crowed a fourth time, and all her senses homed in, locating him on a perch just outside the open skylight. Her head pounded as if she had a hangover. When the next crow came, she reached for her shoe. But forgetting that she had chosen the top bunk and that she was wearing silk pajamas, she slipped from her bed and landed in an awkward pile on the hard wooden floor.

Again, the rooster laughed at her. She reached for her cobblestone-ruined shoes and threw one as hard as she could at the obnoxious bird. To her surprise, the shoe went right through the open skylight and landed somewhere on the roof beyond her view. He laughed at her again, taunting her. She climbed the ladder to the top bunk, trying to position herself for a cleaner shot. She launched the second shoe just as the rooster poised for another jeering insult. This second shoe struck the side of the rooster's perch, knocking him off balance. A great squawking commotion resulted, and Genevieve was in the middle of her victory dance when a knock came at the door.

"It's just me—Ruby," the old woman said, opening the outside door. "I hope you slept well. It occurred to me that I forgot to bring down your farm duds last night. Are you decent?" Ruby looked up at Genevieve standing on the top bunk. "Well, I'm glad to see you're gettin' your exercise, but dancing is probably safer on the ground." She smiled, laying an armful of clothing on the bottom bunk. "Breakfast is in ten minutes. Lorenzo and I would like to discuss a few things with you before we get started with the morning chores to make sure we're all on the same page. Seeing how you were dressed yesterday, I figured you probably don't have the right duds for the job. You can take your pick of these. We'll figure out the rest this afternoon when the kids arrive. You'll find breakfast in the dining hall at the big house. Any questions?"

"Uh, yeah, I assume there's a shower in the bathroom."

"Of course there is, but it's solar powered and won't be warm till this evening. You'll be needing a shower much more tonight than you are right now. Now chop-chop! We got a mess o' work to get done. The kids'll be here soon. I left a pair of boots for you here on the front stoop." Without another word, the old woman turned and left.

Genevieve slid down from the bunk, imagining a pair of brightly colored cowgirl boots like those she had so envied on the models at the Western Design Conference in Jackson Hole last summer. She looked over the clothes Ruby had laid out on the bottom bunk—a pair of worn overalls and a couple of hideous button-down flannel shirts. She balked at the clothing, unwilling to look like a fashion catastrophe.

Instead, she kicked open her suitcase, digging down to the bottom to retrieve her favorite pair of designer jeans and the most fashionable flannel top she had been able to find in New York. She dressed quickly, still imagining the boots on the front porch as she splashed her face with cold water and pulled her hair back with a rubber band.

The sun was nearly cresting the eastern hills, illuminating the horizon with fire, but she didn't see it; her eyes searching the front porch for the cowgirl boots she had imagined. When they weren't readily noticeable she began to wonder if a dog might have carried them off, just as she tripped over a tired-looking pair of rubber boots.

"You've got to be freakin' kidding me," she muttered, angrily sweeping the boots across the porch with her foot. The rooster who had tormented her earlier jumped down from the porch awning and landed in the dewy grass in front of her. He crowed loudly then followed it with what sounded like haughty laughter before turning his tail end toward her and prancing off.

Reluctantly, she picked up the rubber boots, slid them on, and walked up the hill to the big house for breakfast, cursing under her breath with each dewy step.

"Glad you could join us," Lorenzo said with a smile as Genevieve entered the dining hall. He looked over the top of a book and motioned for her to come forward where a single bowl and spoon had been set close to him on the long, whitewashed table. "Mom and I got an early start and have already eaten," he reported. "Have a seat and help yourself. We've already said grace." He closed the book and set it aside. "I trust you slept well. It will be a long day before we're through."

Genevieve straightened her jaw but didn't respond, taking a seat on the long wooden bench.

"Steel-cut oats," Lorenzo said, pointing to the bowl. "The kids from last year grew 'em. You'll get the chance to grow 'em this year."

"I can't wait," she grumbled.

"They would've been hotter a few a minutes ago, but they're still good." He passed her a small ceramic pitcher filled with milk and pointed to a bowl of amber honey. "Mom went up to the phone booth to get in touch with one of the kids to arrange for us to pick 'em up. Please, help yourself. We'll be gettin' started as soon as she gets back."

Genevieve looked down at the porridge in front of her and frowned. She hated all mushy breakfast foods. "I usually just have a cappuccino for breakfast. I don't suppose you have anything like that?"

Lorenzo raised his finger to his chin, looking thoughtful. "I don't suppose we do. Closest thing would probably be the chicory coffee the kids made last summer."

"Is it any good?"

"If you like that sort of thing. There won't be time this mornin'... maybe tomorrow. You better eat up. You'll need the energy."

She looked down again at the bowl in front of her. "I think I'd rather die."

"Suit yourself. The chickens will love it."

The door at the end of the table swung open, and Ruby stepped through it, looking taller than Genevieve remembered. "Oh, good, you decided to join us for breakfast," she said with a smile. "I just spoke to one of the boys. He says he's in Pittsburgh and will be arriving in Niederbipp shortly before ten. I told him to hang tight at the old train station and wait for the rest of the kids to arrive."

"Let the games begin!" Lorenzo said, clapping his hands.

"Not so fast, Pops. There's still mornin' chores to be done, and that talk we're needing to have with this one."

"Where do you wanna start?"

"The cows won't wait much longer. Why don't you take Genevieve with you to the barn, and I'll get the chickens fed and slop the pigs and..." She paused, closing her eyes and shaking her head. "And I guess I'll be remoppin' the ding-dang floor where Miss Hoitytoitypants forgot to slip off her muckers."

Lorenzo looked over Genevieve's shoulder to the trail of fresh, dewy mud she had left across the whitewashed floor.

"Oh, sorry," Genevieve responded lamely. "I guess I'm not used to everything being so dirty."

"Well, around here we try to keep the dirt outside the house," explained Ruby. "In the future, you'll kindly leave your boots at the door."

Genevieve nodded.

"Now, let's get movin'. It's almost seven. I figure we'll be needin' at least half an hour for our chat before you and Lorenzo head off to pick up the kids."

Lorenzo nodded and grabbed his cap from the bench. He got to his feet and came around the table, where he hugged and kissed his wife. "Love you, Mom," he said as he headed out the back door. And as Genevieve followed, sheepishly retracing her muddy footprints, she noticed his socks for the first time—bold stripes on one foot and colorful polka dots on the other.

CHAPTER 7

Adventures in Mucking

We are not merely imperfect creatures who must be
improved; we are rebels who must lay down our arms.
— C. S. Lewis —

The old red barn was no more than a well-thrown stone away from the big house, but Genevieve could smell it before she saw it. She put her hand over her nose to help block the stench.

"I'm guessin' you've never been on a farm, eh?" Lorenzo asked, laughing at her watering eyes.

"I had a pony when I was a kid."

"Is that right? This'll be old hat for you then. I reckoned you for a city girl. I assume you know all about muckin' then."

"Muckin'?"

"Sure, you know, scoopin' poop, cleaning out the stalls…muckin'."

"Uh, sure," she lied, not wanting to admit that the hands at the stable where her pony had been kept took care of all the dirty work and that she had never mucked a stall in her life.

"That's great. I think I'll make you chief mucker. Nobody ever wants that job, but in my humble opinion, it's better than most."

"Uh, thanks, but I'm sure I'll be happy to do another chore."

"Nonsense. A strong, experienced cowgirl like you won't have any trouble at all." He whistled loudly, and from over a mud-covered berm on the far side of the pasture, a pretty brown cow raised her head and came trotting, followed by three heavy-uddered companions, all of them wearing bells around their necks. Without hesitation, they filed into the barn.

"You trained them to come to your whistle?" she asked.

"I'm surprised they weren't already waitin'. I'm sure they're hurtin'. I'm at least a half hour late." He opened the side door and flipped on the lights before showing Genevieve in. He led her to the milking stall and filled the trough with alfalfa and grain. As if on cue, the cows lined up, sticking their heads through the metal bars of the trough. Lorenzo secured leather tethers to their bell collars.

"I'll need some help tying up their tails," Lorenzo said, pointing to the four braided ropes on the wall opposite the trough. He reached for one and motioned for Genevieve to come closer so he could show her how this was to be done. A metal clip at the end of the rope was attached to the long hair at the end of the first cow's tail. "I'll get some soap and water if you handle this," he said, pointing to the other ropes.

In spite of her minimal experience around larger animals, Genevieve felt like a fish out of water. She reached for the next rope and was just about to grab the second cow's tail when to her surprise, it lifted its own tail. She was amazed that the cows were so well trained and was just about to attach the clip when Lorenzo shouted from behind her to get out of the way.

Startled, she backed up as fast as she could, but it wasn't fast enough. A solid stream of what looked like fresh pesto sauce shot out of the cow's rump and hit the wall, narrowly missing Genevieve and splattering all over the floor. It continued to flow, now leaving great splatters across Genevieve's boots and jeans, even hitting her cheeks and shirt before the green stream turned off and the excitement ended.

Thoroughly disgusted, she turned away to find Lorenzo standing behind her, smiling. "I'm sorry, but Ol' Cindy there gave you the answer before I could even ask the riddle. He tried not to laugh. "The riddle is, what do you get when you cross a hungry cow with a field of fresh spring grass."

"You think this is funny?" she asked angrily.

"No, I think it's hilarious," he said, cracking a barrelful of laughter wide open. It took nearly a minute for him to compose himself. Meanwhile, Genevieve dipped her hand into the bucket of warm water he held toward her and wiped the muck from her face and hands.

"These are my favorite jeans," she lamented, looking down at the splotchy, batter-like blobs of green manure. "They're from Saks."

"Didn't Mom bring you some farm duds this morning?"

She shook her head. "Yeah, but I'm not gonna wear crappy clothes like that."

"Oh, I see, so instead you're just gonna make your nice duds crappy?" he said with a smile. "Do what you want. The choice is always yours. We were only hoping to save you some trouble. Now, if you'd tie up those last three tails, we need to get the milkin' done."

He brushed past her with his bucket and rag and began cleaning the udder of first cow. "Any time you're behind a cow and it lifts its tail and arches its back like that, I strongly recommend you get out of way. You can only train an animal to do so much, and unfortunately controllin' its bowels ain't one of those things."

"Thanks for the warning," she said sarcastically.

"There will be many more before the summer's over."

"Are you talking about crap or warnings?" she asked defiantly.

"Both, but I suppose much of that depends on you. Now if you don't mind, turn that crank at the end of the row so neither you nor I have find out what happens when a cow's tail gets loose."

She decided not to ask any more questions and did as she was told. The turning of the crank handle turned the pole to which the ropes were fastened, quickly lifting the cows' tails out of swatting range and making it safer for Lorenzo and Genevieve to work. When the udders were cleaned, Lorenzo taught Genevieve how to prime the teats before attaching the automatic milking machine. By the time the last cow's udder was empty, most of the manure on Genevieve's pants had dried and fallen off, leaving lovely pastel polka dots as subtle reminders of crappy lessons learned.

"What do you do with all that milk?" Genevieve asked.

"You get to drink some, some will be made into cheese and ice cream, and the rest will be sold to buy farm supplies."

"And you have to do this every day?" she asked.

"No, we *get to*—twice a day—morning and night—365 days a year."

"Why would you do that?" she asked after roughly figuring how much time that would consume.

"You wouldn't understand right now, but you will before you leave in September."

After Lorenzo taught her how to rinse out the milker, they let down the tails and unhitched the tethers just as the cows were finishing their breakfast. Lorenzo whistled loudly again, and they all turned to leave, heading back out into the bright day.

Genevieve had pretended she knew how to muck out a stall, but she was more than happy when Lorenzo stepped between her and her pitchfork, offering a refresher course. Two pungent wheelbarrow trips to the far side of the barn later, they had completed the first chore of the day.

"Don't forget to take your boots off," Lorenzo said as they approached the back door of the big house.

She smiled weakly and nodded, placing her boots on the rack she had walked past earlier. They found Ruby in the dining hall, setting the table with starched white linen napkins folded like paper cranes, which seemed entirely out of place on a farm and in a room so sparsely decorated.

"We'll make a milker out of this one yet," Lorenzo said from the doorway.

Ruby turned and smiled. "I knew she'd be a good mucker the moment I laid eyes on her. Well done, child. Are you ready for our little chat?"

"Uh, whatever. Let's just get it over with."

"Very well," she said, looking down at her manure-stained pants, obviously trying not to smile. "Why don't you come around to the front porch where we can keep the scent of the stall outside." She turned her back to finish her work, and Lorenzo motioned for Genevieve to follow. They traipsed around the tall grass of the side yard and up the front steps. It had been dark the night before when Genevieve had arrived, and all of this had been lost on her. Seeing it now for the first time, it was different than she had imagined; still old, but slightly less ugly than she had envisioned.

No sooner had she taken a seat in a squeaky wicker chair than Ruby came out the front door to join them, a tall glass of lemonade in each hand. When she had delivered the beverages, she sat down in the wicker chair opposite Genevieve, a stern but pleasant look on her face.

"You may be curious why I finally agreed to an interview request and why I've agreed to it solely on my terms."

"Yes, as a matter..."

"It's simple," she said cutting her off. "You couldn't possibly understand what happens here each year till you've experienced it yourself. Experience is usually a very expensive teacher. In this case, it costs only a summer's labor, but what it costs in time, it promises much greater wisdom and happiness in return. We open our farm to only twelve lucky souls each year. Six men and six women. When I received Mrs. Galiveto's initial request for an interview, six years ago, I wasn't ready or willing to put up with such a hassle. But times change. I'm not gettin' any younger. Pops and I have been discussing it every winter, wondering how much longer we can reasonably go on. A whole lot o' praying's gone into this decision, hoping we'd know when to let the press in. When one of the girls contacted us on Wednesday to say she was staying home to take a new job, we made the decision to let you in on very strict conditions."

"That's why I'm here?"

"That's the only reason you're here."

"You haven't read my articles? You don't know my work?"

"Do I look like I have the time to read lady magazines?"

"Well, no, but Julia said you chose me to tell your story."

Ruby nodded. "I felt like it was a sign, not that I was even lookin' for one. I had no idea who we'd be getting, but I told Mrs. Galiveto I'd agree to the interview only if whoever she sent would stay the summer. I sent her all the paperwork and contract, and she assured me that your contract with her obliged you to everything my contract would."

"I don't think that's even legal."

"That's none of our business. You'll have to straighten that out with your attorneys at the end of the summer. The way we see it, your obligation to your boss has been transferred to us. Now, that doesn't mean we own you. But a contract is a contract, and there's nothing that you'll be obliged to do that won't be expected from the rest of the kids that will be joining us later today, except one thing."

Genevieve raised an eyebrow, looking a bit worried. "What kind of exception are you talking about?"

"It's simple, really. You may not, under any circumstance, let the others know that you're here doing research for an article. They can know you work for a women's magazine. They can even know you're a writer, but they cannot know that you're doin' research on me, the farm, or this experience."

"Why not?"

"Because the last thing I want is for people to be putting on airs, sayin' stuff they don't mean, hoping to make themselves look like they're someone or something they're not. This experience is all about authenticity. You'll see. It will bring out the best and worst in you, and it needs to. That's what it's all about."

Genevieve looked both surprised and relieved. "That's it? That's all you want from me?"

"That's all we want."

"And you're not going to torture me until I write something positive about you?"

"Actually, that sounds like a good idea, Mom," Lorenzo said.

"No!" Ruby cracked the first smile Genevieve had seen from her. "Listen, I don't want to make a big deal out of this. As far as I'm concerned, you're here because you're supposed to be here. But you'll get no special treatments. I will be as fair to you as I am to the rest of the kids. And in return, I expect you to work just as hard; put your head, heart, and hands into the work; and promise to have an open mind."

"That's it?"

"Well, no, but there's way too much to cover now. The rest of the kids have been preparing for this for several months. You'll be way behind, but there's no way to catch you up now. You'll just have to roll with it and fake it till you make it. I suppose it's probably like any other job."

"Only you don't get paid," Lorenzo added with a smile and a wink.

"Are we in agreement?" Ruby asked, leaning forward and reaching out her right hand with her wrinkled pinky finger extended.

"I guess so," Genevieve said, linking her pinky with Ruby's.

"I'll take that as a yes," she said, pulling Genevieve forward with uncanny strength until their noses touched. "We're gonna learn to love each other, but until we do, don't you dare disappoint me. And if I catch you throwin' shoes at my favorite rooster again, there's gonna be trouble." She smiled and hugged her awkwardly.

"Now you two better get out of here. The kids'll be waiting."

CHAPTER 8

Meet and Greet

Humility is the foundation of all the other virtues, hence,
in the soul in which this virtue does not exist there
cannot be any other virtue except in mere appearance.
– Saint Augustine –

In the time it took Genevieve to pack her bags, strip the bedding from her bunk, and change her clothes, Lorenzo had hitched the hay wagon to the pickup truck and pulled it around to the front of the house. He threw her expensive suitcase into the back of the pickup and they were off, bouncing and bumping up the rutted driveway that separated the farm from the slightly more civilized world.

It took much longer to get back to Niederbipp than she remembered her trip going the opposite direction the night before. There was nothing that looked the least bit familiar, but then she really hadn't seen much of it or paid any attention to what she had seen. She attempted to comfort herself by pretending this was just an oversized Central Park, but when the town of Niederbipp came into view, she was faced again with the hard reality that she was at least a million miles away from anything familiar.

Lorenzo stopped the truck just around the corner from the train station and let Genevieve out with her bags, giving her a ten-minute head start so she could make it to the rendezvous point where each of the summer's participants had been instructed to meet. With her ego significantly deflated by the events of the last twelve hours, Genevieve approached the eleven other people standing on the platform.

"Are you here to meet the matchmaker?" a tall, bespectacled, darker-skinned, thirty-something man asked as she approached the platform, dragging her bag.

"Yes, I am."

"Cool. I'm Greg. I talked to her this morning. She said her husband would be here to pick us up. I'm sure he'll be here any time now. What's your name?"

"I'm Genevieve," she said nodding, trying to be cool but feeling very out of place. "Patterson. That's my last name, just in case you wondered."

"Nice to meet you."

"Have you been waiting long?" she asked, distracted by a forty-something man wearing a well-worn rucksack covered in patches from around the world. She strained her eyes to read one of the patches—*Not all who wander are lost*—and immediately began wondering what kind of weirdos she was going to find here.

"Uh, most of us got here about an hour ago on the Greyhound," Greg responded, interrupting her thoughts.

"Wait, what? You seriously rode the freakin' bus?"

"Well, yeah. It seemed like the most sensible and economic way to get here considering that we weren't supposed to bring cars, right?"

"Oh, right, of course."

"How'd you get here?" asked a freckle-faced woman with ginger hair.

"Huh? Oh yeah, well, my uncle dropped me off."

"He didn't want to bring you all the way to the station?" she asked, her eyes looking down road from where she had just come.

"Shy. He's shy," Genevieve stammered. "Plus, he's my uncle, you know. I didn't really want my uncle dropping me off for summer camp when everyone was watching."

The ginger-headed woman peered at her suspiciously.

"Hey, there's one sweet roll left," a curly-headed twenty-something man said, thrusting an aluminum tray in front of her. "I did a little research before I got here. Neiderbopp has a world-renowned bakery."

"I'm pretty sure it's pronounced Niederbipp," Genevieve corrected him.

"Oh, I've heard it both ways," the guy reported. "Anyway, I saved this for you. We've all had one. We were just waiting for you to show up."

"Uh, thanks," Genevieve said, her mouth watering at the sight of the sweet roll, remembering that she hadn't eaten since the night before. She reached for the sweet roll just as the cry of an old-fashioned ahoogah horn sounded behind her. She jumped, and the sweet roll landed on the platform. With everyone else looking up at the pickup truck, Genevieve did something she had never done in her adult life: she stooped down quickly and swept the sweet roll off the platform in one graceful move, taking a bite before she even stood back up. To her relief, no one seemed to notice. No one, that is, except the ginger-headed woman who expressed her disgust by pulling a very funny face.

"Welcome to Niederbipp," Lorenzo said through the open window before he had even put the truck in park. He jumped from the cab like someone half his age, smiling broadly. "Welcome to Niederbipp," he repeated when he stood next to them on the platform. "I'm Lorenzo, but you can call me Pops if you want. And let's see if I can make my old brain work. You're Greg," he said, surprising the tall man. "And let's see," he said, scanning the crowd, "Susan, and Josh, and Crystal." He shook each of their hands as he continued searching both the crowd and his memory. "James, Ephraim, Sonja, Holly, Rachael." Again, he shook their hands also, looking brightly into their faces. "Spencer, Matt and…" he stood awkwardly in front of Genevieve looking like he was sincerely straining his brain. "Ahh, of course, Genevieve. How could I forget?" He put his arm around her and one of the men and gathered them all into a huddle.

"It's great to have you all here. I'm grateful you've all arrived safely. We'll have plenty of time for questions when we get to the farm. But I have one question for you before we start loading up your things. Which one of you is the fastest on foot?"

They all looked at each other. "I used to run track in high school," Josh spoke up.

"So did I," responded Susan.

"Very good," Lorenzo said, looking down at Josh and Susan's shoes. "Susan, I'm afraid Josh wins today for the most practical shoes to carry him swiftly over the cobblestones." He pulled a twenty-dollar bill from his wallet and handed it to Josh. "In the middle of the town, just down from the fountain, you will find a fabulous bakery: Gottlieb's. I want you to run as fast as you can and procure for us the best tray of sweet rolls you have tasted in your life—a baker's dozen."

"We've actually already tasted the sweet rolls," the redheaded Crystal reported.

Lorenzo frowned. "That's a shame. I was looking forward to seeing your faces as you bit into the best sweet rolls you have ever tasted." He looked sad for a moment before turning back to Josh. "Josh, run as fast as you can. I want to see the joy on your faces as you bite into the best sweet rolls in the world for the second time!"

The small crowd erupted in cheers as Josh dropped his bag and ran down the street.

"I'm sorry we no longer have a bus to transport you in," Lorenzo sighed. "One of the kids borrowed it to take everyone to the drive-in a few years back and filled it up with gasoline instead of diesel. But never fear. We still have our trusty hay wagon, and if I drive slow enough, and no one falls off and dies, we'll all make it to the farm just in time for dinner."

He waited and watched their faces for a moment before he started to laugh. "Only kidding. It's a short drive, only twenty minutes—unless a wheel falls off. Mom will have lunch ready for us when we get there."

"How do you want us to do it?" Greg asked. "Girls in the truck, boys on the wagon?"

"That's a grand idea," Lorenzo replied. "Anyone who's scared of falling out can ride in the cab with me. Luggage can go on the wagon with the boys."

They were nearly loaded when Josh returned, out of breath but smiling as he cradled the second tray of sweet rolls, plus two more in a paper bag for Lorenzo and Ruby. He distributed the pastries and was just climbing on board the wagon when a red motor scooter pulled up next to the truck.

"Looks like you're ready for another fun summer," Jake said, smiling at Lorenzo.

"Indeed we are," Lorenzo replied. "Would you like to join us?"

Jake laughed. "I don't think my wife would be very happy about me visiting a matchmaker. I was just on my way to the post office," he said, thumping on the brown box in the handlebar basket.

Lorenzo nodded and stood next to Jake before raising his hand to the campers. "Ladies and gentlemen, I'd like you to meet the potter of Niederbipp. If you're lucky, you'll get to meet his better half too. They're both talented artists. In fact, you'll be using some of his pottery on the farm."

Jake blushed and nodded. "Have a great summer," he said as he buzzed off on his scooter, but not before smiling slyly at Genevieve, who was trying to hide in the back of the pickup truck.

Crystal was the only woman to take Lorenzo's offer and ride in the cab, leaving Genevieve and the other women to wonder if Crystal was scared of falling out or hoping to get in good with the master of the farm.

Genevieve was tired, but she felt the need to interact with the other four women in the pickup bed. They all seemed a little road worn and weary, but by the time they hit the edge of town, Genevieve could already tell this was going to be way different from any other summer she had ever experienced. She had spent close to ten summers at one camp or another through her growing-up years, and in every case, she had decided during the first hour who would be her best friend. But as she looked around now, she didn't feel like she could make any of them her best friend—no obvious allies, no easy alliances. But neither did she feel any competition with any of them. Not one of them was preening herself in front of the men, hoping to be noticed.

And something else was different. Not one of the men seemed to be showing off. If she understood the situation correctly, each of them was there for the same reason the women had come: they wanted to get married. Genevieve couldn't remember the last time she had met a man who wanted to get married—or who openly admitted it. She had convinced herself that such a breed of man either didn't exist or was so rare she would probably never meet one. It felt strange and somehow attractive to know that six members of this endangered species were attached to the very pickup truck in which she was traveling, men who wanted to be married, presumably to women! She found herself wondering if she was the only woman present who had made that realization.

Before she had time to think about anything else, the pickup truck came to a stop. Lorenzo put the truck in park before getting out and standing at the side of the bed. "Welcome to Harmony Hill," he said. "The phone booth over there is not only our only means of communication with the outside world—besides the mailbox, of course—but it's also officially the highest point in the county—1,352 feet. If you'll look around, it will be quite obvious to you why this phone booth is on several maps of the most beautiful phone booths in the world. The farm's just down the drive here," he said, pointing directly across the street from the phone booth. "This last quarter mile is a pretty rough road. You're welcome to stay and bounce around, but you might have a better experience if you walk. Either way, it's gonna be best if we put the luggage in the pickup truck so it doesn't bounce off the wagon."

They quickly disembarked, stretching and straightening themselves from the ride before forming a line, the men passing the luggage into the back of the pickup truck, where it quickly became clear that if anyone wanted to ride, they would likely be crushed by bouncing suitcases.

Lorenzo went on ahead, and the campers held back, waiting for the dust to settle before lumbering on. "It's beautiful here," one of the women said, and Genevieve was surprised when the rest of the gang nodded and agreed verbally.

"It's way better than I expected. It almost feels like Switzerland," someone said.

"I was just thinking the same thing," someone else offered.

"I heard this town was settled by German and Swiss immigrants— Quakers, I think," said the same curly-haired man who had offered Genevieve the last sweet roll. Without another word, they started off down the rutted path, following Lorenzo's ebbing dust cloud.

"Check out the fence posts," one of the men commented, and for the first time, Genevieve saw the colorful fence posts that she had already missed twice. Each post was different, covered in varying shades and conditions of colored yarn, knit and woven together in unpredictably undulating patterns. Each of the colorful posts was topped with unusual, unidentifiable farm implements. The travelers laughed and marveled as they moved from post to post, admiring the unique creativity that went into each one. As they walked, Genevieve found herself falling slowly behind, watching and observing what was happening.

Unlike her, she realized, each of these people wanted to be here, and unlike her, they were finding beauty and charm on their very first time seeing it. She looked back along the road they'd traveled and realized she had missed an awful lot. In fact, she had missed everything. They were right. From a distance, the farmhouse was in an idyllic Swiss-like setting, the grassy, rolling hills giving way to wildflowers and pastures. There was even a glossy pond not far from the house. She had missed the entire pond! Part of her wanted to join them, but another part, maybe the journalist part, wanted to hang back a few paces and observe the place through their eyes—eyes that seemed to see more clearly and sharply, eyes that were open to more detail and meaning than she had previously made room for.

"Look at this," one of the women said, pointing to the finial on one of the last fence posts.

"It's a shoe," another added. "It looks expensive."

"That's because it's a Christian Louboutin," one of the men replied in a very seductive French accent. "That's a $700 shoe."

"More like $750," Genevieve wanted to say, recognizing the shoe as her own—the shoe she had thrown at Ruby's favorite rooster just hours earlier.

"How would a guy know that from ten feet away?" one of the women asked dubiously.

"My ex-girlfriend left me because I refused to buy her another pair," he responded.

"Seriously?" they all asked in seeming unison.

He nodded. "I know. I was a jerk. I had bought her several pair of Louboutin already, but I just couldn't bring myself to spend that kind of dough when so many people in the world can't even afford to buy Nikes. She told me I was selfish. It's been kind of a sore subject. I guess I've regretted it ever since."

"No, dude, you did the right thing," Greg responded. "That's at least fourteen shades of crazy. No shoe's worth seven hundred bones."

They all nodded and moved on.

"Technically, it's only half that," Genevieve whispered in a tone only she could hear. She wanted to explain that the high price actually included two shoes. But she knew that this fact would be lost on them, so she kept her mouth shut. Still, she couldn't help but wince when she saw the rusty nail that had been driven through the sole, attaching the shoe so crudely to the old fence post.

Genevieve hurried to catch up to the others for the last thirty yards of the walk leading to the large, craftsman-style farmhouse, half hidden by the mammoth cottonwood trees. Ruby was there to meet them, a huge welcoming smile on her face as she embraced each of the campers, calling them by name as if she had known them for years. She welcomed them onto the generous porch, where they all found seats on the wicker furniture and were served tall glasses of lemonade as they chitchatted. Genevieve observed how different their reception was from the rushed and awkward reception she had received the night before. She had blamed Ruby and Lorenzo for that awkwardness, but as she watched them laughing and enjoying their guests, she began to wonder if she had missed something more important.

CHAPTER 9

Orientation

You must understand the whole of life, not just one little part of it. That is why you must read, that is why you must look at the skies, that is why you must sing and dance, and write poems and suffer and understand, for all that is life.

– Jiddu Krishnamurti –

After fifteen minutes or so, they were all shown into the big house; through the warm, homey entry; past the well-stocked library; and into the dining hall, where the table had been set with a broad mixture of stoneware plates and old-fashioned cutlery that looked like it had been collected from antique shops and flea markets across at least four continents. There was a whimsy and joviality about the table, and Genevieve noticed that even the napkin cranes now seemed to fit in with the whole picture in a way she hadn't recognized before.

Despite the eclectic nature of the rest of the table's settings, in the center of each plate stood something that still stood out as peculiar—a fortune cookie.

Ruby invited the campers to write their names on name tags so they could all get to know each other more quickly. Then she prompted them all to choose their own seats at the table. When everyone was seated, she wheeled into the dining room a stainless-steel cart stacked with tureens and lidded dishes of various sizes and shapes.

"Before we begin a new year with this first meal, and in keeping with the tradition that has been passed down through seven generations of matchmakers in Niederbipp, I asked Pops to say grace."

Genevieve watched as some folded their arms, others closed their eyes, and others looked awkwardly at their laps while Lorenzo stood at that the head of the table and thanked the heavens for good food, new friends, freedom to make changes, mercy and grace, and new beginnings. It was simple and sweet and somehow far less awkward than Genevieve had anticipated.

The dishes and tureens were moved to the table, and lunch was served while Ruby explained one culinary tradition from Switzerland, whence her heritage stemmed—that of eating the day's biggest meal in the middle of the day, when the energy consumed could still be put to work rather than sitting in one's belly overnight and doing little good.

Amid the sounds of cutlery and delighted consumption, Ruby explained that every day at noon, the lunch bell would be rung, calling everyone from their work to join together around the table. The meal would be different every day, but today there were bottled beans and carrots, mashed potatoes and gravy, homemade rolls, cornbread saturated with butter and honey, a big roast that was tender and juicy, and a huge bowl of salad. As the diners passed the dishes and tureens around the table, Ruby explained that dinners would generally be much simpler fare, but she left them guessing what that meant.

As they ate, Ruby also told them that everything they were eating had been grown on the farm either this year or the year before. She explained that their work over the coming months would not only include raising the food they would eat themselves but would also include preserving any extra, which next summer's folks would use.

Lorenzo also took his turn explaining how the farm's two hundred acres had been handed down from matchmaker to matchmaker for more than three hundred years. They learned that in addition to featuring fields of wheat, barley, corn, and oats, as well as a sizable garden and orchard, the farm was home to four milk cows; four beef cows; a team of Belgian horses; six pigs; at least fifty chickens; a dozen ducks; a handful of geese; thirty sheep; two alpaca; four cats; one dog; and innumerable mice, honeybees, butterflies, and songbirds—all of which needed to be respected, if not cared for and fed.

When asked for a show of hands of who, if any, had spent time on a farm, only one raised his hand—Matt, a quiet fellow who appeared to be in his early forties and who freely admitted that his experience had been limited to a weeklong stay with an uncle nearly thirty years earlier. Lorenzo suggested that there was no need to be intimidated by what lay ahead but that it was important for each of them to dive into the work and learn the nuances of each of the chores as quickly as possible. He admitted that the first two weeks would be the most difficult—before muscles were toned, calluses and work ethic developed, and a basic understanding of farm life gained.

After that, Ruby explained how all of the daily chores would be divided into six groups of tasks that would be accomplished by pairs— with one man and one woman in each pair. But just as Genevieve noticed the group eyeing each other strategically, Ruby clarified that different partners would be assigned to work together each day, giving each woman a chance to work with each of the men, and vice versa, as they rotated through all the chores. Changes to pairs, she stressed, would not be made without a darn good reason, so it was in their best interest to do their best work and to be nice. With this constant shuffling of workmates, Ruby made it undeniably clear that the strict policy laid out in their contracts—that of making no romantic advances toward any member of the group—must be adhered to with all solemnity until after the end of the summer. This was news to Genevieve, but it suddenly made sense to her why there had been such an obvious lack of flirtation.

Next they reviewed the strict policy of separation of the sexes in the bunkhouses. Only under emergency circumstances would violations to that policy be tolerated. When asked what might be constituted as an emergency worthy of deviation, Lorenzo offered only two—fire and overflowing toilets.

A brief explanation of the bunkhouses was offered next; of particular note were the solar water heaters on the roof of each house. They held only fifty gallons of water each, meaning short showers—no longer than four minutes so everyone could enjoy the warm water. As laundry would be one of the shared chores, and because mornings would always start before sunrise, it was recommended that the showers be enjoyed each evening before bed to keep the sheets clean.

While the subject of laundry was still being discussed, the group was directed to the far side of the dining hall, where wardrobes filled with various sizes of work duds were available to anyone who wanted to keep their own clothes clean. Permanent markers were available to mark one's underwear and other personal items, and Ruby said that every effort and care would be made to get clothes back to their owners. But she also suggested that flexibility and cooperation would be hailed as virtues while they all lived and worked as a family of fourteen.

After quickly offering an overview of the history of matchmaking here on the farm, Ruby explained that one of the long-held traditions passed down from generation to generation was the unique patterns and designs in the knitted socks. These socks, she explained, were intended to not only unify the group but also to eliminate one of the biggest universal sources of familial stress and disharmony—that of sorting the blasted socks.

Instead of sorting in the traditional sense, Ruby explained how all of the socks worn on the farm could be mixed and matched in every conceivable way. She warned them, however, that it was futile to upend the basket in search of a perfect match, acknowledging that she had never created two socks alike and never planned to do so.

In addition, as the sheep would soon need to be shorn, she informed them that they would all have the privilege of helping to dye, card, and spin the wool into the yarn that would become the socks they would wear. In the meantime, they would have full and open access to the socks in the overflowing basket that she had created over the winter.

Again, Lorenzo stood at the head of the table and asked if there were any questions. They all turned and looked at each other, then back to Lorenzo. "Questions will no doubt arise," he suggested. "We welcome them. As many of you will surely share similar questions, we invite you to bring these to our attention during mealtimes, where they can be discussed."

"And what are the mealtimes again?" Josh asked.

"Great question," Ruby replied. "We don't have many clocks around here. We tend to mark our day more by the flight of the sun. Each bunkhouse has an assigned rooster to greet the dawn. As much as they may annoy you," she said, glancing quickly down the table at Genevieve, "do not, under any circumstances, abuse your roosters. We invite you all to meet on the lawn between the bunkhouses each morning, fifteen minutes after the first rooster crows. Chores will begin as soon as you find your partner. Breakfast will be served as soon as it's ready, which is usually about the same time the morning milking is done. Lunch will be served around noon, and supper at about six. Does that answer your question?"

Josh nodded.

"Yes, Rachael," Lorenzo responded, looking at her raised hand.

"Is there any free time?"

"Good question," replied Lorenzo. "Some of you will be able to finish your chores by midafternoon. Others, depending on the day and the chores, will probably not be done until sometime after supper. When your chores are done, you are welcome to do as you please. On the tour we will give you after lunch today, you will find a well-stocked library as well as a parlor filled with musical instruments. You're welcome to nap if you would like or explore the farm or use any of the bicycles and go into town. There will be plenty of time to spend in contemplation, and I encourage you to embrace the solitude of the farm. If you'll listen, you'll discover that even the grass has a voice," he said, smiling.

"As outlined in your packets you received before your arrival, we will be working Monday through Saturday. Sunday is the Sabbath around here, which likely means something different to each one of you. Though the cows need to be milked and the animals need to be fed, we hope you'll make the Sabbath a delight and find joy in whatever observations seem most appropriate to your conscience. Mom and I head to town for ten o'clock church services, leaving at 9:30 sharp. You're all welcome to join us or worship however you would like. The kitchen chores on Sunday will be simpler, and laundry duty will be called off till Monday."

"Uh, where's the TV?" Spencer asked without waiting to be called on.

Lorenzo smiled, looking to the opposite end of the table. "Mom, you wanna take that one?"

"There's no TV," she said bluntly.

"Seriously?" Spencer asked, looking like he might cry.

"Absolutely."

"This is crazy," he mused. "Five months without sports?!"

"I guess you'll have to create your own. There's a box of balls and other sports stuff out in the shed. Help yourself."

He shook his head, looking very disappointed.

"Anyone else?" Lorenzo asked.

Crystal raised her hand. "What's up with the fortune cookies?"

"Ahh, yes. Mom, why don't you take that one, too?"

Ruby got to her feet this time. "Many of you probably wondered the same thing. We've discovered over the years that most folks who need a little wisdom are often not in the right place mentally to accept it when it is given to them directly. But if it comes wrapped in a cookie, the response is usually different. It's still true that a spoonful of sugar helps the medicine go down. The wisdom in these cookies is the collective wisdom gathered over the past three-hundred years of matchmaking on this farm, but Pops and I started this tradition about forty years ago. During the winter, we make thousands of these cookies, filling them with the wisdom of the ages and stowing them away for the next summer. The cookie may be stale, but the wisdom you'll find inside is as fresh as it ever was. *Wisdom cookies*, as we like to call them, will be available at every meal. You're welcome to take them or leave them. The choice is always yours. If you get a piece of wisdom you believe someone else is in need of, it's yours to pass on."

Genevieve watched as everyone at the table reached for their cookie, and she felt compelled to do the same. With the sounds of cookies cracking, she noticed smiles spreading and people sharing in subtle whispers. Breaking up her own cookie, she pulled out the folded message and read.

> Enough is as good as a feast.

She looked up to find Ruby smiling, not at her directly but more broadly across the whole of the gathering as they partook of the wisdom she offered them.

"Now," Lorenzo said when the chatter had quieted down, "we would like to give you a tour of the farm. If you'll stand and clear your plates and cutlery, you can follow Mom to the kitchen."

They all stood, excited to see what there was to see. They followed Ruby out the door and into the adjacent room, which was the kitchen. The room was awash in natural light coming in from the generous windows above the sink and the skylights in the ceiling, illuminating the black-and-white checkerboard tile floor. An old cast-iron stove and oven stood against the far wall. Ruby instructed the group to place their plates into the old farmhouse sink that looked like it had been carved out of a single block of gray soapstone. Dozens of old copper pots and pans hung from the overhead pothanger, casting interesting shadows on the butcher-block countertop of the long, narrow island.

"You'll each have your turn to play in the kitchen," Ruby said. "And if you don't know how to cook yet, you will by the time you leave—at least for fourteen people."

Genevieve nodded, turning to look at the extensive collection of herb jars labeled with hand-lettered stickers; thyme, rosemary, sweet woodruff, paprika, and dozens more. As she turned to leave, she nearly ran into the biggest refrigerator she had ever seen. "Wow," she said out loud.

"Ah, yes. A gift from one of the kids. The delivery boys had a heck of a time getting it through the doorway, but as soon as I saw it, I wasn't about to let them take it back." She smiled and pointed out the door, "To the parlor."

They wandered back to the front of the house, passing two small bathrooms on their way and coming to a halt where the wide front door stood ajar, spilling natural light onto the hardwood floors. "On the left side," Ruby said, pointing, when she had made her way to the front of the crowd, "you will find the library." She ushered them into the cozy space where bookcases lined every wall and books of all shapes, colors, and sizes were displayed. Comfy chairs and a long couch circled an old steamer trunk, several short stacks of books lying on top. "It's all alphabetized and organized by subject," she reported, pointing to the shelf labels—strips of wood with words carved into them.

"Ooh, do you have Jane Austen?" Sonja asked.

"Of course," Ruby said, pointing to the shelves in the far corner.

Sonja smiled and moved toward the bookcase.

"We have them, but the girls aren't allowed to read them," Ruby continued.

"Wwwhhaat? What do you mean?" Sonja asked, turning around and looking hurt.

"Those books are only for the boys."

"I don't understand."

"How many times have you read *Pride and Prejudice?*"

"Oh, at least seven or eight," she reported without hesitation.

"And have you ever met a man in real life who is as charming as Mr. Darcy?"

"Uh, no, definitely not."

"That's the reason you can't read them. You should spend your time while you're here in the action and adventure section over there," she said, pointing.

"Why action and adventure?" Susan responded.

"Look," Ruby said, "it's really quite simple. There's no such a thing as Mr. Darcy, Edmund Bertram, Henry Tilney, or even John Knightley and Captain Wentworth. They're simply fictitious heroes that live in the hearts and minds of the…excuse my frankness…the *possessed* women who read them. Are they romantic? Absolutely! But you'll get more value, word for word, by reading fiction that could feasibly be real; take… this book for example," she said, reaching for a thick book on the fiction shelf.

"20,000 Leagues under the Sea?" Genevieve asked, reading the title aloud and trying not to laugh.

"Okay, perhaps not the strongest case in point, but ladies, let's be honest with ourselves. Our friend Miss Jane was a wild dreamer. Granted, her dreams were very delicious, but she died alone, having never married, holding out for one of the dreamboats she created."

"But wait. If we can't read them, why can the guys?" Holly asked.

"That should be obvious to all of us ladies—for pointers, of course."

"Wait just a minute," Ephraim responded, jumping in. "I read *Pride and Prejudice* and *Emma* 'cause my sister told me they'd help me meet more ladies. I don't know what she was smokin'. If any guy went prancing around in his stretchy pants, talking like a rich boy from the English elitist society today, he'd be laughed out of every bar or dance club in less than a minute flat. Those guys didn't even have jobs! They just strutted around like a bunch of peacocks, expecting the ladies to fall all over them. Give me a break."

"Thank you, Ephraim. You're absolutely right. Still, I think Jane Austen would make great reading for any of you boys, if for no other reason than to better acquaint yourself with your competition. I'm sure it would be more advantageous to be competing against a real adversary, but sometimes your most worthy opponent will be the man in the mirror." She nodded at the ladies as if acknowledging the letdown caused by this traumatic revelation. "Furthermore, if you read the books the boys are reading, you will likewise have a better understanding of what they're looking for, however misguided and completely impractical."

The ladies nodded, acknowledging the wisdom she had spoken.

"Across the hallway is the music room," she said, ushering the crowd to the other side of the entryway. "It doesn't always make sense to have the music parlor next to the library, so I encourage you to be sensitive to each other. You'll notice the sliding pocket doors to each room. We encourage you to use them."

When they entered the music room, there were several audible gasps. "Is that really a Steinway?" Genevieve asked, laying her hand on top of the grand piano.

"You play?" Lorenzo asked.

"Well...no, but I've always wanted a Steinway."

"Wait, you want a big, expensive instrument that you don't even know how to play?" James asked. "Why?"

"They're just so beautiful. My parents have one in their front room. They don't play either, but it makes such a statement, don't you think?"

James nodded, taking a seat on the piano bench. He lifted the cover and exposed the keys. Without hesitation, he began playing an intricate piece from memory.

"Mozart, right?" Genevieve asked.

"Close," James replied sarcastically, trying to keep his cool. "Chopin."

Greg reached for a guitar that hung from the wall and quickly tuned the instrument, playing a few basic chords before launching into "Wild World," by Cat Stevens. He was obviously showing off and feeling pretty good about himself until Rachael stood next to him with a violin and played the exact tune while singing and balancing on one foot. Holly grabbed a red percussion egg and did the best she could to shake it to the rhythm. The others stood back and watched, a few of them singing along the best they could as they looked over the tambourines, pan flutes, a mandolin, a banjo, and three ukuleles.

"Not bad at all," Lorenzo said. "It looks like we'll be able to enjoy some good music this summer."

"Do you play any of these?" Genevieve asked him.

"Sure. You gotta have something to show for long winter nights with no TV," he responded, winking at Spencer.

"Which ones do you play?"

"He plays all of them," Ruby responded. "We both do. And we'd be happy to teach you. Music is always fun, but if you can participate, the fun is multiplied. We also have an accordion and a few harmonicas, but if you want to try those, you'll have to practice in the barn. I'm afraid the cows are far more patient than I am."

They all laughed as Ruby led them back into the entryway. "Lorenzo and I have our private quarters up the stairs here. We appreciate our privacy, but if for any good reason you need us after hours, you can ring this bell that sounds in our bedroom." She pushed a black plastic button, and they heard a muffled ringing above their heads. "We all need our sleep, so please don't abuse it."

They all nodded and, before following Ruby out onto the front porch, took turns glancing up the beautiful wood staircase that led to the private part of the house.

"This is my favorite room in the house," she reported. "On a summer evening when the work is done and the music is right, there's no place quite like it. The evenings are yours, of course, but we'd be honored if you'd like to share them with us here on the porch. There will normally be beverages and hopefully engaging conversation that will allow us to get to know each other better. Lorenzo and I usually hit the hay around ten. You're welcome to stay up as late as you like so long as you don't keep the rest of us up.

"Now, if you'd like to grab your bags, Lorenzo and I will show you to your bunkhouses, where you can unpack your things. We don't have much on the agenda tonight other than the evening milking around five and a light supper about six. If the boys will help with the milking tonight, I'll have the girls help me with supper. Oh, and don't forget to pick up your work duds and socks in the dining hall."

"And if you'd like, we can make some ice cream on the front porch tonight if a few of you will help out by pickin' some fresh berries from the berry patch," Lorenzo added as he glanced up at the sun. "And if we get movin', there still may be time for a siesta."

CHAPTER 10

Settling In

Truth, like gold, is to be obtained not by its growth, but by washing away from it all that is not gold.
- Leo Tolstoy -

The truck was unpacked in no time, and Ruby and Lorenzo led out, holding hands until the path divided in opposite directions toward the two bunkhouses. Ruby gave a brief orientation to the women in their bunkhouse, Lorenzo to the men in theirs. They outlined the nuances of the toilets and showers. Both groups were asked to observe the white walls and the clean surfaces throughout their simply adorned abodes and to plan on returning them in the same, if not better, shape at the end of the summer. Each camper was presented with their own hand-bound leather journal, which Ruby and Pops had made over the winter, along with pens for taking notes and recording their personal experiences, musings, and insights.

Before they were turned loose to unpack and decide who was sleeping where, they were all reminded of the farm's no-electronics policy. If they happened to have brought a phone, they were asked to voluntarily hand it over until September —regardless of its ability to connect with a cell signal. Genevieve watched as each of the women's faces turned down at this announcement. A shudder of panic raced through her own chest as she considered the deprivation of being cut off from the world. Immediately she began plotting a way to somehow keep the satellite phone she had gone to no small effort to procure just for this assignment. But before she could come up with a plan, she remembered that Ruby and Lorenzo had seen her phone the night before at the restaurant and would likely be looking for it.

Momentarily distracted by her phone thoughts, Genevieve's attention was next drawn to the linen closet. Stacks of fitted and flat sheets filled one shelf, pillows and pillow cases on the next, and piles of colorful, handmade patchwork quilts filled the rest of the space. Towels, they were told, could be found in the bathroom.

On their way out of the bunkhouses, Ruby and Lorenzo each took a moment to welcome the group to the farm again and warmly express their confidence in and encouragement to each of them. Reminding them that they had each signed up for a truly life-changing experience, they stressed the fact that their time spent here would be as valuable as they would allow it to be. Then, before they left, they each passed around a basket, gathering up all electronic devices.

And with that, things started much the same way they had for the past three hundred years. The women, in their bunkhouse, looked at each other and quickly began negotiating over who would sleep where, each of them trying to avoid the top bunk until one of them recognized that the bunks were actually detachable and that if they helped each other and sacrificed a little floor space, they could each enjoy a more accessible bed.

The men also soon discovered that the bunks were detachable, but instead of making it easier on themselves the way the women had, they discovered that three beds could just as easily be stacked as two. They quickly achieved the triple-stacking as a team, each of them secretly hoping for one of the two top bunks, which offered nice views through the skylight and the promise of fresher air.

With each house having situated their beds, they moved on to the unpacking of their bags. As everyone but Genevieve had the shared advantage of having received a packing list, they were all well prepared for the small storage space they encountered on the windowless south wall, consisting simply of four built-in, whitewashed cubbies for each woman. She watched as each of the women claimed her line of cubbies, stocking them with simple supplies. Each woman had a pair of jeans, a pair of shorts, a few sets of underwear, an extra pair of durable shoes, three T-shirts, one sweatshirt, a pair of pajamas, and a personals bag.

As she watched, Genevieve knew that there was almost nothing she could take out of her suitcase that would not look wildly out of place here. She tried to look busy, making her bed and fluffing her pillow while attempting not to panic.

"Do any of you want to go up to the big house to look at the work duds?" Rachael asked.

"I'll go," Sonja responded. The rest of the women were quick to join in, and Genevieve was relieved that she could finally open her suitcase without the women seeing its excessive and impractical contents. As soon as she had unzipped the cover and thrown it open, however, she wished she hadn't. The unmistakable scent of recycled spring grass escaped the confined space like methane under pressure, filling the room with its offensively pungent odor. She panicked and ran to the door with the soiled jeans. Looking both ways, she threw the pants as hard as she could into the tall grass at the corner of the house. Running back, she quickly looked over her clothes to see which ones she could use. She grabbed a handful of her delicates and sniffed them, immediately recoiling, recognizing that the odor had saturated everything. She ran to the already-open windows and opened them even farther while she racked her brains for a solution. She knew she had to come up with something—and fast!

Perhaps blaming it on the cows and a change of wind direction?

No, too easily debunked when the doors and windows were shut and the stench only grew stronger.

Lighting her entire her suitcase on fire and blaming it on spontaneous combustion?

No, too dangerous. Plus, the suitcase was Gucci.

A beautiful collection of manure potpourri, nicely arranged in a bowl on the table, with an accompanying note from the men?

Every possible solution she came up with sounded even stupider than the one before.

Feeling hopeless and knowing the women would be returning soon, she turned back to her suitcase. In a flash of pure desperation, she ran to the table that had been pushed to the middle of the room to make room for the beds. Nestled in the bouquet of pens and pencils that had been stuffed into a broken vase, she found an old pair of scissors. Cringing as she considered what she had spent on her fancy tops, she quickly cut off the long sleeves of three of them, trying to make them look less formal. They were also stinky, but she didn't have time to worry about that now.

She ran back outside and pulled her jeans out of the long grass. Then, laying the legs side by side on the lawn, she cut them off a few inches above the knee, eliminating the most despicable of the stains and their accompanying stench.

Looking up, her panic soared into high gear when she saw the women returning from the big house, their arms full of clothing. Running back to her suitcase, she zipped it quickly shut and locked it. With extrahuman strength, she hoisted the heavy bag above her head and stowed it on top of the cubbies next to the others. She hurried back to her bed and was just straightening her clothes when the women came back into the bunkhouse.

"What's that awful smell?" Crystal asked, her face looking much like a shriveled raisin.

"This is a farm, duh," Susan responded, laughing.

"Yeah, but it's in here too?"

"It's everywhere—get used to it," Rachael suggested. She walked past the others who were busy putting the borrowed farm duds into their cubbies. "Ruby said you'd probably need these." She handed Genevieve a large basket full of clothes. "It's too bad that the airline lost your other bag."

"Oh…thanks," Genevieve responded, rolling with it but not at all sure where she was going.

"Ruby told us you're a writer," Susan said. "I got a minor in English, but my dad talked me into getting a safe job, so I went to law school. I've kinda regretted it ever since. Good for you for following your dreams."

"Uhh…thanks," Genevieve responded, her confusion only growing. "What exactly did Ruby tell you?"

"Not enough," Holly chimed in. "You were really in Paris all week, interviewing a fancy purse designer about his fall line? Tell me what it's like! I've always wanted to go there."

"Uh, yeah, it's really nice," she managed, trying to hide her surprise by looking down into the basket.

"That's gotta be a bummer to lose some of your luggage after a trip like that," Sonja added.

Genevieve nodded, lifting a pair of cutoff shorts out of the basket to reveal three simple T-shirts in pleasant colors and what looked like the same pair of worn overalls Ruby had offered her earlier that morning. Feeling a little sick about the clothes she had just ruined, she walked to the empty cubbies and loaded them with the farm clothes from the big house. At the bottom of the basket, she found eight colorful socks and a pair of slightly used, but clean, leather work boots.

"Ruby also said to tell you that you can pick out a sweatshirt," one of the other women said.

Genevieve let out a long breath, suddenly feeling the letdown of her adrenaline rush.

"You've gotta have some pretty crazy jet lag, right?" Holly asked. "Do you want some help unpacking?"

"No, no. Thanks. I got it," she replied, feeling completely unworthy of the help being offered and the kindnesses the women had already extended to her.

Holly smiled and nodded, but looked a little disappointed and was just turning away when she noticed Genevieve's shirts on the bed.

"Are those French?" Holly asked, pointing to the recently short-sleeved blouses.

"Uh yeah, why?" She wasn't lying about that; she knew they had at least been designed in France.

"Do you mind if I take a look at them? I've always been curious about foreign fashion."

"Oh, sure. Knock yourself out."

Holly picked up the top blouse and held it up for the others to see. The sweet woman, who was clearly the youngest among them, turned the blouse around so they could all see that the pastel floral pattern continued onto the back side as well. She was just refolding it when she held it up to her nose and breathed in. "Wow, it even smells like Paris!" she announced.

Genevieve wasn't sure whether she should laugh or cry, recognizing it as the shirt she had worn the day before—the same shirt that been trapped for hours in a methane-filled suitcase.

"Hey, I'll tell you what. If you wanna help me put this stuff away, the shirt's yours,"

"Shut up!" Holly responded enthusiastically.

"No, I'm serious. I go to France at least a couple times a year. It's no big deal."

"Wow, thanks," she said, burying her face in it again.

Genevieve tried not to cringe watching her. "Maybe we should just wash all this before we do that," she said, scooping up the stinky clothes on her bed and throwing them into the empty basket from the big house. "Does anyone know where the washing machine is?"

"I think I saw a shed with a laundry sign on it about half way up to the big house, on the left," Rachael responded. "You might check there."

Holly hurried alongside, and Genevieve found her interest both charming and a little overwhelming. She had plenty of questions about Paris, and Europe in general, which Genevieve was happy to answer. She was surprised at how much Holly knew without ever actually having been there, but her questions were so incessant that Genevieve never had a chance to ask why.

They came to the laundry shed and pushed the door open, but there was no washing machine in sight. Instead, it looked like the shed had been converted into a bicycle-repair shop. When Holly's questions continued unabated, Genevieve decided she didn't need to do her laundry that badly anyway. She left the basket on the steps of the shed, figuring the stinky clothes would be better there than in the bunkhouse anyway. Holly's questions continued, and Genevieve was beginning to feel a little bit bugged by it all when she realized no one had ever asked her questions like this in her entire life. She had been to Europe dozens of times in her lifetime, but no one had ever asked questions like this. They sat down on the grass under one of the ancient cottonwood trees, and Genevieve tried not to grow tired of the younger woman's many questions.

The rest of the women were lounging out on their beds when Holly and Genevieve returned to the bunkhouse an hour later. Genevieve was happy to see them taking it easy, hoping to rest a bit too before they were due back at the big house for dinner prep. But just as they walked in, the other women invited them for a walk around the pond. After the kindness they had shown her and their tolerance with the stench she had introduced to the bunkhouse, Genevieve didn't feel like she could say no.

It was really the first chance they had had to get to know each other since they had arrived, and the dread of the next five months that had kept Genevieve up all night quickly started to feel slightly more manageable. They walked past the large fenced-in garden that was filled with weeds except for a small corner where the ground had been worked and cleared. Here several varieties of lettuce showed signs of recent harvests and young herb plants were growing.

The northern edge of the garden stopped at the bottom of a gently sloping hillside. They followed the trail along the west side of the garden and continued down the meandering path that wound through a variety of heavily laden berry bushes, which Sonja identified for the others as raspberry, currant, gooseberry, blueberry, blackberry, and huckleberry. Excited to try her first blackberry straight from the vine, Genevieve made the mistake of picking a plump red one and popping it into her mouth only to learn the hard way that it definitely wasn't ripe. The sour taste made her eyes water, but she swallowed it anyway, not wanting to draw attention to herself. Sonja explained that most of the berries would not be ripe for another month or more.

Disappointed, they moved on. But not more than a few paces later, they discovered hundreds of strawberries in various shades of red hiding out under dark-green leaves. Crystal removed her straw hat, and the women quickly filled it to overflowing with the fresh fruit, figuring it would be more than enough for the homemade ice cream. They lingered here for several minutes, enjoying the berries and the view of the pond, which seemed much bigger from this vantage point.

Cattails and lily pads dotted the surface of the pond, and the air was alive with all sorts of insects and the acrobatic swallows who chased them. Water skeeters raced across the glassy surface, and tadpoles flopped about in the shallows. Susan stooped to point out fresh prints from raccoon and deer in the dark mud. They were nearly half way around the pond when they were startled by the sight of a lone skunk that was lazily lumbering down the path in their direction. They retreated quickly, laughing like schoolgirls until they were back at the berry patch, where they enjoyed more of the ripe berries before heading home.

They found Ruby already in the kitchen, cutting bread dough into smaller pieces, forming them into loaves, then dropping them into pans before setting them under clean dish towels to rise. Two of the women had helped their mothers bake bread when they were younger, but they both admitted that it had been a long time since they had last attempted it.

Ruby was happy to receive the hat full of berries and to hear about their adventures. She explained to the women that the farm was entirely self-sustaining due to her progenitors' hard work and resourcefulness, as well as her and Lorenzo's continual upkeep and maintenance. With the funds earned from the sale of their extra milk, grain, and hand-knit socks, as well as the proceeds from the farm stand, they were able to purchase the few sundries they couldn't raise or make on the two hundred acres that surrounded them.

After demonstrating how to position the twelve bread pans in the hot oven for maximum efficiency, Ruby spelled out the baking schedule: six loaves of bread every morning Monday through Friday and twelve loaves on Saturday to eliminate the need for heavy baking on Sunday. The women would be welcome to share any recipes they had brought with them for cookies and desserts or to use the vast library of recipes Ruby had accumulated over the years.

While they waited for the bread to bake, the women took turns churning the morning's cream into fresh butter using a hand-crank mixer that had been on the farm for two hundred years. They washed and mashed strawberries for the ice cream and laid out plates of handmade cheddar cheese, farm-cured ham, and summer sausage.

Lifting the trap door on the kitchen floor, Ruby escorted all the women into the expansive cellar, where hundreds of bottles filled with all sorts of preserves lined the shelves of the surprisingly chilly space. There were also wooden bins still half filled with potatoes, onions, and apples from last year's harvest as well as racks of cheese wheels wrapped in yellow beeswax.

As they walked from shelf to shelf, Ruby handed the women quart jars of preserved foods—pears, peaches, honey—and smaller jars of homemade mustard, jams, jellies, and horseradish. These, she explained, had been preserved by the campers from the previous year and would need to be replaced when each fruit was in its season.

Back in the kitchen, the bread was pulled from the oven, filling the room with its warm aroma and making every mouth water. Ruby moved quickly, dumping the fresh loaves from their pans and setting the bread upright on the wooden cooling racks near the open window. She brushed the tops of the loaves with some of the fresh butter, causing them to glow in the evening light.

While Genevieve and Sonja set the table, the other women carried out the food and straightened up the kitchen, washing and drying the giant metal bowl and bread hook from the mixer.

As if on cue, the men arrived from the stall, looking hungry. After washing up, they all sat down together at the long table.

"Well, Mom, I think it's been a good day," Lorenzo said, winking at his wife at the opposite end of the table.

She smiled in response and nodded. "Indeed it has, Pops, the first good day of a new summer. I do believe it's my turn," Ruby responded, bowing her head and folding her hands in her lap. Her words were filled with thanksgiving for good kids and good food and the good earth that provided for all their needs. Prayer was new for Genevieve. Praying over a meal, now two times in one day, was completely foreign, but Ruby's words left her feeling puzzled by the weird sense of peace they left behind.

"En guete!" Lorenzo said, looking down the table again to Ruby.

"Smacznego!" she responded, smiling broadly.

"Those are the traditional Swiss and Polish greetings at mealtime," Lorenzo explained.

"What do the words mean?" Greg asked.

"Bon appétit!" Holly replied, passing him a wooden cutting board filled with thick slices of still-warm bread. No one needed any further encouragement after that as they dived into the mouthwatering spread that was laid before them.

"When you said dinner would be simple fare, I was imagining ramen noodles. *This is awesome!*" James announced, his mouth half full of fresh bread.

"Can we do this every night?" Josh asked.

"You don't think you'd get tired of it?" Ruby responded.

They all shook their heads in unison, their mouths too full for words.

"Then the answer is yes, or at least in some variation."

A muffled, unified cheer rang out, and there was much rejoicing in life's simple pleasures.

CHAPTER 11

Porch Games

To love at all is to be vulnerable. Love anything and your heart will be wrung and possibly broken. If you want to make sure of keeping it intact you must give it to no one, not even an animal. Wrap it carefully round with hobbies and little luxuries; avoid all entanglements. Lock it up safe in the casket or coffin of your selfishness. But in that casket, safe, dark, motionless, airless, it will change. It will not be broken; it will become unbreakable, impenetrable, irredeemable. To love is to be vulnerable.

– C.S. Lewis –

Everyone participated in the clearing up of the dinner dishes. In all, they consumed five loaves of bread, four bottles of fruit, two plates of ham and sausage, a plate of cheese, half a quart of honey, nearly two bottles of jam, and the whole bowl of fresh butter. As they chatted among themselves, they all agreed it was the best "simple fare" they had ever eaten.

Satiated and happy, they poured out onto the front porch to enjoy the evening. After a few minutes of small talk, Lorenzo announced that they would be playing a game while they made the ice cream. Most of them had seen ice cream makers before. Some of them had even used the hand-crank type. But none of them had ever seen one quite like the one Lorenzo uncovered in the back corner of the porch and introduced them to that night.

Looking like a whimsical cow/bicycle/washing-machine hybrid, the Niederbipp Neutralizer was the brainchild of Joel and Linda Hashimoto, two campers who had spent the summer on the farm more than twenty years earlier. Both engineers by training, their first collaborative effort was the Niederbipp Neutralizer, more commonly known as "Bessie." Born out of a need to create large quantities of ice cream while hermetically neutralizing the negative effects of heavy cream, Bessie had been satisfying and entertaining folks for more two decades.

While Lorenzo loaded Bessie's tank with cream, sugar, strawberry mash, and ice, Ruby reported that Joel and Linda married shortly after their summer on the farm had ended. They had four children and went on to cocreate the Mopster—the world's first floor-mopping robot—and the Kat Shack—an ergonomically correct, solar-powered pet entertainment system for people too busy to play with their cats. Ruby retreated to the house for a moment and returned with the Hashimotos' most recent Christmas picture, showing the happy couple and their four teenaged children, all dressed in adorable matching sweaters and reindeer antlers.

With Bessie fully loaded, the game began. Lorenzo called on Greg to take the first heat. Timidly, he climbed aboard the wide spring-loaded bicycle saddle and began pedaling, holding on to the recycled bull horns that took the traditional place of the bike's handlebars. The crank chain turned the old washing-machine tub that had been welded onto the rear of the bike where the back wheel had once been.

As soon as Greg began to pedal, Lorenzo stood by his side and outlined the rules of the game. Whoever was riding the bike had to share his most embarrassing nickname, where he was born, his favorite kind of cookie, and a brief review of his worst blind date. When he was done, he had to call someone of the opposite sex by name to take the next shift, tell the group one thing he had already learned about that person, and one thing he admired about them. Then, before he could completely dismount the bike, the next person had to climb aboard and keep the ice cream drum moving. If the drum ever came to a stop, the two people touching the bike would be required to run to the pond and, using pond mud, finger paint onto each other's foreheads the names of their favorite bands. They were laughing before they could even get started. To help keep things straight, Ruby wrote the items and order on a small chalkboard and propped it on a chair in front of the bike.

Greg started off pretty well. His embarrassing nickname was Jockstrap. He was born in Detroit. His favorite cookie was a Fig Newton. And his worst date met him at a club, rang up a big bar tab, and ended up running into an old boyfriend and leaving drunk with the other guy. Amid laughter, he called Sonja's name, said he had learned that she was a botanist, and admired her for trying the horseradish sauce at dinner.

Trying to keep the drum spinning, Sonja came to the front of the bike and lifted Greg's feet to the pegs that extended out of the front forks. Without constant pedaling, the drum immediately began to slow. Panicked, she yelled at him to stand up on the pegs while she raced around and jumped on the seat. But without anything to hold on to for support but Greg's belt loops, she was way off balance and nearly fell off, to the screaming delight of everyone on the porch.

Awkwardly, and with much effort and laughter from the crowd, Greg was able to dismount without hurting himself. And miraculously, Sonja was able to keep the drum spinning.

Her nickname was the Brainiac. She was born in Guatemala, where her parents had met as Peace Corps volunteers. Her favorite cookie was oatmeal raisin. And her worst blind date asked her to dinner; tried to pay with a check; and before they could even leave, was arrested by the police for check fraud.

Amid laughter and guffaws, she called on Matt. She said she knew he was a Tolkien fan from the patch on his backpack that said "Not all who wander are lost," and she admired the fact that his quiet demeanor seemed to suggest a thoughtful nature rather than simply shyness.

As Matt approached the bike, Sonja surprised everybody by quickly standing on the seat and arching her body high over the frame of the bike. Matt saw what she was doing, and, without needing to be directed, slid in underneath, sitting on the front of the seat to keep from smashing her toes. He began pedaling immediately while Sonja moved her hands from the bull-horn handlebars to his shoulders, steadying herself for a second before jumping down to the floor, earning loud cheers from the crowd.

It went like this for the next forty minutes. By the time the ice cream was ready, everyone's stomach and cheeks hurt from laughing, and Josh and Rachael each had their favorite bands written across their foreheads in mud.

Spoons and bowls were brought out from the kitchen, as well as an ornamental glass jar filled with wisdom cookies. As they waited for the ice cream to be served, they passed around the cookies.

"Is it all right if we read the fortunes out loud?" Ephraim asked.

"It's up to all of you," Ruby replied. "There are a few rules we set, but for decisions like this, it's completely up to all of you to determine what you want to do."

"Then I'd like to propose we spread some of this wisdom around," Ephraim responded. "The way I see it, I could use all the wisdom I can get right now."

Many of them nodded, and no one protested, so Ephraim broke his cookie and extracted the small paper, unfolding it.

> To everything there is a season,
> and a time to every purpose under heaven.

He looked up and smiled. "Sounds a little bit like Thoreau."

"It does, doesn't it?" Matt responded, "But I think it's from the Bible, from Ecclesiastes."

"Very good," Ruby said. "There is indeed a time for everything. When you get to be our age, it seems like time is running faster than ever, and you start to wonder how you're gonna fit it all in. I'm grateful we made the happy memories we did when we were younger."

"We're not done yet, Mom," Lorenzo responded, his arm deep in the drum, scooping ice cream.

"You're right, Pops. Let's keep making memories." She winked at her husband, and the love that passed between them was missed by no one.

"I've got one," Crystal said, straightening her piece of paper.

> Love does not dominate, it cultivates.

"Where is that from?" Susan asked.

"Goethe," Matt responded again. "At least I think."

"Impressive," Ruby complimented him. "You're a reader."

Matt blushed, looking uncomfortable. "I...dabble," he said humbly.

"Well if you're gonna dabble," Ruby responded, "you've chosen good company in the books you read."

"Let's see if you can get this one," Susan said.

> Haste is the mother of imperfection.

Matt shrugged, and no one else took it on.

"That comes from one of the greatest philosophers who ever lived," Ruby said with a smile. "And to the credit of the fairer sex—a woman." She stared into their blank faces for a moment before giving the answer. "She was perhaps the wisest woman who ever lived. Unfortunately, history has largely forgotten her. And with that amnesia, we have lost a great fortune." Smiling back into their perplexed faces, she uttered the name, "Annabelle O'nonomus, often referred to by her devotees as Aunt Ann, and sometimes called by the more ignorant classes Anonymous."

They all laughed.

One after another, they shared the fruits of their wisdom cookies. Discussions followed many of them, and it was collectively decided that the scraps of paper should be collected and saved till the morning, when they could reconvene and write each one down in their journals.

By the time the ice cream was gone, they had all had seconds if not thirds, and it was unanimously agreed to be the best ice cream they had ever tasted.

"Can we do this again tomorrow?" Josh asked as Holly began gathering up the empty bowls and spoons.

"Would you like that?" Ruby asked.

Josh nodded. "If someone had ever told me I'd be hanging out with a bunch of near-strangers on a farm somewhere in the middle of Pennsylvania, eating strawberry ice cream, and talking about philosophy—and loving every darn minute of it, I'm sad to say I would have laughed in their faces."

Genevieve looked around, seeing many heads nod in agreement, and she found herself wondering what sort of strange spell they had all fallen under.

"The agendas for the evenings are all yours to decide," Ruby responded. "As long as the cows keep making cream and the sun keeps turning the berries red— and the company is honest and willing—Pops and I are up for anything."

"Then let's say same time, same place tomorrow?" Josh suggested.

"Amen!" was the common response.

Several of them volunteered to do the dishes while the others lingered on the porch. The small festoon lights illuminated everything with a warm, gentle calm, chasing away the evening chill.

At ten, Ruby and Lorenzo excused themselves, but not before giving each of the campers a hug. As Ruby wrapped her warm arms around her, Genevieve realized it was more hugs than she'd ever received in one day. Confused by the feeling it gave her, she walked out onto the front lawn and kept walking until the light of the front porch faded into darkness. She closed her eyes tightly, trying to fight off whatever it was she was feeling. When that didn't seem to work, she opened her eyes again and nearly screamed at what she saw.

The sky was filled with more stars than she had ever imagined were even possible. Slowly, trying to take it all in, she followed the river of light that cut through the darkness from horizon to horizon.

"It's amazing, isn't it," Holly asked from behind, startling her. She handed her a sweatshirt, which she gratefully accepted, slipping it on quickly.

"It feels like the end of the world, like everything just blew up."

Holly laughed. "My mom used to call it the Highway of Dreams. I think I was ten before I learned it was the really called the Milky Way."

Genevieve nodded, unable to take her eyes off the sky. "I'm a little embarrassed to admit it, but I can't say I've ever seen it before."

"Seriously?"

She nodded. "There has to be like a billion stars up there."

"Yeah, well, scientists estimate a few more than that."

"Really? How many?"

"Last I heard, it was at least a hundred billion, but that number keeps getting bigger as the telescopes get better."

"That's crazy talk, right?"

"I don't know, but I don't have any reason to doubt it. It's pretty big up there. I think it's something like a hundred thousand light years from end to end, but that number keeps getting bigger too.

"No way! Our universe is that big?"

Holly laughed again. "That's just our galaxy. The universe is something like ten billion light years in every direction, and they say it's still expanding."

Genevieve tried to wrap her head around those kinds of numbers but couldn't. "How do you know so much about this kind of stuff?"

"Oh, uh…my mom taught me. She was a pretty smart woman."

"Yeah, it sounds like…wait, there was past tense there."

"Yeah, well, my mom passed away."

"Oh my gosh. I'm so sorry. When?"

"Four and a half months ago."

"Holly, I'm sorry. I didn't know."

"It's all good. It's not really something you wear on your sleeve, right? Nobody really wants to be known as the orphan."

"Wait, your dad's dead too?"

"Well, to be honest I guess I don't know."

"What do you mean?"

"I was adopted when I was two."

Genevieve stared at her, the light of the stars shining on Holly's dark hair as she pieced together the little she knew about her."

"Wait, you said tonight that you were born in Korea, right?"

She nodded. "My mom never married, but she always wanted to have kids. So she found an adoption agency that worked with single women, and…yeah, we became a family."

"Wow, that's really brave of her. I don't think I could do that."

She nodded. "She was the bravest person I've ever met."

"How did she die? Sorry, that's none of my business. If you don't want to talk about it, I…"

"Parkinson's. She was diagnosed when I was nine. She was given ten to twenty years. We got thirteen. I was lucky to have had her as long as I did. She always told me it was our dreams that kept her alive."

Genevieve nodded thoughtfully, putting the pieces together. "And you always dreamed of going to Europe."

Holly shrugged. "I think we got about as close as you can get without actually going there. We watched all the travel shows on PBS dozens of times and went on virtual tours almost every night. I've never been to the Louvre, but I could tell you exactly where to find the Mona Lisa."

Genevieve swallowed hard, realizing that in her many trips to Paris, she had never made it farther than the Louvre's cafe. "Well, if it's any consolation, the City of Lights doesn't have anywhere near as many stars as there are here."

"Yeah, I've heard that. It makes sense, right, with all the light pollution?"

"So why are you here?" Genevieve asked. "Why did you sign up for this? You're young and smart and beautiful. Why don't you go see the world? It seems like marriage would be the last thing on your mind."

Holly nodded thoughtfully, not responding for a long moment, and when she finally did, the emotion was raw. "Because I watched my mom suffer every day of her life."

"Are you talking about Parkinson's?" Genevieve asked, a little confused.

"No, I'm talking about loneliness. She always wanted to be loved. She wanted that same kind of magic that Ruby and Lorenzo have. You saw the way he looks at her, the way he loves her. My mom wanted someone to love. She wanted that! I have no doubt that that's why she adopted me. I know I helped plug that hole a little bit, but it was never enough. As hard as I tried, I knew I could never be enough for her. There were plenty of moments of real happiness, but she always wanted more, always believed there could be more—something that was always out of reach. She was always missing the love of a man. As I got older, I started worrying that she'd sacrificed any chance to get married when she adopted me."

"What do you mean?"

"There aren't many men who are willing to take on both a wife and a child. I don't know if she ever thought that way, but growing up with her, knowing what was missing in her heart—I don't want to miss out on that. I don't want to experience the same emptiness she felt, like she was always missing a piece of life and happiness."

"But I'm sure you've dated, right? You know that most guys are jerks, right?"

"I've dated enough to know two things—that I want to get married so I don't have to date for the rest of my life and that I'd really like to find a guy who wants to be married to me. I made it through college without finding the latter, and I guess before I get swept up in a career and forget what I want, I feel like I really need to explore this and see what happens."

"How did you even hear about this?" Genevieve asked, trying hard not to sound like a journalist.

"My mom's best friend came here about the same time my mom started the paperwork to adopt me."

"Why did she come?"

"Because she wanted the same thing my mom wanted, but she hadn't been able to find it. She had a career and money and adventure, but she said after she'd tried to fill the void with everything else, she decided to give the hope of marriage one last shot. She was almost forty-five and knew the window of opportunity to have kids was rapidly closing. So she took a sabbatical from her job, came here for the summer, and was married within a year."

"She had kids after forty-five?" Genevieve asked. "Shoot me now."

"No, she never got to have kids of her own. But her husband had three kids, and she learned to love them. She told me once that she knows she has no claim on them, but she stakes full claim on the grandkids. I don't know what it is, but there's something in us, deep down in the deepest, purest part of who we are, that wants to be loved—that needs to love—that wants to pass that love on to another generation. Sometimes we go to desperate ends to achieve that. I guess I'd rather do that now when I'm young and sassy than wait till the my ship has passed and I'm drowning in my own sea of what-ifs and how-comes.

"I want to be prepared when and if I meet a decent guy. I want to be able to know one when I see one. I want to be able to run with it when that void in my heart finally meets the piece that can fill it."

Genevieve sighed unconsciously.

"So why are you here?"

She laughed, not knowing how to answer Holly's question. But a big part of her was afraid that the cynic in her would say too much and burst the beautiful bubble Holly had just shared with her. "I guess I'm trying to figure that out," she finally answered. "I'll let you know when I do."

CHAPTER 12

Sunday School

"Let mystery have its place in you; do not be always turning up your whole soil with the plowshare of self-examination, but leave a little fallow corner in your heart ready for any seed the winds may bring, and reserve a nook of shadow for the passing bird; keep a place in your heart for the unexpected guests, an altar for the unknown God. Then if a bird sing among your branches, do not be too eager to tame it. If you are conscious of something new—thought or feeling, wakening in the depths of your being—do not be in a hurry to let in light upon it, to look at it; let the springing germ have the protection of being forgotten, hedge it round with quiet, and do not break in upon its darkness."

- Henri-Frédéric Amiel -

Just like clockwork, the rooster crowed as the first light of dawn cut its way across the farm. A collective, audible moan was heard from all of the women as they tried to fight the reality that morning had come.

"I can't remember. Do we get to sleep in on Sundays?" Sonja asked, sitting up in her bed.

"I don't think so," Susan lamented. "Didn't Lorenzo say that the cows need to be milked...and something about the chickens...and breakfast?"

Fifteen minutes later, they met the men on the lawn between the bunkhouses. Lorenzo and Ruby divided them up, the men going to the kitchen this time and the women going to the barn. While Ruby instructed the men on the finer points of biscuit and gravy preparations, Lorenzo taught the women the importance of rudimentary sanitation before milking cows.

The men were sent out to the chicken yard with two pails of table scraps and basic instructions about egg collecting. They returned with proud faces and a basket overflowing with beautiful, multicolored eggs in a variety of subtle hues. After a guided tour of the cellar, they returned to the kitchen to cook the eggs. Matt, with his more extensive experience as a bachelor, wasn't shy to jump in and get started with some scrambled eggs. He was feeling pretty good about himself until Ruby reminded him that he was now cooking for fourteen.

By the time the women had washed up, the table had been set with the morning's spread. Lorenzo said grace, thanking God for a day of rest, good food, and time to consider their blessings.

As they ate, Ruby reminded them all that she and Pops would be leaving for church at 9:30. There would be room for two more in the cab and at least six in the truck's bed. But she also informed them that there were twelve bicycles in a shed on the side of the house if anyone wanted to bike to church—or anywhere else for that matter. Otherwise, the library and music parlor were there for their enjoyment. Naps were encouraged, and the day was theirs until five o'clock, when the evening milking and dinner prep would begin. As they had all received basic training in both the kitchen and the barn, they could decide which chore they wanted to do, but she asked that no one shirk their responsibility.

Braving the tepid water in the shower, Genevieve quickly washed off two days of sweat while the other women tidied up the bunkhouse. Susan and Holly both decided they wanted to go to church with the Swarovskis, and they sorted through their meager wardrobes, wondering what would be most appropriate to wear. They hurried back to the cupboards in the big house and returned with a couple of very basic skirts and tops, informing the others that there were plenty more to be had if they wanted to join them.

Genevieve was also curious about church, but she didn't decide until after nine that she might as well give it try. On her way back from the big house's clothing cupboard, she ran into Spencer, who invited her to bike to church with him and Matt. She accepted the invitation tepidly, unable to remember the last time she had attended church or been on a bike with wheels.

She quickly changed her clothes, trying hard not to cringe at her limited and wildly unfashionable choices. She looked around for a mirror to confirm how bad it was, but the only mirrors to be found were the small ones above the sinks in the bathroom. These offered only a small window into the truth she already knew. Assuring herself that there was no way she would run into anyone she knew—so far from the civilized world—she hurried out the door.

She found the men waiting for her at the bike corral. They had already dusted off the old bikes and were ready to leave when Ephraim and James showed up, having decided to join them.

They rolled out across the lawn, deciding it made more sense to push the bikes up the drive rather than to try to ride them uphill over the rutted and uneven surface. The five of them reached the pavement just ahead of the pickup, and they waved to the four passengers who were crowded into the cab of the old truck.

"Take a look at that view," Spencer said, looking out over the Niederbipp Valley.

"It's beautiful," Ephraim concurred.

Genevieve was surprised by the beauty but chose not to respond.

The trip down the hill was so exhilarating than none of them even once considered that the same road home would be mostly uphill. Matt took the lead, winding his way down the scenic byway and through the town, trying to keep the steeple in view to avoid getting lost. They rolled into the courtyard just as the bell tower tolled ten. With no bike stand in sight, they leaned their bikes against the retaining wall that led to the elevated cemetery, and they hurried up the stone stairs to the chapel. To everyone's surprise, they found it was nearly full. There was no room for all of them to sit next to each other, so they squeezed in wherever they could. Genevieve sat with Spencer and Matt, and Ephraim and James found a spot a few pews in front of them.

No sooner had they sat down than the congregation stood to sing a cheery song that Genevieve was not familiar with. The old man next to her offered to share his hymnal, which she gracefully accepted, but she chose not to join in singing, distracted by the simple beauty of the chapel. After an invocation given by an elderly woman in a very bright blouse, a man dressed almost like a priest stood at the pulpit and announced that the sermon would be given by the local florist, Gloria.

Void of the usual pomp and circumstance that Genevieve had been accustomed to seeing at the rare religious services she had attended, a tall woman with silver streaks in her jet-black hair stood from the front row and moved toward the pulpit. As she straightened her papers, Genevieve thought how interesting it was that the local florist had been asked to give a sermon. The fact that she was a woman made it even more interesting.

"I've been thinking about what I might say today for the last several weeks," Gloria began, her strong voice resonating off the stone walls. "I've considered all sorts of things, from the miracles of spring to the merciful wisdom of God's plan for each of us. What I thought would be a burden when I accepted Thomas's invitation to speak has become a humbling but delightful honor. It has caused me to think more deliberately, and the sincerity of my prayers has kicked up a notch as I've asked for wisdom and insight. Over and over again, I've come back to a quote that a dear friend shared with me years ago when I was in a tough spot.

"Many of you know that Joseph and I were unable to have children of our own. That was definitely one of the toughest trials we've faced in life, but I realized over the past couple of weeks that in spite of the brutality of that trial, I am grateful for the patience and humility it taught me.

"The quote that I am referring to comes from one of my favorite men of wisdom, Ralph Waldo Emerson. I wrote this quote on my heart many years ago, and recently I invited my artist friend, Amy Kimball, to paint it on the wall above the doorway in my shop to help me remember the truth about every man and woman who comes and goes through that door: 'Every man is a divinity in disguise, a god playing the fool.'

"This quote is powerful on its own, but when coupled with one of my favorite passages of scripture, it blossoms with an even more beautiful meaning.

"From the fourth chapter of John's first epistle, 'Beloved, let us love one another: for love is of God; and every one that loveth is born of God, and knoweth God….for God is love.'"

"Separately, these quotes could provide one with years' worth of meaningful contemplation. But when studied together—when one comes to understand that the things of the divine cannot be understood without love, we begin, I believe, to understand the value of every soul.

"As children of God, He has endowed each of us with a portion of Himself, a seed of greatness and infinite value and promise. But just like any other seed, if that divine seed falls on stony ground, its value is in jeopardy of never being fully realized.

"The problem is that in our natural state, most of us have stony hearts. And in that natural, stony state, none of us are ready to give nourishment to the divine seed that God has planted there.

"Unfortunately, changing the makeup of our hearts is not easy—it's next to impossible to accomplish on our own. For most of us, due to our own pride, it takes years. Indeed, the sad truth is that most of have to be swallowed by a whale, often of our own making, and marinate in our own juices long enough to begin the softening process. Only we can decide when this softening can begin. I believe God stands waiting and anxious like a patient gardener, hopeful that we will open the tall gates of our gardens enough to let Him pass through.

"And once we finally let Him in—oh, the work He has to do. With pick and hoe, He will, if you let Him, dig out the noxious weeds with their deep roots and prolific, cankerous fruits. With the patience of a loving Father, He'll till the ground, folding in mercy and compassion with each turn of the soil. As stones make their way to the surface, he'll toss them to the side and build up a wall to protect against rodents and vermin. And when the ground is finally cleared, he'll conjure the rain and sunshine and patiently wait for that good seed he planted so long ago to finally send out roots and branches and sweet fruits.

"I believe the work that matters most is always God's to do, but I also believe each of us has a role to play in this grand work of the garden of mankind. It seems unlikely that you and I will ever be asked to do the weeding or digging in someone else's garden. But if we're ready and willing, He will call on us to help with the watering and the spreading of sunshine.

"I don't think Jesus was kidding when he gave us a new commandment to love each other. We are told that we will know His disciples by this one act alone. And it's with the light that radiates from that love that the world becomes illuminated, filled with goodness and peace.

"Because He has invited us to love, if we're willing, He'll enlist our help from time to time. And if we're faithful and trustworthy with the work He gives us, He'll enlarge our capacity to love beyond anything we can imagine.

"My friends, there truly is a piece of the divine within each of us. I see it in your faces as I look out at you this morning. I feel it in your presence as I see you on the streets. I'm humbled when I see and feel the spiritual connections we share—connections that tie us to each other and, more importantly, connections that tie us all to our Creator.

"I believe in love. I believe love is the balm of Gilead, the ointment and the salve that cures all sorrow and pain. But it is also the blessing for Babylon that changes hearts and reminds wanderers that they have a home. Love is that perpetual whisper from the Messiah that pricks the hearts and rings in the ears of fallen men and women everywhere, inviting—even pleading—for each of us to return to Paradise. I believe that even the stoniest of hearts can be softened, tenderized, and become fertile ground for the seeds of divinity within each of us."

Genevieve was surprised by this woman's words and the imagery they conjured in her mind. She glanced to her side and saw that Spencer seemed to be completely captivated by her words. She looked past Spencer and saw that Matt was also interested, a small notebook in his lap, a pen in his hand, and a steady look of concentration on his face. She wondered what he had written down and if they both were feeling the same strange sense of calm she was feeling, almost like the physical letdown after a long workout. She wondered if it was some kind of physical reaction to the bike ride, perhaps the drop in elevation from the farm to the town. But the calm she felt was different from any calm she had ever experienced following a workout.

She looked around and saw that everyone seemed to be focused on what this woman was saying. She was even surprised to see a couple of parishioners with tear-stained cheeks. Genevieve tried again to concentrate on what the woman was saying, but she struggled, thinking about her earlier words: the garden, the stony ground, and the seed of divinity that she believed was in each of us. Genevieve had never spent much time thinking about things like this, and she hesitated to think about them now, afraid of allowing ideas so esoteric and spiritual to take the place of the rational, physical reality in which she had always tried to live her life.

By the time the woman sat down, Genevieve had come up with at least five good reasons why people seemed to be bewitched by her words—all of which suggested either some form of desperation or less-than-adequate cognition. The words of the hymn and prayer that ended the service only seemed to solidify her reaction, and she began wondering if she was the only thinking person in the whole congregation.

"I've never heard anything like that before," Spencer said as they stood to leave. Genevieve forced a smile but said nothing. She watched as the congregants poured from the pews and entered the aisles. But instead of leaving the chapel through the tall front doors, many of them surged toward Gloria, the town florist. Surprised by the reaction, Genevieve watched as all four of her male companions left the pews and joined those moving toward the woman.

"That was great, wasn't it?" a voice came from behind her. She turned to see Greg, his hair a frightful mess. "Was hers the only sermon?"

"Uh, yeah," Genevieve responded, a little confused, realizing he must have come in late. "I guess you decided to join us, huh?"

"Yeah, I was planning on taking a nap, but after you guys left, I decided I could sleep later. Is she some kind of pastor?" he asked, nodding toward the woman, who was now surrounded by people.

"I don't think so. She was introduced as the town florist."

"Really?"

"That's what that priest guy said. Why?"

Greg looked up, seeing the man in a black suit chatting with an elderly couple on the side of the chapel. "I heard this was a Quaker town, but this isn't anything like what I expected."

"What *did* you expect?"

"I don't know. Probably a bunch of folks dressed up like the dude on the Quaker Oats box. This was actually way more interesting."

"When did you get here?"

"Just when she was talking about that quote from Emerson—that we're all divinities in embryo…something like that. What did I miss?"

Genevieve shrugged, trying to remember. "I think you got most of it. You could ask Matt. It looked like he was taking notes."

Greg nodded, spotting Matt and the other guys slowly moving down the aisle toward Gloria. Without another word, he left Genevieve and got in line to follow the others.

Genevieve considered leaving, but wasn't sure she'd be able to find her way back to the farm. Instead, she sat down on the pew to wait for the others. As the pews in front of her cleared out, she had an unobstructed view of Gloria greeting the many people who wanted to talk to her. As she watched, she recognized that there was something undeniably lovely about the woman, no matter how deluded she was. She recognized the backsides of Ruby and Lorenzo as they both reached out to embrace the town florist, who smiled and thanked them for coming. She also saw Jake and Amy on their way out of the chapel. But not wanting to be seen by them in such unstylish clothes, she turned her back to them and hoped they wouldn't recognize her.

"Are you ready to head back?" Matt asked, interrupting her thoughts a few minutes later.

She nodded, and the six of them who had biked to town descended the stairs together.

"Do any of you want to explore the town before we head back?" Ephraim asked.

"I do," Greg responded.

"Do you think we can find something to eat," asked Spencer.

"There's only one way to find out," James replied. "Do you want to join us?" he asked, looking at Genevieve.

"I guess I've got nothing better to do," she responded lukewarmly.

They left the bikes where they were and descended the flight of stairs that dropped down from the courtyard to the charming, quiet street below. Colorful geraniums cascaded out of the window boxes as well as the baskets hanging from the lampposts.

"Have you ever seen anything like this?" Greg asked as he looked up and down the cobblestone street, immediately charmed by its beauty.

"Not on this side of the pond," Matt responded. "This looks and feels like a European town."

They all nodded in agreement. Spencer led off, walking down the street past the darkened shop windows. "It looks like everything's closed," he reported. "Even the grocery store."

Matt smiled. "Just like the small towns in Europe."

"That's a bummer," Ephraim declared.

"I was just thinking how refreshing it is," Matt replied. "How cool is that—to have a whole town that can enjoy a day off?"

His comment offered them each food for thought as they walked through the streets, stopping at the fountain, where they drank their fill of the cool spring water. The sound of children playing drew them through the otherwise quiet, narrow lanes. They stopped from time to time, admiring the craftsmanship of the old buildings and marveling at the flowers and trees that enhanced the town with life and beauty. Turning a corner, they stopped and collectedly gawked at a three-story wall that was completely covered with flowering trumpet vines.

As they walked, Genevieve recognized that she was surrounded by five men who had come here in hopes of finding love and with dreams of being married. She hadn't considered that she might have access to the minds and hearts of men like this when she had accepted the assignment to interview Ruby. As they walked and talked together now, she wished she had spent more time working on questions that might help her with her story. But just as she started formulating questions in her head, she remembered Ruby's warning that honesty would be compromised if the others knew she was working on an article for a women's magazine. Feeling a little frustrated, she resolved to take a step back and simply observe for now, with hopes of eventually embedding herself fully.

After nearly an hour, they unwittingly wandered back into the courtyard. Only then did they realize they had walked around in a circle. They sauntered through the shade cast by the courtyard's well-groomed trees and had nearly reached their bicycles when Spencer spoke up. "It looks like there might be an old graveyard up there," he said, pointing to the rusty iron fence atop the wall against which they had leaned their bikes.

They all looked up, seeing it for the first time. Curious, they walked to the stone stairs that led up to the higher ground. When they reached the top, they looked across the plot of land that was crowded with headstones in a wide range of designs. Lichens and moss colored many of the older stones in brilliant shades of green and orange. The graveyard was deserted except for two older women who sat chatting on a bench near the center of the yard, their backs toward the group.

"Look at that tree," Matt said, starting off toward the brightly adorned crabapple tree in the far corner. The brilliant pink flowers burned in the bright sunlight and littered the ground with petals all around the tree. The group followed Matt down the narrow dirt path that jogged its way around the gravestones and past the old ladies. Soon they reached the tree and stood in its shadow. Matt stooped next to a bench at the tree's trunk and cleared the spent flowers from its surface, quickly realizing that it too was a grave marker.

"I've always planned to be cremated when I die," he said as he stood and turned around, looking out over the quaint cemetery and the looming clock tower. "But maybe I wouldn't mind being buried here."

The others nodded in agreement.

"Good morning," a deep, somewhat familiar voice said from the shadows cast by the tall stone retaining wall on the far side of the cemetery.

They all turned in the voice's direction.

The man who had opened the church services emerged from the shadows and walked toward them. "You must be Ruby's summer recruits," he said. "Welcome to Niederbipp."

"How could you tell we're from Ruby's?" Spencer asked.

"I recognized your bikes," the man reported as he approached them. "And it looks like one of you might be wearing my sock's long-lost brother." He lifted the bottoms of his black pants to reveal a set of colorful but definitely not-matching socks. "My name is Thomas."

"Nice to meet you," Matt responded, stepping forward to shake the older man's hand. "Is it Father Thomas?"

Thomas smiled. "Yes and no. Are you in need of a priest?"

"I…I don't think I am today, but you never know about the future," Matt replied playfully, returning the priest's smile with one of his own.

"Yeah, I get that a lot," Thomas said, turning to look at the cemetery. "Births and deaths and an occasional marriage here and there—that seems to be all folks need a priest for anymore."

"I was curious about that," Ephraim said, speaking up.

"You've recently had a death or birth, or you plan to marry?" Thomas asked playfully.

Ephraim laughed. "No, I mean…I guess maybe, but not right away. No, I was just curious…I mean, I don't know much about Quakers, but I didn't think they had priests. When I saw you conducting services…I…I guess I'm just curious."

"Then I commend you," Thomas said, reaching out to shake his hand. "Curiosity is often the gateway to the long path that leads to wisdom."

"Only often?" Matt asked, looking confused.

"Excuse me?"

"You said curiosity is *often* the gateway. Isn't curiosity always the gateway?"

Thomas smiled. "It's always the gateway to something, isn't it, but…" He stopped and looked into the faces of the others; they all seemed to be waiting for his answer. He stepped back, smiling at them. "It's not uncommon for me to get into philosophical discussions in the cemetery with old friends, but I can't say that it's very common with new friends. I'd hate to mistake your questions as an invitation to bore you all to tears. If you're interested in chatting, then I'd like to invite you to come have a seat in my garden. If you're not, well...then I'll invite you to my garden to talk about other things."

"How about if we go to your garden?" Matt asked, turning to the others. "I didn't mean to speak for all of us. Some of you probably want to go back to the farm and take a nap."

"I'm in," Ephraim said.

"Me too," said James.

"I guess I can take a nap later," Genevieve added.

"How far away is your garden?" Greg asked.

Thomas turned toward the church. "If you could toss a stone over the top of the chapel, it would land in my garden. I live in the caretaker's house on the other side. I have a couple loaves of day-old bread and some honey if anyone's interested."

"You had me at bread," Greg responded. "Lead on."

CHAPTER 13

A Garden Discourse

Because God is love, the most important lesson He wants
you to learn on earth is how to love.
— Rick Warren —

They poked around the cemetery for a couple more minutes, giving the priest the time he had requested to tidy things up before they arrived. And while the bell tolled twelve times, they wandered across the courtyard to the humble white house on the other side of the church.

"Come around back," Thomas told them before they reached the open front door. "I'm sorry about the grass," he said, leading the way. "I should have mowed it last night, but the dandelions are so pretty this time of year, it seemed a shame to knock them down in all their glory."

They followed him to the back of the house, where a flagstone patio was shaded under an overgrown trellis. A small table was draped simply in a yellow cloth and adorned with the promised bread and honey, as well as seven mismatched mugs and a glass pitcher filled with amber liquid.

"Please make yourselves at home," he said, motioning to the assemblage of mismatched chairs and stools. "I don't often get visitors. It's a pleasure to have you here. Please help yourselves to the food." As Thomas poured the tea into the mugs, he told them about his wise, old friend, the potter who had created each one.

"Have you lived here long?" Genevieve asked.

"Nearly fifty years. It's a rather long story—probably boring and definitely too long for a day like today. Suffice it to say that I landed here by accident, but I very deliberately chose to stay."

"Do you support yourself with service to the church?" James asked.

"Oh heavens, no," Thomas said, laughing. "I get to help out with the services on Sunday, but during the week I try to make myself useful at one of my other jobs. If you find yourself in need of a priest, you should look for me at the bakery or the library or wherever pipes are in need of an honest plumber."

"You sound as though you might also be a philosopher," Matt suggested, not wasting any time, his hunger focused on something different from the food that had been set before them.

Thomas smiled but shook his head, chewing slowly on a piece of bread and looking like he wondered how he might answer. He had chosen the lowest of the stools in the collection and looked quite humble, his nose nearly reaching the top of the table. "I'm sure that title—philosopher—means many things to many different people," he replied once he had swallowed. "I have no credentials, if that's what you're asking. But I've attempted to be thoughtful most of my life, and I feel like I've been fortunate to be able to find a few golden nuggets of sunshine along the way."

"I like the sound of that," Matt replied.

"How about you? Are you a philosopher?" Thomas asked.

Matt laughed. "No, I'm a...I guess I'm a dentist who's been searching for...what did you call it? *A few golden nuggets of sunshine?*"

"That's a good thing to search for," Thomas replied, taking a sip of his tea.

"But those nuggets are hard to find sometimes, aren't they?" Matt responded.

Thomas shrugged. "If gold came easy, it would be unlikely that we would appreciate its value."

Matt nodded thoughtfully.

"Gold, like wisdom, has value because of its scarcity," Thomas continued. "Some find vast veins of the stuff, while others are satisfied by tiny, glittering flecks. Sometimes it takes a while to figure out that where you dig can make all the difference in your degree of success." Thomas looked into each of their faces. "You're all looking for those nuggets, aren't you?"

"Isn't everybody?" asked Spencer.

Thomas shook his head. "I think it's probably human nature to look for nuggets, but many of us give up and even try to forget that we were ever searching for them when the going gets tough and the common stones of discouragement are so much easier to find. If you're honest with yourself, you know there was probably a time in your life when you gave up the search too."

Spencer looked down into his mug, nodding thoughtfully.

"So what brings six thoughtful seekers to Niederbipp on a glorious Sunday when you could be doing any number of other things?"

"Curiosity," Matt responded without hesitation.

"Oh, that's right. That's where this all started, isn't it?"

"Yeah, you said that curiosity is always the gateway to something."

"Ahh yes, of course it is."

"But?" Matt asked after a pregnant pause.

"There are no buts about it. Curiosity is the gateway to many things."

"Yeah, but you implied there was more to it than that."

Thomas nodded. "Curiosity can be a wonderful thing. It gets the mind thinking outside of its previous borders. And if it's at all sincere, it gets you up off the couch—gets you turning over leaves and rocks and staring into the night sky for answers that only leave you wondering how and why you never thought of things like this before. And if your curiosity continues, so will your desire for learning, discovering, and creating, to the point that time will mean more because there will never be enough of it. And you'll curse your own mortality when it demands that you must sleep and eat when you'd rather be learning."

"And how is any of that bad?"

"Who said that it was?"

"Well, I thought…maybe I misread what you were saying, but it seemed like you were suggesting there was a flip side," Matt said.

Thomas nodded. "Everything has its flip side. Curiosity has the ability to lead men and women to great truths. But like Winston Churchill once said, 'Man will occasionally stumble over the truth, but most times he will pick himself up and carry on.' No, I don't believe that the search for truth and wisdom in and of itself is the answer to the world's problems."

"No?" Matt asked, looking surprised.

Thomas shook his head. "If one is so busy looking for truths that he never takes the time to assimilate the truths he discovers, what's the point?"

Matt nodded thoughtfully. "Okay, I understand that, I think. But isn't it important to find all the truth possible while you're young so you have something to chew on when you're too old to chase after it?"

"What the young chase after, they often chase away."

"Tell me what that means to you."

Thomas smiled. "It means you can chase a butterfly for miles and miles through forest, field, and glen, and still it will elude you. But quite often, if you'll sit very still, the butterfly will land on your shoulder."

Matt shook his head. "But sitting around never brings anybody anything."

"Who said anything about sitting around?"

"But you said…"

"There's a big difference between sitting around and being still."

"Enlighten me."

"Sitting around is self-indulgence and laziness. It's giving in to the natural, mortal man—that which is most base and uninspired about our existence. It allows the physical self to overpower and even bind the spiritual self, robbing it of its promise and potential."

Thomas looked at Ephraim, who was nodding thoughtfully.

"On the other hand," he continued, "being still is neither passive nor impatient. It requires you to look outside of yourself and to recognize your own smallness in the grand plan of creation and then to look within yourself and realize the beautiful, eternal potential and grand design of the human soul. Being still is humility and grace; it's patience to wait expectantly. It's the recognition of that long spiritual umbilical cord that ties us to our Creator."

"It always comes back to that, doesn't it?" Matt lamented.

"You sound disappointed."

He shook his head. "I think I'm past disappointment. A couple of years ago, I might have been upset, but I guess I've come to the realization that nothing else offers any real hope."

Thomas smiled, his face lit up with kindness. "That's a beautiful place to be."

"Maybe, but where do you go from here?" Matt questioned.

"And where do you go if you're not quite there yet?" James asked.

Genevieve could hardly believe her ears—grown men admitting their own fallibility, even weakness. But there was more than that. As she slowly looked at each of them, she recognized a rare humility in each of their faces—a hunger for something more than they had and a willingness to admit their own deficiency.

"Both good questions," Thomas said after taking another sip of his tea.

"Do you have an answer?" Greg asked.

"I think so."

"Would you mind sharing it?" Greg prodded.

"I'd love to, but I fear that doing so would cheat each of you out of your own answers. There's nothing I could tell you that would have the same impact as it would if you received it from a source far wiser than I."

"That's it? You're just going to drop it like that?" James asked, obviously a little peeved.

Thomas shook his head. "I don't feel like I've dropped anything. I'd prefer it if you would see it as an invitation—a key."

"A key to what?" Ephraim asked.

"To whatever it is you'd like."

"If that's the case, I'd like it to be a key to a new Ferrari," Greg said sarcastically.

"Then that's what it is," Thomas responded. He reached into his pocket and withdrew a ring of keys, tossing them to Greg. "There's your key to your new Ferrari. What are you going to do with it now?"

Greg laughed. "If I knew it was going to be that easy, I would have asked for a Lamborghini instead."

"You still can. There's nothing stopping you. That key works the same way for a Lamborghini as it would for a Ferrari."

"I don't understand your point." James responded.

"There are probably plenty of men who would be happy knowing that they had a fancy sports car parked in their garage. But could you ever really be happy with that alone?"

The guys looked at each other, no one sure how to respond.

"My point is that it may be a pretty thing to look at, but I can't imagine that any sports car designers ever hope that the cars they create will sit in garages and never go anywhere."

"Okay, I get it. It would be a lot more fun to drive it than just park it, right?" Greg responded.

"Exactly! But without keys, a car—even a pretty one—isn't much better than a big, expensive paperweight. And if it never went anywhere and you could never even get inside it to check it out, I have to believe you'd probably get frustrated with it, right?"

They all nodded but still looked a little lost.

"But what if you took that key," Thomas said, pointing at the keys Greg had laid on the table. "What if you took that key and went out to your garage every day and started it up—listened to the powerful purr of that big Italian motor under the hood and then took it out for a spin? Maybe you could drive it around town or—better yet—on a cross-country road trip. I guess what I'm saying is that you get to decide. It doesn't even have to be a car. It can be a house or a door or a gold mine. The point of all of this metaphor is that a key that unlocks most doors and starts most engines is going to be far more valuable to you than a key that works only on my front door."

They looked at each other, nodding silently as understanding finally came.

"So what is this key you're offering us?" Matt asked.

"It's probably far more simple than any of you are imagining. It's the key called gratitude."

They all looked surprised.

"I don't get it," Greg admitted.

"Gratitude is the foundation on which all spiritual understanding is built. It is the wellspring of wisdom. It is the mother of all virtues. Without it, people stumble over their own feet, tied down by pride and by indifference toward God, which only further limits their insufferable ambition. They are stuck in purely horizontal planes.

"But gratitude changes everything. It leads us to recognize our connection and ultimately our reliance on something bigger than ourselves. It leads to the development of humility and understanding, and it opens one's horizons—elevating our thoughts and goals while aligning them with the source of all wisdom, grace, and mercy."

Greg shook his head. "I appreciate what you're saying, but I'm sure we all know lots of people who have reached the top without having any connection to God whatsoever."

Thomas pursed his lips and nodded. "But the top of what? Don't forget that this world—as grand and beautiful as it may be—is only God's footstool. For those who put their trust in Him, He promises the blessings of eternity. The prideful and arrogant may build up mansions to elevate themselves, but the Good Book warns us that such people are doing little more than building their castles on shifting sand dunes. Gratitude, with its promise of infinite wisdom and grace, not only offers us mortals a chance to build on an exclusive, rock-solid foundation but it also offers us a mansion within a kingdom ruled by the only truly just King. Compared to that, everything else is vanity and deceit that yields only sorrow and bitterness in the end."

Matt nodded slowly. "So, if gratitude is the key, how does it work?"

"It begins in here," Thomas said, patting his chest, "and if it's sincere, it leads to outward expressions. It opens one's heart to God and gets you counting your blessings, giving thanks to Him in all things—from the food you eat to the very air you breathe. And when you come to the realization that you are indebted to Him for all that you have—then you are finally humble enough to learn wisdom. I am a believer that God is glorified every time we as natural people give up that which is carnal about ourselves and choose instead to begin nurturing the divine seed God planted in our souls."

"That sounds a lot like the sermon that lady gave today," James said. "You must have had this conversation with her too."

Thomas nodded. "We both shared the same teacher. He gave us each the same key I've just given you."

"So it really works, huh?"

"I could tell you all day long, but it would never be enough to convince you. There's only one way to find out."

"Take the key to the garage and start up our engines?" Ephraim asked thoughtfully.

Thomas smiled and nodded. "And drive until you run out of road."

CHAPTER 14

The Uphill Road

All love that has not friendship for its base, is like a
mansion built upon the sand.
- Ella Wheeler Wilcox -

The farm was quiet when they arrived home an hour later, tired and sweaty from their steep ascent. They had pedaled as far as they could before dismounting and pushing the old, heavy bicycles the rest of the way. Few words had been spoken. Genevieve had noticed how each of the men seemed to be lost in his own thoughts. The words Thomas had shared with them had unexpectedly influenced her thoughts as well. She had never had much to do with God. Her parents had taken her to church only a dozen times or so over the course of her younger years. She had attended a handful of church weddings since then. But religion had never been comfortable or in any way natural to her. If it weren't for the way Thomas's words seemed to have affected the men, it would have been easy for her to blow off what he had told them as delusional mumbo jumbo.

For her, gratitude was a new concept—to give thanks to a god she had never known felt completely foreign. To her knowledge, nothing she had could be traced to a divine source. Her grandfather had told her about a distant relative who had arrived in Boston with only a few pennies in his pocket—but from those pennies, he'd built a modest fortune. His experience was the family's one claim to the notion of pulling oneself up by one's bootstraps and becoming something better. But the details of his story had been lost over the generations, and there was nothing in her memory that could tie her family's financial success to any hand of Providence.

By the time she had parked her bike and made her way back to the bunkhouse, she had all but decided that Thomas's words were nothing more than foolishness.

The bunkhouse was empty when she arrived. She took advantage of the quiet and lay down for a nap; she might have slept all afternoon if it had not been for the sounds of bleating sheep outside her window some time later—and the groans of her own stomach. She rose to find the bunkhouse surrounded by a flock of sheep feeding on the surrounding grass, mowing it down.

Curious how the others were spending their afternoon, Genevieve made her way to the big house. She found Holly and Susan at the table writing letters but declined their invitation to join them. After helping herself to leftover biscuits and jam in the kitchen, she made her way to the front porch, where Greg was strumming a guitar and Ephraim was writing in his leather journal. She took a seat on an old rocking chair that offered a commanding view of the expansive front yard and even a sliver of the pond. Crystal, Rachael, James, and Spencer were playing croquet on the freshly shorn side lawn. It was quiet and peaceful, and she found herself trying to remember a more boring Sunday.

Feeling imprisoned against her will—and imagining five months' worth of unbearably uneventful Sundays—she worried she might go mad out of sheer boredom. As she looked at the others, she doubted she would ever choose to have a coffee with any of them—that is, if she could even find a coffee shop around here. She could not imagine a more stark contrast than that between the sedated pace of a Sunday afternoon in Niederbipp and the rush of New York City.

Blind to the acrobatic swallows performing their stunts over the glassy pond, she imagined what she might be doing if she were home. It took only a few seconds to remember that she would be getting ready for her trip to Brussels. She looked down at the ugly skirt she was wearing and wondered what she could have possibly done to warrant Julia's switching her to this assignment, so far away from the glamour and perks of another European fashion show.

Feeling her face flush with anger, she left the front porch to try to walk it off. Of all the writers on staff at the magazine, she knew she was one of the best. Julia had praised her repeatedly for the work she had done. So why this? Why now? The more she thought about it, the more upset she became. She felt betrayed, trapped, and entirely unappreciated. Was this her reward for years of hard work and devotion?

She wandered past the garden, kicking pebbles along the path toward the pond, silently spitting fire with each step. She wanted to sue. She wanted to call her father and get his attorneys involved. They'd find a loophole in the stupid contract she'd signed. They'd find a way to get her off this stupid farm and back to civilization.

Thinking about the nightlife she would be missing in Brussels, she angrily kicked a large pebble. But the pebble did not move; it stubbed her toe instead. With venom in her mouth, she kicked the stupid pebble with her other foot. Wincing in pain and nearly in tears, she looked down to see that the pebble had shifted only slightly. She looked around for a stick, determined that no stupid pebble was going to get the best of her. Dropping to her hands and knees, she scratched away the dirt surrounding the stone, breaking three sticks before she finally unearthed the softball-sized rock.

Angry but triumphant, she awkwardly wound up to toss the rock into the pond. But just as she let go, the earthen bank beneath her feet gave way. Before she could respond, she was nearly up to her knees in thick, black mud—just in time for her rock to land mere feet away from her, splashing dirty pond water all over the front of her shirt. She let out a long string of curses, not holding back as the hem of her skirt wicked up muddy water. She backed up the best she could, reaching for the dry bank. She was teetering on the edge of losing her balance when someone grabbed her flailing hand.

"Are you okay?" he asked.

Genevieve didn't turn to look at him, embarrassed and humiliated.

"Are you okay?" he repeated.

She nodded, feeling stunned. After a long moment of hoping this was all just a very bad dream, she finally turned to look at the man who was firmly holding on to her right hand. It was Matt. "Can you get me out of here, please?"

He nodded and pulled her hand the best he could, scrambling backward in a tug-of-war with the mud. With the sound of a sloshy plop, Genevieve fell backward, knocking Matt over, landing in his lap, and smearing mud all over his shoes and pants.

"I'm sorry," he said, scrambling to his feet. "That didn't go at all like I imagined. I hope that wasn't something valuable that landed in the pond." He took her hand and lifted her out of the dirt. "Are you hurt?"

She shook her head, her anger temporarily halted by the shock of being covered in mud.

"Good, then if you don't mind, I really need to laugh." He put his hand over his face and turned his back toward her as he let out a long and hearty laugh. "That was so funny when you stubbed your toe…bah haha! And to see you sliding down the bank into the mud…bah ha ha!

Oh, and I can honestly say I've never heard that kind of language out of girl before." He turned around, obviously trying to compose himself, but as soon as he looked at the mud splattered on her face, he busted up laughing again.

Genevieve looked down at her mud-cloaked bottom half, splattered shirt, and muddy hands and shook her head. "It's not that funny," she said, trying not to laugh at herself.

"No, it's hilarious!" he roared, sliding again into a fit of laughter. "Remind me to stay out of your way when you're angry," he replied, mimicking the flight of the rock with his hands. "Come on, you have to admit that was funny. I don't remember the last time I laughed this hard."

"You saw the whole thing?"

He nodded, biting his lip to keep from laughing. "From a distance. I couldn't see what you were doing at first, but I was just over there on the bench under the tree."

Genevieve looked past him to see the bench only thirty feet away, hidden in the shade of the willow tree.

"Come on over to the dock where the water's deeper. You can wash your feet off, and maybe your knees, and your hands...and...bah haha."

She laughed again too, and she was surprised how good it felt to be able to laugh at herself. Matt offered her his hand again, and they scrambled up the muddy bank toward the dock. Together they walked out onto the graying planks, to the end of the dock where the water was deep and clean. He sat next to her as she washed the dark mud from her legs. The one pair of practical shoes she had brought with her—her white Keds—were now black.

"Let me see your face," he said as he dipped a corner of his handkerchief into the cool water.

She turned to look at him, and he gently wiped the mud splatters from her nose and forehead.

"You just happened to have a handkerchief in your pocket?" she asked incredulously.

He shrugged. "Habit, I guess. My mom taught me to always carry one just in case I ever made a girl cry."

"Oh really? Does that happen frequently?"

"No," he said, going back for a second time to wipe a smudge of mud from her cheek and another small splatter from her neck. "I'm pretty sure this is the first time I've ever used it for anything besides wiping my nose."

"Wait…what?" she responded, recoiling.

He smiled. "Relax. It's clean, or at least it was before this." He handed it to her, pointing to a smudge on her arm.

"Thanks," she replied. "I'm sorry I got your pants all dirty. It will probably stain."

"It was well worth it," he responded, starting to laugh again. "You looked like you were pretty upset back there."

"Uh, duh! How would you respond if you fell in the mud?"

"Hard to say," he said, obviously trying not to smile. "I was actually talking about the minute before that."

"Oh, that…yeah, it's a long story," she muttered, weakly.

"Well, I think we still have at least an hour before dinner. Wanna talk about it?"

She shook her head. "What were you doing over here?"

"Oh, I was just…writing."

"You're a writer?"

"Yeah, I mean…not really. I've always thought I'd write a book, but I've never done anything worth writing about. I was actually just writing down some stuff about that conversation we had earlier…you know, with the priest, Thomas."

Genevieve nodded. "You like that kind of stuff?"

He shrugged. "What's there not to like? It makes me think."

She nodded again. "So, what did you think about it?"

"Oh, I don't know. I've always been curious about stuff like faith. I like to try to understand what causes people to develop their belief systems."

"What got you interested in that?"

"That's a good question," he responded contemplatively. "It feels like I've always been curious, but I'm sure it was probably influenced by my parents' divorce."

"What was the correlation?" she asked, using Matt's handkerchief to rinse more mud splatters from her knees.

"Well, I was just a kid back then, you know, trying to figure out my place in the universe, and then the only foundation I'd ever known fell out from under my feet. My dad was never really present after that. He'd pop in every couple of years on his way through town, but I guess that not having a dad around, and mom being busy with work...I don't know...I guess I've always had a lot of questions."

"Was he a salesman?"

"My father?"

"Yeah."

"No...uh...no, Dad was an entrepreneur, but it was mostly just manure."

She smiled. "I suppose that means he wasn't successful?"

Matt shrugged, looking out across the pond. "In terms of financial success, no. Dad is the kind of guy who is always two weeks from being a multimillionaire. He must have promised me at least a dozen times that as soon as his ship came in, he'd take me to Disneyland."

"Did you ever get there?"

He shook his head. "I guess the two weeks never came around. He's still at it somewhere. He drops me a line every year or so. I used to imagine him making up for all my disappointments by taking my kids to Disneyland, but I guess I let him off the hook."

"Wait...you have kids?" she asked, looking surprised.

"Yep, six of 'em?"

"Wait, what!?

He rolled his eyes. "No, I don't have kids. That's how I let my old man off the hook."

"You freaked me out there for a second. But it's not too late, right?"

"I'll be forty-four in August. I'm pretty sure that train has left the station."

"Have you ever been married?"

"Nope. I kind of got close once."

"Kind of got close once…what does that mean?"

"Oh, it's a long story. But it's basically the classic story of boy meets girl, boy falls stupid in love with her but doesn't know how to tell her, so boy runs away to try and figure out his life. Then boy wakes up almost twenty years later and realizes he somehow got lost on his way to trying to figure things out."

"Wait, what's classic about that story?"

Matt forced a smile. "I don't know. It happens all the time, right? People forget to say something, and the next thing you know, your life's on a different path than you were hoping for."

Genevieve swished the handkerchief in the water and wrung it out, handing it back to him. "That was how long ago?"

"Long enough to know I'm pathetic."

"Yeah, it sounds like it," she said thoughtlessly, almost impatiently, getting to her feet. "Anyway, thanks for your help. I'm gonna go change out of this ridiculous costume."

Matt watched her go, feeling the full weight of his own patheticness hit him once again. His first hope in coming here was to find a way to get over the woman who'd broken his heart, but so far, opening himself up to be vulnerable had only been met with the confirmation of all that he feared: he was pathetic—a forty-three year-old bachelor whose confidence had only decreased with each passing year. He ran his hand through his thinning hair, forcing a half-hearted smile at his own reflection on the surface of the pond's dark water.

CHAPTER 15

KP

In the arithmetic of love, one plus one equals everything,
and two minus one equals nothing.
– Mignon McLaughlin –

With the evening chores and dinner done, the newly formed
family of fourteen convened once again on the front porch.
The campers took turns on Bessie, churning out a fresh batch of
strawberry ice cream while they played a new game that Pops introduced
to them: Worst Job Ever. It sounded fairly straightforward when he first

described it—pedaling while describing the worst jobs they had ever had. Susan volunteered to go first, but before she could even sit down, Pops opened an old trunk filled with Nerf guns and a variety of ammunition, handing them out to every member of the family. He then set on Susan's head a metal helmet that had been retrofitted with a clear plastic face shield with a curly tipped mustache painted on the front of it. Everyone began laughing immediately as Susan looked cross-eyed at the mustache in front of her.

But Pops was just getting started. Next, he attached a metal plate to the top of the helmet with a couple of magnets, set a red plastic cup on top of the plate, and poured a small amount of ice water from a pitcher into the cup. He explained that while Susan told her story and pedaled old Bessie, the rest of the family would attempt to knock the cup of water off of her head with their ample supply of Nerf bullets.

Over the laughter and the sounds of flying foam bullets, they learned that Susan had once had a job cleaning out fish tanks at a pet shop but was forced to quit after only three days because she had inhaled too much nasty fish water in her pitiful attempts at syphoning. She had nearly finished her story when a well-placed bullet stuck to the face shield directly in front of her nose, causing her to jump and dump water down her own back.

She chose Ephraim to take the next turn, and he was just getting started with his story about washing dishes at Chuck E. Cheese's when someone knocked the cup off the helmet, dumping ice water down his back. He reacted with a jolt and nearly launched himself off the bike, to the delight of the rest of the family.

Spencer followed Ephraim. He nearly got through his story of scooping poop at a dog park, but then he attempted to dodge a bullet, upsetting the cup of water, dousing his own back, and splashing three of the campers closest to him.

By the time they had each taken a turn in the saddle, nine of them had wet backs, and all of them had laughed themselves silly. As they ate their ice cream, Ruby gave a brief description of the additional chores that would begin the next day after regular chores. The garden would need to be weeded, tilled, and planted as soon as possible so the campers could harvest and bottle the tomatoes before the end of the summer. In addition to that, the back forty acres of land that Pops had turned over the week before was ready for planting and would require all hands on deck. Once the garden was in and the grain was planted, only the regular chores would be required, but until then, they would need to plan on rising early and getting to bed as early as possible to enable them to have the energy to get the work done.

Ruby then announced that her primary interviews would be held in the evenings over the course of the next week. These, she explained, would enable her to get to know each of the kids better, focusing on their strengths while also exploring possible weaknesses, dreams, and aspirations. Genevieve looked around, watching as all of the others nodded as if they'd been anticipating this announcement. Once again, she found herself feeling very uninformed and was lost in her imagination when she heard that her own interview would take place after dinner on Wednesday evening. It felt unwise to ask what that meant, deciding instead that she would get the information from the women who went before her. But she was distracted for the rest of the evening when she remembered that she would have been on her way to Brussels right then, anticipating a world of glamour and glitz a million miles away from the stink of a farm and the annoying sound of crickets.

Thus distracted, she didn't hear Lorenzo's invitation to kneel and pray. But the shuffle of the other bodies on the porch alerted her, and so, befuddled, she knelt on hard wooden planks next to the others. Lorenzo briefly explained that ice cream was optional on the farm but that prayers would be offered at mealtimes and at the close of each day, as had been the tradition on the farm for more than three hundred years. He explained that each of the kids would have the opportunity take a turn, praying in whatever manner was familiar or comfortable to them, giving thanks while invoking the continued blessings of God. As heads bowed and some eyes closed, Genevieve looked around, recognizing that she was not the only one for whom prayer was foreign. She noticed that Spencer had his eyes turned to the porch's light as if he were counting the fluttering moths, while Sonja grimaced as if in pain. But Genevieve listened as Lorenzo thanked his god once again for the farm and the summer's laborers. He asked the heavens for sunshine and rain, requested that friendship might continue to grow, and prayed that everyone present might reap the rewards they desired as they sacrificed their time to labor on the farm.

At amen, the porch was again in motion as everyone seemed anxious to get off their knees—everyone, that is, except Matt, who looked lost in thought. While Susan and James volunteered to clean up the ice cream messes, the rest of the family made their way to the bunkhouses to change out of their wet tops and turn in for the evening. Genevieve turned back to see Matt conversing with Lorenzo and was curious what they might be talking about, but her weariness quickly overpowered her curiosity. She wandered back to the bunkhouse and lay down on her bed, her head feeling full and her eyelids heavy as she looked up at the words painted above the doorframe of the front door. *Except the Lord build the house, they labor in vain that build it*. She thought about it for a few seconds before rolling over, wishing she were anywhere else but here.

The next thing she knew she was running—running as fast as she could down the steep slope of a mountainside, her feet getting tangled in the tall grass as she ran, trying to outrun the giant pterodactyl soaring overhead. But she found neither shelter nor relief from his incessant, bloodcurdling cries. And as the monster bore down on her, bearing his razor-sharp claws just inches from her shoulders, she sat up in fright, feeling confused. Again the pterodactyl screeched, and she ducked to avoid his claws, falling back onto her pillow and waking her from her deep, nonsensical slumber. Genevieve was reaching for a shoe to throw at the rooster when she noticed the shadows of her housemates were moving in the low, early light of morning. Reluctantly, she peeled back the covers and shambled across the cold floor and into the bathroom to wash her face.

Never having been a morning person, Genevieve said nothing to the other women and was grateful none of them attempted conversation either until they all left the bunkhouse to head out for morning chores.

"Where are you going?" Sonja asked as Genevieve stumbled absentmindedly toward the barn.

"Uhh, where am I supposed to be?" she muttered, realizing she didn't know.

"I think you're in the kitchen today, right?"

"Am I?"

"I don't know for sure, but I think I'm supposed to be at the barn, and Crystal is taking care of the chickens, and Rachael went to slop the pigs..."

"Right," Genevieve said, changing her course for the big house. She entered the back door of the dining hall, stumbling over the rubber boots that had been left on the rag rug. She cursed under her breath as she caught herself, but she was reminded to take off her own boots, setting them and the others to the side and donning the felted, gray slippers from the partitioned cubbies. She climbed the few stairs and was making her way across the floor when she heard voices and followed them to the kitchen.

"Good morning!" Ruby said with an annoying singsongy voice that forced an involuntary smile onto Genevieve's face.

"Good morning," Genevieve countered, wanting badly to be sassy but deciding to hold her tongue when she saw Greg, who was standing behind Ruby and cracking eggs into an old stoneware bowl. He looked up and smiled, looking tired.

"Since Greg got here first, he got to decide what to make for breakfast. You'll be his assistant this morning. That means you'll get to decide what to make for dinner, and then he can assist you."

She took a deep breath, exhaling loudly. "Fine. What are we making?"

"French toast and oatmeal," Greg reported. "I was hoping for Captain Crunch, but Ruby's never heard of it. Do you know how to cook French toast?"

"Uh, of course," she lied.

"Oh, good. I used to help my mom make it, but it's been a long time. Ruby said she'd help us out if she thinks we're going off the rails, but she wanted us to do our best first. What do you think it needs besides eggs and bread?"

"Uh, maybe milk?"

Ruby nodded, pointing to the large fridge.

"I was thinking cinnamon," Greg added.

Ruby pointed to a tall jar filled with cinnamon sticks on the butcher-block counter. "You'll find the grater in the drawers."

"What do you want me to do?" Genevieve asked, glancing between Greg and Ruby.

"Um, do you want to help me get the eggshells out of here? I'm kind of making a mess."

Genevieve rolled her eyes as she stepped closer to the multicolored eggs to lend a hand.

"Breakfast needs to be served at seven to keep us on schedule," Ruby announced. "You have forty minutes. I'd normally be helping, but Pops asked me to round up the garden tools while he's overseeing the milking. Will you two be okay without me?"

Genevieve glanced at Greg, who nodded unconvincingly.

When Ruby returned thirty minutes later, she looked around as if things were just about as she had expected they would be. The center island was a mess, littered with eggshells and cinnamon dust. Genevieve was standing at the stove, flipping a batch of burnt French toast on the cast-iron griddle. Greg was standing at the other corner of the stove, frantically blowing on the oatmeal as it rose to the top of the pot. It looked like it had already overflowed a couple of times; the spilled-over mess was slowly baking onto the outside of the pot and the stove itself. Ruby moved quickly to open the window above the old farmhouse sink, letting in some fresh air.

"I hope it tastes better than it smells," Ruby said with a face neither of them could read.

"Sorry, we kinda made a mess," Greg reported, as if she hadn't noticed.

"That's all right. You two are on cleanup duty, too."

Genevieve bit her tongue as she turned over another burnt piece of French toast.

"What are we going to do?" Genevieve asked, looking up at the large clock above the window.

"Well, we're gonna eat breakfast," Ruby said, matter-of-factly.

"I don't know if any of this is edible, and I just used the last of the bread," Genevieve reported, almost humbly.

"Oh, believe me, I've eaten far worse," Ruby said. "My constitution goes through a painful reset every year at this time as I get used to you kids and your cooking skills—or lack thereof. I always find myself hoping beyond hope that someday I'll get a batch of kids who've all be trained in the culinary arts, but so far my hopes have been dashed. But fear not!" Ruby said, holding up one finger. "The cellar is still stocked with plenty of jam. You'd be surprised how a little raspberry jam can go a long way in masking the flavor of most burnt offerings."

She smiled kindly at Genevieve before pulling open the cellar door and descending into the dark, cool space below, reemerging a minute later with several jars of crimson preserves cradled in her apron. She set the jars on the counter and walked quickly to the fridge, pulling out several bottles of milk and cream and a large crock of butter. "Yep, butter and jam hide a myriad of sins, at least at breakfast. But you both better learn to use that gas stove before dinner, or we'll have a mutiny on our hands. And that's never a good thing."

Genevieve wiped her sweaty brow, feeling like a failure, but wasn't sure if she really cared. She'd never cooked a meal in her life outside of a few classes she'd taken at the Williams Sonoma test kitchen in Manhattan as part of a story she'd done years before. It had always seemed silly to cook for one. But then it seemed even sillier to cook for fourteen. She already knew she wasn't going to like this—any of it.

Ruby sent them into the dining hall to set the table, and they were nearly finished when the back door opened and the rest of the family began filing in. Crystal and Matt each came carrying a basketful of eggs, and Sonja and Ephraim each carried one side of a milk can. The others wandered in looking at least as tired and hungry as Genevieve felt.

"Who's burning the bacon?" James asked without thinking.

"Oh, it's not bacon; it's Genevieve's famous gourmet mesquite French toast," Greg replied.

Genevieve felt her face flush as she saw the others look at each other as if they were wondering if mesquite French toast were really a thing. She was turning away when she caught a glimpse of Lorenzo smiling kindly as he looked her way from behind them all. Ruby directed the hungry crew into the kitchen to wash their hands, and Genevieve watched as they nervously smiled to themselves and each other as they caught glimpses of breakfast makings scattered across the island, the floor, and the stove. They all moved back into the dining hall, carrying the accessories of breakfast with them to the table.

"I've never heard of mesquite French toast, have you?" Genevieve heard Ephraim whisper to Crystal, and she was relieved when she heard Crystal whisper back that her father made it all the time. They sat down, and Lorenzo invited Greg to say grace over the meal he and Genevieve had created.

It was obvious to everyone that Greg was not nearly as practiced at prayer as Lorenzo was, but his simple words were at least sincere as he thanked God for food to eat and work to do. He asked for a blessing on the food and petitioned that they would all be protected from food poisoning and other less obvious distractions to the work that lay ahead of them.

Then, being careful not to scoop too near the bottom of the scorched pot, Greg served everyone bowls of oatmeal while Genevieve passed around the platter of her now-famous mesquite French toast. To her surprise and relief, she soon discovered that Ruby was right—good jam did indeed cover a plethora of mistakes, or at least enough to make many of those present believe that mesquite French toast really was a thing. Most of them even had seconds.

With the morning chores complete, Lorenzo announced that he would be leading everyone except Mom and the day's kitchen staff into the garden to begin the annual extraction of weeds and prepping of the soil. Though spending the next several hours in the garden sounded like a form of cruel and unusual punishment to Genevieve, the idea of spending the rest of the day in the kitchen cleaning and cooking again and again sounded even worse. And even though everyone helped by carrying their dishes to the sink, the mountain of dirty dishes they left behind felt like an unwelcome gift.

For his part, Greg tried to make the best of it. And as they worked side by side, he confided in Genevieve how happy he was to be here after being rejected three years in a row. His honesty intrigued her. He reported how he had changed over the course of those three years. As he'd waited, he'd recognized how self-centered he had been before; he took the time during the long wait to work on himself and try to become a better man. He had read numerous self-help books; spent hours volunteering at the local Boys & Girls Club; and learned how to knit from his grandmother, who had promised him that knitting would help him slow down long enough to solve all the world's troubles, or at least his own. Eleven sweaters, thirteen mittens, and four afghans later, he had finally been accepted into Ruby's summer program.

Ruby returned from checking on the garden crew just as they were finishing chiseling the last of the encrusted oatmeal from off the stove. She led them into the cool, dark cellar, into the far corner where barrels of grain were stacked two-high, nearly reaching the ceiling. Removing the top of one, she dipped an old wooden scoop into the loose grain and then transferred it into a metal pail. This she carried to a contraption near the opposite wall. The apparatus looked something like a giant, old phonograph, only its bell was turned at an odd angle, facing up. She poured the contents of the pail into the old copper bell before lifting up the front panel of the contraption and sliding the empty pail inside. Then she invited each of them to take a seat on the wooden chairs attached to the sides of a big wooden box. This they did, sliding in front of a bent metal shaft that protruded from both sides of the box just in front of them. They looked at each other, and then, wondering what this was all about, they turned back to see Ruby smiling at them.

"It's good luck to be the first couple of the year to grind the wheat into flour."

"Oh yeah, I've heard about this," Greg said, unable to keep his enthusiasm under control. "I can't believe I'm really here."

"So, how is this good luck?" Genevieve asked, thoroughly confused.

"You don't know about this?" Greg asked.

"No."

"Oh, this is great. My mom's been telling me about this since I was a kid. She was the first one to grind wheat in her year, and it's true…she was the first one in her group to get married."

"Malory Flemming,"Ruby said with a smile. "Your mother was quite the spirited young woman. How is she? I haven't heard from her in a couple of years."

"She's great. Busy with grandkids most of the time."

Ruby's smile broadened. "She must have a dozen by now."

"Fourteen," Greg said proudly. "I've been working hard to be the favorite uncle."

"That's splendid. I don't suppose she told you how this works?"

He looked down at the bent shaft in front of him, placing his hands timidly on the polished wooden handle.

Genevieve, watching him, did the same, only her handle was a good foot taller than his.

With a small grunt, the handle in front of her began to move in a circular motion before stopping. They both looked up to find Ruby smiling.

"It takes a little work to get the timing right—a bit like using a two-person saw or running a three-legged race. This old flour mill has been here in this cellar for probably close to three hundred years. It's ground the flour to make the bread for at least seven generations. Some teams figure it out quickly. Some teams take forever while the whole family goes hungry. I'll leave it to you two to figure it out on your own, as you'll have to figure it out with each of the other kids you'll be teamed up with over the next five months. I'll be waiting for you in the kitchen. But I'll warn you that we have six loaves of bread to bake before anyone can eat lunch. Hungry folks don't like to wait any longer than they have to, so I'd like to encourage you to work together."

They both nodded as Ruby left them in the dimly lit cellar.

"So what do you know about this?" Genevieve asked.

"I don't know a lot, but my mom said it took her and the first guy she was teamed up with most of the day to make a pail of flour."

"Seriously?"

"That's what she told me. She did say it got easier, but yeah...after screwing up breakfast, I don't wanna make it any worse."

"That makes two of us. Isn't there an easier way?"

"Like what?"

"I don't know...like running into town and picking up a bag of flour? There are normal people around here who just buy flour, right?"

Greg laughed. "That would take us at least an hour to ride our bikes down and back, and I can't imagine it being very easy to schlep a bag of flour uphill on a bicycle."

"Well, how hard can this be, right? I mean, if seven generations have ground their flour on this crazy contraption, we ought to be able to figure it out, right?"

"Go for it," he responded, gesturing with both hands to the crank in front of her.

Genevieve pulled the crank toward her, and her hopes rose as it moved several inches before stopping like it had somehow sucked a stone into the works. "It won't go any farther," she said, grunting as she alternated between pushing and pulling.

"Let me try," Greg responded. He wrapped his fingers around the handle and pushed as hard as he could, but the crank turned only a few inches before stopping again.

"This is ridiculous. We could die here," Genevieve muttered melodramatically. "It's gonna be faster to go into town, even if it does take us all day to get there and back."

"No. Let's keep trying. Loads of people have figured this out. It's not rocket science. It's…what did Ruby say? It's like a three-legged race."

"Yeah, well, then it might as well be rocket science! I've been in exactly two three-legged races in my whole life and ended up with broken bones in each one."

"Seriously?"

"Okay, so maybe only one. I broke my nose in the third grade, and in the fifth grade, the girl I was with broke her wrist."

Greg laughed. "Maybe your timing was just off. It takes some coordination and cooperation, but it's really not that difficult once you get the hang of it."

"Really? Are you calling me uncoordinated? I happen to be a dancer—I was a ballerina until I went to college. That takes all sorts of coordination, so don't even give me that. I'm going into town." She stood up and began walking away.

"Hold on! I'm not calling you uncoordinated."

"Then what are you saying?"

"I'm saying that we're not cooperating."

"No duh!"

"Like in a three-legged race, I mean. I won lots of blue ribbons on field day. Even when I got teamed up with guys bigger or shorter than me, if we could cooperate, we usually won."

She folded her arms across her chest. "This isn't a three-legged race."

"No, it's not, but I think the principle might be the same."

"How?"

"Come sit down."

"This is stupid."

"Maybe it is. Listen, if this doesn't work, I'll go with you into town to buy the flour."

"Promise? If it doesn't work, you'll go with me and we won't waste any more time on this stupid thing?"

"Yeah, I promise. Just take a seat."

She reluctantly returned to her seat, but it was obvious that she wasn't happy about it.

"Okay, so let's give this a try," he said. "You push on your side while I pull on mine."

She rolled her eyes and took hold of the handle.

"On the count of three. One. Two. Three. Go!"

Genevieve pushed hard, bearing her teeth while Greg pulled back hard on his handle. To his surprise and relief, the shaft turned much farther than it had before, not coming to a stop until it had moved 180 degrees.

Genevieve grunted as she pushed again and again, but the shaft had stopped turning. There was nothing she could do to get it to move, even elevating herself with her full weight on the handle. "Are you ready to go to town?"

"Not yet I'm not."

"Greg, this is stupid. This thing is broken."

"Are you sure?" he asked, getting off of his chair and walking around to the front of the machine where the pail stood waiting to receive the flour.

"Yeah I'm pretty sure this is a piece of crap," she said as she leaned over his shoulder as he stooped down to look into the pail.

He reached his hand into the bottom the pail, scooping up enough flour to cover his fingertips. "Hey, it works!"

She closed her eyes. "Dude, we've been down here for ten minutes and we've only made enough flour to make a pancake for a grasshopper."

"Okay, but that's our fault, not the machine's. If seven generations have made flour on this contraption, I'm sure we can too."

"Imbecile," she muttered almost silently as she watched him return to his seat.

"Excuse me?"

She shook her head.

"Look, the secret of a good three-legged race team is timing and communication," he persisted. "Someone has to be the counter. One, two, one, two as you work your way down the field. This is obviously a little bit different—we're not going anywhere, just trying to pedal this weird bike together. But I think it's kind of the same principle. When I push, you pull, and when I pull, you push. It's cooperation. It's gotta work."

"And if it doesn't?"

"Then we'll go to town and I'll carry the flour back home."

She shook her head but sat back down on the seat and put her hands on the handle, turning to face him. "Okay, now what?"

"You push and I'll pull. Ready, go!" Again the shaft rotated 180 degrees before stopping. "Now just keep it going. Ready, pull! Push! Pull! Push! Pull! Push!"

After three rotations, the shaft came to a stop again. "What happened?" he asked, pushing on the handle in front of him but making no progress.

"I stopped."

"Why?"

"Because you stopped telling me what to do?"

Greg shook his head, smiling. "Really, a liberated woman like you is seriously waiting for man to tell her what to do?"

She responded by pulling a face and throwing her weight onto the handle again, which moved just an inch or two before stopping.

"Look, it doesn't matter to me who calls it," he said. "But it seems like the only way this works is if we're working on it together...you know...cooperation."

She shook her head. "So you want me to call it then?"

"Sure, have a go. We can take turns if you want."

"Then push!" she said loudly. "Pull!"

Again the shaft rotated, and Genevieve continued for nearly a minute, calling the directions out as the central shaft continued to turn, each rotation smoother than the last.

"Why'd you stop?" he asked as the crank in front of him slowed.

"I'm out of breath."

"Do you want me to take a turn?"

She nodded.

But before he began again, he walked to the front of the machine and looked into the pail. "It looks like we've got about a cup of flour. Only forty cups to go!"

"Shut up!"

"We can do this. It's like going to the gym."

"Yeah, except we're in a cave and there's no CNN and no hot guys to show off to."

Greg laughed. "Would it help if I took my shirt off and pranced around during breaks?"

"Just shut up and push. And it's your turn to count."

The counting continued for the next half hour, each of them taking turns when the other became winded. Greg was beginning to wonder when this would end, when all of a sudden the crank began to turn with hardly any effort.

Genevieve looked at him, surprised. "Did we break it?"

"I don't think so," he said, letting the crank fall from his hands. "I think we must be out of wheat."

He walked around to the front. "It's full!" he said, stooping down to shake the pail and even out the level.

She smiled from her seat but didn't move, feeling winded.

"Come on," he said, reaching out his hand to take hers. "We need to learn how to make bread before everybody's hungry."

CHAPTER 16

Passions of Time

Every man ought to be inquisitive through every
hour of his great adventure down to the day when he
shall no longer cast a shadow in the sun. For if he dies
without a question in his heart, what excuse is there for
his continuance?
—Frank Moore Colby—

They found Ruby in the kitchen as promised, her backside toward
them, her top half inside an oversized metal bowl connected to
an oversized mixer.

"Oh, it looks like you two figured it out," she said, turning to face them and staring at the pail they'd brought with them from the cellar.

"Tell me," Genevieve said, "How was our timing compared to others'?"

Ruby glanced at the clock. "Not bad for first timers. If it takes you this long by the end of the summer, I'll have to wonder if something's wrong. But for newbies, you did okay."

"Wait," Genevieve responded, looking a little bit upset. "How could we possibly have gone any faster?"

Ruby smiled. "There is a big difference between a three-legged race and a dance. And once you learn the rhythm of a dance—how to read your partner—how to know what they are going to do before they do it—then you can tango."

Greg looked thoughtful. "It almost sounds like this is about more than just making flour."

Ruby touched her nose with one index finger and pointed at Greg with the other. "It takes lots of kids half the summer before they discover that every farm activity offers open-minded participants far more value than the simple tasks themselves. If you'll look at every problem as you've looked at this one, all the lessons you have to learn here will come much easier and quicker. For those who are seeking and open to real solutions, they'll always find the writing on the wall."

"So how long do most people take?" Genevieve asked impatiently.

"Some teams take hours their first time. We've even known some who ride the bikes into town and buy the flour, but that usually results in a lot of hungry and cantankerous campers who have to wait too long for lunch. Everybody's got to come up with their own solutions, but some solutions are far better than others."

"So what's the record to beat?"

"Do you mean timing?"

Genevieve nodded.

"Well, the only record you really need to worry about is your own, but since you asked, the record is three minutes and forty-two seconds."

"Impossible!" Genevieve responded, shaking her head.

"Difficult, yes, but not impossible. I should know. Lorenzo and I share that record. Of course, that was when we were younger and more limber. These days our tango is more of a waltz. But it all depends on the music and the level of our arthritic pain."

"Wait, you mean you use that grinder too?" Genevieve asked incredulously.

"Of course. What else would we use?"

"I…just thought you guys must have an easier way."

Ruby shook her head. "We don't ask any of our campers to do anything we don't do ourselves. We've been using the same grinder for more than fifty-six years, seven months a year. We get a break in the summer when the campers are here. It's good exercise for old people too. The way we figure, it's a little bit like climbing stairs—if you do it every day of your life, you can do it forever. But once you believe you're too old for stairs, you're probably too old for stairs. You gotta keep movin' or you'll get old."

Greg nodded, making a mental note of the conversation. "So what's next?"

"Well, it's time to bake some bread," Ruby said, pointing to a recipe written in white chalk on a slate hanging on the wall. "Have either of you baked bread before?"

"Not me," Greg said.

"Does Pillsbury count?" Genevieve asked.

"Hardly! It's not rocket science—at its best it's more of an art/science hybrid, really. Proportions are important, as is the dance of working in the kitchen with others. Like most things in cooking, you get a feel for it over time. The recipe is there as a rule in the beginning and as a guideline as you develop your skills. There will be plenty of variations to come in the future for those of you who are more creative, but this recipe will ensure six decent loaves if you follow it. I've taken the liberty of getting out the ingredients you'll need. You'll have to measure the water."

Following the recipe on the wall, they measured out the water, yeast, salt, and honey, allowing the mixture to sit for a moment until the yeast began rising to the surface of the water. Then they began the task of measuring the twenty cups of flour. Out of fear of losing track, they decided Greg would scoop and Genevieve would count. They had several cups of flour left in the pail when they were done. Ruby instructed them to dust the counter with some of the flour and then to dump the rest into a heavy crockery jar for later use.

Genevieve made what she quickly learned was a common amateur mistake; she hit the power switch a little too aggressively, which threw a cloud of flour into the air and onto the tiled floor. But Ruby was patient with them, and before long the bread hook had worked the mixture into a nice ball of sticky dough. While the dough rested in the bowl, Ruby instructed them to grease the bread tins with butter before adding a fine coat of flour.

With the tins now ready to receive the dough, Genevieve and Greg dumped the contents of the giant bowl out onto the table, the dough blob quickly changing shape as it rolled and unfolded out onto the flour-dusted surface of the countertop. Then, following Ruby's instructions, they massaged the blob into the form of a boa constrictor, dusting it with more flour before cutting it into equal-sized smaller blobs. They kneaded these in turn, folding in the uneven edges to form beautifully rounded, tan blobs of flour-dusted dough that were laid to rest in the greased tins.

Ruby lined the tins up, three wide by two deep, before draping them with a clean cloth. "On a cool spring day like today, they'll take thirty minutes to rise, but in the summer, you'll have to watch them closer. Either way, now is the time to start the oven."

She moved to the black behemoth of a cast-iron oven. Lighting a match, she opened the oven door and turned on the gas, leaning down to ignite the burners. "This ain't your momma's Sears and Roebuck. If you want to keep your eyebrows, light the match before you turn on the gas. This oven can smell your fear and will bite you if you're not careful. If you're unsure of what you're doing, ask!"

Ruby set them to cleaning up their messes while they waited for the bread to rise. By the time they were finishing up, the bread had risen enough to slide into the hot oven. Greg laughed at Genevieve as she daintily handled the bread pans, moving each one trepidatiously to the oven like she was making an offering to the angry gods of a volcano. A windup timer was set for forty minutes, and they backed away from the giant oven, each feeling a sense of accomplishment.

"What do we do now?" Greg asked.

"Well, that depends on what you want to serve on your bread," answered Ruby.

"Humm. How about peanut butter and honey?" Greg replied. "That's my favorite."

"Good choice," said Ruby.

"I was actually thinking smoked turkey and avocado," Genevieve responded.

"Is that right?" Ruby said.

"Yeah, maybe with some sprouts and deli mustard or something."

"While you're at it, why don't we have a side of caviar and a few martinis?"

"Really?" she asked, looking surprised.

Ruby laughed. "Around here, if you want smoked turkey, you've got to smoke it yourself. We can pick up some avocados the next time we're in town if it's in the budget. Sprouts take several days to grow, even in the greenhouse, and as far as deli mustard goes, well, I'm sure I could dig out a few recipes."

"Why can't we just take the truck into town and pick all of that stuff up at the store?"

Ruby smiled. "We could, but with fourteen mouths to feed, it would blow our budget pretty quick."

"How much is in the budget?"

"Well, you're lucky. With the sales from last summer's extra eggs and milk and the sales from my socks, plus what Lorenzo and I have been able to scrimp over the winter, I think we have about $900 after property tax and tithing."

Genevieve looked surprised. "That would be enough to buy gallons of mustard and bushels of avocados every week."

"I don't think you understand—our weekly budget isn't $900. That's our budget for the whole summer. We'll make more, of course, by selling the farm products, but that money's got to last until more money comes in. Taxes are due in December, you know, and there'll be all sorts of other surprises that pop up unannounced—there always are."

"So, wait—are you saying I won't be able to eat avocados for the whole summer?"

"Of course not. But you may have to raise some carrots or pick some berries to trade for that avocado. Avocados don't exactly grow on trees, you know—at least not around here. I think I told you on Saturday that we try our best to be self-sufficient. There are things we can splurge on if we plan for it, but it generally takes sacrifice and planning and aligning the opinions of fourteen people."

Genevieve shook her head. "This is going to be a very long summer."

"Perhaps. That really all depends on you. When you're a member of a fourteen-person family, you don't usually get what you want all the time. But I hope you'll discover that the lessons you learn from sacrifice and negotiation will far outweigh any perceived loss of self-identity and personal desires. It may seem like a lot to swallow in one gulp, but if you take it a day at a time, you'll likely begin to see the beauty and meaning behind it all. Besides, I think we'd all agree that it's better to go without a couple of avocados than toilet paper."

Greg laughed. "Those are the kinds of compromises you talked about in the paperwork, right?"

Ruby nodded. "Those and a hundred million others. Most single people don't realize how inflexible they are until they have to live with someone. Sharing shampoo and toothpaste is hard enough, but learning to share money and a budget—learning to compromise through it all and yield to each other—those are some of the biggest challenges married people face. It's better to learn it here with a bunch of strangers you may never see again than to take your issues of selfishness and inflexibility with you into a marriage with someone you really love. Either way, it's work. But you might as well practice here so every relationship in your future can be blessed. Avocados may seem like a big thing today, but kids and cars and where you'll spend the holidays—it all takes compromise, budgeting, and sacrifice. It all requires flexibility."

"Okay, fine!" Genevieve responded impatiently. "Peanut butter and honey will be fine…but wait, don't you have to buy peanut butter too?"

"Most people do, but you don't have to if you own a farm. Follow me."

They followed her down into the cellar, walking down the dimly lit aisles of preserves. They stopped at a gunnysack. "Greg, if you'll carry the peanuts, Genevieve and I will handle the mortar and pestle."

It was heavier that it looked. Genevieve had seen a smaller version at the pharmacy near her apartment, but she had never used one. When they got back to the kitchen, Ruby explained that peanut butter was nothing more than squashed peanuts. Genevieve and Greg both looked doubtful but accepted the challenge. After dumping in a cup of shelled peanuts, Greg took the first turn. The smooth marble pestle was cool to the touch. He began by smashing the peanuts into crumbles, then working his weight against the large pestle until, just as Ruby had promised, the mixture began blending into an ever-smoother butter.

"Just as good as the Piggly Wiggly!" Ruby said, patting Greg on the shoulder.

By the time the bread was done, Greg and Genevieve had each created a cup of peanut butter, one creamy, one chunky. They kept at it until the bread had cooled long enough to be cut, then they emptied the peanut butter from the heavy mortar into bowls. It wasn't as sweet as the peanut butter from the stores, but with only one ingredient, no one expected it to be so.

After the table was set again, they proudly displayed the fruits of their labor on a variety of cutting boards and set them in the center of the long table along with the bowls of fresh peanut butter and a couple of jars of amber honey and more raspberry preserves. Genevieve was surprised by the sense of accomplishment she felt. She was tired and hot from working so near the blast furnace, but the aroma and sight of the bread felt like a surprisingly big and welcome reward for a morning of labor. And to her surprise, the reward only multiplied when the rest of the hungry campers came to the table, oohing and aahing at what they saw and smelled.

Despite the coolness of the day, everyone was sweaty and tired from their work in the garden and could hardly wait for grace to be said. They breezed through the warm bread and peanut butter in no time, making history of five full loaves. Lorenzo announced that they'd all be given the rest of the hour to relax before the work would resume. Many of them filed out into the shade of the front lawn to catch a quick nap. Genevieve could see from the front porch that the garden had been mostly tilled and weeded, which suited her fine. She wouldn't have to admit that she had never pulled a weed in her life and wasn't sure if she even knew the difference between a weed and young vegetable plant. The porch was cool, and a light breeze refreshed her, causing her to doze off in a comfy chair.

"So, what do you want to cook for dinner?" Ruby asked, setting her hand on Genevieve's shoulder.

"I'm so full I can't even think about dinner right now," she responded.

"Maybe not, but it'll be too late to think about it when everyone's hungry."

"What do you usually have?"

Ruby laughed. "When it's just me and Pops, we usually just have bread and milk, but not many folks in your generation have any appreciation for that. And besides, there's not enough bread for another full meal. The way everyone's working today—and will need to keep working for the next few days—we probably ought to load on the carbs. How about pasta?"

"Uh, sure," she responded, working her way to the edge of the chair. She followed Ruby back into the kitchen, Greg trailing behind as the rest of the campers headed back to the garden.

Before they could begin cooking, there were lunch dishes to be done, but these cleaned up quickly as Genevieve washed and Greg dried. They soon discovered that pasta on the farm meant something very different from what it had meant for each of them prior to their arrival in Niederbipp. Starting with two quarts of stewed tomatoes from the cellar, Ruby instructed them in the lost art of marinara from scratch. She sent them both to the garden with a list of herbs to bring back from the herb corner. Basil, oregano, thyme, and chives. The basil was easy for both of them, but they had to ask Lorenzo to point out the others, having never seen them outside of a spice bottle. And they had to return again to the garden for second helpings when Ruby reminded them that they were cooking for fourteen.

They rinsed and chopped the herbs, as well as garlic and onion from the cellar. When the sauce was finally bubbling slowly on the stove in a big copper pot, they moved on to the pasta itself. To their surprise, they learned that there weren't bags of premade noodles in the cellar waiting to be boiled. Instead, they were instructed in the fine art of pasta making, beginning with flour, eggs, oil, and salt. They each formed a flour volcano into which they cracked their eggs. The mixture quickly became sticky and messy, gumming up their hands as they attempted to knead the dough. When it all finally came together, Ruby instructed them to dust the dough balls with flour and wrap them in clean dish towels before putting it into the fridge to rest. After they cleaned up the counter, she sent them back out to the garden to gather lettuce and spinach. It was the first time either of them had ever seen greens like this growing in a garden. Lorenzo even showed them where they could find a few carrots and green onions still growing from the previous season. They returned to a kitchen filled with the aromas of Italy, and even Genevieve couldn't help but smile to herself as they rinsed the greens and chopped the carrots and onions. By most standards, it was a simple repast, but watching a full meal all come together from scratch for the very first time in her life, she felt like she was part of some crazy bit of magic.

When the salad was finished and placed in a giant wooden bowl, Ruby called them back to the center island to roll out the pasta dough. It was harder than either of them had imagined, Ruby encouraging them again and again to apply more pressure to the big rollers until she was satisfied with the thickness. Then, dusting the thin dough with another coat of flour, she handed each of them a pizza cutter and encouraged them to begin cutting the dough into long strips. Their lines were crooked at first, but they quickly got the hang of it. Before long, they had a large pile of fresh fettuccini.

Looking up at the clock, Ruby instructed Greg to fill a giant pot with water and get it onto the stove to boil while she and Genevieve set the table. While they waited for the water to boil, they sliced the remaining loaf of bread and filled the water pitchers. Then into the boiling water they carefully added the thin strands of dough. As they waited for the pasta to cook, Genevieve realized that she had probably spent more time in the kitchen on this one day than over the entire course of her lifetime. She also couldn't remember ever eating as many carbs in one day, but she felt good, having used those carbs to fuel the physical work she'd performed.

Ruby sent Genevieve to ring the dinner bell, and the kitchen sink was soon overwhelmed with hungry gardeners washing their hands. Crystal offered to say grace, which was quick and simple. And soon plates were filled with beautiful pasta and salad, bringing smiles to everyone at the table. There was plenty of food, enough for anyone who wanted to enjoy seconds, and despite the long day of labor, the conversation at the table was playful and fun.

Before anyone could leave, Ephraim passed around the jar of wisdom cookies, and each of them shared what was written inside theirs.

Crystal read.

Who is rich? He who is content with his portion.

"That's Benjamin Franklin, right?" Matt asked.

"Very good," responded Ruby.

"Here's one," said Ephraim.

> Happiness cannot be traveled to, owned, earned, worn, or consumed. Happiness is the spiritual experience of living every minute with love, grace, and gratitude.

They all looked to Matt for a guess, but he had nothing.

"Denis Waitley, I think," Lorenzo said. "He's a writer and a motivational speaker. You'll find a few of his books in the library."

"Here's one," said James.

> Opportunity is missed by most people because it is dressed in overalls and looks like work.

Again, they all looked at Matt.

"I've heard this one before...Thomas Edison, right?"

"Impressive," Ruby responded. "That was one of the quotes that became pivotal for Pops and me when we took over the farm."

"Wait...what?" Genevieve asked, the journalist in her waking from a nap.

"Let's just say this place needed some work," she said, winking at Pops at the opposite end of the table. "Everything worth doing and keeping always requires more work than you think is necessary. Remember that, and you'll never be disappointed or surprised."

"But wait..." Genevieve started, but she was quickly drowned out by Holly.

> Inaction breeds doubt and fear. Action breeds confidence and courage. If you want to conquer fear, do not sit home and think about it. Go out and get busy.

"This is a good one," she said.

Again all heads turned to Matt. "That sounds a lot like Dale Carnegie, but I'm not sure."

"That's right," said Lorenzo. "You'll find Mr. Carnegie's books in the library too."

"How do you know all these quotes?" Spencer asked, looking quite impressed.

Matt shrugged, looking embarrassed. "I...I guess I've always been a sucker for a short, pithy bit of truth, no matter where it comes from."

"I collect quotes too, but these are really good ones," Crystal acknowledged, looking over Sonja's shoulder at hers. "I feel like I could write a chapter of a self-help book on each one of these."

"Funny you should say that. We've had two of our kids go on to write self-help books after their summers here, using many of these quotes from the wisdom cookies. You can find their books in the library too," Lorenzo reported.

"Sounds like I need to spend more time in the library," Ephraim responded.

"There'll be time for all of that when the planting's done," Ruby replied. "It's always one of the favorite places on the farm. I encourage you all to spend some of your spare time there. Pops and I have always felt that a well-stocked library is at least as important as a well-stocked pantry. If you desire wisdom, you must make the time to feed your heart and brain the same way you take time to eat and nourish your body."

"That sounds a lot like Sonja's quote," Crystal responded.

Sonja nodded. "I was just thinking the same thing. Would you like to hear it?"

All heads nodded.

Everything changes the hour you realize there are exactly enough minutes for the important things in life.

A silence fell across them all as they considered the words.

"Who said that?" Susan asked.

"One of our own, or at least he used to be—a Niederbippian potter named Isaac Bingham. His current residence is in the cemetery adjacent to the church. He was a dear friend to both Pops and me. I don't know if I've ever known a soul who better spent his minutes and hours on the most important things," Ruby offered.

"Boy, that makes me think about how I've been spending my time," Josh responded. "It's feels like I never have enough time to fit in everything I want to do. Maybe I'm not focusing on the right things."

"I was just thinking the same thing," admitted Spencer. "I've always felt like there's never enough time to watch everything I want to watch—I mean, the way basketball season is now running into both golf and baseball. It makes me crazy to have to DVR so many games so I can watch them later. And then I have to avoid the news and hanging out with my buddies so they don't ruin it for me with their highlights." He looked around the room at the blank faces and realized his problems were far different from the others'.

"Not many things are equal across all humanity, but time—time is one of the rare exceptions. We are all given twenty-four hours a day to live and learn and dance and sing," Ruby replied. "What you do with your twenty-four hours determines so many things in life and in the eternities. You have already learned that there are many voices vying for a piece of your time. One of my favorite quotes comes from Charles W. Chesnutt—'There is time enough, but none to spare.' If you'll live each day with that in mind, you'll be able to make much more out of your life than you might if you believed you'd been endowed with all the time in the world. One of my mentors used to say, 'We're awake for at least sixteen hours each day. We ought to have something to show for it at the end of the day.'"

"Is that why you don't have a TV?" asked Holly.

"I don't know when we'd ever have time to use it," Lorenzo replied with a little laugh.

"Why be a boob in front of the tube when you can become a poet, a musician, an athlete, an artist, or a millionaire?" added Ruby. "To the chagrin of some of our campers, we've stocked the music room, library, and sports shed instead of paying a cable bill and buying a big screen. We recognize some entertainment habits are difficult to break, but we've never had even one camper say at the end of the summer that they can't wait to get back to their TV. At the same time, many have left the farm with new skills, talents, and appreciation for their twenty-four hours. More than one of our kids has left with the majority of a novel written. Many others have left with more friendships than they've ever had before, recognizing for the first time in their lives how their mistreatment of time has starved them of the opportunity to grow and expand their minds and talents and circles of friends. One young man admitted after learning to play the guitar one summer that if he'd spent half as much time learning to play an actual guitar as he'd spent playing Guitar Hero, he'd be a virtuoso."

"We were taught by the same mentor," Lorenzo said, nodding to Ruby, "that time would be our friend if we used it to enhance our lives and the lives of others but that it would evaporate and leave us empty if we chose to spend it doing things that brought no honor to it. She always encouraged us to make our lives rich by making every hour count as the bonus that it is. I don't think we understood it then—at least not the way we do now, when we look at each other and wonder how many more hours the good Lord will keep us around before He calls us home. Since we've come to understand the true value of time—that we're all stewards over our own twenty-four hours of each day—I think often how I will respond when I'm invited to stand and give an accounting of how I used those hours. You use them different when you recognize the scarcity of them. They become more valuable than gold. You become compelled to fill them with the things that matter most—love—service—relationships— making good memories to last through the rest of eternity."

"Oh right, so instead of watching TV, you spend your time milking cows?" Spencer challenged.

Lorenzo smiled, nodding slowly. "If I was only milking cows, I might worry that I was using my precious time unwisely."

"Huh?" Spencer asked, looking confused as all eyes turned back to Lorenzo.

"You now have each experienced the basics of milking a cow, right?" They all nodded.

"It takes a little practice to become proficient at any chore, and then, if you're lucky, you can put your brain on autopilot and use the rest of your faculties to solve challenges or contemplate the meaning of life. I can't tell you how many times inspiration has hit me as I've sat milking the cows with a thankful heart, considering the beauties and challenges of the farm."

"I've found the same is true of washing dishes or hanging laundry or feeding chickens or pulling weeds in the garden," Ruby added. "Inspiration is a bird who seeks a welcome nest. And if you're mindful of your time, your brain can become a tree whose limbs are teeming with the nests of inspiration, love, and gratitude. It takes practice, but as you seek to honor the gift of time, you'll find that that there truly are exactly enough minutes for the important things in life. We each have to answer for ourselves the questions about what's important. Entertainment can certainly be part of that, Spencer, but a life consumed by entertainment alone rarely, if ever, reaches the unique potential God plants in every human soul.

"Thomas Edison had it right," Ruby acknowledged, pointing to James. "Hard work, practice, getting your hands dirty, working up a sweat, and getting back up every time you fall—these are all conditions for enjoying the opportunities that await each of us. We have discovered over the past fifty-six years that those who are inclined to seek the easy way or the shortcut inevitably waste the valuable time they have here— and everywhere else, for that matter."

I've got another one along those same lines," said Rachael.

Dost thou love life? Then do no squander time, for that is the stuff life is made of.

"That's Benjamin Franklin again," Matt said softly.

Ruby nodded thoughtfully. "I heard once that time is a fourth dimension and that we cannot truly understand the value of life and its other dimensions until we learn to value time. There's obviously much more that can be said, but for now, I have an interview with Ephraim. Genevieve and Greg, I'm sure, would be appreciative of some help cleaning up the dishes; the cows need milking; and if we're going to enjoy porch time tonight, you might want to think about dessert."

CHAPTER 17

What's in Your Big Fat Bag?

Without love, what are we worth? Eighty-nine cents!
Eighty-nine cents worth of chemicals walking
around lonely.
— Benjamin Franklin Pierce —

It all went much faster than anyone had supposed. It was decided unanimously that since Greg and Genevieve had been sequestered in the kitchen all day without the same interaction as the rest of the family, everyone except Ephraim, who was being interviewed in the library, would go to the kitchen together and then to the berry patch to look for ripe strawberries. Within just a few minutes, the dishes were washed and dried, the counters and table were wiped clean, and the floor was swept.

This was first time in her life that Genevieve, an only child, had ever fully appreciated the power of teamwork. As she watched the others swarming about, doing the work she knew would normally have been hers and Greg's alone, she felt an appreciation for these strangers. Dressed in their humble farm duds and smelling like they'd put in an honest day's labor, they were still willing to help her with hers. Genevieve was surprised by the emotion this selflessness spawned in her. If given the chance to relax on the porch or help out in the kitchen after a long day of work, she wondered what she would do. She felt so ashamed of the honest answer—relax on the porch—that it felt like it thumped her on the back of the head.

As they wandered out into the evening in search of berries, Genevieve lagged behind, observing this odd collection of weirdos who had consciously committed to spend a summer on a godforsaken farm far beyond the edge of civilization. And what was even more strange was that they all seemed to be enjoying it. Even Spencer, the self-described sports nut, seemed to be finding his place in a location completely void of sports. She sat down on the ground, pretending to look for berries, but instead she quietly observed each of the members of this crazy, ragtag group of misfits. They were goofy and so…not New York, acting more like a bunch of kids than adults. Even Matt, the oldest in the group, appeared to have forgotten that he was in his forties; he joyfully bounced about the berry patch like a six-year-old at an Easter egg hunt.

The bowl was soon filled with fresh berries, and Genevieve quickly joined up with the group and added her three small berries to the collection as they walked back to the house. She had noticed earlier that these berries were far smaller than the berries she'd purchased at the markets at home, but never had she eaten any berries that tasted sweeter. Ephraim caught up with them before they made it back to the porch, and he sent Sonja in for the next interview with Ruby. As Genevieve watched her hurry up the front steps, she began to wonder about these interviews, curious about the insights she was missing out on for the story she would eventually write. And so while the others worked on preparing the berries and getting Bessie ready to churn her magic, Genevieve excused herself to use the restroom.

She noticed that the library door was ajar as she walked through the entry. She could hear the muffled voices but couldn't make out what was being said, so she sat down on the stairs, quickly untying both of her shoes and slowly tying them again, trying to eavesdrop on the conversation. But the voices coming from the porch drowned out the conversation she hoped to hear. She'd have to find another way. She'd have to use her skills of sleuthing and snooping to be able to find out what was going on.

"Are you all right?" Lorenzo asked from behind, startling her.

"Yes, uh, I was just tying my shoe," she said, turning to face him.

"Oh, for a minute there I thought you might be spying."

She felt her face flush and looked away.

"It'll be your turn soon enough," Lorenzo said with a smile, placing his hand on her elbow and leading her to the front porch. "Everybody needs their time and space with the matchmaker," he whispered. "You'll see."

Caught in the very act of espionage, Genevieve felt stupid. She tried to make herself useful and was grateful when she was sent into the kitchen to bring ice from the freezer.

Ruby and Sonja soon joined the rest of the family on the porch, and the churning of ol' Bessie began anew. After being asked for a game suggestion, Lorenzo named a few. It was decided they would play a game he called What's in Your Big Fat Bag? He explained that this game was often played sporadically over the course of most summers as each new family got to know each other better. The person on the bike would talk about the baggage they'd been carrying with them for years: the painful details of breakups, daddy issues, mommy issues, obsessive compulsions, addictions, or other challenges they wished to open up about in an effort to rid themselves of the burden of said baggage. "A burden shared is a burden lightened," he suggested. But he warned them that this game, more than any other, usually resulted in tears. But Lorenzo also promised that the sharing of personal vulnerabilities always produced trust, empathy, and encouragement among the family, making fast friends of near-strangers.

The game started slower than the others had. They looked around at each other, waiting for the first brave soul to begin. Rachael finally stood and walked to the bike. She pedaled for nearly a full quiet minute before she opened up about the baggage of depression that had plagued her for all of her high school years and well into college. She admitted that she still struggled with feelings of self-worth. She hated shopping for clothes, because her mother had constantly placed great value on body shape and size. When Rachael was a young teen, her mother was always buying her clothes that she never could have fit into and then guilting her for not dieting, calling her dozens of unkind names that Rachael chose not to share. She also admitted that for the first time in several years, she was happy to not feel like she was squeezing into clothes that made her uncomfortable, and she got the whole family laughing when she asked if anyone wanted to help her start a new line of farm duds branded and manufactured for the general public.

Rachael called on James to take the saddle next. His baggage came in the shape of his parents' messy divorce, which left him and his two siblings being tossed back and forth for most of their formative years, giving him an inability to trust and therefore a nature that was slow to make friends.

Greg talked about becoming addicted to alcohol at fourteen and struggling with it for the next ten years, when he'd finally admitted he had a problem and spent some time in rehab. He was proud to add that he'd been sober for 843 days, but he said his addiction had ruined his self-esteem and made him constantly second-guess himself.

Susan began tearing up before she even sat down on Bessie, and, judging the crowd to be safe, she opened up a piece of her baggage that she said she'd shared with only a very small handful of friends. Her confession brought many others to tears as well; she spoke about her uncle going to jail for sexually abusing her when she was a child. She admitted that it had taken more than a decade of intense therapy but that she had found a way to forgive and move on the best she could, though she still struggled with trust issues and remained uncomfortable even being platonically touched by men.

To Genevieve's surprise, as each family member shared, each of them expressed gratitude for being able to give air and voice to the baggage they'd carried with them. But she was grateful when the ice cream was ready before all of them had had a chance to share, not having any desire to share her own baggage with these weirdos—or anyone else, for that matter.

As they ate their ice cream on the porch that night, a different feeling encompassed the family. Matt explained what he was feeling by comparing it to a PTSD group meeting he had once attended to support a veteran friend who had been struggling with his own baggage. Ruby explained that every kid who had come to the farm over the past three hundred years had carried some form of baggage with them whether they admitted it or not. Even those kids who had grown up in what many might consider ideal circumstances always opened up with deeply sorrowful struggles of their own when given the chance. Ruby admitted she had even considered changing the name of the game to We're All Human, Therefore We Hurt, but the other name rolled off the tongue much easier and therefore stuck.

Walking back to their bunkhouses after evening prayers, Genevieve was surprised when all the women linked arms as they walked across the lawn. And for the first time since their arrival, the talk continued as they showered and got ready for bed, each of them sharing about both the familiar and unique challenges of life—and comforting each other. If there had been any walls between the women before, most if not all of them had been broken down through tears and laughter and through the compassion they extended to each other. And as Genevieve drifted off to sleep, she knew this story was going be different from any story she had ever written before.

CHAPTER 18

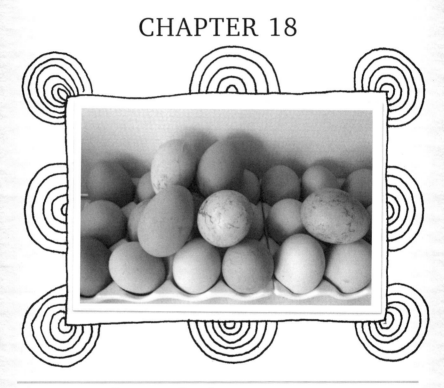

The Truth about Potatoes

To get the full value of joy you must have
someone to divide it with.
- Mark Twain -

The screech of the pterodactyl came early the next morning, and this time it brought friends. The whole fiery sky from horizon to horizon was filled with the dark silhouettes of the squadron, menacing reptiles screeching out their bloodcurdling cries, announcing to the world that it was time for breakfast.

Genevieve sat up, her long hair matted and still damp from last night's shower. She looked around the dimly lit room, consoling herself that the other women looked at least as disheveled as she knew she did. As she dressed, she listened to the women talking about morning chores. She couldn't remember her assignment or her partner for the day. Had she even been given an assignment? Despite the strong resentment she still felt toward this place and the circumstances that forced her to be here, she was surprised by the feeling of suspense and anticipation for what the day might hold.

Josh was waiting for her as the women filed out of the bunkhouse to begin the morning chores. "I guess we're supposed to be partners today," he said with a crooked smile, his face still lined with pillow impressions. "We're on chicken duty, and Ruby says they could use some eggs in the kitchen right away." He handed her one of the baskets and led off toward the henhouse. The chicken yard was already busy with a variety of multicolored hens strutting and pecking at the dirt. Josh held the gate open, allowing Genevieve to pass through, then followed her into the yard. There were still several chickens roosting on the perches and several more hanging out in the nesting boxes when they entered the henhouse. The floor was strewn with straw and feathers, and the aroma of birds was strong. Josh softly pushed aside a bird with his foot, and the remaining birds clucked happily, most of them strutting out the miniature door and down the ramp to the yard.

"Have you ever done this before?" he asked.

She laughed. "No, have you?"

"A couple of times. My grandparents had chickens when I was a kid, and Grandma used to send me out to collect eggs whenever I stayed over." He laughed as he picked up a light green egg, placing it in his basket. "I remember asking her how long she had to scrub the eggs before they became white."

"What did she say? This one looks like looks like it would take a lot of scrubbing," she said, holding up a chocolate-colored egg.

Josh laughed again. "We're such city kids, right?"

"What do you mean?"

"Oh, you don't know?" he said when he realized she wasn't joking.

"What?"

"Most chickens don't lay white eggs."

"Really?"

"Yeah, I mean, I guess people who don't grow up on farms think eggs are supposed to be white, but look at the variety," he said, pointing to a cluster of eggs that had been left in a nesting box.

"I thought they looked strange when I saw them yesterday in the kitchen," she said, "but these are really beautiful." She picked one up and taking a closer look. It was pale pink and still warm. She reached for another; this one was a pastel green with brown specks. After riffling through the straw in each of the twenty nesting boxes, they had collected two basketfuls—nearly sixty eggs, each one different in size and color.

Remembering that the kitchen crew was in need of the eggs, they hurried to the big house, kicking off their boots at the door and hurrying across the floor in their mismatched socks. Ruby met them at the kitchen door and exchanged their baskets for two silver pails of scraps.

"That seems like a bad trade to me," Genevieve said, looking confused as they walked back to their boots. "What are we supposed to do with this crap?"

Josh laughed. "This is food for the chickens."

"What?"

"Sure. What do you expect them to eat?"

"I don't know, but they'll actually eat eggshells and old salad?"

"Yeah, Grandma used to send me out to feed the chickens with all sorts of stuff—old bread, apple cores, potato peels. We humans waste a lot of food, you know."

They weren't even within twenty feet of the chicken yard when all of the chickens raced to the edge of the fence in anticipation of what was to come. Josh dumped his pail over the fence, and a wild frenzy broke out as chickens swarmed the morning's offerings. Josh and Genevieve watched the melee for a moment before Genevieve dumped her pail too, and the whole yard again erupted with enthusiastically clucking chickens diving in for their share of the scraps. Within minutes, there was nothing left.

"Ephraim said they also get a couple of scoops of feed," Josh said, pointing to a barrel on the outside of the fence near the gate. Again, the chickens went crazy as the pair scattered the food on the ground. It was hard not to be amused by the feeding frenzy.

"What else do we have to do?" Genevieve asked when the commotion had settled and the chickens returned to their business of strutting around the yard.

"I'm not sure." His attention was drawn to movement closer to the house. James and Rachael, standing next to baskets overflowing with wet laundry, were just beginning to hang the laundry on the lines that were stretched between two enormous cottonwood trees.

"Can we give you a hand?" Josh asked.

"Uh, sure," Rachael responded, looking winded.

Genevieve followed Josh, and they jumped in to help. Minutes later, Susan and Spencer joined them, having finished the milking. As the lines filled up with wet farm duds and personal items, Genevieve looked around at each of the campers. They seemed to be more than just half-heartedly willing to help each other; they somehow silently recognized that each of them benefited from the others' individual labor. They were just hanging the last of the socks when the breakfast bell rang at the big house. Ephraim and Rachael gathered up the empty baskets and quickly carried them back to the laundry house before joining the others in the breakfast procession.

The dining hall was filled with the aroma of bacon and hash browns, and bowls of scrambled eggs were set on the ends of the table. Ruby said grace, and the campers helped themselves to healthy portions of each dish. The bacon, Ruby explained, had been smoked in the smokehouse the previous January and had been in the deep freeze since then. Because most of the animals on the farm would eventually be used as food or would die of natural causes, she warned about becoming too attached to any of them.

As Genevieve was wondering to herself how vegetarians spending the summer on the farm managed this news, Holly asked that very question. Ruby responded that she'd never turned a vegetarian away but had never had one make it through the first month without relaxing their ideals to conform to the meals on the farm. On the other hand, she said that not one true-blue carnivore had ever made it through the summer without changing their habits and opinions after being involved in the care of the animals. Moderation, Ruby said, was one of the secrets to a happy, balanced life, while extremes of any kind were often directly responsible for most of the world's unhappiness and contention.

To illustrate the need for moderation, Ruby told a story one camper had shared about her mother, who had emphatically determined one day that salt was evil. She not only decided from that day forward to stop cooking with salt, but she also purged her home of every food that listed salt as an ingredient. The food in their home immediately became bland and tasteless, leading to discontent among all the members of the family. When the mother expanded her personal opinions to include a campaign against the use of salt in the schools and the church community, she alienated herself from everyone she loved and everyone who cared about her. The daughter, Ruby reported, traced the destruction of her family to her mother's espousing of extreme ideas.

"Coming to a place of moderation," Ruby said, lifting her fork above her head, "is the only hope we have for finding balance, and in a time when the world is full of extremes and extremist philosophies, there never has been a more important need for people to hold on to the common-sense principle of embracing moderation in all things."

After carrying their dishes to the sink for Holly and Matt to clean, the rest of the crew poured out the front door and headed for the garden. It looked much different now than it had the last time Genevieve had really noticed it. The weeds had been pulled from most of the ground, and dark, rich soil had been turned over and worked until it was free of stones. Pops worked beside the group as they attacked the last of the weeds, throwing them over the garden fence, which had been built to keep the deer and the rabbits from making a quick meal of the gardeners' hard work.

When the weeds had been expelled, Pops instructed four of the men to make a trip to the compost pile to load four wheelbarrows with compost. When Crystal protested that she could do the work as well as any of the men, Spencer volunteered to step down, turning his wheelbarrow over to her. The rest of the crew used pitchforks to gather up the withering weeds around the perimeter of the fence and stack them in piles. The wheelbarrows returned, and under Pops's direction, the men dumped the compost in four spots throughout the garden. As several of the campers worked to mix the compost in with the soil, others filled the wheelbarrows with the weeds and took them to the pigpen and the chicken yard for the animals to enjoy. Genevieve noticed that Crystal didn't protest; she stayed in the garden this time and seemed quite content to allow the men, with their broader shoulders and taller statures, to handle the wheelbarrows.

They laughed at Pops's response when he saw Sonja kneeling in the dirt, working the compost in with her hands. "You're welcome to do that if you want," he said, cracking a smile, "but compost—at least our compost—is rather high in manure." Sonja blushed and quickly stood, making a comical face as she ran to the hose to wash off.

By ten o'clock, the garden was ready to receive the seeds and seedlings. While the men began planting rows of sweet corn against the east fence, the ladies and Pops pushed the wheelbarrows to the small greenhouse. They returned quickly with loads of small plastic pots filled with tomato, squash, melon, and pepper plants. These, he explained, had been started several weeks before, as soon as the daytime temperatures stayed above freezing.

He invited them all to council together about the layout of the garden, noting that it had never, in his fifty-seven years of planting a garden, been done exactly the same way twice. There were many opinions, and Genevieve was beginning to wonder if they'd ever get the plants in the ground when Rachael quietly walked away. Picking up a stick, she began dragging it behind her as she walked over the soil, drawing lines as if she were creating the page of giant coloring book. In the center, she carved a large heart into the soil and deep rays extending out from the heart to the outer fence, taking into account the herb corner and the area where last year's lettuces and carrots were still growing well. They all stopped and watched what she was doing, her feet and the stick marking partitions for the different vegetables.

Genevieve noticed that Pops was smiling as he watched. "I said that it's different every year, but it's always truly unique when an artist steps up with a totally new idea."

The others quickly rallied behind the design, and they began carrying the pots of young plants to the different partitions, spacing them out to see how it might look.

"What did you envision for the center heart?" Ephraim asked, standing next to Rachael as they looked at their work.

"How about potatoes?" she responded.

Spencer quickly looked through the box of seeds. "Sorry," he said, looking up. "It doesn't look like we have any potato seeds."

Pops giggled, placing his hand on Spencer's shoulder. "I take it this is your first time planting a garden."

"How did you know?"

Pops nodded. "Does anyone know the answer to that question?"

"Umm, is it because potatoes come from eggs?" Crystal asked innocently.

Pops nodded slowly, pursing his lips. "Yes, because potatoes come from eggs." But he couldn't keep a straight face, and before he could say anything else, he burst out laughing. The others joined in, though none of them were completely certain why they were laughing; they just had a foggy notion that potatoes and eggs having anything to do with each other besides breakfast was rather silly.

"Let's set the record straight," he said, trying to compose himself. "Potatoes do not come from eggs. They come from other potatoes."

"*So, they like…have babies?*" Spencer asked, looking very confused.

Pops laughed again. "No, not like babies." In between fits of laughter, he managed to send Spencer running to the big house, where he told him he would find a gunnysack on the front porch. Spencer returned a minute later, out of breath, with the sack over his shoulder.

Pops put his hand into the sack and pulled out a big potato with a dozen small white growths poking out from its skin. "What's this?" he asked, holding it up for them all to see.

"A pregnant potato?" Genevieve asked, looking completely uncertain.

Pops smiled and shook his head. "Close enough. Potatoes are the root of the plant, and each of these eyes," he said, pointing to the growths, "has the potential of becoming a potato plant that will produce potentially dozens of new potatoes."

"So you just plant the momma potato, and…" Josh asked, looking bewildered.

Pops smiled and shook his head. He pulled a pocketknife from his back pocket and began carefully cutting the potato into pieces so that each piece had at least one eye. He handed each of the campers a piece.

"So we just plant these, and they become new potatoes?" Sonja asked.

"Yes, but you can't plant these right away. I got some started last week," he said, reaching into the sack and pulling out a handful of squared-off chunks that looked a little brown and withered. "These guys have developed a bit of a skin and are ready to go into the ground. These should be planted no closer than twelve inches from each other and about four inches deep."

After resolving the confusion of where potatoes come from, Pops had a chance to realize who he was dealing with, and things went better. But still there were challenges. Genevieve was a little aggressive with the first tomato plant, ripping the tender plant from the plastic pot like it was a weed, breaking the stem. It became a learning lesson for all of them, and they treated the rest of the plants much more delicately. By the time the lunch bell rang, the garden was nearly half planted.

Matt and Holly were proud to present their fresh bread to the group, though it came with a caveat that they had somehow shorted the recipe by at least half the salt that it needed. A rookie mistake that was made at least once every summer, Ruby explained as she passed the salt shaker down the table. But despite its more bland taste, the bread was still quickly consumed with the pear butter and applesauce that the kitchen team had brought up from the cellar.

After a short nap on the lawn and porch, they all got back to work, finishing up the planting in the garden while Matt and Holly went back to the kitchen to plan dinner with Ruby.

Instead of ringing the dinner bell, Matt and Holly came out to meet the rest of the family and check on the progress they'd made. They were thrilled to find that the garden had been planted and watered in; plants and beds had been labeled with creative stakes; and paths had been trodden down, outlining Rachael's artistic inspiration while also providing access to all the disparate sections and corners of the garden. Though the plants were still small and thousands of seeds had yet to sprout, they each left the garden that evening feeling a sense of collective accomplishment.

Dinner was served in the dining hall, and Matt and Holly did a great job presenting the fruits of their labor: breaded trout, which Lorenzo had caught earlier in the spring and which they had found in the freezer; rice pilaf; wild-green salad, including dandelion, wild-garlic leaves, and edible flowers; and sautéed wild steinpilz mushrooms that Matt had discovered on the edge of the forest. It was much more gourmet than most of them were used to. Spencer admitted that the only time he ate fish was an occasional fish stick, but even he admitted it was way better than he'd expected. Holly, who had made the salad based on the edible plants her mother had taught her, was pleased when several people asked if she could make it again the next time she cooked. But the mushrooms were probably the biggest hit. Even Susan, who confessed she'd never met a mushroom she liked, asked for seconds.

The men seemed to be equal parts impressed and intimidated when Holly told the group that she was just following Matt's lead. He explained that he had learned to love cooking on his many and varied jaunts doing humanitarian dental work around the world. Wild mushrooms had become one of his passions, and he magnanimously voiced his gratitude for being teamed up with Holly for this meal because she shared an appreciation for wild plants and herbs.

They were just finishing up the final remnants of the meal when the timer in the kitchen went off and Matt and Holly excused themselves. When they returned, they asked to be forgiven for making dessert plans without the input of the rest of the family, but they announced that a surprise dessert would be served on the porch after the dishes were cleaned up and evening milking was done.

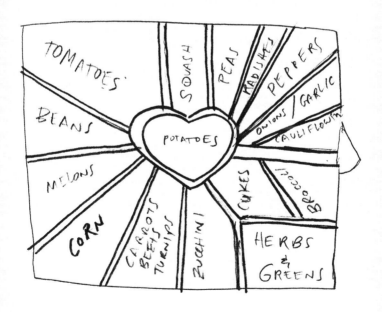

CHAPTER 19

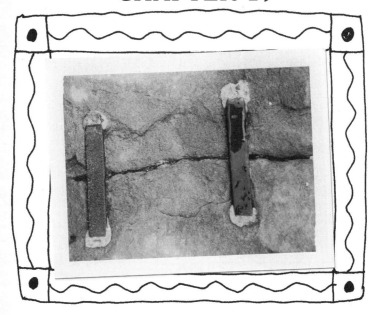

Love and Homicide

*Sexiness wears thin after a while and beauty fades,
but to be married to a man who makes you laugh every day,
ah, now that's a real treat.*
-Joanne Woodward -

With surprise dessert in mind, Pops, along with Crystal and Spencer, wasted no time with the evening milking, returning to the big house just as the rest of the family were finishing the cleanup in the kitchen. To the delight of everyone, the surprise apple crisp, made from the last of the autumn apples, was still warm by the time it was served under generous portions of whipped cream.

Without Bessie to offer a segue into a story or conversation, there was an unspoken restlessness for a moment, when Susan spoke up.

"Do you mind if I ask you a personal question, Ruby?"

"Not at all. Pops and I have a policy that no questions are ever too personal if they are asked with a sincere heart."

Susan nodded. "So…I've been watching you and Pops over the last few days, holding hands, talking together, sharing in the work and duties of the farm without appearing to get upset or push back against the things you don't want to do. Coming from a very dysfunctional home, I guess I've got a lot of questions about all of that, but maybe my first question would be…how did you know you could make it work without wanting to kill each other."

Ruby laughed. "Sometimes in marriage you walk a fine line between love and homicide."

Everyone laughed.

"But in all seriousness," she continued, "I can honestly say I haven't wanted to kill Pops for a least a decade." She looked into the faces of each of the campers, who were looking back at her expectantly. Her head bobbed, looking thoughtful before she spoke again. "Every year this question comes up in one form or another. It's a good question and one you'll each have to figure out for yourselves. Most kids come to the farm with two distinctly different ideas. One of those ideas is what marriage is all about, usually based on their perceptions of their parents' marriage and the family they grew up in. We've watched this change a whole heck of a lot over the last fifty-six years. In the beginning, it used to be rare to have more than two kids out of twelve who came from a broken home. Anymore, it's usually at least seven."

Genevieve watched as many of the others nodded their heads.

"But kids also come to the farm with a whole lot of ideals—some are practical, others are totally not. The trick for everyone becomes sorting out what is real and attainable and what is make-believe and fiction."

"So how do you decide which is which?" Holly asked.

"Let me ask you first what your idea of a good marriage is."

Holly blushed. "I'm a little embarrassed to say. I didn't grow up with a father—my mom adopted me and was always single, so I guess my idea of falling in love and getting married was probably shaped by the media I watched and the books I read. I've always fantasized about finding a Mr. Darcy, but I've never met one yet."

"Yeah, me neither," Rachael muttered.

Ruby smiled and nodded. "The first step to finding happiness in courtship and eventually marriage is to recognize that not one of you will ever marry Mr. Darcy, Prince Charming, or George Clooney. Like I said the other day, boys like that don't really exist, and neither do their female counterparts," she said glancing at a few of the men. "And no amount of wishing or dreaming is going to change that. On top of that," she said, turning back to the women, "the idea that you're a princess and that you're going to set up your home in a castle and live happily ever after without any effort on your part is not only unrealistic and impractical, it is also completely absurd and contrary to at least seven laws of nature. Some of you have already discovered that. Some of you have yet to let that sink in. But I promise that none of you will find peace and joy in any relationship until you know that the person you marry will be a human being and therefore prone to be at least occasionally selfish, stinky, cantankerous, insensitive, lazy, and infuriating. And if you're honest with yourself, you are much the same way.

"The trick is to find ways to love your partner in spite of their weaknesses, hoping and praying that they'll do the same with you. There will be little you will ever be able to do to change the person you marry, but love goes a long way to encourage and inspire small and sometimes great changes and to soften your own heart with patience and endurance. And if the vision you have for them never pans out, you can choose to either wallow in disappointment—which certainly brings no joy—or you can reconcile with the truth that you too are a work in progress and should focus your efforts instead on the things you can change.

"It's been my observation that good marriages—the ones that last and inspire others—there's something consistent with all of them: they encourage each other with love, patience, and kindness. We've observed that the marriages that fail also have at least one thing in common: selfishness—where one or both partners are only looking out for themselves, keeping score, believing they're owed something. The sooner we find out that life is not all about us, the longer we have to be happy. Some people discover this at twenty and enjoy many good decades of happiness. Some people don't figure it out until years later when they finally look around and realize that every interpersonal relationship they have has suffered due to their own selfishness and unrealistic expectations. And then there are some who never discover this truth and die lonely and miserable, believing that they've somehow been dealt an unfair hand and that the world still owes them something."

Ruby reached for Lorenzo's solid, farm-worn hand and gave it a squeeze. "One of the most important secrets I've learned about life is that no matter who you are or how privileged or unprivileged your birth, the world owes you absolutely nothing. You each have been given the gift of life. It's up to you to unwrap that gift and do something extraordinary with it. If that's the only truth you leave with at the end of the summer, then I will be satisfied."

Susan nodded, but Ruby realized she hadn't fully answered her question.

"The truth is that there have been plenty of times over the course of our marriage that we've been angry with each other. But fortunately for us, our love has always endured the moments of frustration long enough for us to remember that love is far more fun than the black holes of selfish and negative emotions. We've known each other long enough for me to know that Pops would never try to hurt me or disappoint me on purpose, but it still happens. My mentor used to tell me that love inside of marriage is a little bit like a bank account. If you each make love deposits every day, there will be plenty of love to go around when you fall on hard times, when the roof springs a leak, or when the wagon breaks down and you need to make a withdrawal. But if either of you holds back and skips making a daily deposit, you shouldn't be surprised if the love is not there when you need it. Love has to be a decision you make every day. You have to decide if you'll let your pride get in the way of letting your love flow freely. You have to decide if you'll build a wall with the rocks life hands you or use them to pave a walkway or build a bridge instead. And I've noticed that even the hardest of hearts can't continue to build walls around themselves forever when those they love continue doing their part to pave walkways and build bridges."

"I like that. I think my parents' marriage would have lasted if they'd each tried to build bridges instead of walls," Crystal said.

"Mine too," added Josh. "But how do you keep doing that forever if the other person doesn't reciprocate?"

Ruby nodded thoughtfully. "It's a sad truth that not all marriages will last, and like I suggested, at the core of those that don't last will always be found a seed of selfishness that was nourished instead of plucked out like the parasitic weed it is."

"There's a reason we wait for all of you to arrive before we begin the work in the garden," Pops added. "Like in many of the chores you'll participate in over the course of the summer, there are plenty of parables in gardening that apply directly to life and marriage, if you'll look for them. When you arrived on Saturday, you walked past an overgrown garden. You spent the last two days pulling out the weeds and cleaning and preparing the soil before you designed your garden and planted seeds. It wouldn't have made much sense to skip pulling the weeds, right? And if we hadn't boosted the nutrients in the soil with compost, the bounty our garden could yield would be greatly diminished. You've done a good job. The garden is attractive, and I know you all have high hopes for what will come from it. But if you neglect your garden, if you don't water and weed it every day, these past two days of hard work will never yield the same quality, variety, and quantity as a well-tended garden could provide."

Pops pointed to the garden as he continued. "Within that fence lies the potential to not only feed this family this summer but also to yield ample fruits to put away enough for the winter, enough for the kids who'll come to the farm next spring, and enough to sell at the farm stand to help pay the taxes to keep the farm going another year.

"There are many lessons you can learn this summer in the garden, but the best ones are the ones you'll take with you as you learn more about who you are and what you want out of life. You may discover some overlooked weeds or that you've neglected to water a certain area. You'll discover that you can get better and bigger fruits if you'll limit the length of the vine. And you'll also face the disappointment when, despite your best efforts to keep them out, the rabbits and raccoons still find a way to get into your garden and make lunch out of your hopes and dreams. If you keep your eyes and heart open, the farm and the experiences you share here with each other will provide you with a firm foundation on which you can build a solid life and marriage."

"If all you see is the work in the garden, the cows that need milking, or the chickens that need feeding, you'll miss out on the big picture," Ruby added.

Matt nodded. "Ask and you will receive, seek and you will find, knock and the door will be opened," he spoke softly.

"Who said that?" Spencer asked.

"Umm…Jesus," Matt replied with a warm smile.

"Oh, right," Spencer responded sheepishly, looking a little embarrassed.

Pops nodded, smiling at the quick interaction between the younger men. "There's something to be said for what Matt just shared."

"I think I missed it," Josh admitted.

"Do you mind sharing it again?" Pops asked.

Matt looked embarrassed. "I…sorry, I didn't mean to sound like I know what I'm talking about."

Pops nodded, encouraging him.

"It's just something that came to mind when Pops was talking about finding meaning in what we're doing here. It is from Jesus, right?" Matt asked, suddenly unsure of himself.

"Yes. And great advice it is," Pops replied.

"I think it goes something like, ask and you will receive, seek and you will find, knock…and the door will be opened."

Pops nodded again, smiling at Matt.

"Yeah, well, it's never been that easy for me," James admitted.

"Me either," Susan added.

Several others nodded in agreement.

"I've often wondered if something might have been lost in that translation of the Sermon on the Mount," Ruby confessed.

"What do you mean?" asked Crystal.

"It's terribly presumptuous to try and put words into the mouth of the Lord, but in my own Bible I've written the word R-E-P-E-A-T at the end of that verse. Most of us don't usually find what we're looking for in the first place we look. And sometimes you gotta knock twice or more before the door opens." She smiled, looking around at all of them. "Look, I believe in a God who hears and answers prayers, but I believe He's also patient with us and never annoyed if we keep asking until we understand. And sometimes the answer is no, and sometimes it's 'not now.' And sometimes God waits patiently for us to do something more than just ask—to throw some passion and action behind our desires. I feel like He's always ready to send the rain along with the sunshine. But I think he sometimes waits to show us the miracle until we've taken the time and made the effort to weed the garden."

"I like that," Holly said. "Repeat. I guess we have to do that with anything to get any good at it, right?"

Many of them nodded.

"Maybe that's been part of my problem," Susan confided. "After the trauma I went through as a child with my uncle and everything…I guess I've been reluctant to ask for help from a god I really don't know."

Ruby patted Susan on the arm comfortingly. "You're certainly not the first to struggle to define your relationship with God, and you won't be the last. Regardless of our experience and the baggage we carry with us, in order to come to a place of spiritual learning, we each must be humble enough to ask and curious enough to seek and diligent enough to knock—and to keep at it until we're ready and can find a place to be still enough to hear the answers He's anxious to give us."

Genevieve shook her head and looked away.

"You disagree, dear?" Ruby asked.

She looked back, surprised to have been noticed. "I don't know if I do or not. I guess I just don't know how, why, and if He—or She—why *They* would even care."

Ruby looked at Pops before turning back to Genevieve. "I think I know how you feel."

Genevieve smiled and shook her head. "I doubt that."

"Why? Because I'm an old woman who's found my faith?"

Genevieve shrugged.

"When you've lived as long as we have, the list of things we haven't experienced is much, much shorter than the things we have."

"And struggles with faith have been part of that, too?" Susan asked.

"Oh heavens, yes. *Crises* would be a better term for the depths of them. *Struggles*—those are part of my everyday life."

"Really?" Matt asked, looking surprised.

"Sure. And the older we get and the closer we get to the grave, to witnessing for ourselves what's on the other side...I don't know if the struggles ever get any easier."

"So why worry about it at all?" Genevieve asked. "What's the point? I mean, we're all somewhere along our path to the grave, right? It seems to me that we'll figure out what's there—or not—soon enough."

"Oh, believe me, I've considered all of that," Ruby replied.

"But?"

"But my heart—when I choose to listen—reminds me there's more to life than just grinding our way through it."

"Huh. Like what?" Genevieve challenged.

"Like joy."

"You don't think joy's just an illusion?"

Ruby shook her head. "No, I don't. I'll concede that happiness can be an illusion—that it can appear quickly and evaporate in a fleeting moment. But joy, I've learned, is something very different."

"I don't understand," said Genevieve.

"What's the difference?" James asked. "Aren't they the same?"

"That's a common misconception, but no—no, not at all. Happiness is nearly as common as the air we breathe, and it's good that it is because life is so much better when there's happiness to share. But joy is something uniquely different. Unlike happiness, joy can't be bought and sold or passed around at a party like a jug of punch. Genuine joy comes as a reward for good living. It takes time to cultivate and grows slowly over the course of many years, being fed by thousands of good choices and sincere acts of kindness. It demands a clear conscience and an open heart and mind. Joy requires us to put away our natural leanings toward selfishness and causes us instead to look outward—to love, to encourage, and to nurture the goodness we find in others. Joy comes from developing kindness and patience for yourself and everyone around you. It calls on us to forgive ourselves and those who've done us wrong, and it pushes us to seek the forgiveness of those we've hurt."

"That's beautiful," Matt responded. "Do you have that written down anywhere?"

Ruby smiled. "Yes," she said, patting her chest, "right here on my heart. You know," she said, turning to look into each of their faces, "knowing the difference between happiness and joy could have saved me a lot of pain and heartache in the years before I came here. I think that's one of the reasons I felt obligated to stay—to help other people learn the truth so they could avoid so much of the sadness I experienced. I spent most of my twenties and all of my thirties wrestling with reason and science on one side and these deep-seated questions about happiness and the meaning and purpose of my existence on the other."

"So what changed?" Spencer asked. "How did you find your answers?"

"Well, I came to the farm."

"Wait, hold on! When did you come to the farm?" Rachael asked.

"When I was thirty-nine years old—May of 1964."

"Wait, I thought this was your family farm," Rachael replied.

"It is. My fifth great-grandmother was the first matchmaker of Niederbipp. The farm's been in my family ever since she and her family homesteaded here in the early seventeen hundreds. I visited the farm once for a family reunion when I was a child, but it wasn't until my great-aunt Millie Smurthwaite invited me to spend the summer with her that I had a chance to live here."

"So you spent a whole summer working here like we are?" Sonja asked.

"That's right. I never imagined taking over, but Millie and her husband George were interested in retiring to Florida, and the summer I spent here convinced me of the vision of what this farm is all about. I'd seen what felt like more than my share of struggles before I got here— struggles that had both driven me to my knees and made me doubt if life even had any meaning at all. I was pretty angry and bitter back then."

"How'd that change?" Holly wondered out loud.

Ruby smiled, looking thoughtful again. "Being able to change and evolve is a critical indication that you're alive. Sometimes all we need is a change of scenery to bring about a change of heart. I couldn't see it where I was—I was too close to really be able to focus on what was making me angry. Looking back, I realize that every day when I went to work teaching other people's kids, I was reminded of all the things I didn't have—all the dreams that were aging out as each year passed without my being married, without having children of my own. My sadness slowly turned to bitterness, and I felt like the God I had prayed to since I was a child had abandoned me. Those were some of the darkest years of my life, feeling completely forgotten.

"And then, late in the winter of '62, I got a letter from Aunt Millie inviting me to spend the summer on the farm. At first I thought she was crazy. As a schoolteacher, I would have the summer off, but leaving before school got out and not being back until a month after school had started—it felt impossible, not to mention irresponsible."

"So, what did you do?" Holly asked.

"The same thing each of you has done—the same thing everybody does who has ever committed to spend the summer on the farm. I made the decision to sacrifice what I *was* for an old dream of what *could be*."

She looked into the young faces of each of the campers as they stared back into her gray eyes. "There are many who give up on the dreams you still hold in your hearts. And there are many others who settle for something easier than their full potential. You will learn, if you haven't already, that putting your faith in the only being in the universe who truly knows your full potential can be frightening. It's a little bit like giving up the steering wheel on a winding road and trusting that somehow you'll get to the destination that's best for you even when that destination may look very different than the place you had in mind. But I promise you that by placing your sincere trust in God's care and following the gentle nudges He gives you along the way, you'll eventually come to a place of happiness that you never could have imagined. The timing will likely not be your timing, but then true faith has never been limited by our plans or conditions. Putting our faith in God, after all, must include faith in the tempo and meter of the one who knows the end of the symphony from the very first note. After fifty-six years of doing this work, I cannot deny one truth—if we can patiently trust in Him and His timing, all true and good things will conspire to bring us greater happiness than we could know in any other way."

Genevieve shook her head.

"You disagree?" Ruby asked patiently.

"It just sounds like a cop-out."

"A cop-out?"

"Yeah. What about grabbing the bull by the balls and making it bow to your desires?"

Ruby laughed out loud.

"What's so funny?"

"It's an interesting—if crude—philosophy, but it seems rather foolish to believe your knowledge and understanding can compare to that of the Creator of the universe."

Pops giggled. "But if you'd like to try your philosophy on for size, ol' Brutus is out in the pasture, and I'd love to place a wager on how he'd respond to you getting fresh with him."

Genevieve shook her head but couldn't keep from smiling as the rest of the campers snickered. "But you know what I mean, theoretically speaking, right?"

"Of course," Ruby responded. "It may be hard for you to imagine, but I was once thirty years old too." She shook her head, turning to her husband. "Boy, it seems like that was only a few years ago."

Pops nodded. "It was."

"Genevieve, you may think your world in the big city revolves around a different star than ours does here, but the longer you live and the more you see, I promise you'll begin to recognize that we're more the same than we are different—that each of us is a spiritual being trying to make sense of the challenges of mortality. If we'll embrace the spiritual within us and align it with all the spiritual light and truth the universe has to offer us, we'll be able to discern between the real and the counterfeit."

Ruby looked into each of their faces before she spoke again. "You each are here because you have a desire to prepare yourselves for what we believe is the most important decision you will make in life. Who you marry, along with the details of where, when, and how, will determine not only your short-term happiness but also your long-term joys. It's a decision that will intimately affect nearly every aspect of every day for the rest of your life. And though there will always be surprises that will pop up along the way, our job is to help you avoid as many of the potential pitfalls as we can. There is never a guarantee that any of this will be foolproof—heaven knows all marriages have their challenges. But in our study of happy, successful marriages, we've found there are commonalities that wind their way through every one."

"And more often than not," Pops interjected, his finger raised, "those are the marriages that are built and continually strengthened on universal principles like compassion, loyalty, faith, mutual respect, prayer, and forgiveness. There will always be those who'll do their best to challenge these ancient principles of matrimonial joy, but most of those folks get burned in the process and usually end up in dark and dreary places. Each of you is free to choose which path you'll take and ultimately what you'll do with the principles we try to teach you here on the farm. But beware that the universal laws of justice rarely allow you to choose the consequences of the choices you make."

"We recognize that this is something we can't convince any one of you to follow, and the truth is we wouldn't want to," Ruby admitted. "But for those of you who care to find it, you will discover, as you sit in quiet places, that in your heart is a seed that was planted long before your birth. And if that seed is given light and truth, it will grow to become a mighty tree that will produce fruits that can bless all your posterity and even the entire world."

Pops nodded thoughtfully. "We've seen a lot of kids come and go over the years, but not one of them has ever left this farm at the end of the summer without discovering that seed of promise within their heart."

"That's what convinced me that I needed to stay," Ruby added. "Discovering that neglected seed for the first time—it was like a light turned on that illuminated everything."

"So, is that what the bench is all about? The one by the pond under the willow? The one with the tile embedded in it?" Matt asked.

Pops smiled. "It sounds like you've been making good use of your free time already."

"Are you talking about the tile that says 'Be still and know that I am God?'" James asked.

Matt nodded.

"There's another one of those benches on the edge of the forest," James reported.

"And another one that overlooks Brutus's pasture." Susan added.

"Yes, and there are nine more of them scattered across the farm," Pops replied. "You each have the better part of five months to discover them. Of course, it's up to you to decide how to use your free time. But I'd like to recommend, if you're interested in discovering the secrets of your heart, that you give yourself the gift of some quality time to consider your place in the universe."

"In each of your applications, you expressed a desire to find a marriage partner," Ruby interjected. "I promise to do my best to help you, but I don't usually let more than the first few days of the summer pass before I try to impress upon the minds of each camper the magnitude of this decision you'll ultimately make. My observations have certainly given me a bias, but I believe that if you'll invite God into your life and include Him in helping you make your decisions, your marriages will be much more likely to succeed. By saying this, I don't mean to suggest that making this important decision with God's help will inoculate you from the sorrows and trials of life. Your spouse, your children, and your grandchildren will each influence your happiness by the decisions they choose to make as well. But by tuning your heartstrings to resonate with the whispers of angels, you'll avoid many of the perils that tear families apart and leave heartache and misery in their wake.

"There's nothing Pops or I can do to ensure you a happy marriage, but we hope to give each of you a bagful of tools that will enable you to choose wisely, to fight your way through the hard times that will certainly arise, and to turn to the one true infinite source of mercy, grace, and love. As you learn and then reflect those divine attributes in your own life, you'll be able to attract sincere individuals who share your values and hopes."

"You're spilling all the secrets at once?" Pops teased.

"I never know how much longer I'll be around," she said with a warm smile. "And besides, you know I don't believe the secrets to a happy marriage were ever intended to be secrets."

"Yes, I do know," Pops said, squeezing Ruby's arm. "You still have interviews to do tonight, don't you?"

"That's right! I nearly forgot. It's Josh's and Crystal's turns tonight."

It was decided that family prayers would be said early so that those who weren't being interviewed could help with the dessert dishes and then enjoy some free time. But before they broke away, Pops warned everyone that the next four days would be long and grueling as they planted seed in the back twenty acres. It would be important to get enough sleep and wake up ready to put in an honest day's work.

CHAPTER 20

Breaking Bad

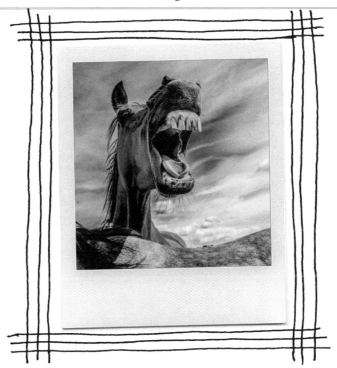

You can find God if you will only seek— by obeying
divine laws, by loving people, by relinquishing self-will,
attachments, negative thoughts and feelings. And when
you find God it will be in stillness. You will find God within.
- Peace Pilgrim -

Genevieve carried her plate to the kitchen but chose not to engage with the others who were discussing the evening's discourse around the sink. Instead, she walked out the front door and just kept walking, not sure what she was feeling but knowing she didn't want to discuss it any further. The sun was setting, painting the high clouds in pastel hues as Genevieve walked past the new garden, which she had to admit looked pretty darn good. She considered walking around the pond, but the memory of Sunday afternoon's mishap made her think twice. Instead, she just kept walking up the rutted drive. The sight of her Christian Louboutin, crucified with a single rusty nail to the top of the fence post, caused her temperature to quickly spike, and she kept on walking, finding it unbelievable that she had been here only four days. It already seemed like it had been a month, and she had nearly five months left in this godforsaken wasteland!

When she reached the main road, she couldn't think of anything better to do than to keep on walking. Remembering that a right turn would take her into town, she turned left instead. The lights of a farmhouse shone across the freshly plowed fields, and a cloud of dust hovered over a corral surrounded by a pipe fence. She walked on, drawn to the sounds of a whinnying horse. As she came closer, she could see the yellow stallion running in circles, kicking and bucking as a man dressed in dusty black pants and a straw hat stood in the middle of the corral, holding what looked like a long whip.

She watched from a distance as the pony bucked and ran erratically, tossing its head and bellowing in defiance. Genevieve came closer to the fence, watching closely to see if the man was abusing the horse, ready to be angry with him. But to her surprise, she didn't see any aggression on his part. She couldn't tell what he was saying, but his voice was calm, hardly audible over the ruckus the horse was making. And to her surprise, the long object in his hand was not a whip. Rather, it was a stick that he used to point the horse in the direction he wanted it to go as it circled the corral.

"Oh, hello," he said, looking surprised to see her. In the waning evening light, his face was pleasant, a patchy beard growing on his chin and cheeks like a hairy chin strap. Looking closer as he continued to turn slowly around the corral, she recognized his simple clothes and style from the county's website, which she had scoured before her trip to find any information she could about Niederbipp. He was the first Amish person she had ever seen in real life, and she watched him curiously.

"Are you the Cartwrights' daughter?" he asked.

"Uh, no," she responded, looking confused.

"Oh, I'm sorry. You must just live in the neighborhood."

"Well, kind of…for the summer. I mean, I…I'm staying at Ruby and Lorenzo's farm."

"Oh, you're here for a summer of matchmaking?"

"Uh, yeah. How did you know?"

"Everyone knows Ruby around here."

"Is that right?"

"Sure. She's a legend. And Lorenzo bought his team of horses from my father when I was just a kid. They're good people."

"I guess."

"Your accent—you're not from around here, are you?"

She laughed. "No, not even close. I'm from Boston, but I live in New York now."

"Whoa! That's a big, crazy place to live," he responded, continuing to lead the horse in circles.

"You've been there?"

"Yes, ma'am. I lived there for a couple of months. That was long enough for me."

"I didn't know Amish folks came to the city."

"We try not to," he responded with a smile.

"There must be a story there."

He nodded, clicking his mouth at the horse. "Have you ever heard of Rumspringa?"

"Uhh, isn't that a German pastry?"

The man laughed. "I wish. When Amish kids are sixteen, they're given a chance to leave their families and communities and experience the English world and decide if they want to commit to joining the church and the community for the rest of their lives. I decided to get as far away from here as I could, and New York seemed to fit the bill."

"Yeah, I guess it would. What did you do there?"

"Oh, after fumbling around, realizing I wasn't well prepared for most jobs in the city, I ended up finding a job driving carriages around Central Park."

"That makes sense—working with horses. Did you like it?"

"Sure, it was nice seeing something different, at least in the beginning. But after a couple of months, I realized I was on a circular track that wasn't really going anywhere meaningful. It was nice to have money in my pockets, at least for a few minutes, and to have more freedom to listen to music and see some of the sights and taste some of the foods, but…"

"But you came back?"

He nodded.

"Why?"

"Because of this," he said, pointing to the orange sky behind her. "And this," he said, pointing to the horse. "And this," he said, pointing to the farm. "You never get beauty like this in New York."

She nodded, looking around her. "So you live here?" she asked, pointing to the farmhouse.

"No." He pointed to the power line that was strung over her head. "That's a sure sign this isn't an Amish house. No, I live about five miles south of here. I'm just here to break this stallion."

The horse bucked and reared, sending more dust into the air.

"He looks like he doesn't want to be broken."

The man shook his head. "They never do at first. The Cartwrights adopted this one from a wild herd in New Mexico. This is probably the first time in his life that he's ever been inside a fence."

"So why did they adopt a wild horse?" she asked, looking confused. "Wouldn't it have been easier to find a tame one around here?"

He shrugged. "Mr. Cartwright said that this one's herd was being thinned, so they drove out and brought him back to keep him from being culled and turned into glue."

"That sounds like a lot of effort. Is it worth it?"

The man didn't answer for a moment, continuing to turn in a small circle as he closely watched the horse. "It's hard to say," he said after a long silence. "But my father taught me that that the true value of a horse can never be realized until he's broken and trained. This stallion is only about three years old. He could live to be thirty if he's treated right, maybe longer. There's no telling how much work a good horse can do in that amount of time or how many foals he can sire."

"But isn't it more humane just to let horses like this run wild and free?"

"It all depends on who you ask. In a community like mine where horses are at the center of all that we do, a horse is almost part of the family. We rely on them for transportation and farming and friendship. If you believe like we do that horses were created by God to work and serve mankind, then you understand that breaking and training a horse gives it purpose and helps it reach a potential beyond just looking pretty."

Genevieve nodded slowly as the young stallion ran past her. "So how do you know when he's broken?"

"When he stops doing that?" the man responded as the stallion bucked again. "It's a process that takes weeks, sometimes months. This is my first day with this one. He's got a strong spirit, and he's probably homesick. Every horse has to come to a place where he's comfortable enough to accept the reality that people like me are trying to make his life better. I guess, in some ways, it's a little bit like Rumspringa."

"In what way?"

"I used to think that the church and the community were confining and restrictive."

"Not anymore?"

He shook his head. "When I saw the way people lived in the city… chasing money while they ignored the people that were right in front of them, drinking themselves into oblivion every night in the name of fun, sleeping around with strangers, doing drugs, basically running around like wild stallions…it all began to look like a race to the bottom of all that was base and dishonorable."

"Hey, there's lots of good stuff about New York, too," she responded defensively. "The art, the culture, the sights. There's always something to do and new things to see."

He nodded. "Everyone has to find their place in the world, and sometimes we have to go far away from our home before we can really appreciate it."

"So why'd you end up coming back?"

"That was easy. After getting robbed at work for the third time, I realized that what once looked like freedom could also bring out the very worst in people. About that same time, I realized that what once felt like restriction and confinement were only efforts to make life happier and less complicated. When I realized I could never imagine raising kids in that environment, I decided to come home, join the church, and be happy with a more simple kind of freedom.

"Okay, but after living in the city, after having so much at your fingertips, don't you feel claustrophobic and depressed surrounded by all of this?"

"No," he responded without hesitation. "I'm surrounded by good people who inspire me to be better every day. I know my wife and children are safe. My farm provides us with our needs, and I can use my talents to make the world a better place. I don't think I need anything more to be happy."

"Wait, you're married?" she asked, surprised. He looked no older than twenty-five.

"Yes. It will be six years in September. We have three children."

"Wow, you didn't waste any time, did you?"

"We try not to. You never know what time will bring. We buried my mom in February. She was only fifty-eight. Time marches on whether you're ready or not."

Genevieve nodded. "I guess I should get going," she said after a long silence, the stallion continuing his protest.

"Have a lovely evening," he responded, nodding to her.

She walked back the way she had come, the low light fading to darkness and new stars appearing with each step she took. As she walked, she considered what the man had said. She had no reason to doubt his happiness or sincerity, but still she couldn't imagine his life— coming home to a place like this after experiencing a full, exciting life in the city.

She was just starting down the drive to the big house when a dark figure approached her quickly. She jumped back, bracing herself for an attack, but the figure breezed past her without even noticing her. As she watched it carefully, her eyes adjusting to the lack of light, she was surprised to hear music. The figure stopped at the road, jogging in place to the beat of the music for a moment and punching the air like he was a ninja. Realizing it must be one of the men, she stooped down and picked up a small rock, tossing it lightly at his back.

He swung around, his hands made into fists, ready to fight. He slid his hoodie back and pulled out his earphones, looking around wildly.

"Relax! It's me, Genevieve."

He let out a long breath and started laughing. "What are you doing here?"

"Spencer?"

"Yeah."

"What are you doing?"

"I was going for a jog."

"In a black hoodie after dark—with headphones?"

"You're not going to tell, are you?"

"What's there to tell?" she asked, laughing.

"I couldn't give up my music, and I haven't been to bed before midnight in years. What are you doing here?"

"I just needed some fresh air."

He laughed out loud. "Are you kidding? A girl from New York ought to be hyperventilating by now."

"Tell me about it," she responded, letting out a long breath.

"How you doin'?"

"I don't know. Struggling to think I'm gonna be in this hellhole for another five months. How about you?"

"Yeah, same I guess—worried that I'm gonna go nuts. I'm sure I already missed at least five good games. I can't even imagine how long it's going to take to go through all my recordings after five months of this."

"What do you mean?"

"Yeah, well, I DVRed every scheduled game that's going to be played in the next five months. I'll miss any playoff games, but I usually have at least one friend I can get those from. Still, the thought of binge-watching five months' worth of sports is already making me sweat."

"It sounds like you might have a problem. What do you do for a living?"

"I'm a sports analyst for ESPN."

"A what?"

"Yeah, I come up with all the commentary that the talking heads discuss on the Sunday shows so they don't look and sound stupid."

"Why can't they do that themselves?"

"Shoot, it'd be impossible to keep on top of everything they have to do. That's where the sports analysts like me come in. We make predictions based on what we see. It's kind of a high-pressure job. Most nights, I lie awake knowing that people decide what games they'll watch and how they'll spend their whole weekend based on what I say."

"For real?"

"Absolutely. This is making me crazy! I knew this was going to be tough, but I had no idea I'd be so far removed from my world. I ran into town last night, hoping to find a newspaper or catch the sports news through someone's open window, but all I could find was the local paper, which doesn't have a sports section. I poked around town for a half hour and couldn't even find anyone watching TV. It's like I went back in time a hundred million years. There's not even a bar or sports club in the area. Some guy told me the closest thing is in Tionesta, and that's like fifteen miles away. I was thinking I might try to get up there on Sunday night and catch the highlights at least, maybe the tail end of a couple of West Coast games."

"That's a long way to go for a sports report."

"Pshaw. I've gone much farther. Maybe you'd like to come with me?"

"To Tionesta?"

"Yeah. By the end of the week, I'm gonna be totally jonesin'. You want in?"

"Do they serve alcohol?"

"Uh, I'd assume so. It's a bar."

"Then I'm in. But how?"

"Didn't you read the packet they sent us?"

"Not very well. Why?"

"It said we can take the bikes into town any evening we want."

"Yeah, but which town? That's thirty miles round trip! Are you crazy?"

"Hey, a guy's gotta do…are you in or out?"

"Who else is going?"

"Josh wants to go. Come on. It'll be fun. I'll buy the first round."

"Deal. I need something to look forward to."

"Great, we'll leave at eight o'clock and should be back by midnight. It'll be awesome."

Spencer offered her a fist bump, which was awkward in the starlight. He continued on with his jog to try to find a newspaper, and Genevieve returned to the farm, grateful to finally have something to look forward to besides the end of September.

CHAPTER 21

Fieldwork

Love teaches even asses to dance.
– French proverb –

The morning came early, but to Genevieve's surprise, she was already awake when the rooster began his morning reveille. Remembering that she was on milking duty with James, she waited for him outside the men's bunkhouse when the women dispersed to their separate chores.

They found Pops in the barn waiting for them to arrive, a bucket of warm water in one hand and a clean towel in the other. After a short course on the proper ways of sanitizing udders, they got to work. James had never done this before, and Genevieve was careful not to give it away that she had already met these bovine ladies and that they had been the ruin of her favorite designer jeans. But as she worked, she was surprised that the stench of the barn was not nearly as bad as she remembered it being that first cruel morning.

After the milking was done, Pops instructed them to fill two smaller cans with milk for the house and then weigh the remaining milk on a giant scale; the needle fell just shy of eighty pounds. Pops wrote the number down on a clipboard and instructed them to use a giant funnel to carefully pour the rest of the milk into a pipe extending from the floor.

When James asked where the pipe went, Pops explained that it all started when the local dairy cooperative began refusing to pick up the farm's milk because driving down the rutted-out drive was turning the cream into butter. The family had counseled together, considering how the loss of milk income would affect the farm. Pops explained that they came up with at least ten decent ideas, including fixing the rutted drive, but the one that made the most economic sense was this one. The pipe was the ingenious idea of one of the women. She'd grown up making house calls with her father, who was a plumber. The farm family had spent a week digging a trench two feet deep and a half mile long, and they laid a pipe that ran downhill to the Hagen's farm, where the milk could be collected year-round by the cooperative truck that was already servicing the Hagens. After the pickup, the Hagens' crew would leave the valve open so the pipe could be flushed and made ready for the next milking.

"I think we all learned a lesson that year," Pops said as he handed each of them a pitchfork to muck out the stalls.

"What, that next time you should listen to the lawyer and not the plumber and sue the cooperative for contract infringement instead of spending all that time digging ditches?" James asked.

Pops smiled. "That's good, James. Spoken like a true attorney. But no, that wasn't the lesson we learned."

"Was it that you should just sell the farm and retire to Florida?" Genevieve snarked.

Pops rolled his eyes. "Tempting, but no, it wasn't that either. I couldn't have imagined it, but digging that trench brought those kids closer together than any group of kids we've ever had. The lesson I think we all learned is that there are always solutions to our problems if we're willing to be creative. I think we all learned that somewhere among all the brains in the family, the right bit of inspiration will be found."

After turning the cows out to pasture, James and Genevieve headed back to the big house, stopping to help hang the last of the laundry along the way. Ephraim and Sonja presented breakfast—giant pancakes with buttermilk syrup. The syrup was so good that the pancakes ran out before everyone was satiated; Ephraim and Sonja went back to the kitchen to make more.

While the pancakes cooked, Pops described the work for the next few days: the planting of oats, wheat, and rye in the acreage just behind the big house. This grain would be harvested in mid-September and was for the campers who would arrive next spring. The ground had already been plowed by a neighboring farmer who rented the majority of the farm's acreage to plant corn, peanuts, and soybeans, rotating the fields each year. But before anything could be planted, the soil needed to be harrowed and the rocks tossed to the side. The work would be divided over the next four days, giving everyone an opportunity to participate in each of the various activities. Pops stressed that if everyone gave it their all, they would be able to finish by Saturday afternoon. But shirking and dillydallying could extend the labor into the next week.

When they had eaten their fill of pancakes, Pops led ten of the campers to the fields while Ruby stayed with Ephraim and Sonja to begin the preparations for lunch.

Their first stop was an outbuilding where a variety of equipment was stored. As they slid open the doors, they found harrowers, planters, and harvesters in a variety of designs, parked like fancy cars on a showroom floor. Pops wove his way through the equipment to a wall where an assortment of harnesses and other farm implements hung from hooks. He handed each person a piece of equipment, and they followed him out the back door to a fenced pasture. He whistled loudly, and two beautiful horses came running from the shady grass on the far end of the pasture. He introduced the campers to Abraham and Sarah, the Amish-trained Belgian draft horse team that had been working together on the farm for nearly fifteen years.

Pops explained that this Abraham, unlike his Old Testament namesake, was not, nor ever would be, the father of nations. The women laughed as Pops explained that this Abraham was a gelding, having been castrated at an early age to keep his hormones from distracting him from his work. As he harnessed the horses, Pops also explained that Abraham and Sarah were twins and that though male-female teams were not all that common, the farm had a long-standing tradition of always having at least one team that was gender mixed.

Sliding open the back doors of the barn, Pops instructed a couple of the men to roll out a piece of equipment he called a harrow, which looked a little like a medieval torture device on wheels. Long, daggerlike pieces of metal extended downward from the frame, and rusty springs supporting a wooden bench were welded to the top. As he taught the group how to outfit the horses with bridles, bits, collars, straps, and harnesses, he explained how the weight would be distributed evenly and humanely over the horses' shoulders and backs. Then, checking that everything was in its proper place and order, Pops called for the yoke. After pointing out the features of this four-foot-long device—the ring in the middle and the iron attachments on either end—he explained how it would keep the horses working in sync with each other. He would attach one end to the front of their harnesses and another to the straps attached to their hindquarters. Finally, he instructed the men to roll up the harrow and attach it to the yoke.

He led the team across the pasture to the gate that led to the field they'd be working for the next few days. "Our first task is to break up the big dirt clods and move the rocks to the edges. I'll need a team to volunteer to take the first turn on the harrow; the rest of you will follow behind, picking up rocks. And don't worry. You're all going to have turns to ride the harrow."

"We'll go first," James said, tapping Genevieve on the shoulder. She wasn't sure what she'd just been committed to, but they climbed aboard and took their seats on the old, weathered bench, looking quite unsure of what to expect. Pops handed each of them a set of reins before flipping the lever at James's side, which dropped the blades of the harrow into the soil. They looked at Pops expectantly, waiting for further instruction. He quietly circled the rig and horses, checking one more time to be sure that the straps and harnesses were correctly attached and ready for work.

"Because this team was trained by an Amish man, they have been trained to respond to German commands," Pops explained. "It will be important that you remember these, or the horses won't respond. If you want them to move forward, you loosen the reins and say, 'Bittah shern.' If you want them to stop, you pull back on the reins slightly and say, 'Danka shern.' When you approach the end of the row, the team will wait for instructions, so you better be together about the direction you want them to go. If you each have different ideas about where you want to go, the horses will get confused and you'll lose their respect. And believe me, you do not want two one-ton horses to lose respect for you. Any questions?"

"Uh, yeah!" James said. "In my professional opinion, this looks like an accident waiting to happen. Isn't there a training course we should all be taking before we put our lives on the line?"

"This is what we call on-the-job training," Pops said, looking amused. "You may have forgotten, but you all signed a waiver when you applied. If you'd like to review it tonight, Mom would be happy to give you a copy. Just relax. Nobody's gonna die. But we do recommend keeping your hands and feet inside the ride at all times, and please stay seated until you have come to a complete stop."

"That's it? That's the training." James asked, his eyes wide open in surprise.

"Yes. We'll be doing this the rest of the day. That bench gets a little hard after a while, so let us know when you're ready to swap with another team."

James looked at Genevieve. "Are you ready?"

"I think so," she lied. "Are you?"

He smiled and shook his head, looking very uncertain. But giving the reins in his hand a little slack, he said the words "Danka shern."

Genevieve followed suit, repeating the command, but the horses didn't move.

"You just told the horses 'thank you,'" Pops reported.

"Is that bad?" Genevieve asked.

"Well, considering that they haven't done anything yet, yes. You'll confuse them. If you want them to go, you have to say please."

"Please?" she asked shyly, looking confused.

"But in German," Pops reminded them. "Bittah shern."

When they tried again, using the right word this time, the horses jolted forward.

As they pulled away, Josh ran alongside the harrow, handing each of them an old straw hat before distributing hats to the rest of the campers.

The group followed behind the harrow, picking up rocks and breaking up the bigger chunks of hardened dirt with their boots.

James and Genevieve started out going fairly straight, but within just a few yards, their line quickly became crooked. Turning to look at the tracks they were leaving behind, Genevieve responded by pulling on the reins. To her surprise, instead of straightening out, the line became even more crooked, and they began veering off toward the forest. Recognizing what was going on, James responded by pulling on his reins, and the rig moved in the opposite direction. He had just started to chide Genevieve for her lack of steering abilities when they realized the rig was now headed for the trees on the opposite side of the field. Genevieve didn't like being chided, neither had she ever been one who tolerated being told what to do. She responded by pulling back on her reins, which of course caused the rig to slowly swing the other direction. This went well for a moment, bringing them back to center, but she quickly realized that the harrow wasn't stopping there; it started heading toward the trees.

"This is ridiculous," James said, looking over his shoulder at their lightning-bolt-shaped wake.

"What are we doing wrong?" Genevieve asked, feeling a little bit frantic as the trees came ever closer.

"Do you think Pops rigged it wrong to make us look stupid?"

"He checked it twice. We both saw him. It's gotta be something we're doing."

James responded by pulling hard on his reins, saving the pair from running into the trees, which he was quick to point out. But like before, the rig went straight for only a few seconds before heading off again in a very crooked line.

Genevieve looked back to find the other campers watching them. She could see the broad smiles on their faces even from this distance. Some of them even looked like they were laughing. She looked back at James, who was sweating and alternating between giving his reins slack and pulling them in, but it made no difference—their line not only continued to be crooked but it also got worse the farther they drove.

Without warning, Genevieve started to laugh, which only seemed to make James more frantic.

"What's so funny?" he asked, turning to look at her.

"We're pathetic. It reminds me of my parents."

"Your parents are farmers?" he asked incredulously.

She laughed again. "No, but they've never been together."

"Your parents are divorced too?"

"No, they're together as far as living under the same roof goes, but if it weren't for the prenuptial agreement, I'm sure they would have split a long time ago. You said your parents are divorced, right?"

"Yeah. So what?"

"Didn't you say something the other night about being bounced back and forth between them?"

"Yeah. It sucked. Why?"

"Was it kind of like that?" she asked, pointing at the mess they were making of the plowed field.

He stared at the field for a moment before nodding. "Yeah, it was a lot like that, actually."

Genevieve watched him closely, recognizing the sting the memories still carried. "Why did you come here this summer?" she asked, suddenly remembering why she had come.

"Because I want to get married, but I want to make sure it's not the kind of marriage my parents had." He turned and looked at the mess they'd left in the field. "We should have let another team go first, huh? I'm sure they're totally laughing at us."

"Yeah, they are. But they'll have their turns soon enough." She pulled on her reins to keep them from hitting the trees on the side of the field, but just as before, the rig only began heading back the opposite direction in an equally cooked line. James scooted to the far side of the bench, experimenting to see if shifting his weight might help steer the rig in a straighter course. As he moved, Genevieve looked down at the bench between them, noticing something she hadn't seen before. Reaching out, she ran her fingers over the carved indentation—two characters. B1. At first she wondered if it wasn't a brand, but looking closer at the bench, she knew it was nothing more than an old board that had probably been replaced a few times over the life span of the rig.

She wrestled with her reins again as she moved to the far side of the bench, hoping to at least bring the springs into equilibrium if not to right the harrow's course. But it didn't take long to realize that their efforts were doing nothing to create a more steady, straight line.

"Should we let someone else have a chance?" James asked, looking frustrated.

"You wanna give up that easily?"

"How long do you want us to make fools of ourselves?"

She shook her head, feeling discouraged as the horses continued their meandering path. "It can't be that hard," she muttered, looking down at the carving on the bench.

"It obviously is. What are we supposed to say to stop this thing again?"

She shook her head, uncertain. But the carving in the bench caught her eye again. "What do you think this is?" she asked.

"It's an absolute disaster!" he responded, looking again at the line they were leaving in the field.

"I mean this," she said, pointing down at the bench.

"Is that the model number?"

"I don't think so. This has been carved by hand. B1. Does that say anything to you?"

He looked at her blankly. "Should it?" he asked, taking off his hat and mopping his brow with his forearm. The sweatband of his hat was exposed for just a moment before he put it back on his head, but in that brief moment, she saw something that intrigued her. She reached across the bench and took his hat off.

"Hey, what are you doing?" he asked, looking perturbed.

"Look, something's written there."

He took a closer look. "'LONG AND WINDING IS THE PATH THAT'S TROD ALONE,'" he read slowly, some of the words faded more than others, making it difficult to read. "Is there something written on your hat too?"

She leaned in, inviting him to take it off while she held his reins. "It says, 'IT IS NOT GOOD FOR MAN TO BE ALONE.'"

"What does that mean?"

"I don't know, but there's something else," he said, running his thumb over a particularly worn part of the sweatband before looking up, then down at the bench, then back at Genevieve.

"What is it?"

"B1"

"What?"

"That's what it says, just a B and a 1. And look," he said, turning back to his own hat. "There's one here too."

"And you're sure it's not a brand or part of a label?"

"Positive. It's faded, but it looks like it was written with a Sharpie."

She looked down again at the carving on the bench. "Let's try something. Slide toward the center."

He looked at her funny but did what he was told. She slid over as well until their shoulders touched. James laughed. "Really, you think this is a good time for this?" he teased.

"Relax, young stallion! I'm not getting fresh."

"What *are* you doing?"

"Look," she said, pointing to the center of the yoke that the harrow was attached to.

He squinted, trying to see what she was referring to. And there it was, stamped onto the metal band that attached the ring to the wood: B1. "What do you think this is?"

"You haven't had a turn to cook yet, have you?"

"No, why?"

"Ruby said something about…something like…for those who are seeking and have an open mind, the writing is always on the wall. It's not exactly a wall, but it seems like there's gotta be something here. Show me what's written in your hat again."

He pulled it off and read it again. "'Long and winding is the path that's trod alone.' What does yours say again?"

"'It is not good for man to be alone,'" she responded, not needing to look again.

He sat back, their shoulders touching again. "Okay, so alone is bad, but…oh my gosh, we're stupid."

"Hey, speak for yourself."

"B1," he said, pointing to the yoke. "B1. *Be one!* Get it? That's what that yoke is! It makes two horses with different agendas work together.

It ties them together. Look!" He pointed to the yoke. "And look at that," he said, lifting his reins loosely above his head with both hands. "I'm not controlling the horse in front of me."

"What?" she asked, looking confused.

"Lift up your reins."

She did, and to her surprise, she noticed that each of her reins was attached to the right side of both Abraham and Sarah.

"You control the right and I control the left. We've been fighting against each other the whole time, thinking that just one person could control the horses."

"I was thinking Abraham was just being stubborn," she admitted.

"I've been thinking the same thing about Sarah. But it's us, isn't it?" He laughed out loud.

"So, now we know what doesn't work. What do you want to try next?"

He nodded thoughtfully before pointing to the yoke. "I think that has something to do with it. It's like it all ties together—our heads—our butts—and the horses, whose heads and butts are already together, right?"

"I'm not going to sit on your lap," she said, laughing."

He smiled and shook his head. "I don't think you have to. Maybe if we just acted like we were one person instead of two, it would bring the right and left together. It would be one."

"Why don't you just take my reins," she said, offering them to him.

"I don't think it works that way."

"What did you have in mind?"

He looked at her reins and then his before leaning back against the back of the bench and putting his feet up on the bar in front of them, encouraging her to do the same. He turned and smiled at her. "It already feels better, doesn't it?"

"Uh, I don't know if you've noticed, but we're in the middle of a freakin' field, and we're still making very crooked lines. It reminds me of an Etch A Sketch."

They laughed together at the mess they'd made of the once nicely lined field, now carelessly scribbled on by a couple of clueless rookie plough kids.

With their hips and shoulders together, they found it was easier to check the tension on the reins and keep it all equal. Instead of fighting each other, working independently, and choosing opposite extremes, they found that by talking to each other, they could actually make the rig go straight for the first time. They smiled and waved to the other campers, who cheered as the harrow passed. After making a perfect U-turn at the end of the field, they trotted up alongside the rest of the work crew.

"Danka shern," they said together, giving a slight tug to the reins. The rig came to a stop just in front of the crew.

"Who's next?" James asked. He turned around to face them, obviously amused when nobody seemed immediately interested.

"I guess we could go," Matt said, tapping Susan on the shoulder. They traded places, each of them taking a set of reins.

"Do you have any tips?" Matt asked humbly.

Genevieve smiled at James and then glanced at Pops, who very subtly shook his head. "Only one," she said, turning back. "Remember that sometimes one is better than two."

With the utterance of two poorly pronounced German magic words, the rig took off again. And as the campers watched in amusement and anticipation, the harrow very quickly veered off course.

CHAPTER 22

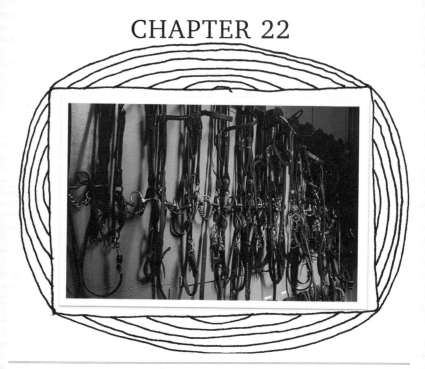

The Interview

...Love is the oil that eases friction,
the cement that binds closer together,
and the music that brings harmony.
– Eva Burrows –

By the time Ephraim and Sonja arrived at the field with Ruby, toting picnic baskets and a couple of jugs of lemonade, the last pair was taking their turn on the harrow. The field was a mess. With only a couple of straight lines to brag about, the rest looking like a jumbled bowl of spaghetti.

"Looks like it's been a productive morning," Ruby said with a generous smile.

"Hey, we've got some great rocks," Pops responded, pointing to the fresh piles of various-sized stones that lined the edge of the field.

"I don't see why Ephraim and Sonja don't have to suffer this humiliation," Crystal chided.

"Oh, they will. That's why we brought lunch to you. Nobody misses out on harrowing day," Ruby reported.

After watching Greg and Holly finally make their first straight line and come to a stop, the rest of the family ushered Ephraim and Sonja to the rig. As they all looked on knowingly with furtive smiles, Pops gave this last pair the same basic instructions the rest of the group had received. But as the gang watched them leave, they were all disappointed when, after making only a few minor corrections, Ephraim and Sonja quickly began making the straightest lines yet.

"That's a good idea," Susan said, pointing toward the back of the harrow as the pair passed the first time. Genevieve looked to see that Ephraim's right arm was draped over Sonja's shoulders, while her left arm wrapped around his back, resting on the top of the bench. They all watched in admiration and surprise as Ephraim and Sonja made four perfect passes across the breadth of the field, erasing the messes the rest of them had left behind, before coming to a halt in front of the family. A roar of applause rose up as the two gracefully dismounted the harrow.

As they picnicked on the edge of the forest, they all talked about the experience, laughing at each other and themselves for their slowness in catching on. But there were also compliments given and congratulations shared—because each team had ultimately discovered the secret of creating a straight line. Admiration was equally showered on Ephraim and Sonja. Someone asked what their secret was in figuring it out so quickly, and Ruby answered for them, praising them for their work in the kitchen and announcing that their record at the flour mill would be a tough one to beat, rivaling many of the best records that had been set in summers past. Though that information was essentially meaningless to the half of the family who had not yet experienced the flour mill, it made Genevieve think.

Throughout the rest of the meal, Genevieve watched Sonja and Ephraim. They had met each other only a few days before and had worked as a team for only a few hours, but there was already an energy—almost a visible chemistry—that had somehow formed between them. More than just the physical connection they all had witnessed while the two drove the harrow, there was another connection—a kindness and gentleness that seemed like it almost filled the air they shared. As Genevieve considered her experiences being teamed up with Greg, Josh, and now James, she realized there had been nothing like this between her and any of those teammates. It made her curious.

When Ephraim and Sonja were given another chance to ride the harrow before heading back to the big house to work on dinner, she noticed that all eyes seemed to be upon the pair, as if everyone else had also witnessed the energy and shared a collective curiosity for what it was.

Just as it had been with them the first time, Ephraim and Sonja made the work look easy. Genevieve recognized that that there was a beauty and a grace they shared in accomplishing something that had seemed so void of beauty and grace when she and James had been in control. With these thoughts in her head, it was hard to concentrate on the rocks she was supposed to be moving to the edge of the field, her mind and eyes constantly distracted toward Ephraim and Sonja.

After the pair created five more perfect lines, the harrow was turned over to Genevieve and James again, and Ephraim and Sonja went back to kitchen duty. With the knowledge and experience they had gained on their first go, and from watching the success of Ephraim and Sonja, they worked much differently. In fact, it barely seemed like work at all. They communicated more openly with each other this time, even lightly embracing each other as they'd seen modeled. They created their first consistently straight lines, paralleling the others.

The exercise continued, each team adding several lines before passing the harrow on to a different couple. And for those who weren't riding, the piles of stones on the edges of the field grew bigger and bigger, mingling with rocks that had been tossed aside by generations of other campers just like them.

Before Ephraim and Sonja came out to call everyone to dinner and take one more turn on the harrow, finishing up the last few lines in the field, each of the teams had had three turns to hone their skills. There was a shared sense of accomplishment as they looked out on their work. The lines were straight. The field was clean. The soil was ready for seed.

Together they stripped the tack off the horses, hanging it all back in the barn. Pops handed each of the campers a couple of sugar cubes and encouraged them to thank Abraham and Sarah for their work and gentle patience. As they walked to the big house that night, there was a very different feel among the group. Three days of shared toil and experience had united them into something far different from the strangers they'd been just days before. And though they came from different backgrounds, education levels, and even ethnicities, none of that seemed to matter in this moment. Somehow through the shared experience of sweat, blisters, fatigue, and unfashionable farm duds, they had come together to form something much different from a group of strangers.

Genevieve fell back, waiting for Pops to catch up. "Is it like this every summer?"

Pops smiled, nodding. "Yep, every summer. Some groups are quicker to gel than others, but they all come around. It's magic, isn't it?"

"I don't know if I'd go that far," she responded, not ready to give in. "But I'll give you that it is unique."

Pops laughed. "You're a difficult person to impress, Genevieve Patterson, but I promise you that you ain't seen nothin' yet."

After they all kicked off their boots and washed up, they sat down to a full meal of roast beef, mashed potatoes and gravy, Ruby's famous mustard pickles, bottled beets, steamed carrots, and even hot rolls. After sharing a round of wisdom cookies, they broke for evening chores. James and Genevieve returned to the barn with Pops for the evening milking while Ruby had her interview with Matt. The rest of the campers self-selected between kitchen duty and the berry patch to get ready for another evening on the porch.

Spencer randomly drew a card from a rubber band-bound stack of possible activities Pops handed him, and announced that the game for the evening was called Sharks, Bears, or Tyrannosaurus Rex. As he had with the other games, Pops explained that this one had been created one summer at least a decade earlier with the combined efforts of a paleontologist, a marine biologist, and a park ranger. The person riding Bessie would try to keep a straight face while family members drew on their personal fears to come up with the most insane ways to die, all of which must include being eaten by either a real or fictitious animal. The person who stayed on the bike the longest without smiling would earn herself an extra scoop of smashed strawberries on her ice cream and would be entitled to hang on to the very unique trophy until the game was played again and a new champion determined.

It seemed straightforward enough and proved to be very fun. Greg was the first to pedal, but he didn't last long, losing his stoic composure when Holly mentioned maggots. Crystal was up next and was doing pretty well until James began talking animatedly about a very vivid dream he once had as a child in which he had gone camping in the Australian outback, had fallen into a pond, and was slowly nibbled to death by a crazed and rabid platypus. Matt fell at Ephraim's mention of hummingbirds that sucked people's brains out through their ears. And Sonja had everyone in stitches by exposing her fear of being dragged into a lake and eaten alive by the giant squid that her brother had always taunted her about.

Susan was ultimately the winner of the game that night and was presented with the hideous trophy, a sun-bleached and varnished skull of a rather ferocious-looking badger, which could either be hung on the wall or worn as a necklace. She opted instead to leave it in the music room so everyone could enjoy it. As they ate their ice cream, they continued to share their stories of impractical fears. For Genevieve, it was the first time in her life that she had ever admitted her fear of snakes, and she was pleased that several of the women and at least two of the men admitted to being afraid as well. As she watched and listened, she was surprised by two things—that talking about fears made them feel smaller and that the act of exposing one's vulnerabilities to other vulnerable humans enabled connections to be shared and trust to be built.

When the ice cream was gone and the conversation turned to the need they all felt for a shower, they broke for the evening, sharing in the cleanup before heading to the bunkhouses. Genevieve was on her way out of the big house with the women when Ruby stopped her, reminding her of her interview. She followed Ruby into the library. The room's only illumination was a lamp with a colorful stained-glass shade that stood on a squat table between two wooden-framed armchairs with seasoned-leather cushions.

"Please have a seat," Ruby said, pointing to one chair and taking a seat in the other. "How are you liking it so far?"

The question surprised Genevieve. It had been only twenty-four hours since she had wandered up the rutted lane, feeling trapped. "I'm not sure," she responded, feeling more than a little confused by what had somehow softened her hard feelings in the hours since. But she wasn't sure if she wanted to admit to any of that. "It's not as totally terrible as I thought it would be," she finally said.

Ruby nodded, staring into Genevieve's face until she looked away. "But?"

"What do you mean?"

"There was just a little hesitation there. I sensed a 'but' was coming. It's not as totally terrible as you thought it would be, but…" Ruby said, as she if were anticipating something more.

"I guess I just thought it would be worse, that's all."

"I see. When would you like to begin the interview?"

"Oh, I'm ready. Go ahead."

Ruby smiled. "I'm ready when you are."

"Excuse me?" she asked, looking confused.

"I promised you and your boss an interview. I'm ready now."

"Oh…I," she stammered, feeling stupid. "I thought you were interviewing me. Isn't that what you've been doing this week?"

"Yes, it is, but you're different, right? You're the only one who's not here of your own volition. I wouldn't want to waste your time with questions that have no relevance or application to what you're here for. Now, what questions did you have for me?"

Genevieve felt stupid. She had written a long list of questions before she had come, but she didn't quite know where that list was, let alone remember what was on it. "Uh, I'm sorry, I…I'm not prepared for this. I didn't know…"

Ruby smiled but shook her head. "We won't be having interviews again for at least a month. Will that give you enough time to sort through your thoughts and come prepared next time?"

"Yes," she said, looking away.

"What would you like me to tell your boss about your progress on your story?"

Genevieve's face registered surprise, then concern. "Do you think she'll contact you?"

"She already has. I've spoken to Mrs. Galiveto twice since you arrived. That satellite phone you brought with you has proven to be very helpful. Thank you."

"What? You've spoken to Julia?"

"Yes, twice. She's a rather astute woman, isn't she?"

"What did she say?" Genevieve asked, looking a little desperate.

"She mostly just called to check on your progress. I told her you were interviewing me tonight. I'm sure she'll be checking in tomorrow or Friday. Is there anything you'd like me to tell her."

Genevieve leaned forward, covering her face with her farm-worn hands. "Tell her I'm making progress," she mumbled.

"Excuse me?"

Genevieve dropped her hands into her lap, staring down at her once beautifully manicured nails that were now chipped and broken. Shaking her head, she brushed her hands over her dusty overalls, realizing how far she'd fallen since Friday. "I can't do this."

"What can't you do?" Ruby asked, leaning in closer.

"This, this, this!" she responded, pointing from her overalls, to Ruby, to the farm. She looked like she was about cry.

"Well, you've already committed to me and your boss that you'd do this. Julia says she's holding a place for you in the November issue of your magazine. From what I understand, your job and your housing situation are both on the line if you don't follow through."

Genevieve shook her head.

"Dear, how can I help you?"

She looked up, surprised by not only the question but by the tenderness in which it was asked. "Can you stall her?"

"Probably, but not forever. I've been away from your world for a long time. I'm afraid I've become too honest to be able to whip up a yarn that's believable. What would you like me to say?"

"That I'm working on it. That I've been working hard at getting people to trust me so I can get the story. Oh, and tell her that I learned how to milk cows and feed chickens."

Ruby smiled. "Do you think that would help?"

"I don't know," she said, looking desperate. "It's all I've got."

She nodded, reaching over to squeeze Genevieve's hand until she turned to look at her. "Listen, dear, I know this isn't where you want to be."

"But?"

"Excuse me?"

"Wasn't there a 'but'? You said you know this isn't where I want to be, but it sounded like there was something else."

Ruby shook her head. "I don't know what to say. You're here. And from the sounds of it, a lot's riding on you staying here through the summer. I guess the only real option is to stop thinking you're better than the rest of these kids and jump in—really become a part of them. Put it out of your mind that you're different or better or somehow other. I think you've been here long enough to realize you're not much different than any of them, that you have strengths and weaknesses just like they do. In my interviews so far, I've encouraged each of them to begin focusing a conscious effort on feeding their strengths and starving their weaknesses. If you don't know what yours are or which is which, I'd like to encourage you to spend some time discovering what's in your own soul."

Genevieve took a deep breath, exhaling slowly as she wrestled with the emotions inside her. Ruby stood and offered her a hand, pulling her up with a surprising strength before wrapping her arms around her in an embrace. "You're gonna be fine, and the summer will be over before you know it. My advice to you is to make this time count for something extraordinary."

Genevieve nodded and pulled back, mumbling a thank you before walking away. She walked out the front door and was down the stairs before the first tear fell. She felt overwhelmed by emotions too big to ignore. Anger. Frustration. Fear. Helplessness. They were all there, simmering just beneath the surface, ready to explode like a boil. She walked across the lawn to the bunkhouse, the happy sounds of the women filling the room. She put on a smile as she gathered up her towel, pajamas, and clean underwear and headed for the showers.

She had just worked the shampoo into her hair when the water turned cold. Instead of jumping out and screaming like she was tempted to do, she stayed under the water, crying at her lot in life as she shivered uncontrollably, punishing herself until her tears ran out.

She found the women dressed in their night clothes, their hair wet, huddled around Rachael's bed as she sketched in a notebook.

"You should see what we're doing," Holly said.

Genevieve tossed her dirty clothes into the hamper and rubbed her arms, trying to make the goose bumps disappear as she wandered over, far more interested in going to bed than being sucked into a lame project. To her surprise, however, the sketch looked good, and despite her mood, it was impossible for Genevieve to not acknowledge Rachael's talent. She watched as each of the women made suggestions, Rachael responding by adding details and even color with a small set of colored pencils.

"So, what are you going to do with this?" Genevieve asked, obviously confused as she looked down at the whimsical, colorful design.

"We found some paints and brushes in the closet over there," Holly announced. "Rachael's going to help us design a mural for that big wall."

Genevieve looked at the big wall and tried to imagine it. "You can do that?"

"It's been done before," Crystal replied. "There was a piece of paint that was peeling off next to my bed. I pulled on it and...look!" She slid her bed back from the wall, revealing what looked like a pile of leaves that had obviously been painted there. "And there's another section over here," she said, pointing toward the top of her bed, where a small piece of an undersea-themed mural peeked out.

"My overalls today had splatters on them from every one of those paint colors," Sonja added. "We're obviously not the first to think white walls are boring."

"We already talked to Ruby. She said we can do whatever we want as long as we paint it all back to white at the end of the summer," Susan added. "Is there anything you want to add?"

Genevieve took a closer look. There was an island and an ocean filled with colorful fish. The sky was tinted in warm hues, and a giant tree grew out of the middle of the island, stretching out its limbs to support an elaborate tree house. "Looks like you're going for a Swiss Family Robinson theme, right?"

"Actually, we were thinking more Peter Pan," Rachael responded.

"Either way, you probably need some pirates!"

Holly clapped her hands and looked quite happy with the idea. "Do you think you can paint one that looks like Johnny Depp?"

They all seemed to like the idea of a pirate who looked like Johnny Depp watching over them as they slept at night. Before the lights were turned off, plans were made to get started as soon as the fields were planted, when the promise of more free time would become a reality.

CHAPTER 23

Laundry Day

Life is short, and we never have too much time for
gladdening the hearts of those who walk this way with us.
Oh, be swift to love. Make haste to be kind.
– Henri F. Amiel –

The chatter continued long after the lights were turned off, but Genevieve chose not to participate. Instead, she chose to be angry. She was angry at her boss, angry at Ruby, angry at the stupid rooster who'd be waking her up long before she was ready. She was angry that her nails had never looked worse, angry that the pitiful excuses for clothes she had to wear highlighted none of the curves with which she'd been so well endowed. And her anger only thickened when she remembered that none of the stupid men had even glanced at her. Most of all, she was angry that she had to be here—had to do this—had to pretend to be nice to all these idiotic people. After silently screaming every vile and wretched word she knew, she finally fell asleep, fantasizing about burning down the farm, going rogue, and running away with Johnny Depp.

But dreams never last forever.

She was standing on the deck next to Johnny as he masterfully piloted the Black Pearl into the sunset. She was wearing her favorite dress—yellow, cotton, lots of buttons that helped accentuate her figure. Johnny was just leaning down to kiss her when his stupid parrot screamed out at the top of his tiny parrot lungs, "Icebergs at twelve o'clock! Icebergs at twelve o'clock!" But the icebergs disappeared, and so did the dress, and so did Johnny. And Genevieve was once again in the cruel, real world, still feeling the chill of last night's shower.

She sat up, the anger she'd gone to bed with still stewing as she dressed in her frumpy overalls, a faded T-shirt, and mismatched socks. She slogged out the door with the laundry basket overflowing with stinky laundry and towels. She felt a little bit better when she saw Ephraim emerge from the men's bunkhouse with a laundry basket as well. He was no Johnny Depp, but of all the men, he seemed to possess the most innate charm.

"Good morning," he said, looking very tired. A serious rooster tail stuck out sideways from the back of his head.

She nodded. "So I guess it's you and me today, huh?"

"Yeah, and I heard this chore is a little tricky. We should probably get right to it," he suggested, leading off to the laundry shed.

"Uh, I don't think that's a laundry shed," she suggested before they had even reached it. "I poked my head in there on Saturday, and it looks like it's just a storage room for old bikes.

"That's exactly what the guys said, but they said something about it being more than it appeared. Let's check it out."

Ephraim pushed open the door, but just as Genevieve had warned, it looked nothing like any laundry room either of them had ever seen before. Instead, a big utility sink stood in one corner, and in the middle of the room stood a couple of old bicycles without wheels. The bike frames had been welded to an I-beam, and they faced two big wooden barrels that sat atop what looked like giant gears. The bicycle chains were each attached to a sprocket that had been welded to a single rod, which in turn attached to a series of gears, shafts, belts, and other parts that Genevieve could only guess had come from a car or tractor.

"This looks interesting," Ephraim said, dropping his basket onto the cement floor and looking up at the instructions written on a board above the barrels:

1. Collect laundry from the bunkhouses and the big house.

2. Sort laundry, darks and lights, into the two barrels.

"I'll go get the laundry from the big house if you want to start loading the barrels," he said and then disappeared, leaving Genevieve to wonder in silence about the strangeness of this place.

Ephraim returned before she had finished loading. He added Ruby and Pops's laundry, as well as the dish towels and washcloths from the kitchen, to their respective barrels.

They looked back to the wall for further instructions.

3. Add a cup of soap to each barrel.

They each looked around for a bottle of liquid detergent or fabric softener, but all they found was an old aluminum measuring cup, a cheese grater, and a bar of what looked like homemade soap that been formed in a bread tin. Genevieve lifted the bar of soap to her nose. It had a pleasant scent—lavender and mint. She looked at the grater and shook her head. "Why can't they make anything easy around here?" she muttered, handing the bar of soap to Ephraim.

"Mmm, this smells good!" he exclaimed. "And I bet it works way better than shampoo."

"What?" she asked, laughing. "You use shampoo for laundry? You know that's not a thing, right?"

"Well, yeah. I mean, I wouldn't recommend it…it basically covered the whole laundromat floor with bubbles, and I'm not sure how clean it got my clothes. But it was a good experiment. At least I know now, right? Have you ever used bar soap for laundry?"

"No. Never. You?"

"Maybe in college. I don't know. Anyway, do you think we just drop the bar in the barrels and hope for the best?"

"Uhh, no," she laughed. "I'm pretty sure that won't work." She pointed to the marks left on the corner of the bar where it had obviously been pushed across the grater's rough surface. "Do you want to hold the cup or do the grating?"

"Oh, I get it. I'll grate. I worked at an Italian restaurant one summer and was good at grating parmesan. This ought to be easy."

While Genevieve held the cup over the barrels, Ephraim grated, quickly filling the cup twice. While she spread the soap, he moved on to the next step—filling the barrel with water. This was accomplished quite quickly with the aid of a hose connected to the nearby water valve that came up through the floor. When the water reached the prescribed level in each barrel, they moved on to the next step, each sitting down on one of the wide-load bicycle saddles.

Anxious to get things moving, Genevieve pushed down on the pedal of her bike, but it didn't move. She responded by standing on the pedal and exerting all her combined strength and weight, but still the pedal refused the budge.

"It says we have to engage the gear," Ephraim said, pointing to the instructions. He smiled at her, pointing to the old gearshift handle that rose out of the gearbox on the floor between the bicycles. He pushed the handle forward till it clicked into place. Again Genevieve attempted to make her pedals move, and again she failed. "This is a piece of crap," she grumbled, turning to Ephraim, whose interest had been distracted by the mechanics of the contraption.

"No, this is actually a brilliant idea," he responded as he dismounted, following the chain to the sprockets, to the shared rod, to the gears and driveline that ended at the giant set of flywheels connected to the barrels.

"If it's so brilliant, why doesn't it work?"

He looked distracted as his eyes worked backward from the barrels, following the gears and driveline back to the rod to which each of the sprockets was connected. "This is ingenious," he said, laughing to himself. "Do you know what this is?"

"Uh, a torture device?"

"This is the answer to all the world's laundry problems." He said this as if in deep thought, as if he hadn't even heard Genevieve.

He sat back down on his saddle before turning to her. "I think this must work the same way the flour mill works. It takes two people to get the flywheel moving. Try it now," he said as he pushed down on his own pedals.

To her surprise, the crank began turning. It rotated only a few times before it stopped. She looked at him to see if he had stopped pedaling, and she was surprised to find him smiling as he stared at the red metal lever that was leaning slightly in her direction.

"Wait," she said, finally connecting the dots. "You're an engineer, aren't you?"

He nodded, obviously still distracted by the mechanics of the contraption.

"So why did it stop?"

"Because it reached the end of the cycle."

"Are you kidding? The barrel only turned like a quarter of a turn. There's no way it got anything clean yet."

"I agree."

"Wait, you do?"

"Yeah. You've got to push that lever back in my direction."

She responded, pushing the lever until it clicked. With the click, the pedals were able to turn again, but like before, they rotated only a couple of times before they stopped. She was about to complain, when he pushed the lever back. Again, the pedals were loosed and able to rotate.

"Are you getting this?" he asked.

"Uh, not really. This just seems like a ridiculous amount of effort. What does this thing even control other than the pedals?"

"Don't you get it? It's an agitator."

"Well, mission accomplished! I'm officially agitated," she said, looking upset.

He laughed out loud. "No, what I meant was, it controls the agitation. This lever is a torque reset interrupter."

"A what?"

"It breaks the flow of the torque and allows it to be reset to enable the agitation to take place."

"Look," she replied, looking flustered. "You don't have to make stuff up just so you can look smart."

He laughed. "No, I'm serious. Watch the barrels," he said, pointing.

Together they pedaled four rotations, the barrel moving about 180 degrees before the pedals locked. He pushed the lever back toward her, and the pedals were free to turn another four rotations as the barrel turned back 180 degrees. He turned to her and smiled. "Pretty amazing, right?"

"Uh, I'd rather just push a button and walk away."

"Well, yeah, but this is an engineering masterpiece!"

She shook her head but couldn't keep from smiling at the look of awe on his face. "You probably thought the flour mill was impressive too."

"Absolutely. Do you have any idea what these machines could do if we could get them into the hands of people around the world?"

"Uh..." she said, and then she laughed. "I don't mean to burst whatever balloon you've been sucking helium out of, but there's this thing called electricity..."

He laughed. "Sorry, what I meant to say is the *underdeveloped* world. Did you know that almost 20 percent of the world's population lives in areas that don't have any electricity at all and another huge number of people are really limited in the amount of electricity they can use? Machines like this could change lives."

She looked unimpressed. "Okay, but that doesn't change the fact that we have two whole stinkin' barrels of wet clothes and we're making no progress!"

"You're right. First things first. Let's get this thing going."

"How?"

"It's just like the flour mill…well, kind of, right? It just takes some coordination and cooperation, maybe a little rhythm."

"Rhythm? I don't know if you noticed, but we're sitting on stupid bikes without tires that are supposed to be part of a freaking washing machine. And we've got two barrelfuls of soggy, stinky clothes. What do you care about rhythm?"

He smiled, looking amused by her attitude. "There's rhythm and music in everything if you're looking for them."

She shook her head, thinking he was nuts, and was just about to get off her bike and start washing the clothes by hand in the utility sink when she glanced up at the instruction board. Written across the bottom in fine print, she saw something she hadn't seen before. She read it once, then twice, before turning back to Ephraim. "I hate to admit it, but maybe you're right," she said, pointing to the message.

He squinted, reading it out loud:

'Happiness is not a matter of intensity but of balance and order and rhythm and harmony.' Reverend Thomas Merton.

"Have you ever heard of Reverend Thomas Merton?" she asked.

He shook his head. "But Ruby did tell us yesterday that the writing is on the wall. If it worked for the flour mill, it will probably work for this too."

"Wait, what did Ruby tell you?"

"You mean she didn't tell you?"

"Tell me what?"

"That the writing was on the wall?"

"Yeah, she told us that, but I thought it was just a trite phrase."

"So you didn't read what was written on the beam right above the flour mill?"

"No, what does it say?"

He smiled, looking up at the phrase he'd just read. "Something similar to that?"

"What does it say?"

"She asked us not to tell the others. Apparently we were the first ones to find it. That's why we were able to make it work so fast."

"What?!"

"Yeah, she told us it was one of the secrets—that it made more sense if we figured it out ourselves. You'll be there again soon enough, right? Look for it. I think we better just concentrate on that one right now," he said, pointing to the instruction board.

"So, what kind of rhythm do you think that's referring too?"

He looked thoughtful for a moment, looking down at the pedals and then the lever before turning back. "Did you ever take piano lessons?"

"My parents tried to make me, but I hated it. Why?"

"You know what a metronome is, right?"

"Isn't that the thing that sits on top of the piano and ticks back and forth?"

"Yes. It's to help with timing—with rhythm. Without it, it's easy to get off, and then the music sounds more like noise. It gives it order. It's kind of a different application, but I think it would work here too."

She folded her arms across her chest and shook her head. "This is so stupid."

"You don't even want to try?"

"Don't let me stop you."

He nodded, pushing down on the pedal, but it didn't move. He pulled on the lever and tried again, but nothing—it simply wouldn't turn.

"I told you, it's broken," she said with a sassy voice.

He looked back up at the instruction board, silently reading the quote written across the bottom. "Balance, order, rhythm, harmony," he said, turning to face her.

"What about it?" she challenged.

"Okay, so we're balanced on these seats, there's order to the machine, but we're obviously lacking both rhythm and harmony."

"You think this is a recipe?"

He shrugged. "Have you got any better ideas?"

She shook her head. "This is so stupid."

"Look, I'm kinda hungry, and I'd like to get on with the day. I get that we're not exactly gelling here, but can we figure this out?"

"You don't think this is broken?"

"I'm not convinced that it is. We got it to move, right? And three other teams have made it work so far. Can we maybe see if applying a little harmony and rhythm might change things?"

She shook her head. "What do you want me to do?"

"I want you to help me count."

"How's that going to help?"

"I don't know, but trust me." He looked at her pedals, her right foot higher than her left, the same as his. "Okay, when I say go, I want you to push down with your right foot and keep going as I count, okay?"

"Whatever."

"Go!"

She pushed, and to her surprise the pedal turned as he counted.

"One, two three, four." At four, he pushed the lever to her side and continued counting. "One, two, three, four." But the pedals stopped. "On four, you have to push the lever back."

She did it—late—but she did it, and the lever clicked into place. He counted as they pedaled again, flipping the lever back to her side. It went slow at first as they got the rhythm. But the counting soon got faster, and the barrels began making real progress. They turned back and forth, finally with a respectable agitation and rhythm.

He looked up at the board, looking for further instructions as he continued to count.

7. Wash clothes for at least fifteen minutes.

8. Drain dirty water.

9. Fill barrel with clean water and work again for five minutes.

10. Drain water during spin cycle.

11. Crank clothing though rollers.

12. Hang clothing on line.

Before long, the rhythm of the machine had become almost natural and didn't require counting. They drained the soapy, dirty water by opening the four spigots at the bottom of each barrel. Then, closing the spigots again, they refilled the barrels with fresh water for another round of agitation and rinsing. The spin cycle was accomplished by opening the spigots again and using the gearshift to engage a different drive that allowed the barrels to spin like centrifuges at a very fast clip until no more water came out of the spigots.

While Genevieve and Ephraim wrung out any extra water by running the clothing though two heavy rollers attached to a hand crank, Ephraim carried on about the simple beauty and merits of the washing machine's design. He was still elucidating how it could change the world as they hung the laundry on the line. But Genevieve was tuned out and barely listening, her mind wrapped around the hope of Sunday evening, when she would be able to forget for a couple of hours that the farm even existed.

CHAPTER 24

Chariot Races

Everything that needs to be said has already been said.
But since no one was listening, everything must be
said again.
- André Gide -

Ephraim and Genevieve were the last to arrive at the big house, having taken so long with the laundry that they'd missed out on getting help from the others on their way to breakfast. The feelings of magnanimity that had been shared by the campers the previous day seemed to have declined sharply. Everyone moved about a little more slowly, looking tired and sore. Even the morning prayers, offered by Rachael, came off sounding flat and hollow.

Breakfast was served by Susan and Spencer. They announced that because the previous morning's pancakes had been such a hit, they had decided to repeat the menu. Spencer proudly announced that in celebration of the beginning of NFL spring training, he had attempted to create the pancakes in the shape of little footballs. Other than Josh, who gave a little hoot, the campers seemed less than impressed, and the odd-shaped pancakes were consumed without any extra enthusiasm.

As they were finishing breakfast, it was announced that, unlike on the previous days, Pops would stay to help out with the kitchen work and Ruby would be leading the teams in the fields. And so, following breakfast, Ruby marched the campers back to the barn.

After opening the barn doors, she instructed the men to roll out the planters. These machines looked a little like double-wide shopping carts, each with four large wheels and a pair of funnel-shaped aluminum canisters that sat toward the back. The planters, Ruby explained, were heavy and somewhat awkward to maneuver, requiring the teamwork of four individuals to control. She invited them to walk around the machines as she described their parts and functions.

Two sets of handles protruding from the back would be used help stabilize the pair who worked the back end as the cart rolled over the tilled soil. This pair would focus their attention on the seed depositors— dual discs with stubby metal fingers, designed to quickly and accurately drop the kernels into the dirt exactly two inches deep and two inches apart. This pair would also be responsible to make sure the seeds were covered with dirt to ensure they wouldn't be eaten by birds or exposed to the elements.

The majority of the power would be provided by the pair on the front end, but because there was only one team of horses and three planters, each of the human pairs that had been assigned to work together that day would have a chance to rotate through. Ruby explained that because this would require even more coordination and cooperation between pairs than all of the previous activities, it would be necessary to do a series of dry runs before the seeds were added to the hoppers.

As they began outfitting the horses with the tack they'd worn the day before, the reality that they would be doing the same work as the equine team began to set in. When the horses were attached to one of the planters, Ruby directed the campers to attach an eight-foot chain to the front of each of the other two planters. To the opposite end of each chain, she instructed them to attach a yoke similar to the one attached to the horses, though smaller.

After an awkward effort of pushing and pulling the carts to the field, Ruby offered them only a few words of direction. Try to make straight lines. Rotate regularly to avoid exhaustion. Keep hydrated. And try to have fun. She then informed them that she needed to run an errand but that she'd be back by lunch to check on their work and to see if they were ready to add seeds to their hoppers.

While the others discussed how they'd divide the teams, Genevieve stared out at the field, feeling as if it had somehow grown larger overnight. She had never imagined the work that went into creating a slice of bread. But now that she'd ground her own flour and baked her own bread and was now standing in a field that would soon be planted with grain, she had a completely different appreciation for it all. Turning back, she learned that Ephraim had volunteered them to be the first to pull one of the carts. Matt and Crystal made up the rest of their team. They all aligned their cart with the straight rows of dirt in front of them, and then Ephraim and Genevieve lifted the yoke off the ground and moved forward until the chain was taut.

"Ready?" Matt asked, looking over the tall grain hoppers.

"As ready as we're gonna be," Ephraim said.

"Then giddyup!"

Ephraim looked at Genevieve and smiled before turning back to Matt. "That's not the magic word."

"Oh, right. Bittah shern?"

Ephraim nodded, and they leaned forward against the yoke, feeling the full weight of the cart behind them for the first time. They had moved only a few feet when Genevieve adjusted her hold on the yoke, causing the cart to veer off to the left. Ephraim responded quickly, trying to right them, but within just a few paces, it was obvious that this was going to be harder than any of them had imagined. They readjusted the yoke, but with Ephraim being nearly a head taller than Genevieve, the yoke that lined up with his waist was uncomfortably at the same level as her chest. And lowering the yoke to the level of Genevieve's waist meant that it fell uncomfortably across his groin. The weight of the cart and the resistance it added to the chain and the yoke made it impossible for them to ignore that this whole scenario was physically problematic.

They struggled to keep the cart moving in a straight line, fighting each other over the positioning of the yoke while nearly completely ignoring the field in front of them. Long before they reached the opposite end of the field, they had discovered two things—that the wheels of the cart rolled much more easily when they were straightly aligned with the rows and that keeping the wheels aligned with the rows was a nearly impossible task.

"Can we trade with you guys?" Genevieve asked, already feeling spent and frustrated as they came to a stop at the far end of the field.

"Fine by me," Matt responded, turning to Crystal for approval.

"Yeah, whatever," she said. "It would be tough to do any worse than what we just experienced, right?"

"I guess we'll find out soon enough," Matt said, obviously trying to offer a more diplomatic response to Ephraim and Genevieve's performance.

After repositioning the cart for the return trip, Matt and Crystal took up the yoke, and Ephraim and Genevieve were happy to move to the back.

"Maybe it can be worse," Crystal said, unkindly pointing and giggling at the other human-powered cart which had not yet made it halfway across the field.

"Let's see what you got," Ephraim said. "Bittah shern."

The cart lunged forward but struggled much the same as before. When Ephraim laughed, Crystal glanced backward with a dirty look before pushing harder against the yoke, which only caused the cart to run farther off course, bouncing over several rows of dirt before coming to a stop in the middle of the field.

"You're not even trying," she said loudly, turning her frustration on Matt.

He forced a smile. "I'm sorry. You were pushing so hard, I was having trouble keeping up."

Genevieve and Ephraim slumped behind the hoppers, trying to hide their smiles, but their action was ill timed. The cart took off again and then stopped abruptly, causing both of them to hit their foreheads on the hoppers in front of them. Genevieve cursed loudly, which only caused the stunned Ephraim to laugh even more. She was about to karate chop the hopper, but then she noticed something she hadn't seen before. The writing was subtle and difficult to see, but it was there. She turned to Ephraim and saw that he too had just discovered some writing on the hopper in front of him.

"What does yours say?" she asked as the cart lunged forward.

He struggled to read it as the cart bounced. "I think it says 'Eat cabbage on anchovies and…buy another cup.'" He looked up. "Does that make any sense to you?"

"No!" she laughed. "Not at all. How hard did you hit your head?"

"Hard!" he said, rubbing his forehead. "What does yours say?"

She looked down at the bouncy inscription, trying to read it. "'Correction does much, but encouragement does more.' Goethe. That makes way more sense. What does yours say again?"

"It says, uh…" But he couldn't read it, the hopper bouncing too much as they rolled on, way off course.

"Let me see," she said, trading places with him. She peered more closely, focusing until the words became clear. "'Encourage one another and build each other up,'" she read slowly. "Thessalonians 5:12."

Ephraim nodded. "That's a relief."

"What is?"

"Well, cabbage gives me gas, and I absolutely hate anchovies."

"Thanks for the warning," she replied with a smile, but she looked confused. "What do you think this means?"

"I don't know," he responded. He pointed to the common word that had been etched into each of their hoppers. "Encourage. Maybe that's part of our job, too." She looked forward, watching as Matt and Crystal continued to struggle to get the cart lined up with the rows. "How are we supposed to encourage them when they suck so bad?"

Ephraim tried not to laugh. "We weren't much better."

"Yeah, so?"

"So, it would have been nice to hear some encouragement rather than a snarky comment, right?"

"I guess so, but…"

He looked behind them at the tracks they were leaving in the field. "We've got nothing to lose, right?"

She shrugged.

Ephraim nodded, looking thoughtful as he trudged behind the bouncing cart. "Come on, guys! You're doing great!" he yelled out over the top of the hopper.

Crystal glanced back, shaking her head before extending her hand above her shoulder, her vertical middle finger waving the internationally recognizable one-finger salute.

Genevieve laughed at Ephraim's dejected face, but he didn't give up.

"Okay, so maybe *great* is too strong a word," he responded. "But, hey, you're doing good! We're moving in the right direction—mostly."

Crystal shook her head, but they could both tell that she was smiling.

"We're almost to the other side, and then you can encourage us with whatever words you want. Come on! Come on!" he continued.

They rolled to a stop at the edge of the woods, a good ten paces down the field from where they would have landed had they gone straight. Josh and Holly, who had been steering the cart behind the horses, rolled in just seconds later, finishing their third lap.

"We're never going to get this field planted," Josh declared, looking at the zigzag lines they'd left in the dirt.

"Not at this rate," Crystal added, looking tired and depressed.

"Okay, Johnny Raincloud and Debby Downer! We're just practicing, right? This is supposed to be fun, isn't it?" Ephraim responded, obviously trying to be positive and obviously annoying everyone with his unbridled optimism.

They all looked at him like he was nuts. The distant sound of someone cussing turned their attention to the last cart, which had just begun the return trip from the other side of the field.

"I've got an idea," Ephraim said, sounding way too happy.

"Does it involve a tractor?" Genevieve asked.

He shook his head.

"How about an ice pick? Or maybe a shotgun?" Crystal whined.

He laughed. "No. I was thinking maybe we could try an experiment."

"What kind of experiment?" Crystal asked impatiently.

"Did you notice the words that were written on the hoppers?"

"What words?" asked Holly.

"These words right here," he pointed, reading each of the sayings again so they all could hear.

"I don't think ours says anything," Josh responded, walking back to take a closer look. "Hey, there actually is something here." He rubbed his finger across the dusty etching as the others gathered around him. "This one says…'Be the change you wish to see in the world.' And this one says, 'By encouraging the best in others, we discover the best in ourselves.'"

Ephraim nodded. "I was thinking that it's pretty easy to pick out what sucked in each of the teams, right?"

"Actually, Abraham and Sarah did pretty well. They were a lot faster than you guys," Holly teased. "We've already done three laps."

"Okay, but they've been working together for years," Crystal said. "And they're two-thousand-pound horses. It's hardly the same thing. Besides, your lines aren't much to brag about."

"Anyway," Ephraim said, stepping between the women, "I'm sure you've noticed that everything we've done here at the farm has centered around a team—around creating a sense of teamwork—working together to get something done, right?"

They all nodded.

He pointed to the words written on the hopper. "Isn't a big part of teamwork about encouraging others on your team?"

Crystal and Holly looked at each other before nodding reluctantly.

"I know we live in a world where we're constantly competing to be the best at everything, but if there are winners, that means there have to be losers."

"What's your point?" Crystal asked.

"My point is that I'm tired of being a loser. I didn't come here to keep being a loser. It may be this bump on my head," he said, lifting back his hair to expose a giant blue goose egg, "but I was thinking we need to enlarge our team."

"What do you mean?" asked Crystal.

"I mean we're all on the same team, right? We have the same goal— to get this stinkin' field planted. We're teamed up with our partners today. But tomorrow those teams will be different, and we'll either be doing the same task or a different one that ultimately benefits all of us, right?"

They all nodded.

"Okay, so let's see what a little encouragement can do."

"What did you have in mind?" Matt asked.

"I want to see what might happen if we encouraged each other rather than razzing each other about our weaknesses and bad performances."

"I don't know how that could make much difference," Holly responded doubtfully.

Ephraim shrugged. "There's only one way to find out." He turned his focus to the cart still struggling on the field. The line it was leaving in the dirt was even more crooked than the rest. "Follow my lead," he said as he cupped his hands to his mouth. "Come on, guys, you can do it!" he yelled loudly.

Matt followed, yelling out across the field. "Come on! You're getting closer."

Holly rose to the challenge, joining her voice with the others. "You're almost here."

The others joined in, and to their united surprise, the struggling cart began to right itself, the team on the back echoing the encouragement as Sonja and Greg struggled at the yoke. Even from this distance, the group could see smiles forming on the pair's faces as the encouragement and enthusiasm became contagious. And what surprised everyone even more was that Sonja and Greg's line became straighter and their speed faster as encouraging words flew from both directions.

There was a loud roar as the cart came to a rest next to the others. High fives and hugs were given and received, and everyone shared in the small yet joyful triumph.

"I thought we were going to die out there," Sonja said, leaning on Greg for support.

"So did I," Greg admitted. "You guys were so much faster. How did you figure it out?"

They all turned to Ephraim, who pointed to the goose egg on his forehead. "I found something when I hit my head. We both did," he responded, turning to Genevieve.

"Ruby keeps saying the writing's on the wall, right?" Genevieve offered. "I thought that was just an expression at first, but maybe it would make more sense to look for that writing in the beginning so we don't have to waste so much time."

Sonja nodded. "You're referring to what's written on the yokes?"

They all looked at her funny.

"Do you mean the B1 from yesterday?" Matt asked.

"Yeah, that too, but I just noticed a minute ago that there was something different on the yoke we're using today."

"I didn't see anything," Holly said.

Sonja laughed, leading the others to the cart that had just been dragged in. She lifted the yoke so they could all see before reading it.

"'Head, heart, hands.' I was concentrating so hard on trying to go straight that I didn't see it until just a minute ago."

Greg looked over everyone's shoulders. "That's interesting," he said thoughtfully.

They all turned to him.

"You know something about this?" Rachael asked.

"I might," Greg replied. "My therapist calls it the cornerstone of her therapy regimen."

"What does it mean?" James asked.

"Well, our heads contain our thoughts and our intellect, right? And our hearts contain most of our emotions and desires. And our hands make it possible to tie everything together with our physical actions. She calls it a holistic approach, and she claims that everything in life works better when those three things are aligned."

Many of them nodded thoughtfully.

"I was just remembering how that was the standard that one of my professors used to apply to every piece of artwork we submitted in our portfolios," Rachael said.

They all turned to her expectantly.

"I think it's from a quote from Saint Francis," she said, looking shy now that all eyes were on her. "It goes something like, 'A person who works with their hands is a laborer. A person who works with their hands and their head is a craftsman. But a person who works with their hands, their head, and their heart is an artist.' My professor was known to trash any work we turned in that didn't exhibit a united consideration of all three."

Matt took hold of the yoke, wiping away the dust that obscured the sharpness of the thoughtful design, all three of the words sharing the same H.

"What are you thinking?" Holly asked.

He looked at her before scanning his eyes over the rest of them. "I was just thinking about the similarities between this and the B1 from yesterday."

They waited for more.

He looked thoughtful for a moment before he spoke. "You realize we're not just planting grain, right?"

Crystal laughed. "I hope not, because we really suck at it."

Matt nodded, looking out at the crooked lines they'd left across the field. "I guess none of us have had a chance to try our hand at each of the chores yet, but it seems like all of the ones I've participated in so far have been designed to help me think differently."

"What do you mean?" James asked.

"You've seen it—there's a pattern to all of the chores. We have to work together. We have to acknowledge our weaknesses. It's not all about strength or speed. Sometimes it's just about endurance, it's about taking the time to figure it out, it's about looking for the hints and details like this one that usually make everything work out so much better. But if we find those hints at all, it's usually not until we're exhausted—until we've made fools of ourselves."

They all nodded.

"Crystal and I really sucked at this," Matt continued, holding up the yoke. "It was almost like we were going in two different directions—not really pulling together." He laid the yoke on the ground before walking to the horses' yoke, where he saw something he hadn't seen before. "I thought that maybe the problem was just that Crystal and I are built so physically different, you know? I'm tall and klutzy. She's shorter and stronger and definitely more graceful. It just seemed like an impossible match."

"Yeah, it obviously is," Crystal responded. "What about it?"

"I guess I was too distracted yesterday to recognize it, but look at the differences in the horses."

They all stood at the rear of the horses and saw what he saw for the first time.

"Wow! They're really different," Holly said. "I didn't see that before."

"I didn't either," James added. "Abraham's at least a good four inches taller, and Sara's backside is substantially wider."

Rachael laughed out loud. "You may not have noticed, but most species have similar differences between the sexes."

James blushed. "As I was struggling with Rachael, I remember thinking it'd be easier if we were both the same size, like the horses who were doing laps around us. But they're at least as physically different as we are."

"Yeah, but that's what the yoke is supposed to do, right?" Genevieve questioned. "Doesn't it make them work together? Isn't that what we all discovered yesterday?"

"Yeah, but if it works for them, why doesn't it work for us? These yokes are smaller, but they're basically the same thing, right?" Rachael asked.

While the rest of them discussed the possible differences between the yokes, Matt walked back to the yoke on the rig he'd been pulling, finding the same branded mark they'd found on the other one. He stepped over the chain attached to the planter cart, and, holding just one side of the yoke, he pulled the chain tight. They all watched as he leaned against the yoke. With the chain pulled taut, applying pressure to just one side was obviously awkward, the yoke wanting to twist out of his hands. He moved, standing in front of the yoke with the chain centered between his hands. He pulled, leaning backward. As he exerted all his strength, the cart rolled forward a few inches before his feet slipped on the loose dirt and he nearly fell.

They all laughed at his failed attempt.

"What are you trying to do?" James asked.

"I'm reminding myself why I came here—why we all did."

They looked at him blankly.

"Isn't this why we're here?" he asked, holding up the yoke. "We're interested in finding someone to share this yoke with, someone who'll help us slog through life, who'll be our partner in facing the joys and challenges of life. If I had to, I might be able to pull this stupid thing across the field by myself, but I've been doing that long enough to know I don't want to—not anymore. I'm tired of being alone."

Genevieve watched as everyone nodded.

"So, what are you going to do about it?" James asked.

Matt looked down again at the yoke. "Well, today I'm going to work on uniting my head, heart, and hands. I don't know if I've ever done that. There's always been at least one of those three that's been afraid to commit. And after I get that figured out, I think I'll start looking for a woman who's trying to live her life the same way—who's looking for someone to be one with."

Crystal nodded slowly. "So, do you want to try this again?"

"Absolutely. Which team wants to give it another try with us?" Matt asked.

"We'll go," Holly said, tapping Josh on the arm.

Together the four turned the cart around and headed out across the field. Unlike during their first time, Matt and Crystal weren't fighting each other. By communicating, they quickly compromised to find a mutually comfortable height at which to hold the yoke as well as a speed that worked with their different leg lengths. Within just a few dozen paces, they were walking a straight line as Holly and Josh cheered them on from behind.

The rest of the campers took courage and quickly got the other rigs back onto the field. To everyone's surprise, they were not only able to stay mostly on course but also to increase their speed with each pass. While the pairs in front focused on the lines they walked and on keeping their yoke partners happy, the pairs behind focused their voices on encouraging those who were towing the weight—not only of their own rig but of the other ones too. What had once felt like a directionless competition quickly changed as they began to recognize their shared objective.

CHAPTER 25

Britches of Shame

You had better live your best and act your best and think your best today; for today is the sure preparation for tomorrow and all the other tomorrows that follow.
– Harriet Martineau –

B y the time the lunch picnic arrived, the campers had all but eliminated the crooked lines they'd made in the field on their first attempts, straight lines flowing once again from forest to forest.

Ruby stood with her hands on her hips, silently watching the work continue as the gentle breeze teased her white hair, her simple housedress and apron fluttering. Genevieve watched from behind the hopper. Ruby looked pleased, almost proud. They parked the carts and gathered in the shade, where the food had been laid out on picnic blankets.

"Good work, kids!" Ruby said, offering them all a generous smile. "You might be ready to start planting."

"Nooo," Pops responded. "Nobody's ever planted on the first Thursday."

"I think these kids may be an exception," said Ruby, pointing to the field.

He looked it over from one end to the other and turned back, looking very surprised. "What will we do if we finish our work early?"

"We'll go have some fun," Ruby responded.

"When do you normally plant?" James asked.

"Ideally, we always try to get the grain in this first week, but there are often delays. Sometimes because of rain or snow or troubles with the kids, we don't get the work done until the beginning of the third week," Pops reported.

"What kinds of troubles?" Sonja asked.

"Oh, all sorts of troubles. Mostly not getting along. Not figuring it out. You wouldn't believe the messes we've had out here—kids driving the planters into ditches, getting into fights, scaring the horses."

"And don't forget the time a couple of the teams decided to have a chariot race and ended up in the woods with a couple broken bones and stitches," Ruby reminded him.

He shook his head. "That was a bad year—same year as that fist fight, right?"

"Between a couple of the guys?" Matt asked, looking surprised.

"No. It was actually between a couple of the girls—jealousy, as I recall."

"Those were the same girls who nearly burned the bunkhouse down," Ruby added. "I've never been so close to sending anybody home."

"So, what did you do?" Holly asked.

Pops laughed out loud. "We talked it over, and Mom came up with a plan. As I recall, it was called Operation Britches of Shame."

"Sounds bad," Crystal responded.

"Oh, it wasn't terrible. Mom dug out a pair of her uncle's old overalls and performed a little fashion magic, sewing on a couple of extra legs. The girls had to spend all their free time looking like conjoined twins until they figured it out."

They all laughed.

"How long did that last?" Matt asked.

"It only took them two days. They figured out they had more in common than just an interest in olive-skinned business types. They married brothers, didn't they?" Pops asked, turning to Ruby for help.

"Twins. We got a Christmas card from both of them last year. They're both grandmas now."

"That's right! Patty and Jill, wasn't it?" he asked, looking uncertain.

"No, Peggy and Jane," Ruby corrected. "When you have more than six hundred kids, it's hard to keep them all straight. Somehow they all get married off, though, even the brawlers and the troublemakers. This farm has a way of calming people down and settin' 'em on a different path."

As they ate, Ruby asked how they'd figured out how to make the planters work. Ephraim and Genevieve explained how they'd discovered the writing on the wall, Ephraim showing his goose egg like a badge of honor. Sonja and Greg talked about the head, heart and hands, explaining the meaning they'd discerned to Spencer and Susan, who'd spent the morning baking bread and had missed out on all the fun in the fields.

Before Spencer and Susan went back to the house to start working on dinner, everyone watched as the pair took the helm of one of the planters. With Matt and Crystal on the back end shouting encouragement, everyone was smiling as Spencer and Susan drove the cart nearly straight across the field. The rest of the family hitched up and joined them for the second lap. Even Holly and Josh, who were without a cart, ran alongside them all and shared encouraging words. They even made Genevieve smile when they complimented her on the way she made her overalls look so sassy.

"I think we've had a change of plans," Pops said when they all returned. "We've never done this before, but you guys have impressed us with your ability to work together. We think you're ready to plant seed."

They all looked at each other, sharing a look of surprise and excitement.

"It often takes a full day to seed this field with three planters, but at the rate you kids are working, it's feasible this could be accomplished by dinnertime. Mom and I have just been talking. How would you feel if we unhitched Abraham and Sarah, got you started, and left Spencer and Susan to fill out the last team?"

"Who'd cook dinner?" Susan asked.

"We would," Pops said, taking Ruby's hand.

"You think we can do this without supervision?" Matt asked, looking uncertain.

"We'll stick around for the first few laps, but yeah, we do."

"So, what will we do tomorrow and Saturday if we finish today?" Sonja asked.

"Well, we'll still have chores. Those never go away," Ruby said. "But if we get our work done, you can enjoy some free time. Or we could hitch up the wagon and go down to the river if you want. You get to decide. I think we told you the first day you arrived that we don't dictate how you spend your free time. We only ask that you use it to make your world a little better, and a good dose of recreatin' definitely fits the bill."

"Hey, we could visit that pudding-mold museum that we saw on Sunday," James suggested.

"I think I'd rather take a nap," Genevieve responded.

"Whatever you want. It's all up to you," Pops said. "Now, let's get this field planted."

Pops took the men to the barn to bring out the heavy bags of grain; Ruby marked the divisions on the field for the different types of grain; and the women turned the carts, staging them at intervals down the field. With everybody working together, preparations went very quickly. Creating a single-file human chain, they walked across the field and back again, producing two easily discernible lines that would separate the different grains from each other. They returned back to the carts and filled each hopper with the grain indicated—wheat, oats, or rye. And then, with Ruby and Pops standing next to their horses, the group headed out, more united than any group of campers had ever been on their first Thursday.

After setting the horses free in their pasture, Ruby and Lorenzo stayed and watched, amazed by the teamwork that was set in motion, each planter rotating without its drivers waiting to be told what to do. They could hear the campers' cries of encouragement across the field, and the couple smiled at one another, Ruby looking up at her husband, who was nearly a full head taller.

"This is the one we've been waiting for, isn't it?" Pops asked.

"I think it might be. But time will tell."

They wandered back through the woods to the big house, feeling grateful for another year, another batch of kids, another round of hope for the future.

CHAPTER 26

The Debut

Two are better than one; because they have a good reward for their labor. For if they fall, the one will lift up his fellow: but woe to him that is alone when he falleth; for he hath not another to help him up.
– Ecclesiastes 4:9–10 –

The woods around the field were casting long shadows across the dappled rows by the time the campers were finished with the planting. Ruby and Pops had come to watch after they'd finished with dinner preparations, and they were surprised to find that the enthusiasm among the campers was still going strong. Sitting on a bench that overlooked the field, they watched as the first campers in their long history on the farm planted grain on their first Thursday. They wondered aloud if the promise of a little free time had been the impetus for the unique behavior or if the hidden truths the kids had discovered much faster than previous groups had enabled them to see the bigger picture.

They watched with enjoyment as the campers encouraged each other, collectively extending the stamina and endurance beyond anything the two of them had ever witnessed. And from what they could tell, there was nary a shirker among them.

Dirty, blistered, but somehow still simmering, if not bubbling, with enthusiasm, the campers returned the planters to the barn before heading back to the big house, somehow looking more united than most campers were at the end of the summer. The water in the sink ran dark like chocolate milk as they washed up, and they laughed at each other as they pointed out the lines of dust and sweat that encrusted their faces.

After grace was said, the six chicken potpies Ruby and Pops had made were ravenously devoured within minutes in the dimly lit dining hall. Everyone seemed more anxious to get showered and into bed than to be distracted by talk. The evening chores were quickly divided, one group heading out to take down the laundry and another to take care of the cows. The rest stayed to help Spencer and Susan with the dishes and kitchen cleanup. Ruby decided that the interviews she'd scheduled with Rachael and Josh would be postponed until after breakfast the next morning.

Though the shower ran cold when she still had shampoo in her hair, Genevieve hardly noticed, the cold water feeling good on her aching shoulders and feet and on her sunburned arms. Being the last to shower, she found the bunkhouse silent after she braided her hair, everyone asleep except Holly, the youngest, who was apparently more interested in writing in her journal.

Despite her physical fatigue, Genevieve couldn't sleep. She stared up through the skylight at the growing number of stars as she considered the events of the day. She wished she'd been wearing her Fitbit to track what she knew had been at least forty thousand steps. But for the first time in recent memory, the thought of posting the number of steps she'd walked on social media seemed somehow less than important. She had accomplished something—something real. Those steps hadn't been made on a treadmill in a gym while she mindlessly watched CNN or listened to one of her favorite podcasts. They'd been made while she was actually doing something—turning her physical strength into clean laundry and a field of grain that would someday be made into bread.

As she considered this, she realized that even if she had the ability to post how many calories she'd burned, no one in her social media circle could possibly understand or appreciate any portion of the day's activities. How would she describe doing laundry with a bicycle, or taking the place of a team of horses, or even playing cheerleader while pushing an oversized shopping cart over a bumpy field? There was nothing in any of that to brag about—no accomplishment that anyone would understand. It was work. Dirty, hard work. And despite the fact that her nails only retained a small amount of the bright red polish she'd arrived here with, she couldn't deny the strange sense of accomplishment she felt at having exercised every single muscle in her entire body.

But even with that sense of accomplishment still vibrating in every cell of her body, it all fell apart when she realized where she'd be if she hadn't come here. The glitz and glamour of Brussels Fashion Days, showcasing the latest and most opulent in high fashion, was such a sharp contrast to all that surrounded her here that she found the feelings of anger once again bubbling up inside her. She closed her eyes, trying to imagine all that she was missing, and fell asleep with the imagined scents of expensive perfumes somehow drowning out the unsavory smells of the farm.

Next thing she knew, she was waiting backstage for her turn to walk down the runway. The French avant-garde designer, whose name she couldn't quite pronounce, had met her at a cocktail party the night before and, after complimenting her on her rare physique and beauty, had invited her to be his model. It was all she could have dreamed of, playing princess on an international stage while fashionistas and paparazzi from around the globe indulged in this feast for the eyes.

She looked down, checking her dress one more time, and was shocked to find that this wasn't the dress she'd donned in the dressing room. Frantic, and with just seconds to go before her international modeling debut, she looked into the full-length mirror, wondering how this possibly could have happened. The dress, hideous blue satin with impossibly big shoulder pads, bulged in all the wrong places. Her hair was done up in a messy bun, but it could hardly be seen because of the enormous blue satin wrap that was piled up on top of her head, making it look like she was trying to balance a yoga ball. Turning to look at the giant satin bow on her backside, she noticed the dress's slit. It went far too high and exposed legs that looked as though they hadn't been shaved in years.

"Miss Patterson, the stage is yours," said a short man dressed in an English butler's uniform. He pulled back the curtain. Panicked, she forced a smile and peered out onto the runway, trying to guess how many steps she might take before she'd be back. With her very first step, however, she realized that she really should have paid more attention to her shoes. The walk was short, her mismatched shoes—one stiletto, one flat—making it very difficult to balance. And before she had made it even halfway down the runway, a twist of an ankle sent her flying into the audience to the uproarious laughter of everyone present.

She sat up, feeling embarrassed. She gathered the hideous dress around her, the laughter continuing unsympathetically. "This isn't the way it's supposed to go!" she yelled.

Again, there was laughter.

"How is it supposed to go?" Susan asked.

Genevieve opened her eyes, but she couldn't make sense of anything she saw. Her quilt was wrapped around her tightly, making her feel claustrophobic, and she fought with it, trying to free herself.

"Are you okay?" Holly asked.

Genevieve glanced around the room. All of the women were watching her, looking worried or amused—or both.

"Are you okay?" Holly repeated, kneeling down to help free her from her quilt.

"I'm...I've never been so glad not to be in Brussels."

"Yeah, I feel the same way," Sonja said, looking amused. "Tell us about your dream."

While it was still fresh, Genevieve recited the dream to the women, as they all got dressed for the day, the laughter growing as each detail was added. The men, including Pops, were all waiting outside the women's bunkhouse door and listening to the laughter inside. Of course laughter like that has to be explained, and by the time they'd finished their morning chores, the whole family had heard the story and shared in the laughter.

Crystal and James served breakfast—oatmeal with honey, and a generous side of scrambled eggs. When he'd finished his breakfast, Pops stood at the end of the table and announced that while Mom conducted her interviews, the rest of the morning could be used for free time. He listed many possibilities, including reading, journaling, napping, playing, and cycling. Crystal and James, as the day's KP staff, would be baking bread as well as working on a Crock-Pot dinner that the family would be able to enjoy later without too much preparation. And he announced that for anyone who was interested, the pickup truck along with the hay wagon would be leaving at one o'clock for a jaunt to the river, where they could swim, relax, or try their hand at the bungee board—the invention of a couple of the campers a few years back.

Genevieve was more interested in spending the day napping and relaxing in the bunkhouse, but when it was clear that everyone else was planning on heading to the river, she reluctantly decided to join them even though the closest thing she had to a swimsuit was a pair of cutoffs and a T-shirt.

After breakfast, the campers scattered, some to the music room, others to the pond. On her way to the bunkhouse to rest, Genevieve noticed Matt, his journal under his arm, heading down a path she'd never walked before. Curiosity overcame her. She hurried into the bunkhouse for her own journal and followed after him, giving him enough space to avoid letting him know he was being followed.

The path meandered through the woods, and Genevieve fell back when she realized she couldn't follow closely without the sounds of crunching leaves alerting Matt. But after a hundred yards, the woods eventually opened to another field that looked like it had been planted at least a month earlier, the tall green growth just beginning to show signs of grain heads.

She stopped for a moment and watched the color of the field undulate as the grain moved with the breeze—like an ocean of soft greens and blues. Mesmerized by the magic, she might have forgotten what she was doing if she hadn't heard the distant sound of Matt's whistling, mimicking the call of a songbird. Not wanting to lose him, she picked up the pace, following him around the edge of the field until he stopped at a bench that stood in the shadows of a sprawling oak.

Even from a distance, she could see that his eyes were closed, and she considered leaving him alone, not wanting to interrupt him. But then she remembered why she was there, why she'd come to the farm in the first place. There was a story here, and she needed to figure out exactly what it was.

As stealthily as she could, she closed the gap, quietly sitting down on the opposite end of the bench. When he didn't move for over a minute, she touched him lightly on the arm.

"Are you okay?" she asked.

He opened his eyes, looking a bit startled. He looked at her, obviously surprised. "Yeah, I'm fine. Just enjoying the sounds of nature."

She nodded, sitting back against the bench.

"What are you doing here?" he asked bluntly.

"Oh…I was just exploring the farm and saw you sitting here. Why are you here?"

"I was just looking for a place to think."

She nodded, looking out at the field. "What are you thinking about?"

"I was just reminded of an experience I had last summer in the Tibetan foothills."

"Really? Why'd you go there?"

He turned his body to face her. "I spent a month there with Dentists Without Borders."

"Was it amazing? I've always wanted to go there," she lied.

"Really?" he asked, looking very surprised. "Why?"

"It just sounds so exotic."

"Hmm. No offense, but you don't strike me as the exotic sort of gal."

"Is that right?" she asked, looking offended. "What kind of *gal* do I strike you as?"

He looked away, obviously worried that he'd already said too much.

"I'm serious," Genevieve pressed.

He smiled but shook his head. "You definitely don't strike me as the kind of gal who'd venture off to Tibet."

"Why not?" she asked, looking offended again. "I go on adventures."

"Yeah, to Europe maybe. But I wouldn't expect a girl like you to know the difference between Tibet and Timbuktu."

She wasn't sure if she did, but she didn't want him to know that. "A girl like me…what the hell is that supposed to mean?"

He shrugged. "I've been wrong many times before, but that's just the way it looks. You strike me as more of an *indoor girl*—a tourist, not an explorer."

"Well, you'd be surprised," she lied again. "You didn't strike me as such a judgmental jerk, but it's nice to see your true colors before we have to spend any more time together."

"Funny you should say that. Aren't we supposed to work together tomorrow?"

She looked away, realizing he was right.

"Look, I'm sorry. I didn't mean to offend you. I was just surprised that Tibet was even on your map, that's all. It's not exactly a destination for people like you."

She looked at him and shook her head. "People like me? Unbelievable! You don't even know me! You have no idea who I am. How can you tell what kind of person I am if you've never spent any time with me? It's no wonder you're still single."

He laughed, looking sincerely amused, which only made her more angry. "You wouldn't last ten minutes in Tibet. Stay home. It's safer there, and you won't have to worry about your nails or your hair or where to go shopping. Paris, Milan, Monte Carlo, maybe Berlin—those would be a better choice for you."

It was hard to argue. He had her pegged, but she still wanted to poke his eyes out with what was left of her fingernails.

"Relax," he said, reaching out to touch her on the shoulder, which she avoided by leaning out beyond the far end of the bench. He smiled again, but it wasn't a haughty smile. He looked out at the field and shook his head.

"What?" she asked.

"I'm sorry. I didn't mean to offend you. I guess I'm just trying to figure you out."

"Really? So you call me an indoor girl?"

"Am I wrong?"

She scowled.

"Tell me I'm wrong, and I'll take it all back."

"You're wrong!"

He smiled a rather charming smile. Nearly a full week's worth of stubble on his ruggedly handsome face showed the first signs of gray. "Why are you here?"

"Excuse me?"

"You heard me. Why are you here?"

"The same reason you are," she lied again.

"Really?"

"Quit acting like you doubt everything I say."

"Okay, give me the real answer, and I will."

"What are you talking about?"

"Genevieve, I overheard your interview with Ruby."

"You what?"

"Yeah. I was in the music room. I'm sure I didn't hear everything, but it's obvious that you're here for a very different reason than I am—than the rest of us are. Your whole temperament is different. You've got this pissy little attitude that makes you look like you think you're better than everyone else. The rest of us are grateful to be here, but you…you act like you can't wait to get out of here. What's eating your yak?"

"What's eating my what?"

"What's eating your yak?" he asked again, smiling this time. "It's a Tibetan saying. It means 'what's your beef?' So, what's your problem?"

She shook her head, not wanting to get into this and knowing full well that she shouldn't. "It's personal."

"Oh, I'm sure it is."

"What's that supposed to mean?"

"Look, eleven of us are here this summer for the purpose of getting ready for marriage. We want to be here. We're opening up. We're taking risks. We're allowing ourselves to be vulnerable. And then there's you. You show up unprepared. You haven't read the contract. You avoid sharing anything personal. Your heart's not really in it. You act like a poseur, a fraud. I'm just trying to figure you out—trying to figure out why you'd torture yourself by spending a summer on a farm that you obviously hate. I'll freely admit that I'm slow about many things, but I'm not stupid. I'd call you a spy, but Ruby seems to know what's going on and hasn't outed you yet. I'm just trying to figure out why."

Genevieve took a big breath and let out a week's worth of air, feeling desperate. She turned and looked at him and was glad to find no evidence of malice in his eyes. His questions, she knew, were fair. He was obviously observant, and she doubted she would be able to create a story on the spot—at least not one that he'd believe. With resignation, she turned back to the field, feeling defeated. "Okay, you got me."

"What does that mean?"

"It means I'm…I'm a poseur."

"Why?"

She looked uncomfortable "Will you promise not to tell the others?"

"I don't know if I can promise that."

"Fine. I don't care if you do. Maybe I'll get kicked out and everything will be better."

"What's that supposed to mean?"

She took a deep breath before letting it all come out at once as if it had been under pressure. "I'm a writer. I work for a women's magazine that's been trying to score an interview with Ruby for twenty years. I came out here thinking the interview would last a day—maybe two, tops. I'm not even sure how it happened, but somehow I got conned into…into this," she said, motioning to her overalls and rubber boots.

"You're supposed to be in Brussels at a fashion show?"

She looked at him, surprised. "How did you know?"

He nodded, offering her a kind smile. "That's what your dream was about, wasn't it?"

"What did you hear?"

"Only what you told the girls this morning—only what Sonja shared with me while we worked on the laundry. It was a good laugh. Thank you."

She forced a smile, but there was something more that he wasn't saying. "What else?"

"Have you ever had a tooth pulled or a cavity filled and experienced nitrous oxide?"

"Maybe when I was a kid. Why?" she asked, wondering where this was going.

"I've noticed that my patients—my patients who live in industrialized countries where such luxuries are available, I should say—I've noticed that they often come out of their procedures having had vivid dreams. Sometimes they're laughing. Sometimes they're crying. I don't claim to know how to interpret dreams, but when Susan told me what you'd told the girls this morning, I knew you were in conflict with yourself."

She looked surprised.

"Look, when my patients started sharing their dreams with me, I spent a few years studying the psychology behind dreams. Very few of the things we dream about are ex nihilo—out of nothing. What we go to bed thinking about often plays a role in our dreams whether we want it to or not. There's something there in that dream of yours that you ought to examine a little closer."

"Like what?" she asked, looking concerned.

"Well, off the top of my head, like why you were dressed the way you were. Like why your shoes didn't match. Like why you fell off the runway. You're a poseur. You've put on a costume, but it's obvious that you're not being truthful to yourself or anyone else."

She looked surprised. "Okay, so if you're so smart, what would you tell me that my dreams meant if I said I was being chased by pterodactyls?"

He thought for a moment. "I'd say you're worried about living a lie and you're afraid you're going to get caught."

"Wait, you got that out of pterodactyls?" she asked, looking completely shocked.

He laughed. "No, I don't know anything about pterodactyls. You're probably just afraid of birds…maybe…roosters?"

"Oh my gosh, I hate that stupid bird," she admitted. "I tried to kill it the first morning I was here. I think I actually grazed it with my shoe."

He nodded slowly, thoughtfully. "It wouldn't be that shoe on top of the fence post, would it?"

"You know about that?"

"No, but it seems to have figured into your dream, right? No wonder you were off balance. You couldn't find the right shoe."

She looked incredulous, nervous. She was grateful she hadn't mentioned her dream about Johnny Depp to anyone. "So, what are you going to do?"

"It depends on what you're going to do. It's not fair for the rest of us to be baring our souls if you're just sitting in the corner taking notes and giving it a half-assed effort."

She shook her head, looking worried. "I promised Ruby I wouldn't tell anybody about this. I was just supposed to go along with everything, you know—fit in. It's maddening. I don't fit in. I'm not interested in getting married. I don't belong on a freakin' farm. Maybe it would just be better if you told everyone so she'd kick me out."

"Why haven't you left already?"

"Because my job is riding on this interview—my job, my apartment, my travels. They have my freakin' cat! Oh my gawwwd, I hope they're feeding her. I didn't realize it before, but my whole life might literally revolve around this job."

"Then it sounds like you better figure this out."

She leaned over, bouncing her forehead slowly on the top of the back of the bench.

He stopped her. "So, I'm just guessing, but that's probably not going to help."

"You have a better idea?"

"Yeah. Put your heart into this. Stop giving it a half ass," he laughed. "Decide right now to start giving it the full ass."

She smirked. "I don't know if I have it in me."

"Then give up now. Go home to your cat. I don't really care what you do, but I don't think it's fair for you to ruin this experience for the rest of us. You need to quit being a poseur and go one way or the other, but you can't keep doing what you're doing. You're really bad at it, and everyone's going to catch on."

"Wait! Has anyone else said anything?"

"You mean besides the fact that you're difficult to work with."

"What? Who said that?"

"Every one of the guys. We may all be slow in our own ways, but we're not blind, Genevieve. When you're throwing in your whole heart and someone else tosses in a half ass, you notice. There's a huge difference. Look at the way Holly jumps in. Her heart's totally in this."

"Holly's twenty-two years old."

"And I'm forty-three. Your age is no excuse."

She shook her head. "So why are you doing this?"

"This?" he asked, motioning between the two of them. "Or this?" he motioned much bigger, as if to include the whole farm.

"Both, I guess."

"Because I'm tired of living my life alone. Because I'm tired of pretending."

"What do you mean?"

He let out a long breath, and when he spoke, she noticed that all of the confidence she had seen in him since the beginning seemed to be all but gone. "I'm tired of roaming around the world pretending that I'm happy, pretending I don't want to be tied down to a home and a family. I'm tired of not being honest with myself. It's taken me a long time to get here, but as hard as I've fought it, I can't get a picture out of my head."

"What picture are you talking about?"

He smiled, glancing at her sideways. "I suppose it's more of a dream…not as strange as pterodactyls or mismatched shoes, but it's this picture in my head of me sitting down with my family on a Sunday afternoon and talking and laughing with my wife and kids."

His words surprised her. "Sounds like a Norman Rockwell painting."

He smirked and nodded. "It's the ideal American family, right?"

She nodded. "Do you think such a thing still exists?"

"I don't know, but I want to believe it does. I want to believe I can find it."

"Do you think other single guys want the same thing?"

"Oh, we may not admit it, but I'm pretty much convinced that we all do."

"Why do you say that?"

"It's hard to generalize all the men of the world, but this last November and December, I was doing dental work at a Buddhist monastery just outside of Kathmandu. I became friends with one of the monks there—Bruce."

"That doesn't sound like a Buddhist name."

"Yeah, well, it was the English name he chose for himself. Bruce

Lee. Real creative, right? His English was really good, and he took it upon himself to serve as my interpreter. We spent a lot of time together. I had always had this romanticized idea of spending my time contemplating the meaning of life and having great philosophical and spiritual conversations. But it was a lot different from how I imagined it would be."

"In what way?"

"I guess it just opened my eyes to the loneliness of monastic life. A lot of the young men were there because they had nowhere else to go—no money for marriage or business or education. The reality of being surrounded by men twenty-four hours a day, 365 days a year—I realized very quickly that it's totally overrated."

"Did Bruce like it?"

Matt shook his head. "How could he? It was depressing. He was one who didn't feel like he had any other options—other than a ragged life of poverty."

"But isn't monastic life a life of poverty anyway?"

"Sure, but at least at the monastery he had two meals a day. It's tough enough to live in poverty, but no one wants to live a life without love. His only hope was that if he lived a life of service, the gods would grant him a better life in his next incarnation."

Genevieve shook her head. "Sounds hopeless."

"Yeah. I felt the same way. Of all the things I've seen and all the people I've met over the miles and years, Bruce made me think more about where my life was going than anyone else."

"How so?"

Matt looked out at the field for a moment before responding. "I don't think I'll ever forget this one crazy-cold night as I lay nearly freezing to death on a bamboo mat in that old monastery. I found myself thinking about the hope of love. For Bruce, because of his dire poverty and lack of opportunity, he believed love would always stay beyond his reach. And yet the yearning for it was still there. It made me take a hard look at what I'd been doing for the last twenty years. Unlike Bruce, I had a long list of possibilities, things that I could do, places I could go. I had chosen the life I had because it was mostly uncomplicated and generally exciting, or at least it had been until I really took a close look at it. I've tried to live a good life—tried to use my talents and education to help other people around the world. But I realized that a lot of my choices have been made mostly out of avoidance."

Genevieve looked confused.

"I justified not getting married because I've had this notion that it will get in the way of me being useful to society. I somehow talked myself into believing I was living some higher cause. And I'm sure I was probably self-righteous about it. But being there in Nepal, surrounded by men—men who, if given different circumstances and opportunities in life, would choose to marry and have children and dream bigger dreams..."

He shook his head. "I guess it made me realize that I've basically been living a monastic life for most of the last twenty years. And I'm not any smarter or wiser than I was when I was twenty-six and first embarking on this crazy journey to try and figure out who I was. Coming to that realization—that I'd lost the last twenty years of my life and was no closer to figuring anything out—really made me want to do something different.

"I guess the clincher for me was bumping into an old classmate from dental school at the airport in Atlanta on my way home from Nepal." Matt smiled and shook his head at the memory. "He was this goofy kid from Idaho—the only one of my classmates who showed up to dental school with a wife. He was the only one to graduate with kids—at least any legitimate ones. And there he was with his wife of twenty-five years, heading off to visit their first grandchild."

"Seriously?"

"Yep! Forty-eight years old and a grandpa. There's nothing like bumping into a reality like that to make you feel like you've missed a big part of what life is all about."

"That looked appealing to you?" she asked, trying not to sound too incredulous.

"Parts of it, yeah. It was hard not to be jealous. I mean he was still a goofy kid from Idaho, but he'd somehow grown into his goofiness. His wife was better looking than I remembered, and she looked really happy. He had a flourishing practice—working four days a week—and was pretty much finished raising his four kids. I've thought about him at least a hundred times since then. Somehow he's living the life I've only dreamed of."

"Don't you think he might have been jealous of all your adventures?"

"Maybe, but he still has plenty of time to do all of that, right? Plus he has a wife and kids to share his life with. I remember thinking when I was in my twenties that forty sounded ancient. But now that I'm here, recognizing that I spent the most energy-filled years of my life pursuing adventures instead of family, I feel like I did it all backward. I know they say that comparison is the thief of joy, but as I sat there looking at the joy my old classmate has in his life, I realized that this is the kind of joy I'd always wanted. I was just too afraid to chase after it—to commit to it. He could have great-grandkids before my kids even graduate from high school. I guess it made me panic a little bit, realizing how much time I've lost and how narrow my window of opportunity is to attempt to do something about it."

"So, even with your limited time, you signed up to spend a whole summer here?"

He nodded. "I worried about that too. But I spoke to a couple who had been matched by Ruby, and it seemed like the best way to go. I didn't feel like I had any time to waste on nonsense. I decided I wanted to enter a marriage without any debt, so I got a job working for a dentist in Little Rock so I could finally pay off my student loans. I started asking around about dating services and found out that my boss's brother got matched by Ruby. The whole family had nothing but good things to say about his experience. I feel really lucky to have gotten in on my first time applying. Did you know Greg applied three years in a row before he finally got in? That would have killed me. I guess I must have sounded desperate enough in my essay for them to take pity on me."

Genevieve nodded somberly but said nothing.

"I've got a lot riding on this. We all do. If this doesn't work out for me…" He shook his head. "The thought of being a bachelor dentist for the rest of my life feels…hopeless."

He turned and looked at her to make sure she was listening. "Look, I'm anxious to do what I can to make up for lost time. And I'm sorry if it sounds selfish, but I don't want people like you getting in my way. I'm sure your article is important for you, but you have eleven other people here who are looking at this as something that's far more important."

She nodded slowly but didn't look at him.

"You may not want to be here, but here you are, taking the place of hundreds of people who wish they could be here—honest people like me who want to be married but haven't figured it out yet. You have to do what you have to do, but if you stand in the way of the rest of us, if you don't start giving it your heart, you're going to have a lot people who think you're a fraud. I doubt that will do much to help you produce a decent article."

"Okay."

"Okay what?"

"I'll put in more effort. I'll try harder. But can you promise me something?"

"What?"

"Will you promise not to blow my cover? I've worked my whole life to get to this point, and I don't want to watch it all fall apart."

He stretched out his hand to shake hers. "I'll hold my tongue if you follow through, but I think I speak for the rest of us when I say we're not going to let you stand in the way of what we want out of life. Don't ruin this for us. We've been working our whole lives to get here too."

CHAPTER 27

What It's All About

Life should not be a journey to the grave with the intention of arriving safely in a pretty and well preserved body, but rather to skid in broadside in a cloud of smoke, thoroughly used up, totally worn out, and loudly proclaiming "Wow! What a Ride!"

– Hunter S. Thompson –

Matt left Genevieve there on the bench feeling sheepish. She realized she had been so concerned about her job and the life it afforded her that she hadn't given much thought as to how her attitude might be affecting the others. Almost one week in, she knew she had little choice other than to be committed to finishing out the summer. If she wanted her job, she had to stay. If she didn't want her job, she had no home to go home to. She had already considered calling her dad many times, but she knew he wouldn't understand.

As an only child, she hadn't been aware of how spoiled she'd been until her freshman year at college, when she'd had to deal with roommates for the first time in her life. It hadn't been pretty, and it hadn't ended well. A fresh start at Syracuse University for sophomore year had been much the same. The school was a better fit, but she'd had a hard time making friends. Even the surprise birthday party she'd secretly thrown for herself had been a disaster, with only two people out of sixty showing up. She might have taken notes and made some personal changes, but that would have required her to be start being nice. And she wasn't about to change her attitude toward all the ignorant people that surrounded her. A focus on academics was more important anyway.

A handsome donation from her father to the university, in addition to her association with a sorority (though somewhat chilly), scored her some contacts after graduation. But over the next few years, her systematic slashing and burning of a series of bridges helped flip a switch of addiction she'd sworn to herself she'd never allow to be flipped. She couldn't be completely blamed. It came so naturally, almost as though it were in her genes—and it probably was. Friends had been hard to find, but she was a fun drunk and had learned that even a little alcohol made social situations easier for her.

She liked to think she was more like her father when it came to booze. He had been very successful in his career. There had always been money to spare but, in reality, not a lot of love. Her mother had spent most of her life staying busy with Junior League, bridge club, and other society clubs in Boston, but Genevieve had rarely seen her completely sober. Her mother's drinking never seemed to be a problem for her father, who spent increasingly more time away from home as the years passed.

Though their home was big and beautiful and the apartment in Paris was stunning, time spent with her parents had turned into a depressing chore and one that she tended to avoid as much as possible. She made it home for Christmas but not a lot else; her job and life in Manhattan offered an easy excuse to stay away.

But life in the city also had it challenges. In the nearly six years she had been with the magazine, she had already been to Europe eleven times. The trips were fun and glamorous in the beginning, but they had recently begun leaving her wondering about her future. She would be thirty in September. The eight years since she'd left college had passed quickly. And though there was much to be proud of and happy about in her career, she had started to wonder how long that would continue. She had observed that, with the exception of Julia, there weren't many women in her profession who were older than forty. She had already seen many of her colleagues take a "break" to have a family, only to move to the suburbs and never be seen or heard from again.

Julia was a woman who had inspired many to believe they could have it all. After sending the last of her three children to high school, she had come back to take the helm of the magazine when the last editor had retired to spend more time with her grandkids. Julia was strong and passionate and successful. Her husband was supportive and present, which had always impressed Genevieve. She had seen him many times waiting patiently in the lobby for his wife to finish her work for the day. Genevieve had heard from other staff members that he was at least as ardent a feminist as she was; he was always encouraging her to lift her voice in the cause of equality and moral fairness. And it had been rumored that he even occasionally wrote on hot topics for the magazine under the female pseudonym Chelsea Banks, a blending of his grandmothers' names.

Sitting on the bench, overlooking the fields of grain, and being lulled into a sense of calm by the undulating sea of grass, Genevieve considered her own aversion to marriage, which had certainly been shaped by many influences. It had always seemed like the most stable environment for raising children—that is, if the marriage was strong and partners reliable. But marriages like that seemed to be the exception. With divorce as common as it was around the world, she had found it difficult not to be skeptical, if not cynical. And that cynicism only grew when dates and love interests were as few and far between as they had always been for her. It was far easier to be cynical than to dream about marriage or to ask herself probing questions about why she wasn't even dating. She couldn't recall ever feeling the way Holly felt—anxious to be married. But even some of the less enthusiastic desires that had been expressed among the women seemed foreign as well. The idea of being stuck with a dumb, useless man simply seemed so much less enjoyable than spending life as a single, successful career woman. Sure, there would be no one to share her lows with, but there would also be no one to steal her thunder and slow her down. And the last thing she wanted was to be slowed down.

She stood up from the bench and began slowly walking back to the bunkhouse. In some ways it felt nice to be able to share the burden of truth with someone. But as she walked, she also thought about Matt's reasons for coming here. He was different from the men she knew. He wasn't only looking for commitment; he was anxious to commit. He wanted a family. He was far older than anyone she'd be interested in, but he was handsome and educated and thoughtful and probably still had enough life in him to make someone happy. She wondered what role, if any, he might play in her article. She remembered that she'd be working with him tomorrow and began hoping for an opportunity to ask a few questions.

The women had already changed into their swimsuits and were hanging out in their cutoffs and cover-ups by the time Genevieve made it back to the bunkhouse. When asked if she'd be joining them, she admitted she'd somehow forgotten a swimsuit. To her surprise, the women rallied, coming up with several options for her to borrow. She had never borrowed a swimsuit in her entire life, but after her talk with Matt, she could see it would look rude to turn them down. So she settled on a mismatched tankini that seemed to fit just about right.

The men and Pops had just finished rigging up the trailer when Crystal and James returned to their bunkhouses, having finished both lunch and dinner preparations and looking quite ready for an afternoon at the river.

With everyone ready and anxious to experience the river, they unanimously decided to eat lunch at the river so they could leave without delay. Ephraim grabbed the guitar while Pops sent Greg and Spencer to the sports shed to bring out the bungee board and a braided coil of rope along with the bag of Frisbees and assorted Nerf balls. As Pops drove and Ruby rode shotgun, the campers walked to the top of the drive to avoid being scrambled or tossed from the wagon as it passed over the rutted way.

Genevieve paused to look around when they reached the top of the hill. The day was clear and bright with only a few clouds in the sky. There was a lightness in the spirits of the entire group as they climbed aboard the same trailer that had brought them here less than a week before.

As Pops drove slowly down the winding road, the group took turns pointing out things they'd missed on their first ascent up Harmony Hill. As the town of Niederbipp came into view with its charming buildings silhouetted against the surrounding woods, Genevieve listened as many of the group expressed a desire to spend more time exploring their larger surroundings.

The road flattened out soon after the river came into view. They pulled onto the highway but hugged the shoulder, continuing to drive slowly for a mile or so before pulling off the road. They reached a picnic area situated in the shadow of a bridge that spanned the river. Some of the men were in the water before the rest of the group had even unloaded the picnic. The water was cool but refreshing, and at the taunting of the men, a few of the women waded in up to their knees, bracing each other and squealing as the mud oozed between their toes.

To their surprise, they found that the peanut butter and honey they had enjoyed at the farm tasted even better at the river, though lunch was soon forgotten as the serenade of the water called to them. While they swam, they watched Pops walk to the middle of the bridge with the rope and the board. He attached one end of the rope to the guardrail and the other end to the board before tossing the board into the river. Then to everyone's surprise, he did a backflip off the bridge into the river, landing it perfectly.

Pops swam to the board, which had already floated downriver with the current, and he grabbed hold of the rope. The current continued to push him downriver while the bungee rope grew tighter and tighter. They all watched, unsure of what to expect. A moment later, Pops jumped onto the board, changing the angle of resistance by making the board parallel to water. The result was breathtaking. The board, with Pops on it, shot at least a hundred feet upstream, gliding effortlessly over the surface of the water, stopping only when the momentum had been spent. Pops, along with the board, sank below the surface, rising a moment later to the applause of all present. He swam to the shore before bowing to the ladies and curtsying to the men.

"Show-off!" Ruby said, wrapping her arms around him and kissing him on the forehead.

"It's your turn, Mom. Go show those boys how it's done."

"What, and lose my dentures again? No, thanks. I learned my lesson last year. I'm retired from bungee boarding, remember?"

"That's right." He kissed her back.

The men didn't need any encouragement, racing to the board in the water. Spencer was the first to reach it, and the other men backed away, letting him take his turn. The bungee rope stretched out again with the current, and Spencer, anxious to put on a show, jumped onto the board. He stayed on for only a few dozen feet, however, before losing his balance and going down hard, his face leaving a wake across the water before he let go of the rope.

Greg was quick to try next, making it most of the way back to the bridge before going over the front of the board.

Holly beat Josh to go next and made the women proud by not only going the full distance but also waving to everyone on the shore while she did it. Matt gave his best effort and had everyone in stitches as he zoomed past them, the back of his shorts exposing his half-moon. Ephraim kept the laughter flowing without skipping a beat by picking up the guitar and breaking into song with Creedence Clearwater Revival's "Bad Moon Rising."

The men, as is the case with any men around the world when confronted with water and women in swimwear, did their best to show off their athletic prowess by jumping off the bridge over and over again until they were all waterlogged. After drying off on the grass and soaking up some sun, they were at it again, this time with the Nerf balls, and a variety of associated hijinks. But before long the games had somehow morphed, as such games often do, into a belly-flop contest, which all the women agreed was just plain stupid. They refused to participate.

Josh was the clear winner of that contest, not only ending up with the largest percentage of his body looking like a vine-ripened tomato but also knocking the wind out of himself and having to be rescued by Susan and Rachael, who didn't hold back their opinions about how moronic the whole game was.

But everyone had fun. Even Genevieve, who had never before attempted any water sports that required either coordination or that she get off the beach, got into the spirit of it and was quickly recognized as the bungee-board runner-up among the female competitors—though only three of them attempted it. Even Ruby, dressed in a rather colorful swimsuit for a woman of so many decades, enjoyed a romp in the water, relaxing in a near-weightless state until her hands and toes had pruned up, finally matching, she joked, the rest of the wrinkles on her body. Ephraim serenaded the family with classic rock-and-roll favorites, and they all sang along when they knew the words.

"I just realized that this is the most fun I've ever had on the water without alcohol," Ephraim said after finishing a set.

"Yeah, me too," said Sonja. "I didn't think it could be this fun. It must be something in the water."

"Yeah, I was just thinking the same thing," Genevieve admitted.

"We hear that every year," Pops reported. "It's crazy, but lots of kids have never experienced anything like this without a few beers in 'em."

"So, what's the secret?" Ephraim asked.

Pops laughed. "I think you've already discovered it. Funny thing is, it's one of the best kept secrets in the world. You'll all wake up in the morning with all the memories of the fun you had here and none of the headache. And you won't have to worry about the stupid stuff you may have done, except maybe Josh, who'll be feelin' that belly flop for at least a week."

Sonja nodded but looked confused. "So why do we think that we always have to have alcohol in order to have fun?"

"It's called failure of the imagination," Ruby said. "Don't worry. You're not alone. Everyone who spends any time here eventually comes to the same realization—whether they drink or not—that they've been underusing their imagination for way too long. Stepping away from the TV, video games, and cell phones—it's like people begin to see the world in color for the first time. It's like they begin to think. You wouldn't believe the changes people make in their lives when they start excising their creative muscles—many of them for the first time since grade school."

"That's right. You've already experienced the wonders of Bessie and the bungee board and Big Bertha—our washing machine," Pops pointed out. "All of those things were invented right here in Niederbipp by our kids. They had some bright ideas pop into their heads once they'd sobered up and were able to think clearly. All you need is a little time and sunshine, some spare parts, and a healthy dose of imagination."

"So, that's where all the games we've been playing on the porch came from, right?" James asked.

Pops nodded. "Inventions by the kids from past years, every one of them."

"And you haven't even seen the best ones yet," Ruby added.

"What are the best ones?" asked Holly.

"They're the ones the world is waiting for you to invent," Ruby responded. "We have a list of good ones, but every year we're surprised when kids come up with new ones. Basketball and football don't hold a candle to Loveball or Cheesehead or Voluminous Vagabonds."

"And don't forget Stinkbait, Portuguese Penguins, and Octopus Rugby. I still laugh every time I think of the kids who invented Octopus Rugby, and that was something like five years ago," Pops added.

"Seven. And I still laugh too—all that mud. That poor girl... Meghan...mother of two as of last Christmas." She stopped to laugh. "One of a kind that one. One of a kind. I swear somewhere right now there are people who are still giggling over her performance that night."

"Oh, and remember..." But Pops couldn't get it out before tears began welling up in his eyes. His words turned into hysterical mumbles as he and Ruby laughed themselves silly.

The laughter was contagious, and even though the campers had no idea what they were laughing about, the sight of two ancient people in colorful swimwear laughing their butts off made it impossible for any of them to keep a straight face.

"That's the one to beat," Pops said, tears still wet on his cheeks. "Invent a game that's better than Octopus Rugby, and we'll give you the farm."

"We'll have to. The laughter would kill us both."

"I don't know if I've ever made up a game," Holly said. "Have any of you?"

"Yeah, but I bet it's been twenty years," Spencer replied. "We played it all summer. I don't remember the rules, but I remember it being incredibly fun."

"What was it like?" Sonja asked.

"There was a basketball and a Hula-Hoop and a couple of brooms..." But he couldn't finish before he was laughing, ensuring everyone in between fits of laughter that if he could remember how it worked, it might be the most fun game any of them had ever played.

"'We don't stop playing because we grow old; we grow old because we stop playing,'" Ruby responded.

"Who said that?" Rachael asked

"I think that's George Bernard Shaw, right?" Susan answered. "And he should know. He was ninety-four when he passed away."

"Yes, and he was still busy living until the day he passed away. We're hoping to go the same way," Pops reported.

"What does that mean to you?" asked Sonja.

Pops looked at Ruby, patting her on the hand. "Ol' Ben Franklin said that some men die at twenty-five and aren't buried until they're seventy-five. It's as true today as it was in his time. Life is meant to be lived—every day of it. Most people our age are retired and sittin' around doin' nothin'."

"Most people our age are dead," Ruby corrected.

"Well, that's true too. But we learned a long time ago from watchin' our peers that when you stop climbing stairs, you stop being able to climb stairs. And when you stop dancing, you stop being able to dance. Then you just get old and fat and tired. That ain't livin'. That's just breathing—takin' up space. Some people make that decision when they're still in their twenties—stop working on themselves, stop caring about what they do, stop reading and stretching and being thoughtful. That ain't livin'. In no way is that livin'. That's not only failure of the imagination, that's failure at life. And the main cause of that is always the same—they stop playing. They stop getting up and moving and finding joy in life."

"We decided a long time ago that we'd keep swimming in the river and dancing our way through life, accepting every day as the gift that it is," Ruby added. "I think that's what life is all about—to adjust your eyes and heart to be able to find something to be happy about every day—to learn to love God, yourself, and others—to learn to laugh in the face of fear. That's the recipe for joy as far as I can tell. It's simple, and it doesn't cost much more than consciously maintaining a good attitude. That's what living is to me. That's what it's all about."

CHAPTER 28

Insecurities Revealed

Be kind whenever it is possible. It is always possible.
— Dalai Lama —

The evening porch gathering was even more lively than those that had already been experienced. Holly drew a card from the deck of already-invented games, randomly choosing a game called Iggly Wumpus. Invented in the summer of 1998, the game, as the card outlined, required the day's teams to be paired up. They would stand on either side of Bessie, and each of them had to have one hand touching the seat at all times and one hand on the bull-horn handlebars. Each would use one foot to pedal the bike while supporting themselves with the other foot.

This sounded fairly straightforward, and Crystal and James had just stepped forward to give it the first try when Ruby suggested that there were more instructions, which Holly quickly discovered on the back side of the card.

Ruby retreated into the house, returning a moment later carrying a shoebox with Iggly Wumpus written on the side. Inside were two long sticks, each with a lipstick tube attached to one end; the other end of each stick was attached to straps that were to be fastened around the player's head and chin so that the lipstick end pointed out. Crystal and James attached the sticks to their heads. As they each donned safety goggles, Holly read that the goal of the game was to keep Bessie's pedals moving while you take turns trying to apply lipstick to your partner's lips. A three-minute hourglass would be turned over, giving each partnership a chance to apply the lipstick using only the muscles in their necks. Spectators would score the couple on a scale from one to ten based on accuracy of application, teamwork, coordination, and creativity. Winners for the evening would retain the hand-carved Iggly Wumpus medals hung from neon shoelaces until the next time the game was played. A medal could also be traded in for an extra bowl of ice cream.

The competition was immediately fierce and hilarious. Josh promptly missed Crystal's lips, applying a dab of lipstick to her nose, which got everyone laughing. The laughter only made his accuracy worse, making her look like a demented clown. But Crystal returned the makeover with one of her own, giving Josh stripes of war paint. Genevieve and Spencer did much better, quietly agreeing ahead of time that the one who was applying the lipstick would focus on that task alone while the one receiving the lipstick would concentrate on keeping the pedals moving. Spencer's accuracy was impressive, but Genevieve only managed to apply a small slash of color on his lips before the sand ran out.

It went on like this for the next half hour. Even Ruby and Pops took a turn, which they did surprisingly well, only to be beaten by Susan and Greg, who swept in like old pros, applied each other's lipstick with startling accuracy, beat the timer, and were still able to bring the ice cream to completion. Twelve people with faces smeared in lipstick rose from their seats with great noise and fanfare to congratulate the clear winners. And the noise and laughter only continued while they all enjoyed their ice cream, unable to look at each other without at least snickering.

As the laughter and fun continued, Genevieve looked around at this ragtag group of weirdos and was surprised by the strange sense of connection she felt toward each of them. She knew something was different, but she couldn't pinpoint exactly what it was. As she scanned all of their faces, she stopped at Matt's, realizing he was looking at her. He smiled weakly and nodded before looking away. She tried not to think too much about it, but as she walked back to the bunkhouse that night, she had to admit that his little lecture that morning had changed the way she looked at all of this.

For the first time in a week, Genevieve wasn't awoken the next morning by pterodactyls or even embarrassing stunts. Instead, she dreamed she was lying in a field of wildflowers, looking up at the poofy white clouds as they twisted and morphed into animals. A biplane dragging a sign zoomed in and out of the clouds, and she strained her eyes as she tried to read the sign: WELCOME HOME.

It wasn't pterodactyls, but it wasn't exactly doves either. The message was warm but not entirely comforting. She considered talking to Matt about it but decided against it when she met him outside the women's bunkhouse for morning chores.

They headed out to the garden to weed and water. It had been four days since they had all worked here together, planting the seeds. She was surprised to find tiny rows of green growth popping up through the dark soil. Having forgotten what had been planted and where, she consulted the signs. Radishes, carrots, peas, onion, and squash had already made their debuts. And the tomato and pepper plants were all noticeably bigger.

After pulling any obvious weeds, they each took a watering can out into the corners of the garden, working their way toward the heart-shaped center, tending to each of the areas that had been planted. As she worked, she tried to think of questions to ask Matt, but despite her usual prowess at interviewing interesting people, she found it difficult formulating a question that was both sensitive and smart.

"Thanks for talking to me yesterday," she said before she could think about it.

He looked surprised. "You're not upset about what I said?"

She shook her head. "I get it."

Matt nodded, still looking tired. "Thanks for jumping in and trying to have more fun yesterday. I think it was the first time that nobody could accuse you of not being invested."

"Yeah, well, maybe it was the first time since I arrived that I wasn't wishing I was somewhere else."

"Not even a fashion show in Brussels?"

She thought for a minute. "I'd be on my way to Milan right now. I was planning to work on a story about a cobbler who still makes all his shoes completely by hand. I was actually looking forward to that one."

"Will someone else pick it up?"

"I don't know." She walked back to the spigot to fill her can, and he followed her.

"I'm sorry," he said softly.

"For what?"

"Well, among other things, for calling you an indoor girl."

"Hey, you know…it was true. I'll admit it. You nailed it."

He smiled. "I know, but that's not what I was getting at. It may have been true, but it wasn't kind. I have this goal to be kind and…"

"Wait. Back up. You have a goal to be kind?"

He looked up from his watering can before quickly looking away. "I'm sure it sounds stupid, but you were right yesterday."

"I was? About what?"

"You said something like…it's no wonder I'm still single."

She couldn't keep from smiling. "Sorry, that wasn't very kind either."

"No, but it was true."

"So I guess that makes us even then. We both said unkind but true things, and we're both sorry we did. It's okay. I'm over it."

He nodded. "I'm glad you're over it."

She watched him for a moment. "You're not, are you?"

Matt shrugged. "I don't know. Probably not. I overthink a lot of things. It's one of the perils of being single for forty-three years. Not a lot happens in my life, so I tend to overthink everything. I guess what you said was a little too much truth."

"Wow, I'm…sorry. I…didn't realize. Tell me more about your goal."

"To be kind?"

She nodded.

"Oh, it's just…I've been thinking about my weaknesses since my interview with Ruby. I've got a lot to work on. I don't know if she suggested the same thing to you, but she told me that if I'd open my heart and allow the universe to talk to me, it would tell me what I needed to work on. That was the first answer that came. I decided I'd work on that."

"How's it going?"

"Obviously not very well. I've been keeping track," he said, pointing to the backs of his hands, where several lines had been drawn with a blue pen.

"What do those mean?"

"On my left hand, I mark the times I was kind, and on my right hand, I mark all the times I was not. I obviously have a long way to go."

"My dad used to say we're our own worst critics."

"Yeah, but no one else knows what's in our heads. I've got a lot of issues. I started making a list, and it's pretty overwhelming."

"Do you think you might be overthinking this too?"

"Oh, I'm sure I probably am. But if I don't start working on them now, I don't know if I ever will. I came here thinking I was ready to get married, but after just a week, I'm realizing why I'm still single. Our little chat yesterday really hit that home."

"Seriously?"

He nodded. "You're right. I am a jerk."

"Whoa, why are you being so hard on yourself?"

"You mean besides the fact that I'm forty-three and single, I'm full of personal flaws and insecurities, and I haven't had a real girlfriend in close to twenty years?"

"Okay, but you've traveled and read lots of books and helped people. That ought to count for something. It might not be everything you want it to be, but you've had a good life as far as I can tell. *Buck up, little camper!*"

He laughed. "You're too young to know that reference."

"What reference?"

"Buck up, little camper."

She looked at him blankly. "My dad used to always say that."

"Oh, that makes me feel really good."

"What?"

"It's from a dumb movie—*Better Off Dead*. It came out when I was a kid—in the mid-eighties, maybe."

"Yeah, that was before I was born."

"Ouch!" he feigned, stepping back a few paces with his hand clutching his chest. "Thanks for the reminder that I'm an old man."

"Hey, you still got some life left in you. You're keeping up with the younger guys."

"Just barely. Look, I don't expect you to understand any my madness. I shouldn't have even brought it up. I really just meant to apologize for being a jerk. I told you yesterday that it's not all about you, and then I made it all about me. I'm sorry."

"Matt, I'm over it. We're good."

"You sure?"

"Yeah. Stop overthinking things. Let's just move on. Tell me more about why you came here."

"Are you asking because you want to know, or are you asking for your story?"

"Does it matter?"

"Maybe. I'm pretty sure I don't want to open a magazine in a dental office somewhere next fall and read about this loser named Matt Farnsworth who couldn't get his crap together."

"I could print your phone number at the end of the article. We have a distribution of over a million. It might be a good way to meet girls."

He laughed. "Thanks, but that would just alert a million more women to the fact that I'm an idiot."

"Matt, you're not an idiot. You're probably the best read and no doubt the best traveled of any of us here. I may be curious why you're here for my story, but I'm no less curious personally."

"I already told you yesterday."

"Yeah, you said you were tired of being single, of…what was it?… telling yourself you were happy roaming the world by yourself?"

He nodded.

"So, what makes you think life's going to be any better after you're married? It just seems more complicated to me."

"Isn't there even a little part of you that wishes to love and be loved?"

"Maybe."

"I mean, yeah, for sure it complicates things—having to listen to someone else's opinion and work around someone else's schedule. That will definitely require some getting used to after not really doing either for most of my life. But when I really stop and think about it, I recognize that I've been ignoring a primal urge for my whole life."

"Are you talking about sex?"

He shrugged. "I'm sure that's part of it, but I'm really talking about love—about friendship and companionship and a desire to breathe the same air with someone for the rest of my life."

"That doesn't sound smothering to you?"

"No. It's hard to explain, but I have this strange sense that there's someone who'd rather be sharing a life with me than going it alone. The last thing I'd want to do is smother anyone, but I do want a connection. I want to connect with someone on an intellectual, spiritual, and, yes, physical level. I want to share my life with someone. It's ridiculous traveling all over the world and having no one to share my adventures with, no one to laugh with, no one to share my fears and sorrows with. I have this crazy idea that if I could just meet the right person, all that loneliness and pain would go away."

Genevieve raised one eyebrow. "I can't tell if you're looking for a lover or a savior."

He shook his head and turned away. "Maybe that's my problem," he muttered.

"That you don't know which one you want?"

"That my expectations are too high."

"Yeah, how fair is that? You want friendship, sex, intellectual stimulation, spiritual connection, and companionship, *and you're offering what in return?*"

He looked stumped. "All of that, plus…financial support—adventure—a graying middle-aged man who's not afraid to admit he leaves a lot to be desired."

She nodded slowly, skeptically. "It's probably a good thing you're a dentist."

"Why's that?"

"Because you really suck at sales. No offense."

He nodded. "That's on my rather long list of weaknesses too." He reached into his back pocket and withdrew a piece of paper, unfolding it. "Yep, it's number eight," he said, pointing out to her where he had written:

8. Poor self-esteem that usually leads to undervaluing myself as a man, a human, and a potential spouse.

"Hey, at least you're honest—and humble. That's better than most men I've had occasion to mingle with."

"Really?"

"Yeah, if I could take that attitude and put it into a man my own age, there might just be some attraction, regardless of what he looked like."

He looked down at his list. "I never considered that my weaknesses could be potentially attractive."

She shrugged. "It all depends on the woman, really. What's a weakness in one woman's eyes could easily be sexy to another. My boss reminds us of that at nearly every staff meeting. In the end it's all about marketing—marketing and timing—which I suppose really have to go hand in glove if they're ever to be met with any positive results. I guess I've never considered it, but maybe those truths apply to dating and marriage too."

He nodded, looking over his list before folding it up and putting it back in his pocket. "I came here thinking I was finally ready for marriage, but since my interview, I've been pretty much preoccupied with this list."

"Have you ever considered that maybe you're concentrating on the wrong thing?"

The question seemed to surprise him.

"I get that it's probably noble to work on your weaknesses, but I thought I remembered Ruby saying something about needing to feed our strengths too."

He looked at her for a moment before reaching into his other pocket and pulling out another piece of paper. He handed it to her. She unfolded it and found the word Strengths written across the top of the page. Only one item was listed:

1. I'm a good dentist.

She turned the paper over, looking for more, but the other side was blank. She looked up at him, surprised. "Give me your pen," she said, pointing to the pen sticking out of the top pocket of his overalls. He handed it to her, and she leaned him over so she could write on his back. She wrote several lines before handing him the paper.

2. I am determined.

3. I am smart.

4. I have a good memory for wisdom.

5. I am a seeker of truth.

6. I am humble.

7. I am interesting.

8. I am honest.

9. I am a hard worker.

10. I am compassionate.

11. I am a good observer.

12. I am easy to talk to.

13. I am a good listener.

She handed him back the pen and paper, which he glanced over quickly before looking back at her.

"I wasn't asking for praise."

"I didn't mean to give any. I was just making observations."

He glanced down at the list again. "Thanks," he said, looking humble and overwhelmed. "This is really nice."

"It's all true, isn't it?"

He looked at the list again, taking a deep breath. "I want it to be. Those are all good things, right?"

"Yeah! Just work on more stuff like that. If you get even better at those things, I'm pretty sure the self-esteem issue will take care of itself."

He nodded. "That reminds me of something I read once—something like, 'When all you retain is lovable, there's no reason for fear to remain with you.'" [1]

She thought about it for a moment before she spoke. "Yeah...so I'm still trying to figure out why you're here."

"What do you mean?"

"I mean, I can see why the other guys are here. No offense to them, but they need some serious work. I'm just wondering why you couldn't have met someone on the other side of this fence and be living happily ever after. I mean, I get that you lack some self-confidence, but I just don't understand why you couldn't turn that all around and find a smart girl who'd fall for you."

"It's not that simple, as I'm sure you're aware. I've got baggage."

"Like what?" she asked incredulously. "Are you addicted to porn?"

He looked surprised. "No!"

"Have you served time?"

"No!" he laughed

"Are you a eunuch?"

"Not the last time I checked."

"And you're not gay?"

He raised an eyebrow. "Would I be here if I was?"

"And you're not a creeper or the lead singer of a polka band?"

He laughed. "I actually did take accordion lessons one summer when I was thirteen. Does that count?"

She smiled and shook her head. "So, what's the baggage?"

He looked at her and then looked down at his watering can. He didn't look back up.

"Matt?"

He glanced up at her and exhaled slowly, letting out seventeen years' worth of breath. "I've never told anyone about this."

"Why not?"

"Oh, I don't know. I guess I've never thought it was a good idea to go around telling people my biggest regrets," he responded sarcastically.

"Do you have a list of those too?"

He thought for a moment. "It's a small list, but they all revolve around her."

"Oh, your regret is a female?" she teased. "Does she have a name?"

He looked away but didn't respond.

"Matt, this is obviously a big deal. If you don't want to tell me, I totally get it. I'll just mind my own..."

"Promise me this won't end up in your article," he said, cutting her off.

"I promise."

"Naomi," he spoke softly after a moment.

"Excuse me?"

"Her name was Naomi. Naomi Richardson."

"Did she die?"

"No!"

"Did she dump you?"

"No, it wasn't like that. I...I don't know if she even knew."

Genevieve looked confused. "What didn't she know?"

"How I felt about her."

"Wait...what? You never told her?"

He shook his head. "Not everything...actually, maybe not much. Definitely not enough."

"Why not?"

He looked flustered. "Because I was an idiot! Because I didn't know what I was doing and definitely had no idea what I was feeling. I'd never had any experience with real love before. We spent six months working together in Tennessee, went on a handful of dates, enjoyed some very innocent romance, and somehow that's been enough to haunt me for the rest of my life."

"So, what happened? Why'd you let her go?"

"Because I was scared."

"Of what?"

"Of tying myself down. Of becoming my father. Of losing my independence. Of not being able to provide financially for a family. Of failing. You name it, I caught it.

"So you still think about her?"

"Well, it's not like I just sit around and daydream about her all day, but yeah, I think about her often, probably too often. Whatever we had—

that connection—it was unlike anything I'd ever experienced before—or since."

"And does it still hurt that you didn't do more to make it work?"

He nodded, but he looked as if her question surprised him.

"I think maybe I might know how you feel."

"Oh really?" he asked doubtfully.

"I'm still trying to forget a guy I fell hard for six years ago when we were both interning one summer for a small paper in Alexandria," she said, shaking her head.

"Genevieve, I can appreciate your pain—and that you're willing to listen to my pitiful story—but the difference here is that I gave up on trying to forget Naomi a long time ago. I've resigned myself to the fact that it's just not going to happen."

"That's not good news at all."

"What do you mean?"

"I've been telling myself that it's got to get easier—that time will pass and my heart will change and it will somehow get better. But no matter what I do, he's always there in the back of my head, taunting me with his charming blue eyes and the memories of all the time we spent together. I regret at least three times a week that I didn't follow him to San Diego at the end of that summer."

"Why didn't you?"

"Because of the job offer I had in New York. I didn't realize at that point what taking a job on the other side of the country from him would mean for our relationship. I naively thought that we'd be able to continue our relationship, but…"

"What happened?"

"Geography happened. And then the timing that had brought us together in such an incredible way slowly turned against us. After months of just being incredible friends, he finally kissed me about a week before we went our separate ways. I've relived that moment in my head at least a hundred million times. He took a job with a literary agency, and I got busy working for the magazine. We called and texted every day for months, but the distance was ridiculous. It just got harder and harder to communicate as work picked up for both of us—and the three-hour difference in time zones…I've played it out a thousand different ways in my head, hoping beyond all reasonable hope that I could've created a different outcome, but…"

"So…it's over?"

She nodded solemnly. "He called me one night to tell me he'd met someone in his yoga class—some bimbo architect chick who made him feel…what was the word?…*alive* or some nauseating bull crap like that. He said he didn't want to hurt me, but he felt like he needed to see if this other relationship had any possibilities."

"And it did?"

Genevieve shrugged. "That was the last time I spoke to him. Last I checked on his Facebook page, like a week ago, he had just posted a picture of their newborn son. He's been married four years! Four freakin' years, and I still find myself thinking about him way more often than my therapist said is healthy."

"You haven't dated anyone else since then?"

She shook her head. "No. I mean, sure I've had drinks with a few guys, but as far as falling in love—as far as creating that kind of connection…I'm busy and complicated and…"

"And?"

She shook her head again.

He looked at her for a moment, recognizing for the first time that there was something familiar in her eyes—some unforgotten bit of anguish that still resided just below the surface. "Do you ever find yourself looking for him in the faces of strangers?

She looked surprised by his question. "I feel like I've been chasing shadows ever since that last phone call. I know he's married and has a kid, but yeah, I still find myself scanning every room I enter, looking for those blue eyes. I once followed a guy for two whole blocks because he looked like Charlie from behind." She laughed and shook her head.

"I even imagined some crazy scenario where he was in town for a book convention and was secretly hoping he would run into me. It was pitiful."

"It wasn't him?"

She shook her head. "Just some random guy who had the same haircut. I felt so stupid, following him into a shop, spying on him over the racks of clothes to see if it was really him, trying to imagine what I would say to him."

"I've done something similar dozens of times over the past seventeen years," Matt said, swallowing hard and forcing a smile. "I still have a recurring dream that we pass each other going opposite directions on escalators in a busy shopping mall. By the time I get off and hurry back to find her, she's done the same thing, and we pass each other again, our fingers briefly touching before I lose her in the crowd."

Genevieve smiled at the picture he'd painted. "What would you say to her if you ever caught up to her?"

Matt turned and looked at the garden thoughtfully. "I've had this discussion at least a million times in my mind, but I'm sure I'd still probably fumble badly if it came right down to it. I've spent seventeen years looking for her in the faces of every woman I've ever met or even passed on the street. I'm embarrassed to admit I even carried her picture with me for at least a decade. I'm sure I still have it somewhere."

"Why are you embarrassed about that?"

"Because I'm sure she's someone's wife—someone's mother. I knew her for this tiny little window of time, but that time is so far gone. When I think about it, it's ridiculous that she still haunts my thoughts and dreams. Her kids could be in high school by now, for crying out loud."

"Wait, you don't know what happened to her?"

He shook his head.

"You've never looked for her on social media or anything?"

He looked at her incredulously. "I'm forty-three years old. As far as I'm concerned, social media is just one more chance to prove both my social and technological ineptitudes."

"But what if she's still single?"

He raised one eyebrow. "A beautiful, talented, outgoing woman like her is not going to be single."

"You don't even want to know?"

"Of course I want to know, but not enough to stalk her on social media." He shook his head, staring out blankly across the garden. "Part of me wants to know, and part of me is just happy to know that she dodged a bullet. I would have made a lousy husband seventeen years ago. The most noble thing I've probably ever done is to spare her that disappointment, but I regret that I never gave her any closure—that I never had any for myself. I regret I wasn't a bigger man."

"What does that mean?"

He shrugged. "It means I left without saying anything. I don't know...I guess it was the pressure. Things moved faster than I was ready for, and when she took me home to meet her folks, I…"

"You didn't like them?"

"No, I...they were amazing—truly great people. They seemed like the perfect family. Her older brothers were all successful. Her parents had been married for forty years. They lived in a cute house in the suburbs with a white picket fence, and her mom planted pansies in the garden."

"What's wrong with that?"

"I was wrong with that. I felt like a mutt in a purebred world. I had a ton of student loan debt. I came from a messy family who lived on the wrong side of the tracks. I was insecure and immature, and I didn't feel like I had anything to offer."

"So, what did you do?"

"I left her a note that said I'd be back as soon as I figured it out, and I disappeared without leaving a forwarding address."

"Where did you go?"

He laughed, shaking his head. "I've been wandering around the world trying to figure it out."

"'Not all who wander are lost,'" she mused, remembering the patch she saw on his bag the first day.

"No," he acknowledged, "but some of us truly are. It's taken me a long time to admit that. I've had some great adventures and seen some amazing stuff, but when I'm honest with myself, I know I'm about as lost as a guy can get."

"It surprises me to hear you say that."

"Why?"

She shrugged. "You just seem to have it figured out. You're obviously educated and well read."

He chuckled. "Some of the most educated people I know are also the most lost. I'd trade it all to be twenty years younger and have a chance to figure it all out earlier."

Genevieve nodded, emptying the last of the water from her watering can onto the tiny radish seedlings. "How would you do it differently?"

"What, the last seventeen years?"

She nodded.

"I'd open my mouth. I'd tell people how I felt about them. I wouldn't allow my fears to stand in the way of my dreams and happiness."

"Do you still love her? Naomi, I mean?"

"Pfff. I never stopped loving her," he said without hesitation. "Someday our paths will cross again."

"And then what?"

"And then…then I'll thank her for the good influence she's had on my life, apologize for walking away without a better explanation…and ask her to stop haunting my dreams."

"You really loved her, didn't you?"

He shook his head, setting down his watering can. "I don't know anymore."

She waited for him to say more.

"That was a long time ago. I knew her for just a few short months."

"But you're still thinking about her seventeen years later. You still love her."

He nodded solemnly. "I wonder sometimes if I'm in love with her or if I'm in love with her ghost—that beautiful girl she once was seventeen years ago. I fell in love with her in the prime of her life—when I was in the prime of mine. Time plays tricks on our minds. The memories I have of that time are somehow sharper today than they were even fifteen years ago, which hardly makes things easier and only serves to keep my regrets fresh and in the forefront of my mind."

"You don't even want to check and see if she's still single?"

"Look, there's absolutely no way she's single. And even if she were, I'm sure she would have forgotten me. I'm really not that memorable."

"Matt, you had a connection with her that you've remembered for seventeen years. You don't think she experienced at least some of that? She's probably wondering what happened to you. You should at least look her up. If she's married, then you can move on. But if she's single…"

"What if that's my baggage?"

"Huh?"

"What if that's my baggage—not really wanting to know?"

"You don't want to know?"

"No. I mean yes. I do. But sometimes…"

She waited, but nothing more came. "Sometimes you'd rather be left to your dreams than reality?"

He looked surprised, but he nodded.

"So how long are you going to carry that baggage and do nothing about it?"

He closed his eyes and shook his head.

She laughed. "That's exactly what I told my therapist."

"What?"

"Yeah, she keeps asking me how long I'm going to keep paying her to listen week after week to the same pitiful story about how I can't get over Charlie."

"Wait, I thought you said yesterday that you don't even want to get married."

"Did I?"

"Yep. I'm pretty sure that's exactly what you said."

"Well, that doesn't mean I don't want to *be* married."

"Huh?"

"It's all semantics really. I think most people would probably like to be married, but all the hassle of getting married…that part really sucks. If I could just skip all that crap and get to the good stuff…"

Matt laughed.

"You can't tell me you'd choose the trouble of going through all that crap if there was a way to avoid it, right?"

He looked at her incredulously. "The only other option I'm aware of is an arranged marriage, and that certainly doesn't look any better than marrying for love, even with all the challenges love brings to the equation."

Genevieve nodded slowly, looking disappointed. "My therapist says the same thing."

"Does she give you any advice about how to get over it?"

"Yeah, they told me I just need to fall in love with someone else and get on with my life."

"They? You mean you go to more than one?"

She nodded, looking a little embarrassed. "I've been to three different ones, but they've all basically said the same thing. It's like they all went to the same school and are equally insensitive to the idea that Charlie's my soulmate. I know it sounds pitiful, but he's been the standard that I've used to measure every guy I've ever even seen in the last six years. I'm sure it sounds ridiculous, but he ruined me."

Matt shook his head and leaned his back against the fence. "I've never known anyone who's had the same experience I've had."

"Oh, and I'm sure that's probably a topic you bring up with friends and strangers all the time, right?" she said sarcastically.

He shook his head. "I told you, I've never talked about this with anyone."

"Maybe we should."

"Excuse me?"

"Yeah, maybe we should. There are ten other people here who seem to be fairly open about their lives. I wonder if any of them have experienced anything like what we've experienced. It might be worth asking."

"Are you ready to look like a fool if they haven't?"

"I've got nothing to lose. You?"

He shrugged.

"Then follow my lead," she said as she set down the watering can and wandered back to the big house for breakfast.

1. Helen Schucman, *A Course in Miracles* (New York: Viking: The Foundation for Inner Peace) 1976

CHAPTER 29

Detecting Scuds

Love is like playing the piano. First you must learn to play by the rules, then you must forget the rules and play from your heart.

– Anonymous –

Genevieve could smell it before she could see it—smoke. It was bad, too. Matt ran ahead, throwing open the screen door and running into the house without removing his muddy boots. Genevieve followed him into the kitchen, the acrid smell wafting about in the hazy smoke that filled the top half of the kitchen.

"Is everyone okay in here?" Matt asked, coughing as he waved the smoke away from his face.

"Yeah, we're fine," Josh responded sheepishly as he stood next to the giant oven, its mouth agape and billowing with smoke from its dark interior.

"We're just making bacon the old-fashioned way," Rachael reported nonchalantly before offering a cough.

Matt rushed to the window above the sink but found it was already open. Josh reached into the oven with an oven mitt and pulled out a smoldering tray. Thin, dark strips of charred nonsense continued to spew noxious, gray fumes.

"What happened?" Genevieve asked, stepping closer to the window in hopes of finding some fresh air.

"It was Josh's idea," Rachael said, coughing again. "Said it was the way his grandma used to make it."

"What the Sam Hill is going on in here?" Ruby screeched, standing in the kitchen doorway.

"I'm sorry," Josh said weakly.

Ruby rushed to the tray, wrapping her hand in her apron before grabbing it and hurrying out the back door. They all followed her, nearly knocking her off the edge of the porch when she stopped abruptly and dropped the tray onto a weathered table.

"I'm getting too old for this," she said, wiping her brow on her sleeve. "Don't cook the bacon too hot, I said. What'd you do? Crank it up to the inferno setting?"

Josh cowered. "I'm sorry. I...must have bumped the knob while I was flipping pancakes."

"I'd say," she responded, turning to look at the still-smoldering burnt offering. She took a deep breath of the fresh morning air. "Is everyone okay?" she asked, not turning to face them.

"Yes, I think we're all fine," Rachael responded after glancing quickly at all of them.

"Good. Please tell me you aren't burning the flapjacks too."

Josh frantically retreated back into the house. He returned a moment later, balancing a tall stack of ebony-colored pancakes on a spatula.

"Congratulations," Ruby said, turning around to face Josh and Rachael. "You have become the first team this year to narrowly avoid burning down the big house—though it smells like you did burn it down. And you two have become the first to volunteer to mop the floors," she added, looking down at Matt and Genevieve's mud-caked boots. "It was all going so well. I knew it would have to come back to normal sometime."

"I'm sorry," Genevieve offered.

"Of course you are," Ruby said, cracking a smile. "Of course you are. And it's just bacon and a little mud and a house full of smoke. It'll all be okay…in a few weeks."

They each continued to apologize as they followed her back into the kitchen, where she opened the windows even wider before flipping the oven and stovetop knobs to the off position. She looked up at the smoke still hovering in the kitchen and began to laugh. She laughed hard for nearly a full minute, breaking the tension as the others nervously joining in.

Breakfast was served: a rather small plate of pancakes that had somehow avoided the incinerator. But even several jars of berry preserves couldn't tempt the campers whose noses and appetites were turned off by the scent of charred food, substantially dampening the overall mood.

"Can I ask everyone a question?" Genevieve asked when a pause occurred in the conversation.

"You got a bee in your bonnet?" Pops asked from the end of the table.

"Maybe," she responded, not entirely sure if she knew what that meant. "I…I mean Matt and I, we were wondering if any of you have experienced what my therapist calls *recurring baggage delays*?"

They looked at her blankly.

"What I mean is, have you ever felt like your current love life—or lack thereof—is being affected by a former love interest whom you can't seem to get out of your head?"

She watched as several campers' heads bobbed, while others seemed uncertain how they should respond.

"Matt and I were just talking this morning, realizing that we've kind of kept some old emotions trapped inside our hearts that may have made it difficult for us to move on."

"My therapist calls them Scuds," Greg replied. They all turned to look at him, and he suddenly looked shy. "Yeah, they're basically the romantic equivalent of those missiles that can be moved and launched from anywhere, especially when you're least expecting it—like on almost every first date I've had since a particularly painful breakup, seven years ago."

Genevieve nodded slowly, thinking about that. "So, I guess I might get where you're coming from. But we are talking about people—former romantic interests or exes—who are somehow still holding on to a piece of our hearts even though we may not have seen them for seventeen years."

Greg nodded slowly.

She looked into the faces of everyone at the table and was surprised to see a common look in each of them.

"We have this discussion every year," Ruby said, "but I've never heard them called Scuds. I like that. They are bombs after all, aren't they? Some of them lie dormant for years before they explode. Some of them are persistent, never letting you sleep or find any peace. And they're far more common and powerful than anyone ever imagines."

"You've experienced them too?" Matt asked, looking very surprised.

"Yes," she said, looking down the table at Pops.

"And so have I," Pops added.

"Wait, you can say that out loud in a marriage?" Sonja asked.

Ruby nodded. "It's not often easy to talk about, and some couples never do. But those who do will often find that their friendships and marriages are strengthened. Others might find bits of jealousy that can't be weeded out, sometimes for years. But Pops and I have always felt that honesty is a far better policy than burying emotions in hopes that they'll just disappear. They rarely do on their own."

"But you must have gotten over those things decades ago, right?" Ephraim asked.

"It all depends on what you consider *getting over*," Ruby responded. "If it means we've moved on, done our best to heal and recover, and learned to love each other in profound ways, then yes, we've both, I think, *gotten over it*. But if you're asking if we still remember the feelings we once had for other people, then the answer for both of us is a resolute yes."

"Seriously?" Holly asked. "You each still have feelings for someone else?"

Ruby pursed her lips and nodded. "Those feelings have changed, of course. We've been married for more than fifty-six years. Everything changes over the course of that kind of time. But true and sincere love for another human being causes one's heart to change—to stretch—to expand."

"And once your heart's been stretched, it never goes back to the way it was," Pops added. "I once fell in love with a girl—Marni. We were too young to marry, still just teenagers, but that girl changed my life—changed my heart—changed the entire orbit of my soul. She loved me, and that love helped me believe in myself. There was a time that I couldn't have imagined my life without her."

"So, what happened?" Crystal asked.

"She married my friend George Reeve. Did the same glorious thing for him that she did for me. They had five children and twenty-one grandkids. They're both gone now—passed on a few years ago."

"Doesn't that make you at all jealous?" Rachael asked, turning to Ruby.

"What's there to be jealous about? I'm grateful for that girl. She changed Pops's orbit so it crossed mine at just the right time in my life. If it hadn't been for Marni, we might never have met. My orbit had been changed by a man as well."

"Two of them, actually," Pops interjected.

Ruby nodded. "He's right. And I loved them both."

"Did you marry either of them?" Genevieve asked.

"No. I wore one's ring for three years while he was serving in Europe during World War II."

"What happened?" Crystal asked "Was he killed in combat?"

"Nearly. He spent six months in a hospital in England recovering from shrapnel wounds. Richard was a good man. Unfortunately, I wasn't the only one to recognize that. Absence often makes the heart grow fonder, but sometimes it makes the heart grow fonder for another person."

"So he fell in love with someone else?" Sonja asked, looking quite upset.

"Yes. The beautiful English nurse who cared for him. He never came back to the States. He sent me a letter a few days before he married her, asking me to forgive him. It was a rather cruel kind of closure. He was married before his letter reached me. That was a tough blow. But if it hadn't been for that blow, I might never have gone to college. I might never have taught school."

"What about the second guy?" Spencer asked.

"Ahh, yes. Michael," she responded, smiling at his memory. "He was a veteran too. Most men were back then. He was a Fuller Brush salesman. Tall. Blond. Handsome. And the kind of man a girl looked forward to taking home to meet her parents. A real sweetheart and gentleman. Wrote me dozens of postcards and letters from his travels. We went together for nearly four years. He made me believe in myself again after Richard broke my heart."

"Why didn't you marry him?" Holly asked.

"The easy answer is that he never proposed."

"So, what happened?" Holly pressed.

"I was offered a teaching job in Ohio, and Michael had obligations that kept him in Poughkeepsie. I loved him dearly for the man he was—for the confidence he restored in me. But I never loved him the way I imagined I'd love a husband. I was never attracted to him the same way I was attracted to Lorenzo. I'm sad to say I broke his heart."

"Because you didn't love him the same way he loved you?" Matt asked.

"That's right. I'm sure we could have made it work. I probably would have stayed and married him had he proposed, but when he didn't, we both moved on with our lives. He married Anne Browning, a classmate of mine, about a year later. She was a much better match for him. We stayed in touch over the years, but they're both gone now too. Most of my old friends are. But I'll always be grateful for the good Michael inspired in me. Even though the romance lacked the spark I needed, I'll always love him for his friendship and encouragement."

"Are you threatened at all by that, Pops?" James asked.

Pops shook his head. "I've never doubted Ruby's love for me. We've both loved other people, and we became better people by loving them. They ultimately helped us become better for each other. When you look at it that way, there's no room for jealousy—only gratitude. A heart wants to love. That's its job, and it's limited in its ability to love only by the head attached to it. I've learned in my long life that the more love you can surround yourself with, the happier your world is. You can look at your past relationships as mistakes and failures, or you can open your heart and be grateful for the love lessons you've learned that have better prepared you for that person you get to love for the rest of your life. I decided more than fifty years ago that I'd much rather go through life being grateful than jealous. That's made all the difference in my life—in our life."

"I like that," Sonja said. "I'm generally a jealous person. I broke up with a really great guy a few years ago when I couldn't get past the fact that he'd been engaged before. How do you get past that kind of jealousy?"

"You allow yourself to recognize that you're a better person because of the people you've loved and who've loved you. And you open your eyes and heart and allow the same to be true of others," Ruby said.

"That sounds a little bit like what my therapist calls TPOTT," Ephraim reported.

"What's that?" asked Josh

"It stands for *the power of the three*. She said that in most cases, a man's life is profoundly shaped by three women—his mother, the woman he ultimately marries, and the woman or women who help the poor guy get to the point where he's worth marrying. She said most men, if they're honest with themselves, will recognize that their lives have been profoundly shaped by those three women."

"I've heard the same idea many times," Ruby said. "And the same is similarly true for women and their fathers, husbands, and the men they date. To try to forget the third is like cutting off a leg of your three-legged stool. It's to deny the very history that made you. I'd suggest you embrace all the good you've learned from those relationships and let the sorrows and disappointments go before you head into a marriage. Sort through the baggage, take out the good, and let the rest go."

"Pff, easier said than done," Genevieve responded. "I've been going to a therapist for years to try and let it go. I don't know if I'm any closer today than I was when I started."

"Sometimes you have to burn it out," Pops said with a wild smile.

"You think they're ready for that?" Ruby asked.

"I don't know why not. This year's campers seem to be figuring things out faster than most, and the house already smells like smoke. We might as well get on with it."

The two glanced at the campers, who all looked as if they were wondering where all of this was leading.

"It's a whole month early, but people and circumstances should always be more important than calendars," Ruby replied.

"What are we talking about here?" Spencer asked. "A fire walk? I did one of those once. It was awesome. My feet were blistered for a week!"

Holly looked scared, and Rachael shook her head.

"No, it's nothing like that," Pops reported. "You're gonna need your feet all summer. No, it's a ritual called the Burning of the Sorrows. It may or may not have pagan roots, and it traditionally takes place on the evening of the winter solstice. But we've modified it to the summer solstice to fit our schedule. It's been done here on the farm for close to two hundred years."

"What is it exactly?" Ephraim asked.

"It's simple, really. You take your sorrows, fears, troubles—any of the things that have been bugging you and bringing you misery—and you write them down on a piece of paper and burn them in the bonfire," Ruby responded. "Some kids like to talk about their sorrows before tossing them into the fire. Others just like to watch them burn. For some it's a somber practice, but others find a way to dance as they watch their sorrows go up in smoke."

"So how soon can we do that?" Susan asked.

"The schedule's all yours," Ruby responded, looking across the table. "It really depends on when you all would like to do it."

"Can we do it tonight?" Susan replied.

Ruby looked at Lorenzo. "I don't see why not. We don't have any plans. What do the rest of you say?"

They all agreed that purging their sorrows would be better done sooner rather than later, and so, following Susan's lead, they collectively began making plans for the evening bonfire.

CHAPTER 30

The Burning of the Sorrows

Love is everything it's cracked up to be
....It really is worth fighting for, being brave for, risking
everything for. And the trouble is, if you don't risk
anything, you risk even more.
– Erica Jong –

Despite the inherent sense of freedom that came from having the chores done and a day of leisure ahead of them due to their speed at planting the fields, the general mood on the farm was rather sober as each of the campers considered their offerings to the evening's upcoming fire. Spencer, after stewing over his list of sorrows, sneaked away to chop some wood, only to find Sonja and Rachael had beat him to the punch and had already accumulated a growing pile of split wood. But not to be turned away, he found a hatchet hanging in the shed and slowly began producing an impressive collection of kindling from a few of the logs the women had split. Matt showed up with a pocketknife and reduced the kindling even further to thin strips of tinder. Before lunch was ready, nine of the twelve campers had found their way to the woodshed; taken turns with the axes, the splitting maul, the hatchet, and the knives; and built a large pile of firewood near the fire ring.

Josh and Rachael served lunch on the front porch. The family seemed to all be lost in their thoughts. Matt had collected several pages of notes, as had Susan. Spencer teased them both, suggesting that their advanced years had provided more regrets and sorrows. But he backed down quickly with his teasing when he noticed that Holly's long list of sorrows rivaled even Matt's and Susan's, leading him to take a closer look at his own list and add several pages to it.

Though it was a rather somber way to spend an afternoon, each of them found the exercise cathartic in some way. Genevieve, for her part, spent a few hours on the bench at the far end of the pond, her backside going numb before she had filled both sides of several pages and let go of many years' worth of tears. She returned to the bunkhouse exhausted and found Rachael, Susan, and Holly working on the mural and quietly talking. She watched them for several minutes as she listened to them sharing history and comforting words with each other. And as she did so, she was surprised to recognize that she shared many of the emotions they expressed. She even picked up a paintbrush for what she knew was the first time in more than twenty years and helped the women fill in the less artistically critical segments of the sky and sea. She even surprised herself as she recognized her uncanny ability to mix paints to create beautiful colors. Sonja and Crystal joined them, and by the time the dinner bell rang, the women had bonded over the mural and the sharing of their sorrows and the emotions that went with them.

They followed the sounds of male voices to the backyard. The men were just finishing construction on a surprisingly realistic sculpture of a dragon built entirely of the firewood they had all chopped earlier. Fourteen chairs had been taken from the front porch and now encircled the dragon, which stood in a fire ring made of rocks. The dragon was filled with kindling and looked like it was ready to be ignited.

Though the smell of smoke still lingered strongly in the big house, Josh and Rachael redeemed themselves from their earlier assault on everyone's olfactory senses; for dinner, they offered up a fantastic lasagna accompanied by salad and breadsticks. The sense of melancholy they each had experienced over the course of the day was greatly lightened as they ate together, but the unspoken shared sense of anticipation for the bonfire silently encouraged them to quicken their consumption.

Sharing quickly in the evening chores, the family was soon circled around the dragon, ready for the event to begin. Ruby stood in the center of the circle and raised her hands, waiting for silence to fall.

"I'm reminded of an old proverb that states, 'We need not fear being eaten by dragons but rather being pecked to death by chickens.'" She paused as if she were waiting for the words to sink in. "Each of you has carried the burdens of sorrows, and like the chickens in this proverb, they've likely been nibbling at you for far too long. What we are doing here tonight can and probably should be repeated often. The universe has many ways of ridding the soul of sorrows, and fire is a universal symbol of purification and cleansing, burning off the dross to reveal what is true and pure and right. Before we light the fire, I invite each of you to consider the burden of your individual sorrows. From your interviews and conversations, I have learned that many of you have visited therapists to help you through these sorrows, with mixed results I'm sure. What we are about to do tonight is to open your heart to all that you have learned from your battles with your individual chickens. I encourage each of you to look one last time at the notes you intend to burn. I'm certain you will find many sorrows, but before you let them go completely, I encourage each of you to consider the good things you have learned from them. In some cases, you may not appreciate that good for some time to come, but among all the bitter that life has to offer us can be found some of the sweetest gems of understanding. These will allow you to love and empathize with and comfort others.

"As you marry and raise children of your own, you will find that sorrows are a universal and unavoidable part of mortality. If you haven't already noticed, there will come a time in the near future that you'll find that your sorrows have enabled you to understand the sorrows and burdens of others. We are human, therefore we suffer. Every religion in the world attempts to give meaning to that sorrow and suffering. Pops and I share a belief that all pain is temporary and no burden is too great to be diminished, if not completely eradicated, by the love of God and the Atonement of Christ. As you seek for truth and understanding, we only want to encourage each of you to open your heart to the healing that God offers each of us. The mortal world will always know sorrow, but within each of us is something more than mortal. And that something secretly knows the familiar wisdom of every truth the universe has to offer you. We encourage you to embrace both the wisdom and the truth and to refrain from becoming content, complacent, or lethargic. Apathy is just another word for death, and it smells much the same. We're only alive when we are growing. And continual growth can only be achieved through constantly feeding that part of us that's eternal. But if you learn anything tonight, I hope it will be this—that your sorrows need not define you and that your future is only as bright as your faith.

"What we do tonight may have some psychological power to lift our burdens, but this ritual will always pale in comparison to fully embracing the idea that you are a child of God and have therefore been endowed with innate potential and gifts—hope being the first among them. I encourage you to embrace the hope that's within you and allow it to lead you to a better life. If you'll take that hope and feed it, it will grow to become something that will sustain you for years to come."

Ruby pulled a handful of matches from the pocket of her apron and walked toward Susan, inviting her to take a match. Then she moved on to Sonja, Greg, and the rest of the campers. When they each had a match, she instructed them all to move forward, strike their matches on the rocks, and ignite the dragon.

The tinder and kindling were dry and ignited quickly. Most of the group placed their lit matches near the feet of the dragon, but Spencer raised his match to the kindling that came out of the dragon's mouth. They all watched, mesmerized by the sight, sound, and smell of the fire as it grew bigger and hotter, smoke and flame slowly engulfing the effigy.

"If you don't mind, I'd like to go first," Ruby said, moving closer to the flame with a small piece of paper. The others stepped back, most of them taking their seats. "I've been thinking about this one sorrow for several months, and I'm ashamed it's taken me this long to be ready to be done with it." She glanced sideways at Pops before looking back to the dragon. "I let this eat me up for way too long."

She held up the small piece of paper. "I'm ashamed to admit that this woman has been dead for more than a decade and I've still held on to some sadness associated with unkind things she said to me more than fifty-six years ago. It's silly that I've hung on to this for so long, but the words she said cut deep at the time. She told me, indirectly, that I was selfish to marry a man who still had the potential of having children when my potential for childbearing was already over. I stewed on those unkind words for way too long, and I'm sorry I did. They brought me only sorrow and hard feelings toward her. So tonight I'm letting it go— fifty-six years too late." Ruby moved closer to the fire, extending the piece of paper to where it was suspended over the flame. "Shirley Jane Fielding, rest in peace. Your unkind words will bother me no more. I forgive you for being unkind, and I set you free." She dropped the note, which immediately caught fire, its smoke mingling quickly with the rest of the smoke rising into the sky.

Ruby, before taking her seat next to Pops, announced that the rest of the evening was all theirs to do with as they pleased. The campers looked around at each other to see who would go next. After a moment, Susan rose from her chair and walked toward the fire, several sheets of paper in her hand. She spoke briefly and generally about the trauma associated with her uncle's abuse, explaining that several years of therapy had freed her from most of the demons, but she spoke openly about how eager she was to be rid of the remaining pain and memories so she could move on and get married without the shadows haunting her. She recognized that she was a survivor, but she also confessed that the events that had brought her so much sorrow had also made her a stronger, more intuitive, and sensitive woman and friend. As she dropped her papers into the fire, she bowed her head in silent prayer, looking up a few moments later with a serene smile on her face and a beautiful aura of calm surrounding her. She returned to her seat, where Greg and Sonja squeezed her hands and patted her shoulders.

Genevieve was the next to rise. She walked to the fire with her small stack of loose papers and shared with the group much of the story about Charlie that she had shared with Matt. She spoke briefly of her parents' loveless marriage and how she had come to recognize that these two burdens—lost love and a poor example from her parents—had tainted her views and thoughts about marriage. She admitted her prior narrow-mindedness on the subject and expressed a desire to move toward something different and better. She fed the paper to the flames one page at a time, admitting that her sorrow and regrets had kept her from recognizing a silver lining—if there was one to recognize—but she expressed hope that this exercise would allow her to move to a point where she might begin to accept that some good could come of everything.

Matt squeezed her hand as she sat down. He rose with his own stack of papers. He expressed a list of regrets that had kept him from being able to see clearly, admitting that his vision had been short and clouded and that his priorities had been misplaced. He shared with the group some of the details about Naomi that he had shared with Genevieve, but this time he expounded on how his lack of action and communication had haunted him for seventeen years. He rolled his notes into a round tube and lit one end, watching the torch burn slowly before dropping it all into the growing pile of coals that was once the dragon.

Ephraim approached the fire with just one piece of paper. He lifted it up to show a name written across the top of the page, explaining that it was the name of his former best friend. He had offered Ephraim's girlfriend a ride home from a party three years earlier when Ephraim had needed to stay late to handle a dispute with a neighbor. His friend and girlfriend had kept the secret from him for three weeks, but together they admitted that they'd fallen in love with each other over the course of several months. They asked for his blessing. Blindsided, he now admitted how hurt he was to lose both his best friend and his girlfriend; the two had quickly married and moved Colorado, doing irreparable harm to his mojo. He confessed that the event had caused him to have serious trust issues with every woman he had met since, and the only good that had come from the sorrow was that he'd had more time to focus on his career, which he wasn't sure qualified as a blessing—or a curse. He crumpled his paper into a ball and tossed it hard into the heart of the fire, setting lose a plume of sparks that rose into the darkening sky.

James gave Ephraim a high five before approaching the fire himself. Because he usually successfully maintained his rugged persona, he seemed surprised by the flood of emotion that escaped in sobs as he spoke of his parents' divorce when he was a teen, their subsequent second marriages, the endless fighting and bickering among his parents and step-parents, and the unfortunate role he had tried in vain to play as peacemaker among his parents and siblings. Marriage, he confessed, had scared him for many years. But throughout it all, he'd remained hopeful of finding a different way, one in which he could secure a brighter, more peaceful future full of love and mutual respect. He held up a list with several names of women who had broken his heart, but before tossing the paper into the fire, he admitted that the day's reflection had allowed him to recognize that each of the women had also helped him believe he was worth something more than he'd previously considered.

Greg stood and thanked Ruby for making him apply three years in a row, recognizing that he hadn't been ready three years earlier. Instead of focusing on the things he'd written on his papers, he chose instead to express his gratitude for the personalized challenges Ruby had sent him each year along with his rejection letter. He admitted he had hated those challenges. But he had found wisdom in them and had done his best to comply, recognizing that he was much better prepared because he had ultimately chosen to listen. He stuffed his sheets of paper in between the burning logs and stayed to watch them burn as if he were making sure none of his sorrows could escape. When he seemed satisfied, he returned quietly to his seat, tears staining the big man's cheeks.

Holly shared her sorrows of losing her mom and never knowing her birth parents. She too wrestled with emotions as she spoke of her seemingly innate sense of loneliness and several failed attempts at romance. She admitted that her experience on the farm over the course of that week had given her a chance to think about herself and recognize many things she wanted to work on, her lack of self-esteem and her emotional neediness being at the top of the list. But she was also gracious, gushing with gratitude at being able to spend the summer with such quality people. Before offering her notes to the flames, she flipped through each page as if she were checking to make sure she hadn't forgotten anything. Then she fed each sheet individually to the fire.

Sonja opted out of saying much about her sorrows. Instead, she ripped her paper into small pieces and threw them bit by bit into the fire as part of a mock interpretive dance, bringing smiles and laughter to everyone.

More laughter, tears, and thoughts were shared as each member of the family burned their sorrows. Darkness fell, and the circle became smaller as they moved their chairs closer to the glowing embers, their faces warm and painted orange by the flames. Crystal was the last to share her sorrows, and the discussion that followed helped each of them to recognize the power of letting go and moving past those things that had kept them from experiencing a fullness of joy. Genevieve recognized that the exercise left each of them aware of the fact that they weren't alone, that the trials of mortality, though varied, were universally experienced by everyone present. Genevieve furtively looked into the glowing faces of each of these weirdos and truly saw them for the first time. There was a power and resiliency hiding just beneath the surface that had been exposed through their shared vulnerabilities. It was a beautiful thing to see—each of them fully exposed and emotionally open. But it was unlike anything she had experienced before. There was no shame. There was no fear of looking foolish or naked or defenseless. A week ago, these people had been strangers, but somehow they had stealthily become something more, something closer.

As she watched and listened to their banter, Genevieve wondered how she could write about this, the very thought of it feeling like such a violation of trust. She could tell that this would surely be the most difficult story she would ever write. She remembered why she had come, anxious to expose Ruby—the acclaimed matchmaker of Niederbipp—as a fraud. It was going to be a quick interview. She'd be in and out in a day or two. She looked across the fire into the animated, happy face of the woman she had come to destroy, and she felt ashamed. There was no hint of malice in Ruby's face, only goodness, honesty, generosity, and kindness. But there was also humility. Genevieve tried to imagine Ruby's picture in the magazine. The juxtaposition of her wrinkled skin and her simple housedress and apron with the flawless plasticity and high fashion of the models Genevieve generally interviewed and wrote about could not have been more contrasting. She couldn't recall the magazine ever showing an image of a woman over fifty, let alone ninety. Ruby was better suited for the cover of *National Geographic* than any fashion magazine she could think of. And yet there was a beauty there that couldn't be ignored. It was real. And it ran much deeper than any beauty Genevieve had ever seen before.

Genevieve turned to Pops, who was staring into the coals as if he were hypnotized. He looked tired and worn yet pleasant and content, basking in the glow of the evening's beauty.

Genevieve was about to look away when she noticed Pops's hand reaching out and gently taking Ruby's hand, his large, farm-worn thumb gently gliding over her knuckles, polishing the thin gold band on her ring finger. There was a tenderness there that intrigued her. Had her parents ever held hands? If they had, it must have been long before she was born. She couldn't remember ever experiencing that kind of tenderness, even with Charlie. She tried to look away but couldn't. She continued staring at the glint of the coals reflected in that small, simple gold band.

This was different from any image of matrimony she had ever seen before. Young, beautiful brides and their dapper grooms were commonly found among the pages of her magazine and scores of others. But in this moment of clarity, she knew this was an image she would never forget. This is what marriage was really about. This is what commitment looked like. This was longevity—decades of patience, love, and gentleness. This love was tried and true, forged in the refiner's fire and polished by what she imagined to be a million acts of kindness and selfless service.

She stared at their hands for a long time, lost in her thoughts. She wondered where to begin with her story, certain she could write nothing that would be able to accurately depict the beauty and grace of this moment.

CHAPTER 31

A Common Parable

At first glance it may appear too hard.
Look again. Always look again.
– Mary Anne Radmacher –

It had been so long since she'd smelled the scent of campfire in her hair that Genevieve breathed it in deeply as she lay upon her pillow, recalling the sweetness of the night before. She rose with the other women as the cock crowed again. Collectively they tried to remember how the morning chores were shared on the previous Sunday.

They shambled out of the bunkhouse, rubbing their eyes and yawning. The men were waiting for them, looking every bit as tired.

After talking briefly among themselves and remembering that the laundry and the garden were considered nonnecessities that could be put off until Monday, they divided up, heading to the barn, the chicken coop, the pigs, and the kitchen. When the cows were milked and animals fed, the campers congregated in the kitchen for oatmeal and scrambled eggs.

Pops announced that the pickup truck would be heading to church at 9:30 if anybody wanted to join them. The rest, he said, could go by bicycle or enjoy the day of rest however they wished.

They knew the showers would be cold this early in the morning, but the smell of campfire on their hair and clothes sent them all scrambling back to the bunkhouses to do their best to clean up before church. To Genevieve's surprise, all of the women decided they'd attend services, making for a chaotic time in the bathroom.

As Genevieve dressed, she realized that it had been a whole week since she had worn anything that made her feel like a woman. The one simple summer dress she'd brought with her felt like a luxury item after a week of wearing denim farm duds. She was surprised that after a week of eating more carbs than she'd ever eaten in her life, the dress somehow seemed to fit even better than it had the last time she'd worn it.

"Are you still in for tonight?" Spencer asked when he caught up to her at the bike shed.

"Huh?"

"Tionesta. Eight o'clock, remember? The sports bar?"

"Oh, right. I forgot about that."

"You still want to go?"

"Uh, sure. It's not like I have anything better to do," she responded, surprised by the toughness of her words.

"Cool," he responded, offering a charming smile.

"Are you going to church?" she asked.

"Yeah. I wasn't going to, but Matt talked the rest of the guys into joining him. What about you?"

"Yeah. Again, it's not like I have anything better to do, right?"

He nodded, rolling out one of the old bikes.

Ten bikes and riders left the farm, making it to the top of the drive before the pickup caught up with them. Pops drove, Ruby rode shotgun, and James and Crystal braced themselves on the wheel hubs in the pickup's bed.

Just like last week's ride, the journey into town was exhilarating, but Genevieve was slow to fully appreciate it, remembering the steep climb back up. As she rode, she was surprised by the sense of discontent that seemed to increase as they rounded each bend in the winding road. It felt like a bad case of waking up on the wrong side of the bed, but she thought it odd that the feeling would hit now, when she'd already been awake for several hours. She tried to push it away, recalling memories of the campfire the night before. But even the scent of the smoke in her hair, which she had enjoyed earlier, made her angry now after both shampoo and conditioner had failed to remove it. She rolled on with the others, her mood only becoming more sour. The churchyard was already crowded when they rolled through it. They leaned their bikes against the cemetery wall and straightened their hair and clothes before climbing the stairs to the chapel.

"Welcome back," Thomas said, greeting them each at the door with a warm smile and a handshake. "I'm glad you decided to join us again. I think you'll be pleased with the good news of the day."

"What's the subject?" Matt asked.

"My favorite parable."

Matt nodded. "Are you giving the sermon?"

"Unfortunately, yes, but I assure you that the message is far better than the messenger." He smiled warmly. "Please come in."

The bright chapel was filling up quickly, and they all moved down the center aisle, Matt leading the way. They spotted Ruby and Pops, along with James and Crystal, sitting near the front, but their pew was already filled. Matt chose a pew near the middle of the chapel that had room for all of them, and they were just sitting down when the organ music began filling the air with beauty.

Genevieve sat silently, sandwiched between Greg and Susan. She looked around, trying to discover the source of her discontent. Her eyes rested on Matt's open journal. The word GRATITUDE was scrawled across the top of the left page, and dozens of things were listed beneath, filling up most of the right page as well. Seeing this reminded Genevieve of the talk they'd had with the priest the week before at his home. Gratitude, she remembered, was what the old man suggested was the beginning of wisdom. She glanced sideways as Matt uncapped his pen and wrote down several other things he was grateful for. Ice cream, bicycles, fresh morning air, new friends. She tried to read what else he had written. Oatmeal. Scrambled eggs. Warm showers. The list went on, two pages nearly filled with everyday things—small things—things she had never even thought to be grateful for.

She sat back in her seat and looked toward the front of the chapel, struggling to understand what she was feeling. She glanced again at Matt's list, trying to think of things she could be grateful for. Her job? Her job, she remembered, had sent her here! Her apartment in Manhattan and her cat? She didn't know if she'd ever see either her apartment or her cat again. Her parents? She let out a long breath, feeling stuck under a pile of messes she couldn't change.

"Are you okay?" Susan asked.

Genevieve forced a smile and a nod and closed her eyes, trying to imagine a happier place.

Her thoughts were soon interrupted by the priest cheerfully welcoming the congregation. The congregation stood and sang a song that felt entirely too cheery for Genevieve's temperament. An invocation was offered by an old man wearing overalls, and then the eyes of the congregation settled on Thomas, who stood at the lectern unpacking his bag of books and notes.

"Friends, it's good to be with you this morning. I have spent the last few weeks considering what I might share with you today, and the answer finally came while I was unclogging Jolene Ericson's sink on Wednesday evening. I'm not sure if there was any correlation between the sink and the inspiration that came, other than the work gave me a chance to be still and listen to God's whispering voice. The answer that came left me feeling grateful and alive as I remembered the hundreds of times I've had to relearn over the years that God stands anxiously at our doors, knocking and hoping we'll let Him in. I don't know about you, but I worry sometimes that my life is so busy and chaotic that I don't always hear the knock when it comes. And then there are the times, I'm embarrassed to admit, that I look out the peephole, see who it is, and carefully walk away from the door as quietly as possible, not feeling like I'm in the mindset or have the time to entertain a guest."

Genevieve noticed that several heads in the congregation were nodding at the priest's words. She also noticed that his words felt honest and sincere, somehow putting her at ease with the realization that she wasn't the only one who wrestled with things of a spiritual nature. The fact that this man was a priest made his message all the more palatable. He was a human, after all, struggling with something that felt universally human.

"I was reminded of one of my favorite parables this week—for a reason that I'm sure was in no way connected to fixing the sink. It's been one of my favorites because the depth of meaning and the lessons behind it seem to be fluid, changing as I change, growing as I grow, constantly reminding me of my own fallibility—not that such reminders are either comfortable or pleasant. And I suppose that's the magic and beauty of Christ's parables—they reach us all in unique ways wherever we are in our many and varied struggles with mortality.

"I understand this parable very differently today than I did when I was at the seminary nearly fifty years ago. It's the parable of the Prodigal Son from the fifteenth chapter of Luke. I'm certain there is no one here, excepting perhaps the children, who have not heard some version of this parable before. And I'm certain each of you has your own idea of what this parable is all about. I do not wish to alter those ideas, only to add to them—for whatever it may be worth. Those of you who have your Bibles with you, please join me in Luke."

The hushed sounds of rustling paper echoed throughout the hall. The priest waited for a moment until it was quiet. "You're welcome to read along in scripture as I offer a bit of a contemporary spin on this old tale." He looked up over the tops of his glasses before turning back to lectern. "There was once a wise and generous father who had two sons. The younger of the two, after looking around at his father's wealthy estate—as well as at all the work the estate required—begins putting together a plan. He's probably heard that the grass was somehow greener on the other side of the country and wants his share of it. So the young man goes to his father, expresses his desires to see the world, and rather impatiently demands that he be given his inheritance early so he can enjoy it while he's still young and handsome.

"Now, before some of you old-timers begin thinking this sounds awfully familiar, I will remind you of George Shaw's quote that "Youth is the most beautiful thing in this world—and what a pity that it has to be wasted on children!"

The congregation chuckled in response.

"But youth is also a time of gaining understanding. If we're lucky, wisdom is also gained through the experiences of our younger years, but unfortunately, wisdom is never a guaranteed hallmark of experience. Many of us find ourselves returning to the same lessons again and again. Unfortunately, I think this must have been the case with the prodigal. His father, a man with both experience and wisdom, tries, I'm sure, to point out to his younger son that his older brother is happy and enjoying his work on the estate. But the boy cannot be persuaded to think differently about his future. He wants out. He wants his money. He wants to be able to exercise his free will; however, he wishes to do so without scrutiny or questions from his family. He wants to be his own man and do his own thing.

"And so, shortly thereafter the young man sets off. He makes his way to the far-off city, where he quickly falls in with the party crowd, who are known to be particularly accepting and nonjudgmental, especially toward those who have cash in their pockets.

"Things go well for the boy at first. He has lots of pals. He enjoys wining and dining the ladies. He enjoys shopping sprees and lavish living. He thinks he's sucking the marrow out of life but is very slow to recognize that in reality he's just choking on the bones. Time passes. Life is lived. Fortunes are squandered, and wisdom proves elusive.

"And then one afternoon, the boy wakes up on the floor after another night of partying. His head is pounding, but he realizes there is also pounding coming from the door. He drags himself off the floor and opens the door. It's his landlord. He informs the boy that the neighbors have been complaining about all-night parties and strange odors. The rent, he says, is already ninety days late, and he hands the boy an eviction notice—effective immediately.

"Stunned into sobriety, the boy panics. He contacts all of his friends, hoping they'll have the money he loaned them or allow him to borrow some money until he can get back on his feet. But he quickly learns that nobody loves you when you're down and out.

"Abandoned by his friends and turned out of every pub in town, he turns to panhandling. He stands at the entrance to the city with a sign that says, 'Will work for food.' After the boy endures several days of being roughed up and spit on by passersby, a farmer takes pity on him, inviting him to come and work on his farm. He can't pay much, just a little food and a hayloft for a bed in exchange for an honest day's work. Desperate and hungry, the boy agrees and follows the man home.

"But the boy, who bucked against learning the virtues of hard work when he was on his father's farm, has a hard time fitting in on this farm too. After the boy messes up every job he's given, the farmer recognizes that he is effectively unskilled and hopelessly pitiful. There is only one job he's capable of not screwing up—feeding the pigs.

"In a time and place where bacon is appreciated for all its deliciousness, we may not fully appreciate the depth of the boy's degradation when he is relegated to caring for pigs. Those to whom Jesus spoke the parable would have understood. Among the Jews, working with pigs was considered the dirtiest of dirty jobs. Beyond being filthy and stinky, the animals were and still are considered taboo among the Jewish people. And not only does this boy have to work with these animals, scripture suggests he lives with them and is actually envious of the food they have to eat.

"Jesus used this imagery, I believe, to suggest that the boy had fallen as low as he could fall. He had hit rock bottom. But as this and other parables suggest, rock bottom is a pretty great place to begin building a sure foundation. And scripture tells us that it is on that rock bottom that the *boy comes to himself.* It may not have happened immediately. It rarely does. Growth, wisdom, true understanding—if they are real and sincere—must be accompanied by meekness and humility. These virtues rarely come either easily or naturally. Many of us have to marinate in the juices of our own foolishness and the sad results of our own pride before we can begin to appreciate the merits of these noble virtues.

"I have learned by watching myself and others that most of us have to experience loss before we can learn to appreciate anything. This parable seems to concur. It is only in the depths of humility that this boy begins to see how far he has fallen—that he begins to see all he has lost. And it is in that lost and fallen state that he begins to remember the comfort and joy he once knew in his father's house. He looks around at his clothes, his surroundings, his quality of life and is humble for perhaps the first time in his life. Hungry and emaciated, he remembers that even the humblest of his father's servants had plenty of food to eat. And so, swallowing what is left of his pride, he picks himself up out of the mud and begins the long journey home, ready to submit himself to the will of his father and become a servant in the very home where he'd been raised.

"That journey home must have been a sobering one. I should have mentioned that to make matters worse for this young man, there is a famine in the land. Food is scarce. Hospitality is lean at best. He is no doubt dirty and ragged and stinky from his time working with the pigs. It's hard to wash off the stench of pigs, even with the fruitiest of soaps—which certainly would have been in short supply. But he presses on, holding on to the smallest glimmer of hope that his father will have compassion on him.

"I'm sure he worries what kind of reception he will receive when he arrives. He has nothing to show for the time and treasure he has squandered. His youth and good looks have been lost to living the party life, gallivanting from one carnal pleasure to the next, and then living with unsavory swine. He is washed up, broken, starved, defeated, and demoralized. And yet there is enough memory left in him of the good times he'd enjoyed under his father's roof to keep a flicker of hope burning within him as he trudges toward home one dusty, painful, humiliating step at a time."

Genevieve looked down the row and saw that everyone had their eyes on the priest except Matt, who looked as though he were feverishly taking notes in his journal. She wondered what he was writing, what he was getting out of the sermon, what this all meant to him.

"My favorite part of this parable," the priest said, looking up from his notes, "is what comes next. Surely this boy travels many miles on his own, but according to scripture, when he is still a great way off, the father sees his lost son, has compassion on him, and runs and embraces him, overwhelmed with joy and mercy. This implies to me that the father had not given up hope that his son would someday return. He kept a vigil, patiently waiting, endlessly watchful, and undoubtedly prayerful that his son would return.

"The son, full of shame and contrition, is quick to admit that he's lost his inheritance, that he's been foolish and reckless, and that he feels unworthy on many levels to be called his father's son. He humbly submits himself, begging instead to be a lowly servant. But the father, ever quick to forgive, calls for the best robe and a ring for the boy's finger, and he has shoes put on the boy's bruised and dusty feet.

"This treatment is certainly far beyond anything the boy could have expected or even imagined, but the father is only getting started. He calls for the butchering of the fatted calf and orders a feast to be prepared with music and dancing and great rejoicing for the return of the son who had been lost for so long.

"It's while this party is going on that the other son, the loyal and dutiful older brother of the prodigal, returns from his work in the fields and, upon hearing the merriment, inquires of the servant to discover what's going on. When he learns that the party is for his brother—the same brother who left the farm and abandoned his family to chase after the lusts of his heart—the older brother is angry. Perhaps he is feeling underappreciated for all the work he has done, for his loyalty and steadiness. He doesn't understand what the big deal is. Sure his brother is back, but he wasn't much fun when he was there the last time. And yet his father is showering him with love and affection and a party, the likes of which the older son has never had for himself.

"Miffed and bubbling with jealousy, the older son refuses to go into the party with his family. The father comes out, and the older brother carries on, surely saying something about life being unfair. Scripture says the father *entreats* his eldest son to come and join the party. I had to remind myself of that word—entreat. It means to *beg or to plead with*. But at this moment, the older brother is more concerned about the lack of fairness than he is about love or forgiveness or the fact that he hasn't seen his brother for probably many years. In that moment, jealousy and envy take the place of understanding. In that moment, instead of showing compassion and mercy, the older brother is also guilty of stoking the fires of what Paul refers to as the *natural man*.

"Paul, in his first epistle to the Corinthians, says, 'But as it is written, Eye hath not seen, nor ear heard, neither have entered into the heart of man, the things which God hath prepared for them that love him. But God hath revealed them unto us by his Spirit: for the Spirit searcheth all things, yea, the deep things of God. But the natural man receiveth not the things of the Spirit of God: for they are foolishness unto him: neither can he know them, because they are spiritually discerned.'" [1]

Thomas nodded, scanning the congregation before returning to his notes. "As a one-time vocal enemy of the church, Paul would have known firsthand this truth of which he spoke. He understood the natural man's propensity toward pride and his perpetual inclination for irreverence and ridicule toward all that is holy. Jealousy and envy are just two of a natural man's innumerably inherent vices—vices we are all subject to as mortals.

"This concept of a natural man is an intriguing one. From all I have been able to surmise, this natural man is the cause of all our woes. It is insensitive to and rejecting of the Spirit of God. Where there should be love and reverence, the natural man breathes out hate and enmity.

"I'm sure I didn't understand the depth of meaning behind this parable when I first heard it as a child. Perhaps I still don't. What I understood then was that the compassion of the boys' father was heartwarming and generous. What I understand now is that I hope and pray for the same treatment. And what I see today that I did not see in my youth is that both sons—the loyal as well as the unfaithful—were in need of repentance, of a change—even a broken heart and a contrite spirit.[2] They both needed to shake off the natural man—their carnal tendencies—and humble themselves to the point that they could hear and listen to the still, small voice of the Spirit of God. I find it compelling that the fruits of that spirit were outlined by that same Paul who rejected those fruits for years until his eyes were opened to love, joy, peace, gentleness, goodness, faith, meekness, patience, and so much more.

"The paths to God—to mercy—to understanding—are as many and varied as we are. God does not and will not give up on us. Like the father in the parable, He waits and He watches for us to return to Him. And it's been my humble experience that when we are still a great way off, feeling overwhelmed and broken, He comes running to lift us and embrace us and show us more mercy and grace than we could ever be worthy of.

"In the end, even the very most loyal and dutiful among us still stands in need of repentance and forgiveness, if for no other reason than our own self-righteousness and pride. We all must be meek and humble before we're willing and able to learn. Those virtues may come naturally to some, but I have yet to meet anyone for whom those qualities arrived as unearned gifts. For most of us mortals, I daresay that pride, egotism, arrogance, and narcissism seem to constantly stand in the way of our spiritual progress.

"I, like many of you, have experienced the pain and sorrow that come from being compelled to be humble. It's no picnic. I've learned that though it requires much toil to build one's house upon a rock, it's far easier than having one's house ripped from its unstable foundation and blown to bits by the inevitable storms of life. The simple truth is that the temporary ease and pleasure of a home on the sand can never compare to the security and longevity of a home with a rock-solid foundation.

"We are creatures who seek comfort. We like the smooth road without any bumps or excessive dust. But the road to truth is rarely free of bumps and is never comfortable. For most of us it's challenging and even upsetting. It requires us to give up what we are for the hope that we might become something better. As truth enlarges our minds and capacities, it also stretches us, often pulling us in uncomfortable directions as it challenges previously held beliefs and goals. If we submit our hearts to truth's power and influence, it will lead us in new directions, to summits we never could have seen had we remained stagnant or unyielding.

"So if truth is so desirable and beneficial, why doesn't God make it easier?" Thomas took a dramatic breath, panning across the congregation before returning to his notes. "I've been asked this question many times over the years. I remember one young mother asking me why, if following the way of truth were so worthwhile, God wouldn't just force us to do it, the way she exercised dominion over her child. I've thought about that question many times over the decades, and I'm convinced that God forces no one to truth. To do so would be contrary to every law of heaven. But that in no way suggests He doesn't love us or care about our decisions. Repeatedly throughout scripture, He invites us to ask, seek, and knock, promising that with time, patience, and perseverance, answers will come.

"God will never force us to heaven. He will never force us to choose good over evil. Instead, as the prodigal discovered, God creates opportunities for us to come to ourselves, to become aware of truths that can open our eyes and hearts and lift us out of our squalor. With mercy, love, and compassion, God patiently waits and watches for us to turn toward truth, toward home, toward Him. I have learned through personal experience and through observing the lives of others that coming to oneself is a key to unlocking the door that leads to joy. There may be other ways to get there that I'm not aware of. Surely mankind has been searching for alternative paths to joy since the beginning. Some alternate routes have successfully provided some semblance of happiness. But to my knowledge, that happiness has always been short lived and painfully temporary.

"C. S. Lewis, himself an atheist turned believer, said in his book *Mere Christianity:* 'God made us: invented us as a man invents an engine. A car is made to run on petrol, and it would not run properly on anything else. Now God designed the human machine to run on Himself. He Himself is the fuel our spirits were designed to burn, or the food our spirits were designed to feed on. There is no other. That is why it is just no good asking God to make us happy in our own way without bothering about religion. God cannot give us a happiness and peace apart from Himself, because it is not there. There is no such thing.'

"This is the lesson the prodigal was compelled to discover as he sat wallowing in the mire of his own making. God does not leave us, but we are pridefully inclined to leave Him. He never turns his back on us the way we turn our backs on Him. His mercy is ever present, waiting patiently for us to awake and arise and inherit all the promises of heaven. And though the road back home may be long and steep, the promised mercy, grace, and blessings—without exception or hesitation— are available to each of us."

Genevieve carefully considered Thomas's words. It was more religious straight talk than she'd heard in her entire life. She found it compelling and thought provoking, yet as she sat there in the pew, she found there was a part of her that remained resistant to fully embracing it. She looked around, noticing that all eyes remained on the priest except those of the congregants who were taking notes. Matt had filled several pages in his journal, and Sonja and Holly were busily writing notes on small pieces of paper they'd pulled from their purses.

The sermon continued for another fifteen minutes, but Genevieve couldn't focus, her pride once again overshadowing any potential meekness. She was smarter than this, and she wasn't going to fall to victim to the opium of the masses. Still, as she tuned in and out of Thomas's sermon, she continued to find his words weighty and nearly persuasive.

Genevieve's thoughts were interrupted by the music of the organ and the singing of the congregation. Susan held a hymnbook for them to share, but Genevieve didn't feel much like singing. She was restless, unsettled, itching to get out.

She made her move immediately following the benediction but quickly found that the aisle was clogged with throngs of congregants surging forward. Finally breaking through, she stood at the back door alone, watching the congregants mill about, talk to each other, and converse with Thomas. As she turned around to leave, she noticed that Matt was still in his seat, his head down as he continued to write in his journal.

1. 1 Corinthians 2:9-10, 14
2. Psalms 51:17

CHAPTER 32

Gumdrops and Straight Talk

The greatest good you can do for another is not just to
share your riches but to reveal to him his own.
— Benjamin Disraeli —

Genevieve left as quickly as she could, bounding down the old stone steps. Weighed down with the dread of spending five more months here, she considered jumping on her bike and going, going—anywhere. She needed to get out—away from here—away from this clean air—someplace where she could figure out what she was feeling. She was discouraged as she approached the bikes, however, and discovered that the nearest women's bike was deep in the pile. On a different day with a different outfit, it might not have been a problem to use a men's bike. But she knew that her dress would not work with the crossbar, and she did not care to make a scene by rearranging all the bikes to get to hers.

She looked around, searching for another escape, and remembered the cemetery just feet away. She bounded up the steps and through the rusty metal gate, making her way quickly through the headstones to the bench that was hiding in the shadows of the crab apple tree. Sitting down, she closed her eyes, breathing deeply; her heart pounded in her ears as it slowly regained its normal pace.

"It looks like you're having a tough day."

Startled, Genevieve opened her eyes to find a frail-looking woman just within the tree's shadow. Dressed in a gingham skirt and a dark sweater, she was leaning on a cane.

"Are you all right?" the woman asked.

"I think so," Genevieve responded, taking a deep breath. "Just getting some air."

The woman nodded, moving surprisingly quickly and sitting down next to Genevieve. "This is a good place to do it. I've been coming here for more than seventy years to do that very thing. I'm Hildegard." She extended a soft, wrinkled hand, which Genevieve took hold of as if it were made of delicate porcelain.

"Pleasure," she lied. "Your accent...I can't place it. Where are you from?"

"Germany originally, but Niederbipp's been my home for more than eighty years."

"This town seems to have more than its share of older folks," Genevieve said, hoping the woman would take a hint and leave her alone, but the woman only laughed.

"When you're young and your skin's still tight, you don't think it will ever happen to you. But age and gravity catch up with all of us. You'll see."

She smiled a rather disarming smile, showing teeth that Genevieve knew were too straight and too white to be her own.

"I think I saw you here last week, didn't I?"

Genevieve looked more closely at the old woman, trying to remember if she'd ever seen her before. "Uh, you might have."

"Yes, I thought so," she said, her eyes sparkling. "You were here with several other kids. I thought I recognized the bicycles. You're from Ruby's place, right?"

She nodded.

"Ruby's a friend of mine. We don't see much of each other during the summer months when you kids are on the farm, but we share a talent for skipping rocks. You might not believe it when I tell you, but we were once rivals in the annual Niederbipp rock-skipping competition."

"Not anymore?" Genevieve asked, amused.

"Nope. A few decades ago, we realized that we were the only ladies left in our age bracket, so we decided we might as well be friends. We turned out to be better friends than we ever were rivals."

Genevieve nodded, wondering if this woman, with her unusual friendship with Ruby, might offer any unique insights for her article. "She didn't by any chance match you with your husband, did she?"

"Oh no. I was married and widowed at least twenty years before Ruby ever made Harmony Hill her home."

"Oh…I'm sorry."

"Thank you. That was a long time ago. I've come here to visit my husband's grave nearly every day since then."

"He's buried here?"

"Right over there," Hildegard said, pointing with a crooked finger to the six white government-issue crosses that rose from a manicured patch of sod.

"He was a veteran?"

"Yes. He died in France with his five best friends. That year, 1944, was a bad one for this town. Six of us were made widows before September was through. I have the distinct and unfortunate honor of being the last of the Niederbippian World War II widows."

"I'm sorry," Genevieve repeated soberly.

Hildegard shrugged. "Good genes, I guess. Sometimes I think they're too good. It gets rather lonesome being the last of anything."

Genevieve nodded, not knowing what to say.

"Are you enjoying your time here? I reckon it's probably a lot to take in, isn't it?

"Yeah."

"Well, if it's any consolation, you're not the first young lady I've found sitting on this bench feeling overwhelmed."

"Really?"

"Sure," she said, patting Genevieve's knee with her wrinkled hand. "The road to happily ever after is never as quick and straight as any of us would like it to be."

"Do you actually believe it even exists?"

"Me?" The old lady let out a long breath before shaking her head. "I've been around long enough to be a little doubtful."

"Really?" Genevieve replied, surprised by the woman's frankness.

"My personal experience is limited, but I was married long enough to learn that marriage is never a cakewalk. I've been an observer of people my whole life,and I've seen enough to know that the only easy marriages are the ones you don't know very well. If you haven't learned it already from Ruby, I'm sure you will: marriage takes work. It takes grit. It requires tenacity and patience and an ability to bite one's tongue sometimes when yelling feels more natural."

Genevieve shook her head, feeling even more overwhelmed. "So, what's the point?"

"Pardon?"

Genevieve looked into the woman's kind, gray eyes. "I've always been the sort of girl who considers things like patience and kindness to be weaknesses. And if I want to yell, chances are the whole block's gonna hear it."

"Spirited one, are you?"

"Oh hell yeah!"

Hildegard patted her on the knee. "That's lovely, dear."

"Excuse me?" she asked, wondering if the woman had actually heard her.

"That only means there's a certain kind of man you should avoid."

"I don't understand," Genevieve replied, thoroughly confused.

"Sure. So you're a yeller and tend to be strong willed and hotheaded. There's nothing terribly wrong with that."

"Wait—there isn't?"

"Well, I wouldn't want to live with you, if that's what you're asking. But that's only because I tend to lean the same way."

"You?"

The old woman smiled. "You sure as tootin' don't outlive all your friends and relatives and get to be ninety-eight years old by being nice all the time."

Genevieve stifled a laugh. "You're not at all what I expected."

"Oh, were you expecting me to be a nice old lady who keeps gumdrops in her purse?"

"Well yeah, kind of."

Hildegard laughed, opening the golden clasp of her small handbag and pulling out a couple of gumdrops. She offered one to Genevieve and popped the other one into her mouth. "Sometimes it's best not to surprise people," she mumbled, "but I still like gumdrops. I've learned that opinionated girls with fire in their bellies rarely grow up to be docile lap dogs. It's just not in our nature, is it?"

"Well, no…" she said, taking a bite of her gumdrop while she tried to figure out where this woman was coming from. "So, I'm curious about something you said…something about knowing what kind of guy I should avoid."

Hildegard nodded slowly, chewing her gumdrop. "Yep, do you see it?"

"I'm not sure. What did you mean?"

"Oh, girly, you know what I mean. Would you want to be married to someone exactly like you?"

"I can't say I've ever thought that much about it."

"Trust me. It'd never work. An impatient hothead should never marry another impatient hothead."

"Why not?"

"Are you kidding? Could you imagine the mess their kids would be?"

"I'm not sure."

"No, no, no. I'm surprised Ruby hasn't already taught you this. It's one of her secrets, you know?"

"Is it?"

"Sure. I know you're not asking for advice, but I'm gonna give you some anyway."

Genevieve laughed in spite of her grumpy mood.

"Remember that no matter how well you're matched, chances are he'll have at least a few habits that annoy the heck out of you. And when that happens, I want you to remember this little talk you had on this bench with the lady who's old enough to be dead a few times over and might be senile. Remember this—for everything you find annoying in your husband, there's at least one thing he finds annoying about you. You can focus on those things, or you can spend more time making out—but you can't do both. It's a pretty basic rule, but it's truth. So if you'd rather make out than sleep on the couch, keep your dang mouth shut."

Genevieve laughed again. "Yeah, you're definitely not at all like what I thought you'd be."

Hildegard pursed her lips and nodded. "That's exactly what my husband told me about a month after he married me."

"Is that good or bad?"

She shrugged, handing Genevieve a bag of gumdrops. "It just is. You think you get to know someone during dating and courtship, but it's all just really a big fake out, right? Putting on your best face, putting your best foot forward—I'm sure you know the drill. Proposals are made. Wedding bells ring. And then one morning soon after the wedding, you wake up next to a snoring, smelly stranger, and you have to admit you don't know this person as well as you thought you did."

Genevieve tried not to laugh. "Is that the way it was for you?"

"Of course. My husband and I courted for nearly a year, but I never knew what a hot mess he was. Most men will never admit it, but let's face it—most of them are. And the truth is, we ladies usually aren't much better, especially the longer we go without men in our lives. We get a cat, then two or three, and pretty soon we turn into crazy cat ladies. Heck, I should know. I've got three myself. They've helped dull the pain of the void Jonas left in my life, but if I'm honest, they're really lousy substitutes for a husband." Hildegard shook her head, giving Genevieve a chance to consider her own recent feline acquisition.

"There are plenty of substitutes, but in reality, we're all looking for marriage," Hildegard said softly. "To love and be loved by another human—it's what we're made for."

Genevieve nodded slowly, feeling another prick of grumpiness.

"I applaud you for being here, for taking control of your life and future."

"Huh?" Genevieve asked, looking confused.

"Being proactive, I mean—coming here to improve your life and your chances of success in marriage. I'll tell you, if I were twentysomething again, I'd be right there with you." She patted Genevieve on the knee again. "You're too young to recognize the power of regrets, but when you get to be my age and have spent the last several decades thinking way too much about them—along with the thousands of what-ifs and too-bads—your perspective is a little different. I'm convinced that God gave us life intending that we'd share it."

Genevieve sat silent for a moment, feeling increasingly irritated. She grabbed a handful of gumdrops and filled her mouth with them, trying to keep herself from saying something rude. But she was soon distracted by the sunlight focusing on a redheaded woman standing on the top step of the church. She knew it was Amy—she didn't have to look twice. She sat back, hoping not to be seen. The last thing she wanted was to have to pretend to be nice. As the old woman continued to ramble, Genevieve watched as Amy descended the stairs, holding the hand of her husband. She was surprised by the envy she felt at that moment. She tried to forget the image as the old woman continued to talk. But Genevieve didn't hear anything she had to say, her mind in a different place. After a few minutes and without warning, she stood and handed the old woman the bag of gumdrops. "I gotta go."

Hildegard smiled and nodded. "Remember what I told you. It's much more fun to make out than it is to fight all the time. If you'll remember that, you'll save yourself a whole lot of trouble."

"Thanks for the advice," she said, turning to go. As she wove her way through the tombstones, she decided that seeking refuge in a cemetery was probably a silly thing to do.

CHAPTER 33

The Road to Tionesta

If you break your neck, if you have nothing to eat,
if your house is on fire, then you got a problem.
Everything else is inconvenience.
— Robert Fulghum —

There you are," Spencer said, looking up as Genevieve unlatched the gate. "We were looking for you. The others already went back to the farm."

"Thanks for waiting," Genevieve responded.

"Sure. I was actually thinking that it would be silly to go all the way back to the farm just to have to travel the same roads again later. What do you think about going now?"

"You mean to Tonkaneesta?"

Spencer smiled. "Or Tionesta."

"Right," she replied, letting out a long, drawn-out breath. "It's a sports bar, right?"

"That's what I heard. We could probably be there by the time the game starts if we leave right away."

"And they have drinks, right?"

"Well yeah, it's a bar. Why else do people go to a bar? I mean, besides to watch sports?"

"It couldn't get any worse than going back to the farm, right?"

Spencer smiled charmingly. "That's what I was thinking. Are you in or out?"

"I thought Greg was coming."

"Yeah, he wussed out. Said he needed a nap or something. You don't have to come if you don't want to."

"No, I want to, but I don't have any clothes to change into."

"Yeah, neither do I," he said, looking down at his khaki chinos.

"And you're buying the first round, right?"

"That's what I said, didn't I?"

"Yeah. Just making sure."

"You're in?"

"What the hell. It's only fifteen miles, right? I used to do that all the time in my spin classes."

"Cool. Let's go. I think we could be back by dinner if we're fast."

The day was still fairly cool as they pedaled their old bicycles, following Highway 62 in a winding northeasterly direction. The town of Niederbipp faded quickly as they followed the Allegheny cutting its crooked path through the pastoral landscape; the farms soon gave way to thick old-growth woods. Big, white clouds raced across the sky, painting the pavement, trees, and river with moving shadows.

With his long legs and muscular build, Spencer held a physical advantage over Genevieve and led the way, driven by his passion for sports. She managed to keep up the pace for some time, but after what she guessed was five miles, she felt winded and thirsty and began to lag behind. Spencer seemed anxious and impatient, and so after another mile or so, she told him to go on without her and promised to catch up.

She didn't have to tell him twice. She continued on the best she could but soon found herself alone, the deserted county highway void of any cars on this lazy Sunday, making it feel like a surreal, apocalyptic landscape. It wasn't long before she began to wonder where she was going and why she had come. Her mouth became so dry and her backside so sore that a nap in the bunkhouse began to sound like a far more attractive way to spend the afternoon.

Her discouragement only grew, however, when she saw the old, dusty placard for Bill's Tavern nailed to a tree. Billiards & Drinks. 12 Miles ahead in Beautiful Tionesta. Twelve miles! It had been years since  she had spent any real time on a bike with wheels, but she was certain she had ridden more than three lousy miles. She pushed on, riding harder and hoping to catch up with Spencer. But after what she guessed was two more miles, she rolled to a stop in the shade of a giant maple, feeling spent. The highway climbed gently in front of her, wrapping around a bend and disappearing into the woods. She was thirsty and hungry. Her throat was dry. Her cute summer dress was drenched in sweat, and she could feel her face pulsating with heat with each heartbeat. She looked around, hoping to find water if only to cool down her face, but she quickly realized that the river was not to her right as it had been. She tried to remember the last time she had seen it, but she couldn't, her head feeling cloudy.

After catching her breath, she pushed on, driven by her thirst for a cold, stiff drink. Standing on her pedals, hoping to gain some mechanical advantage, she had nearly made it to the top of the hill when she heard a pop. Immediately, her right foot slipped off the pedal, and she stubbed her toe hard on the pavement below. Throwing her weight to try to keep from toppling over, she flew forward, slamming her ribs against the handlebars while bumping her left shin against the other pedal. Somehow she avoided falling over, but she knocked the wind out of herself. She doubled over in pain, managing to make her way to the shoulder of the highway, where she collapsed onto a patch of tall grass.

After dry heaving for several minutes, her ribs pounding in pain, she was finally able to sit down and assess the rest of the damage. The tip of her right shoe had been ripped open, exposing a bloody toe. A giant, blue-green goose egg had formed on her shin and was pulsating with pain. She was dirty and sweaty and sore, and she had no idea where she was and no way to call for help. And on top of all that, she was alone. Anger began swelling up inside her. She was angry at Spencer for ditching her, angry at the stupid bike, angry at the stupid road and this stupid county and her stupid job that had sent her here. She was angry at Thomas and angry at Hildegard and angry at the whole stupid town of Niederbipp. She was angry at Ruby and Lorenzo and their stupid farm and all the stupid people who'd come here for the summer. She was angry at her boss and this stupid assignment and all the stupid things she'd had to do all week. She felt broken—finished—kaput!

She was unable to control her emotions, and the floodgates burst open. The tears rolled down her cheeks with complete abandon. It was ugly. She knew it was ugly, but she didn't care. She was sore and tired and more broken than she had ever been in her entire life. She felt hopeless and helpless.

As she picked at the final remnants of her nail polish with her calloused, farm-worn hands, she recognized that the beauty she had spent so much time and money cultivating and preserving was worth nothing on this dusty, godforsaken highway so far away from anything familiar or civilized. She felt abandoned, forgotten, forsaken. Unable to conjure even one positive thought, she cried again. She was miserable. She wanted to die. She stared into the woods for what felt like an hour until even her tears were gone.

A mosquito landed on her upper arm, and she watched as it drove its thin, pointed nose into her flesh. Again her anger flared, and she slapped the bug, killing it. She brushed its corpse off her arm but noticed another mosquito on her leg. Not ready to get up but not ready to be eaten alive either, she struggled to her feet and hurried to her bike, anxious to get away. She lifted her bike out of the gravel and pushed it back onto the pavement, but she knew immediately that something was wrong. Startled at first by what looked like a long, black snake, her first thought was to ditch the bike and run. But taking a quick closer look, she realized it was the bicycle chain, broken and dragging.

With one more thing to be angry about, she reached down and yanked on the chain. It was greasy and dirty, and when her hand slipped, the chain left a black streak across her palm and fingers. The stubborn chain barely moved, still stuck on the teeth of the crank. Her anger growing, she yanked the chain again, leaving a second ugly streak on her hand. She threw the bike down on the opposite side of the highway, attacking the chain with both hands, which proved far messier than she imagined, both her hands quickly becoming covered in black grease. She grunted and cursed and pulled and finally freed the chain from the teeth. Feeling good about her minor triumph, she kicked a rusty paint can that had been lying in the grass—and immediately wished she hadn't.

Within seconds, what looked like a thousand angry wasps exited their home in that paint can and were in attack mode, swarming anything that moved. It took Genevieve a moment to realize what was happening. The yellow wasps began dive-bombing, getting stuck in her hair and flying up her dress. She ran the best she could down the middle of the highway, swatting and slapping every wasp she could reach. She felt a sharp pain on her cheek and another on her thigh, but she knew she couldn't stop, her adrenaline carrying her as far away as she could go. After a hundred yards, she could still hear the buzzing of the wasps. Trying to avoid more stings, she continued to slap at her face and limbs—completely oblivious to the fact that she was spreading the grease from her hands onto every part of her body and dress.

After another hundred yards, she began to slow down; she was out of steam. As her adrenaline began dropping and pain started coming from too many throbbing places on her neck, legs, and arms, she cried out in horror. But the wasps wouldn't quit. Desperate to get away, she noticed a pool of water on the side of the road. Without thinking, she ran into the pool only to find that it was mostly mud. But she didn't care, the pesky wasps continuing to hound her. She found the deepest spot she could, burying most of her body in the dark, cool mud. Grabbing handfuls of the mud, she smeared it over the rest of her exposed skin, trying to escape the wasps' painful assault. But she could still hear them. Several of them were stuck in her hair, driving her crazy with their incessant buzzing. More desperate than ever, she took a deep breath before leaning forward, burying her head in the murky, muddy water.

She held her breath for as long as she could, and then she surfaced, gasping for air. She listened carefully. Even with her ears half filled with mud, she could still hear the buzzing coming from her mud-bogged hair. She bunched her hair together and plunged her head into the muddy water again and again until the buzzing seemed to cease. She waited, sitting still and listening intently. The buzzing had really stopped. Slowly, cautiously, and aching, she rose from the mud. She tried to move, but her feet were buried deep in the dark, stinky bog. Instead, she knelt and tried to crawl on all fours, making slow but steady progress. Finally she collapsed on the side of the bog.

She might have cried, but she was completely out of tears. She looked down at her dress, one of her favorites, and knew it was ruined. Her limbs ached from the wasps' poison. Scared, hurt, and chilled, she wondered what she was going to do. It was then she realized that the mud had sucked off her shoes. She looked into the black water and knew it would be nearly impossible to find them.

Stunned into complete and total sobriety, Genevieve tried to imagine her options. She knew it would be hours before anyone would try to find her. She didn't know for sure how far she had come since she had seen the sign for Bill's Tavern, but she guessed Niederbipp was still closer than Tionesta. She figured that when she didn't arrive at the tavern, Spencer would probably decide she had returned home. And by then, he might be too drunk to be helpful anyway.

For the first time all day, she heard a car on the highway. She scrambled up the mud bog's shallow embankment just as a pickup truck heading south passed by, but the driver didn't notice her. She looked up the road to her bike and could see even from this distance that hundreds of wasps were still buzzing around it. She knew that a bicycle without a chain was pointless enough, but a bicycle without a chain paired with a rider without shoes was completely hopeless. With no phone and no farmhouse in sight, she began walking back the way she had come, one painful step at a time.

CHAPTER 34

Awakening

We must be willing to let go of the life we've planned
so as to have the life that is waiting for us.
-Joseph Campbell -

Within twenty minutes or so, another car passed, this one heading north. Genevieve tried to wave it down. Though the vehicle slowed, as soon as the driver saw Genevieve, she sped off, looking frightened. Genevieve looked down at her mud-caked skin. The mud was beginning to crack as it dried, and she realized that even the best Samaritan might be reluctant to help out a woman who looked as awful as she did. And so when the road finally began paralleling the river again, Genevieve nearly ran to the water, anxious to wash the mud from her hair and skin. Her feet were tender as she crossed the river's stony bank.

She was just kneeling to dip her hands into the water when she heard the sound of another automobile on the highway. She stood and waved, but to her surprise, the passengers in the car only smiled and waved back as they motored on.

Frustrated, she knelt again and was about to dip her hands into the cool, clean water when she saw her reflection for the first time. She shook her head, dried mud cakes falling from her hair as she stared at the disgusting swamp monster before her. Desperate to be rid of the mud, she cleaned her hands the best she could. The mud fell away quickly, but the grease from the bicycle chain remained. She picked up a smooth stone about the size of a bar of soap and began rubbing it between her hands, trying to get rid of the grease. It was slow and painful, and she was soon shivering and worried that she might be going into shock from the wasp stings. But she kept working, stepping into the river so she could wash her legs. This soon proved to be pointless, her filthy dress spreading new mud on her legs as quickly as she could wash it away. She knew she had to go in deeper.

Reluctantly, she waded farther into the river, her tender feet gingerly testing the bottom. She walked until the water was up above her waist. She was already chilled, and the thought of going any deeper was completely unattractive. Squatting, she tried to rinse her hair, but she quickly lost her footing as the current tugged at her dress, pulling her downstream. She panicked. As her feet slid across the slippery rocks and mud, she found it ironic that after all she had been through today, she was going to die by drowning in the river.

The current carried her a couple hundred feet downriver before she was able to find her footing near a large, sun-bleached log that had been stripped of its bark. Fearing another fall, Genevieve looked around to make sure she was alone before she stripped off her dress, eliminating the drag from the current. She threw the dress over the log, using its hem as a washcloth to clear the mud from her arms, legs, and neck before working on her face. As the mud washed away, she was shocked to see the painful, swollen circles around each of the wasp stings. She counted twenty-three of them on her legs alone but could tell from the pain and heat on her back that there were many more that she couldn't see.

Her hair was a disaster. She did the best she could to rinse out the stinky mud, but without shampoo and conditioner, it simply clumped together into four tangled dreadclumps. She tried running her fingers through them but gave up when she realized that the remaining grease from her hands was only making it worse. She looked down at her underwear and bra, once white, now unsightly and permanently stained black and brown by the mud.

A million miles away from the civilized world she knew, Genevieve looked over her polka-dotted body and couldn't help but laugh. As she imagined watching a video of her last three hours, she had to laugh even more. She laughed and laughed, more than she had ever laughed at herself in her entire life. She was just beginning to think about getting out and walking the rest of the way back to Niederbipp when it began to rain. This only caused her to laugh more. Of course it's raining, she thought to herself.

As she waited for the rain to stop, she realized that the cool water of the Allegheny soothed her stings, and so she stayed, her body acclimating to the temperature of the water until she was no longer cold. The rain continued, sprinkling at first and then pouring down. The water droplets danced all around her, and the clouds came down low, touching the treetops on the surrounding hills. As she sat and watched nature's display of beauty, something in her began to soften.

Thunder echoed off the hills and rolled down the river, followed by a flash of lighting as the rain fell even harder. Genevieve looked up at the marbled clouds overhead, giant raindrops falling onto her face and into the water all around. The surface of the river frolicked like it was host to a million tiny dancers. She opened her mouth and tilted her head way back, catching the raindrops in her mouth. She laughed in spite of herself, imagining how angry she would certainly have been if she'd been caught in this storm on a bicycle. But this was somehow different, somehow enjoyable. For the first time in her entire life, she sat still and watched with awe and wonder the power of a thunderstorm. And what had once seemed so intimidating and unpleasant quickly became one of the most exhilarating experiences of her life. She felt alive and rejuvenated, even tempted to get out of the water and dance in the rain.

After twenty minutes, the storm passed, drawing open the heavens behind it. The sun cut its way through the parting clouds, briefly leaving a rainbow that spanned the river. Genevieve tried to remember the last time she had seen a real rainbow. It had certainly been years if not a couple of decades. She looked around, charmed by the small, low, puffy clouds that seemed to be tied to the tops of the trees with kite string. At the call of a bird, she turned her head to the banks of the river, where she noticed for the first time the wildflowers that grew there. She realized she had walked right through them and hadn't even noticed—thousands of flowers in gold, white, and blue.

Her attention was drawn to another bird, a big, white one with a long neck, wading through the shallow water on the other side of the river. Its long, orange beak pointing forward, the bird moved rhythmically with a stealthy grace, pausing briefly before lunging forward into the water. When he came out with a wriggling fish in his beak, Genevieve cheered. The giant bird glanced at her briefly before swallowing his lunch whole, his catch continuing to wriggle as it descended his throat.

As Genevieve lay on her back, floating weightless in the water, she was reminded of a memory from a time long ago, long before life became complicated with work and deadlines. She had learned to swim at Lake George the summer she was five or six. She remembered the simple joy and freedom she had felt when she was finally confident enough to not freak out when the water encircled her face as she floated on her back next to her mother. She smiled now, just as she had then, remembering those beautiful, simple days, so full of wonder and possibility.

In the silence of the moment, Genevieve realized how far away that life was now, and it wasn't just because her parents had sold the lake house to finance a flat in Paris. Life had become complicated. There were bills to pay and ladders to climb and deadlines to meet. Those simple joys had been pushed aside for the bigger dreams she'd chased. But she realized in that moment that she couldn't claim to be any happier after achieving those dreams and climbing those ladders than she had been as a six-year-old girl learning how to float on her back in the summer waters of Lake George.

She closed her eyes and she was there again, dressed in her favorite swimsuit—yellow and blue stripes. Her parents were happy, her father just beginning his quick and successful ascent up the career ladder as a partner in an investment banking firm. The money had been nice. It had afforded her small family many luxuries, but it had come at a cost. Things like that always do. Her father was rarely present, causing her parents to grow apart emotionally to the point that Genevieve had often wondered if the money was the only reason they stayed together.

As she considered these things, Genevieve recognized that the state of her parents' marriage had played a big role in the development of her opinions about men, about marriage, about life and dreams and her path forward. Like snowballs rolling downhill, those opinions had gathered mass, becoming bigger and bolder with each passing year, influenced, no doubt, by the hipster culture in Manhattan and the hookup culture she had observed around the world. Marriage, committed relationships, even any flavor of commitment in general had seemed to be on an irreversible train to oblivion.

But things were different here. She had been thrown into a group with eleven weirdos who not only wanted to be married someday but were also willing to sacrifice five months of their lives to achieve their ultimate goal. It bucked all the trends she'd spent her adult life observing. And the strange thing was that they were normal people—mostly— not fanatics or crazies or old-fashioned zealots. They were just people who were looking for someone to love, looking to be loved, looking for commitment—and ready to work at becoming the best versions of themselves in order to obtain what they sought.

She had referred to them all week as weirdos, but as she lay there in her underwear in the middle of the Allegheny River, she laughed again at herself, realizing that maybe they actually weren't so weird after all. They were seekers. They were dreamers. They were magic-bean buyers. But unlike some people she had known over the years who had claimed to be idealists, these ones were willing to do the work to achieve their dreams. They had bought a bag of magic beans, had buried them in the garden, and were anxiously tending to their seedlings, throwing their time, their sweat, and their hearts behind their faith. It was refreshing and beautiful and inspiring. Who was she to be a critic and a naysayer against a pattern that had worked for hundreds, if not thousands, of happy couples?

As she considered this, she began to realize for the first time that maybe what they wanted and what she wanted weren't all that different. The only difference, she decided, was that they believed in what they were doing and she was full of doubts. Or at least she had been. But something was different now. The world felt new and hopeful and better. There were still a million questions and a million more things to learn, but she felt different. For the first time since her arrival, she wanted to be here. She wanted to make this work. She wanted to discover where this might lead.

CHAPTER 35

Coming Home

*Courage does not always roar. Sometimes courage is
the quiet voice at the end of the day saying,
"I will try again tomorrow."
- Mary Anne Radmacher -*

The sun was getting lower in the sky when Genevieve finally decided it was time to head back to Harmony Hill. As she wrestled to don her wet dress, she thought of how ironic it was that the promise of an escape from her reality on the farm had somehow brought her to a place where she was willing, maybe even wanting, to embrace that very same reality. The polka-dot wasp stings scattered over her body were still red and swollen, but the pain was mostly gone. Still, the thought of a long walk home without any shoes sounded painful and unpleasant.

With her dress finally situated, she began walking back through the shallows. It was then that she saw it for the first time—a black inner tube. With one side of it wedged under the fallen log and armfuls of driftwood piled up against it, it would have been easy to miss. Stepping gingerly over the loose rocks, she walked past it, thinking how sad some kid must have been that such a great inner tube had been lost in the river. She was halfway across the stony banks when the idea occurred to her. She stopped, looking back at the river, struck by the realization that it ran parallel to the road all the way back to Niederbipp. Maybe she wouldn't have to walk after all.

She nearly ran back to the log, pulling away the driftwood to expose and free the tube. It was dusty and slightly low on pressure, but it was an inner tube on a river that was headed in the right direction.

Genevieve was almost giddy as she waded back into the river, carrying the tube on her shoulder to where the water was deep enough and the current swift enough for her to test whether this could actually work. With childlike abandon, she jumped aboard, her bottom sliding naturally into place in the tube's center. The current immediately began carrying her downstream, and she quickly discovered that she could easily navigate her position in the river's flow by only nominally paddling her arms.

The river was slow and lazy, but the late afternoon was still warm, the air perfumed with the scent of rain. Giving in to the inner tube's design, which invites riders to recline and relax, Genevieve floated effortlessly down the river, taking in all the natural beauty that surrounded her. A few cars passed on the highway, and she waved to them, imagining their passengers being at least somewhat envious of her choice of activity for a lazy afternoon.

But the quiet stillness also allowed her to continue to ponder, to observe, even to be grateful—activities that had never been a part of her life before. Somehow the anger and resentment of her earlier rant had been drained from her body and mind, replaced with something far more peaceable. She realized it had been more than a week since she had posted anything on social media. She laughed at herself as she considered how her followers might comment if they could see her now, this fashionista gone rogue, sporting newly acquired dreadlocks and floating on an inner tube down the middle of a river. She laughed even harder when she imagined what they might say had they seen a video of her jumping into a mud bog and purposely spreading mud over all of her exposed skin and hair in her attempt to avoid a million angry wasps. She was grateful no one would ever see that video. And the gratitude only multiplied as she considered her series of unfortunate events. She was grateful that the mud had been right where she needed it. Grateful for the river to wash off the mud. Grateful that somehow between the mud and the river, the pain of the stings had diminished.

As the river rounded a bend, she saw a cyclist on the highway, heading downriver. Recognizing his khaki chinos, she yelled at Spencer, waving from her tube, but he neither saw nor heard her. She could see, even from this distance, that the cord from his earbuds ran down his neck and into his rear pocket.

She lay back in the tube, realizing how wrong she'd been about him. He was undoubtedly the most handsome and charming of the men at the farm, but she recognized that he was also the most clueless and self-absorbed. She knew his invitation to join him in Tionesta wasn't a date, but still, he had ditched her on a remote country road so he wouldn't be late for the first pitch. She was certain it had been several hours since then. She wondered if he had even worried about her or if, when she hadn't shown up, he'd wondered what might have happened to her. She was enough of a feminist to know she didn't need him. But a little courtesy and consideration would have gone a long way, even if she had encouraged him to go on without her.

She remembered the conversation she'd had with Hildegard at the cemetery earlier—something about learning what types of men she couldn't marry. Was this what she had been talking about? She didn't want to be judgmental, but she knew that even though Spencer had some of the obvious physical attributes she considered important in a husband, the idea of having to play second fiddle to sweaty athletes on the other side of the country sounded completely disagreeable. Surely there would be a woman somewhere who could appreciate his physical beauty and handsome salary enough to overlook his all-encompassing sports obsession, but Genevieve now knew it was a deal breaker for her.

Another hour passed, along with several miles of tree-lined banks, before the town of Niederbipp came into view, rising up the hillside from near the river's edge. Genevieve stared at the town as she slowly floated past it, taking in its beauty and charm. The town was nearly out of view when the bell in the church tower tolled seven times and Genevieve realized it was later than she thought. She contemplated getting out of the river immediately, but then she remembered the bridge they had visited on their excursion on Friday. She recalled that the road to Harmony Hill joined the highway not far from there. She stayed her course until the bridge came into view, and then she began paddling toward the bank.

"There you are!" she heard a familiar male voice say from overhead. She looked up to see Matt smiling at her from the bridge. "We've been looking all over for you."

"Who has?" Genevieve asked, scrambling out of the tube and into the shallow waters.

Matt disappeared from atop the bridge. He reappeared on the river's far side, where they had all picnicked on Friday. "You look like you've had a tough day," he said, a broad smile spreading across his face. "I'm sure any of the girls would have loaned you a swimsuit so you wouldn't have to wear your Sunday dress down the river."

She smiled as he extended his hand, which she took as he helped her onto the bank.

"Are you okay?" he asked, looking into her eyes.

She forced another smile, nodding as she tossed the tube onto the gravel. "It's been quite a day."

"Were you attacked by mosquitos?" he asked, pointing at the welts on her face and arms.

"Wasps, actually, but thanks for noticing. What are you doing here?"

"Looking for you. We all are."

"What? Why?"

"We heard from Josh that you and Spencer were headed for a tavern somewhere, but he said you'd be back by dinner. Spencer got back over an hour ago—said he'd found your bike on the side of the highway but no other sign of you. He got home looking frantic—and maybe a little buzzed—so it was hard to get the story straight. Ruby and Pops and a bunch of the others jumped in the pickup truck and headed out immediately. The rest of us got on our bikes and spread out. We've all been worried sick. I'm glad you're okay." He looked her over before stooping to take a closer look at the cut on her toe. "This doesn't look good. What happened to your shoes?"

"It's a long story, and you wouldn't believe me if I told you," she said laughing loudly enough to surprise Matt. He stood looking at her closely as if he were trying to determine whether she might be delusional.

"I think we better get you home," he said, looking worried. He unbuttoned his shirt and took it off, exposing his clean white T-shirt. He wrapped the shirt around her shoulders. She gladly accepted, feeling chilled. Then he pulled out a handkerchief and, for the second time in as many Sundays, wiped mud from her neck and cheeks. She looked into his face as he focused his attention on the mud still caked around her hairline, his handkerchief quickly becoming soiled. His eyes were kind, and there was a tenderness about him that she hadn't noticed before.

"I don't remember the river being this dirty," he said with a curious smile. "I assume there's more to your story than an afternoon jaunt down the river on an inner tube?"

She laughed again, but the chill of her wet dress sent a shiver down her spine. "I wish there was more I could do," he said, looking hesitant. Then, without warning, he stepped forward and wrapped his warm arms around her, holding her until she stopped shaking.

"Let's get you home. I'm not sure how to get word to the others that you're okay, but at least you can get out of your wet clothes. Have you ever ridden sidesaddle on a bike?"

"I'm not sure."

"It's not the most comfortable thing in the world, but it's going to be better than walking on bruised and bloody feet."

He led her to his bicycle and showed her how to sit on the crossbar of the old cruiser in a way that would still give him enough room to pedal. She held on to the handlebars with one hand to help balance herself. Then he pushed off, rolling slowly down the highway, asking her frequently if she was okay until it was clear she had found her balance. They began the long ascent up Harmony Hill, and Matt pushed hard until he couldn't pedal any farther. Then, without missing a beat, he swung his leg over the back tire and continued to push the bike up the hill as he walked, one hand on the seat and the other on the handlebar. This worked well for a hundred yards or so until they reached the steepest part of the ascent and he had to pause.

"How do you feel about sitting on the saddle," he asked, sounding winded. "I can push you up this hill, but I think it would be easier from behind."

"Of course," she said, wincing as she hopped down onto the rough pavement. He gave her a moment as she tried to find the most modest and dainty way to mount a men's bike in a dress. When she was situated and secure, Matt began pushing again.

"So, tell me about your day," he asked calmly.

She skipped much of the bike ride, picking up at the broken chain, the wasps, the mud, losing her shoes, and turning into the swamp monster. They laughed together when she told him about the woman she'd tried to flag down, the one who'd driven away quickly, looking as though she feared for her life. She told him about lying in the river for hours until the wasp stings were less painful. He marveled at her good fortune of finding a runaway inner tube and complimented her on her creative resourcefulness in using the waterway instead of the highway to avoid damaging her feet, even though she likely would have been found earlier—and already be home by now—had she stuck to the road.

"Do you believe in fate?" she asked after a pause in the conversation.

"Fate? I'm not sure," he responded, sounding out of breath. "Why do you ask?"

She shook her head and was silent for a moment. He waited patiently for her to respond. "I've never spent much time thinking about my place in the universe," she said, starting again. "I guess if I'm honest, I've mostly just been driven by ego and money and position."

"Aren't we all?"

"Maybe. I guess what I'm wondering is if maybe the universe wanted all of these things to happen to me today…if it was fate."

"I guess I could be convinced. What are you thinking?"

"Well, in spite of the seemingly endless string of catastrophes, I can't remember ever feeling more…enlightened, for lack of a better word."

Matt laughed. "I've never considered that catastrophes could be a highway to enlightenment, but maybe there's something to that."

She nodded. "This has been without question the most difficult week of my life. I feel like I've spent half of the week wondering how I got here and the other half trying to psych myself up to somehow endure a summer in hell."

"It's really been that bad?" Matt asked incredulously.

"Yeah, but something happened down there when I was lying in the river."

He waited for her to continue, but there was a long pause. "What happened?" he spoke softly.

"I'm not sure. It's like there was a…connection—probably the closest thing I've ever had to a spiritual experience of any kind."

"Are you sure you weren't in shock from so many wasp stings?" he teased.

"Absolutely sure! It was strange; I was more present and open than I've ever felt before."

"I've felt something similar all week."

"You have?"

"Yeah."

"Do you know what it is?"

"I'm not sure, but I might."

"What is it?"

"Do you really want to know?"

"Uh, yeah. Why not? It's not like some kind of demonic possession, is it?"

He laughed. "Not at all. In fact, I think it's probably the exact opposite."

"Huh?"

"Genevieve, I don't know this for sure, but I think that what you experienced today really was something spiritual. It felt like love, right?"

"Actually, yeah," she said, sounding surprised. "How did you know?"

"Well, love is one of the fruits of the Spirit."

"What do you mean?"

"Sorry. I'm still trying to figure this out myself. But the Apostle Paul, in a letter he sent to the believers in Galatia, listed some of the characteristics of the Holy Spirit. He called them the fruits of the Spirit."

Genevieve nodded slowly. "We're talking Trinity stuff here, right? Father, Son, and Holy Ghost?"

"That's right. But the way I understand it, most of us usually only experience God through the messenger—the spirit of love, joy, peace, gentleness, that sort of thing. I'm obviously not an expert at any of this, but if I had to guess based on my own experience, I'd say that the feeling of love you experienced was an outpouring of God's love for you."

"Wait, seriously?" she asked, turning around.

"Yeah, I think so. It took me a few years and a whole lot of reading and research to understand what was going on, but yeah, that's the way I understand it. For me, it seems like I feel it only when I go looking for it—when I take the time to just shut everything else out and connect with that...that spirit of love, for lack of a better way of explaining it."

"No, that makes sense. I can't say I was really looking for it, but this afternoon was the first time in recent memory that I was ever really what could be considered *still*," she paused and looked over her shoulder. "That's why you went to that bench the other day."

"Yes."

"And that's what you were doing last Sunday...when you pulled me out of the mud?"

He laughed. "Yeah, what is it with you and mud anyway?"

She shook her head, turning around to look at him. "That's what those tiles in the bench mean, isn't it? The ones that say 'Be still, and know that I am God.'"

"That's the way I understand it, yes. It's a scripture, you know."

"It is?"

"Yeah, from Psalms somewhere."

"Do you understand it?"

"I feel like I do a little bit more every time I put it to the test."

"What does that mean?"

"I don't think I really understood it this way until this week— till I saw those tiles on every bench on the farm—but it feels like an invitation."

"What kind of invitation?"

"Like an invitation to be still, to sit and listen and see if you don't experience something...something like what you experienced today. That's what this summer is about, right? That's what it said in the paperwork?"

"I never got that paperwork, remember? What did I miss?"

"Something about this experience being about developing the whole self. That's why part of the commitment for the summer is to work on yourself physically, emotionally, mentally, *and* spiritually. The paper said that they're interested in all of us entering into marriage with our eyes and our hearts wide open. That's what I heard from my boss's brother, the one I told you about who spent the summer here a few years back. He was really open about how the experience helped him get ready to be a partner in a marriage that mattered. The guy was agnostic before he came here. His very Christian family all said he came back a totally different guy—faithful, happy, compassionate."

"And that all happened just because he spent the summer here?" she asked dubiously.

"No. He told me it happened because the farm gave him the opportunity to come to himself."

"What does that mean?"

"I don't think I understood it either until Thomas's sermon today—the Prodigal Son."

She nodded for a moment and then shook her head. "Remind me of the connection. I was a little distracted."

"Sure. So, after wasting his inheritance, the prodigal kid takes a job feeding pigs."

"Oh right."

"Yeah, so as he's sitting there in the muck and stench, he begins to remember how good he used to have it in his father's home?"

"That's right. I remember that part."

"I'm not sure if it was something Thomas said or if it was something I felt, but it struck me that maybe we all have to find ourselves in the muck of life before we look around, come to our senses, and realize that our choices have taken us to places we don't want to be. It seems like that's part of human nature—that most of us, if not all, have to get to that point. We all have hit rock bottom and bounce our thick heads along the hard, stony ground before we can finally look up to see that there's something more—something better."

Genevieve nodded soberly. "So, do you think that's what happened to me today?"

"I don't know. I guess time will tell."

"What do you mean by that?"

He stopped pushing, and Genevieve realized they'd finally reached the summit. He walked past her to the front of the bike, where he sat down on the front wheel and rested his arms on the handlebars. He took a minute to catch his breath, admiring the golden light of the evening on the valley below.

"I didn't understand any of this really until a few months ago, just before I sent in my application to come here. I don't think I ever would have made the effort to do this if it hadn't been for that conversation with my boss's brother. I felt like I was lower than I'd ever been before—broken, hopeless, lost."

"You?"

He pursed his lips and nodded, looking her in the eye. "He told me something that I'll always remember, and after hearing Thomas's sermon today, I think I might know where he got it. He told me that rock bottom is a pretty great place for God to begin building a sure foundation."

She listened, mulling over his words for a moment. It reminded her of something, and she searched her memory, landing on the quote written above the doorway in the bunkhouse. "What does it say above the doorway in your bunkhouse?" she asked, wondering if the men's might say the same thing.

He smiled and nodded. "It says, 'Except the Lord build the house, they labor in vain that build it.'"

"It says that over our doorway too. Do you know where it comes from?"

"Yeah, it's from Psalms."

"Psalms? You said that's from the Bible, right?"

Matt nodded thoughtfully for a moment. "I never thought about that until just now, but I think most of them were written by another prodigal son."

"What?"

"Yeah, they were written by David. You know, the same guy who killed the giant Goliath."

"Really? Why did you call him a prodigal?"

"You don't know the story?"

"I don't think so."

"It's pretty compelling, actually. The guy went from being a simple shepherd to the king of Israel, and then he fell for a married woman and lost his way."

"Wow! Did he ever come back around?"

"I think so. I think that's what the Psalms are all about—about staying close to God and allowing Him to help us build a better life."

Genevieve nodded, looking thoughtful. "So, do you think the psalm over the doorway and the tiles on the benches are tied together?"

"I was just wondering the same thing. It makes sense, doesn't it? Being still allows us to get to know God, and that relationship allows us to build our lives on a solid foundation."

She nodded, taking a deep breath. "Thank you," she whispered, squeezing his arm.

"For what?"

"Well, for more than just bringing me home."

"Sure," he responded, looking confused.

"I obviously didn't appreciate it until this afternoon, but you're a true gentleman, Matt. I think you must be the last of your kind."

He smiled shyly and looked away.

"And thanks for the talk the other day on the bench. I didn't want to hear any of it, but I needed to hear it. It's given me a lot to think about. Thank you."

"You're welcome. I hope I wasn't too hard on you."

She shook her head. "You were right. I was being selfish. I didn't want to be here, but when I was lying in the river, I decided that I need to be here. I don't know if it's fate that brought me here, but I've decided I'm going to put my heart into it and see where it takes me." She squeezed his arm again until he looked her in the eyes. "Thank you for being my friend."

"You're welcome," he replied. "Let's get you home so I can go tell the others you're safe."

CHAPTER 36

Reunion

Love is the master key which opens
the gates of happiness.
- Oliver Wendell Holmes -

Genevieve had used up all the hot water by the time the mud was finally rinsed from her hair and the conditioner had worked its magic on her dreadclumps. Finally warm and clean, she dressed in her pajamas and slowly walked up to the big house on bruised feet to wait on the front porch for the family to return. Darkness fell, the stars began shining, and still she was alone on the farm. She began to grow nervous, knowing everyone was looking for her. She felt helpless. But somewhere in her heart there was also a strange sense of peace.

As time continued to pass, she did something she hadn't done in twenty years. She prayed. She prayed that everyone would be safe, that they'd all make it home soon, that they wouldn't hate her for being here—warm and clean and comfortable—while they were out trying to find her. Her prayers turned to gratitude—gratitude for the things she'd learned that day, for the chance to be at the farm, for new friends, for seeing a different side of life. Rubbing the swollen lumps that remained on her legs and arms, she even thanked God for the wasps that had brought her to a place where she could see and hear and experience all the beauty she had neglected to recognize before.

The guilt she felt at being comfortable continued to taunt her, but then an idea popped into her mind. She knew the family would be returning home hungry, having missed the evening meal on her behalf. Forgetting her sore feet, she got up and wandered into the big house, turning on the lights as she made her way to the kitchen. Several loaves of bread were waiting to be cut next to a couple of jars of jam. As she cut the bread, she thought about each of the campers. She had worked with all the men and rubbed shoulders with all the women and was grateful for the patience and kindness they had extended to her despite the attitude she knew she had given each of them. She set the table and was just finishing laying out the bread when she heard the distinctive ahoogah horn coming from the old pickup truck.

She hurried as fast as her sore feet could carry her, throwing open the screen door and hobbling down the front steps. Five people on bikes were illuminated by the headlights of the pickup as it drove down the lane, several other bikers glowed in the tail lights, and a few more campers rode in the pickup's bed. Pops continued to honk the horn all the way down the bumpy drive until they all rolled into the front yard, safe and sound.

Holly was the first to embrace her, nearly knocking Genevieve off her tender feet. But the others were close behind, the embrace turning quickly into the biggest group hug she'd ever experienced. There were smiles and questions and commotion as everyone spoke at once.

"Quiet!" Ruby shouted over them all, and everyone turned to look at the small woman with a big voice and an even bigger heart. "Let's take this party inside. I'm starving."

Again the noise erupted as everyone continued to try to speak at once. They carried Genevieve into the big house, making their way to the kitchen.

"It's already in the dining hall," Genevieve yelled over the din, which was nearly as loud as a New Year's celebration, and the family responded like a slow-moving Chinese dancing dragon.

Genevieve looked into each of their faces as they found their seats, feeling a great outpouring of appreciation for each of them. Pops offered a prayer, thanking God for a meal to share and for everyone's safe and happy return. As they ate, Genevieve told them all about her series of unfortunate events. They laughed until they cried as she described being chased by angry wasps. Josh ran to the pickup truck and returned with a single shoe, still caked in heavy mud, that they had pulled from the bog. They laughed again as Josh described poking long sticks into the mud because his imagination had led him to fear that Genevieve may have been swallowed by the quicksand-like sludge.

Ephraim offered a visual aid of his own, pointing to the single wasp sting he'd received on his forearm when he'd pulled Genevieve's bike from the grass on the side of the highway. They all gasped when Genevieve pulled back her sleeves and lifted her pajama legs to reveal the red polka dots that were scattered across her skin. But she had them in stitches again as she described the smearing of the mud and the swamp-monster scare. She also explained how the river had soothed her stings and how she'd made it all the way back to Niederbipp without being spotted or having to walk. And she openly poured out praise for the kindness of the gentleman hero who had so graciously escorted her home.

Matt looked embarrassed by all the attention, especially from the women, who looked at him with a new kind of respect. Susan was quick to point out that he had not only brought Genevieve safely back to the farm, pushing her uphill, but had then turned around and headed back to let everyone know they could call off the search. Josh got them all laughing again when he told them that after pulling Genevieve's shoe from the bog, he'd stripped down to his boxers and was about to jump into the swamp to recover her body. He was saved from the mud by Matt's timely arrival.

They learned that Ruby and Pops had driven all the way to Tionesta, with Spencer riding uncomfortably between them, as they'd collectively tried to piece together the whole story. After hearing the lengths each of them had gone to in search of Genevieve, Spencer apologized to the whole family, especially Genevieve. Contritely, he pulled the headphones and small iPod from his pocket and laid them on the table, apologizing again and admitting that his contraband had kept him from being fully engaged and present. He promised there would be no more trips to the Tionesta tavern—or any other tavern, for that matter. Genevieve noticed that despite what felt like a sincere airing of his regret, the women especially appeared dubious and guarded as Spencer spoke. She guessed that only time would tell if trust could be restored.

About the same time the bread and jam had all been eaten and the milk had all been drunk, the family collectively began to look as tired as they all felt.

"Tomorrow begins a new week," Ruby said after observing their mutual fatigue. "You'll of course be divided into different teams for the chores you've already experienced. And now that we've all got the basic hang of things, we'll be adding a few additional chores, but they'll be fun. We'll be preparing the farm stand for the season, and this week also begins the cheese-making process. But I also insist that you begin taking time for music and reading and fishing."

"And don't forget letter writing," Pops replied.

"Yes, of course, we mustn't forget letter writing," she said, winking at her husband across the long table. "I want you all to know that Pops and I are proud of each of you and the work you've put in this first week. Thank you. We hope you've learned a little bit more about yourselves in the process—your personal strengths and your weaknesses, your likes and your dislikes. You arrived as strangers just over a week ago, but tonight..." She paused, looking into each of their expectant faces before she continued. "Tonight you became family. Somehow this happens every year at some point. We'll take it however it comes, but this will go down in history as the first time we came together out of nearly losing a member of the family to the Allegheny mud bogs."

The family smiled and laughed again.

"Tonight you have proven your love and your loyalty to each another. It may be hard to believe, but I promise you that over the course of the next four and a half months, your love and loyalty will be tested as well as nurtured, evolving into something even more beautiful than what we feel here tonight. If you haven't experienced it before, *this* is the stuff all great families are made of. Remember this. Remember what this feels like. Look into each other's faces and see what it looks like."

A tear rolled down Genevieve's cheek, but she looked into each of their faces, feeling grateful. Though there were still many unknowns, she felt like there was also a tangible thread that bound them together. Ruby's words echoed in her heart—*this is what family feels like.* Sandwiched between Susan and Ephraim, she took hold of one of each of their hands and squeezed. They each in turn reached for the hand of person next to them. This continued until the long table was encircled by a ring of clasped hands—Ruby on one end, Pops on the other, and twelve former strangers forming the friendliest ragtag family any of them had ever known.

"Remember this night," Ruby said. "Remember this when you're working with your teammates in the fields and in the garden and in the milking barn. This is what harmony feels like. And the truth is, if you'll remember what this feels like, it will never be far away. You can find it again and again."

Ruby smiled across the table at her husband of fifty-six years, and the campers marveled at the energy that passed between them at that moment, electrifying the room with a palpable sense of love. No one had yet released their clasped hands, and Genevieve looked again into each of their faces, feeling a unique sense of love for each of them. And in the nurturing silence that hovered around them, her heart spoke to her with a calm and gentle voice that only she could perceive: *This is why you're here.*

To be continued.

ABOUT THE AUTHOR

God. Family. Art. Stories. With his head, heart, and hands, Ben Behunin tries to bring his passions together to make the world a little more kind, thoughtful, and beautiful. A potter by day and a writer by night—and whenever he can get away with it, Ben maintains a studio just inches away from his home in Salt Lake City, Utah. He and his wife, Lynnette, are the happy parents of two teens, Isaac and Eve.

Information about studio visits and the Behunin's semi-annual home tours is available at www.potterboy.com.

Personalized books can be ordered
at www.potterboy.com.
There, you can register for the email mailing list
to receive updates about upcoming books, shows, and events.

Ben enjoys hearing from his readers.
You can reach him at benbehunin@comcast.net
or through snail mail at:

Abendmahl Press
P.O Box 581083
Salt Lake City, Utah 84158-1083

For speaking engagements including
book clubs, funerals and inaugurations
call 801-883-0146

See the short video Quin Boardman created about Ben at
www.hiveseries.com

For design information, contact
Bert Compton at bert@comptonds.com

 benbehunin

 niederbippboy